BRIDE OF SHADOWS

A CRONUS SOCIETY NOVEL

RHEA WATSON

CONTENTS

Cover Designer: Angela Camilla @ Cat Cover Design
Editorial: One Love Editing
Paperback ISBN: 978-1-989261-18-7

TROPES AND TRIGGERS

Triggers: violence, gore, medical trauma (past), toxic family dynamics

Tropes: Praise kink, insta-love (from the harem), destiny and fated love, morally grey heroes, violent to everyone but soft for each other

Cronus Society

SERIES DETAILS

rhea watson

Cronus Society is a paranormal reverse harem romance series that features standalone novels set in the same fictional world. In it, the supernatural are still a secret to the majority of the human population.

Cronus, however, operates in the shadowy grey area between mankind and the paranormal. The secret society researches, studies, experiments on, and fights any supernatural creatures who want to rebel against the status quo... or start an apocalypse.

In some novels, Cronus is a blessing. In others, it's a nightmare. It all depends on the characters and their relationship with the society.

Some tropes you as a reader can expect in each book:

- Heroine-only POV
- Insta-Love (usually from the harem)

- Heroes who take on more "monster" forms when they lose control or shift

Happy reading! xoxo

FUTURE CRONUS SOCIETY ROMANCES

Kissed by Death
(Fallen Angels)

Cambion
(Demon Hybrids and Hellhounds)

From the Ashes
(Phoenix/Dragon Shifters)

Cerberus Down
(Mixed Reverse Harem)

Faery Tale
(Human/Fae)

BRIDE OF SHADOWS

Cronus Society: a shadow organization operating in the grey between humanity and the secret supernatural world. To some, Cronus is a monster. To others, it's the only defense against a paranormal apocalypse.

All my life, I just wanted to be normal.

Not sick. Not broken.

Normal.

And I tried my best. No matter how crappy I feel, I've always been an expert at grin real wide and bear it. I landed my first job at Cronus thanks to a stellar GPA, not Dad's rank within the organization. I did the grunt work, paid my dues, and never, ever complained.

Three years later, I earned my spot in the intake department, processing all things supernatural when they arrive at headquarters. These days, I love my job. I'm *good*. Respected. Unflappable, even.

Then three shades fall in my lap.

Arawn, Draco, and Balor...

They gleefully terrorize other intake officers from their containment cells, but when I go in alone, they purr like kittens. One word and these monsters become men so hauntingly beautiful, so dark and deadly, and so, *so* irresistible it hurts.

They claim to know me.

They claim to love me.

But demons lie. I don't buy it for a second—

Until they kidnap me and drag me into the shadows, hellbent on proving that the worst lie of all... is the one I've been living.

CHAPTER ONE

You know what they never tell you about in sex ed?

Boob hairs.

Like, the thick, angry jerks that pop out of nowhere, usually around your nipples. One day, nothing. The next? Hair. Just one—one little asshole poking out your skin, all dark and hard and thick, waiting to horrify any dude lucky enough for under the bra access.

Not that I...

Not that there was a dude.

Just...

Ugh.

Lips pursed, forever unimpressed with my body on the days it pulled this crap like it didn't dump on me enough as it was, I tugged off my shower cap and tossed it on the bathroom counter, then went for my tools in the cabinet over the toilet. Surrounded by the thick, hot steam of another glorious scalding shower, I rooted around the little organizer bins for my tweezers, then plucked the damn thing out. It put up a fight, like it had grown roots in my left boob overnight, but eventually caved, and I tugged it out with a grunt.

Yeesh. Definitely longer, blacker, and thicker than the little tip poking out had implied. Gross.

Naked and air-drying, I lifted the toilet lid with my toes and dropped the scoundrel inside, then flushed it with a tweezer salute. Farewell, dick.

The usual hit of morning nausea struck just as I nudged the lid shut again, and after tossing my tweezers back in their rattan basket, I went for the litany of meds stacked neat and organized in the medicine cabinet next to the mirror. One from each bottle, eight total, every morning, huge squishy capsules filled with... stuff.

Stuff to keep my immune system from eating itself alive —I dunno. Dad explained the nuances to me years ago, the nitty-gritty science behind everything, but at this point, as soon as symptoms hit, I just shoved stuff in my mouth and swallowed. The pharmacy stickers screamed to take all this with food, but meh. My appetite just wasn't a *thing*. Never had been, and so long as I met my daily nutritional requirements with Dad's precooked meals, he wasn't concerned.

I slashed at the foggy mirror, my ritual always the same: swallow the meds, confirm an empty mouth, take a mental snapshot. Dad used to make me show him I swallowed everything—now it was just habit, my reflection of an empty mouth and too-sharp canines a reminder for later when he inevitably asked if I'd taken the medication I did every day, without fail, for the better part of twenty-five years.

Like, *I* knew I'd taken it, but something about his tone, the way he scrutinized me—I always second-guessed myself.

Always needed to flash back to *this* moment, my mouth's reflection in the fog.

Kind of embarrassing, really, and not a story I whipped out at office parties.

With that sorted, I snagged my crumpled towel off the counter and wiped the lingering damp from my skin, then opened the bathroom door to air out the steam. The second I ambled into my bedroom, the same room I'd had since I left the base hospital at two days old, he shouted at me.

Squawk.

I jumped, fully expecting it because it happened daily—but the little feathery jerk always got me.

There, in one of my windows, like clockwork—a raven.

The raven, biggest in the flock.

Or, I suppose, the *conspiracy* of ravens—that was the term for a bunch of them, and for some reason, a conspiracy twenty strong had lived in the trees outside my bedroom for years.

Desk lamp on, the hazy sunrise taking care of the rest, I peered around the bathroom door to scowl at him, at the tone he took this morning... like I was running late or something.

"Morning, perv."

He always caught me naked. *Always.* We were the last colonial on the street, and, given my bedroom perched in the upper southeast corner, all windows facing the ravine, I never bothered with curtains. We might be squished in with all the other high-level Cronus families on Cedarcrest Drive, but back here, it was just sturdy sugar maples with the most beautiful fall canopies and gangly white birches that always looked so sad by comparison. Thick grass and lush undergrowth, wildflowers in the spring, and nothing but a white blanket through the tree trunks in the winter.

Just me and nature back here.

And ravens.

This one didn't have a name, but somehow I knew him —bigger talons, sharper beak, a fluffier head than the rest of his conspiracy, and a brighter spark of intelligence in his black eyes. Towel wrapped around and tucked securely under my arms so I wouldn't flash him again, I tiptoed out and offered him an exaggerated frown for startling me.

Cheeky jerk just made a ruckus and hopped back and forth on the white window ledge, his croaking noises almost like laughter.

Like he was in a playful mood this morning.

If I could loll around in the trees all day, in a forest full of food on an active army base with plenty of opportunities to scavenge, no work or responsibilities, I guess I'd be feeling pretty playful at 6:00 a.m. as well.

Instead, I drifted into my walk-in closet, dragging yet another restless night's sleep like iron shackles, clinking and clanging and weighing me down. Fortunately, his crack-of-dawn routine came and went like clockwork, and with my breakfast smoothie chugged, my shower done, and my meds taken, next came the outfit I had laid out last night: pressed black slacks, slouchy and not the most figure-flattering but *very* professional—in Dad's opinion, anyway—paired with a crisp white button-down, the navy-pinstriped pattern about as risqué as I went for work attire. Support bra and granny panties for long days on my feet, plus a thick pair of comfy socks and I was good to go.

Swiping my brush off my dresser, I sock-slid my way across the hardwood to the same desk I did homework on for twelve years. Clutter cleared, memories in every ding and chip, the thrifted vintage writing desk a friend's dad had sanded and painted turquoise for me when I went through a turquoise phase in the eighth grade was neat and orderly these days. Just my laptop and a tin of pens, plus a few stacked ringed notebooks. I plopped into the chair that creaked up a storm if you so much as looked at it wrong, then lifted open my laptop and waited for it to boot up while working on a few of the more persistent knots at the back of my head.

Rrrrwaaaakkk.

Joined seconds later by my black-feathered friend. The raven had swapped one windowsill for another, his talons marking up the wood, this one his favorite. How many years had he sat out there while I stressed over trig or rewrote a lit essay again and again until it was *perfect*?

Too many.

Grinning, I watched him hop and brushed my hair, then lazily logged in to the secure Cronus server to access today's intake schedule.

No one had ever said it to my face, but, logically, people must have figured I got my position in Cronus because of Dad. Maybe they were right to some extent: Dad was my biggest supporter, really pushing me to fly as high as I could in the secret organization. Still, I'd finished high school with top marks and spent years in the various labs and departments doing grunt work. My stripes were *more* than earned by the time HR assigned me permanently to the intake team. I'd paid my dues, and I loved the work.

Loved getting up before dawn every morning.

Loved walking into the research facility.

Loved... meeting supernatural monsters.

Creatures the rest of humanity had no idea existed, right there, in the shadows. Your volleyball coach could be a shifter or the overnight orderly a vampire. They looked like us. Talked like us. Acted like us—but they weren't... *us*.

Cronus Society, a global organizer that technically didn't exist, was our first and last line of defense. We studied the supernatural, some tests performed on volunteers or paid subjects that fit a very specific brief, others forcefully detained because they were preying on way too many humans to stay secret. They'd collected data for ages, maybe even centuries, and with good reason.

In the grand scheme of things, humans did *not* sit cozy at the top of the food chain. Supernatural creatures, for the most part, were stronger, faster, brighter, and more powerful in every way that counted—yet humanity had the numbers. Our population surpassed theirs tenfold, but if they ever decided that living on the periphery of our world just didn't cut it anymore, we were screwed.

But Cronus—the work we did, the trials we ran, the dangers we eliminated—was here to make sure that never happened.

That the ordinary folk, the ones who thought Fort Beacham was just a standard army base, would never have to witness the horrors *we* had recorded at our facility and countless like it around the world.

Having logged in to the server, password and ID tapped one-handed as I finished my brushing, a little box popped up demanding a onetime numerical code for continued access. My phone pinged on the bedside table, and I rolled the old girl with her squeaky hinges and deflated seat and horrible lumbar support across my childhood bedroom to the twin bed that could probably do with an upgrade and grabbed my Cronus-issued cell.

The raven, meanwhile, watched for a beat—then tapped insistently on the glass. Demanding little thing. Smirking, I wheeled back and undid the latch, then lifted the window panel about two inches. A rush of cool, dry autumn air accompanied his beak, and as I entered the number code with one hand, I grabbed a random pen with the other.

"Hello, handsome," I whispered affectionately, passing this morning's gift over. Dad *hated* the conspiracy that called our ravine home, which meant when he asked why the heck I never had any pens on hand, I made up some story about people borrowing them at work.

He didn't need to know I gave them away, one by one, to a bird every morning.

I figured out the best way to quiet this one's croaky antics in tenth grade when he got a little too obsessive over pens with the shiny exteriors or fluffy feathers at the end. Now, he begrudgingly accepted the basic black and blue ballpoints, snapping this morning's up and twisting out of the window opening. Fully upright again, I watched the oddly graceful brat dance the Pen Dance along the ledge. Once my laptop screen flashed to the main portal, however, I pushed everything else aside and went into today's schedule.

Given intake was so unpredictable, we only knew the days we were working in advance—the *what* we were working with varied. Some days we had a full pack of something with sharp claws and scary teeth to process. Others, like today, consisted of a single appointment on my timetable.

Cool.

It'd give me time to catch up on paperwork, maybe help in the lab—

Wait.

I clicked the yellow bubble on my digital timeline for more details, and up popped a square listing the when and the where.

But not the what.

When—eight o'clock, standard start time.

The where?

Sub-level Z.

My heart sank.

I... had never been that deep before.

The more dangerous the monster, the further underground they were housed.

A cold sweat erupted over my palms. Sub-level Z— bottom of the bottom.

I...

On yearly evals, Cronus HR had complimented me on the rapport I built with new arrivals. It was our job to get medical samples and as detailed a history as we could, along with anything else noteworthy about the individual at the time. At twenty-five, I'd been on the team for three years— and unlike a lot of my coworkers, I liked to *talk* to whatever beastie was on my roster, make them feel safe. Not everyone wanted to be here, and even those who had applied for a paid study found the white walls of their new home—cell —intimidating.

I loved my job.

I was *good* at my job.

But...

Sub-level Z was for intake officers with way more experience. Like, at least two or three pay grades higher.

This had to be a mistake.

I mean, they hadn't even listed what I'd be processing.

No. Shaking my head, I closed my laptop and pushed away from my desk—but lacked the strength to actually stand up. No, no, this was *definitely* a mistake.

But if it was a mistake, why were my hands trembling?

Why did it feel like I couldn't catch my breath?

Why did I feel so insignificant and embarrassed?

Face hot and knees weak, I caught my pale reflection in the window, then focused on my morning visitor. He had dropped the pen, celebrations over, and shoved his beak back through the opening, the black curve slightly parted.

"Gotta go, bud," I muttered, nudging the slightly too intense bird out. "See you tomorrow."

Another croaky *squawk* and a few insistent taps on the glass serenaded me as I locked the latch, grabbed my phone, and finally found the nerve to stand. There should have been comfort in my surroundings: this *was* my childhood bedroom, painted recently to reflect a more adult sense of style in all black, white, and grey. Fake plants—couldn't keep real ones alive for the life of me—and rattan baskets to hold spare linens. Fairy lights in the corners to make it extra cozy before bed. A breathtaking view of the forest in full fall outside from any of the four generous windows across the two corner walls.

But I was still shaky while I crossed the muted hardwood, death-gripping my phone as that niggling lifelong insecurity screamed *Mistake!!* over and over again, drowning out the darkness deep down that believed someone like *me* could conquer the world.

I padded downstairs on the tips of my socked toes, still accustomed to moving quietly from the good ol' days when Dad worked all-nighters at the Cronus hospital. By now, I knew which stairs creaked and which ones groaned as my hand ghosted down the banister. Our colonial might have reflected Dad's minimalist style, but it was the same as every other Cronus staff house on the street: three bedrooms upstairs, one for me and one for Dad, plus his home office. First floor for the kitchen, formal and casual living rooms. Throw in two en suites upstairs and a powder room down here, plus a creepy basement that was always cold and damp, and it was home.

The military families, meanwhile, had a suburb of

bungalows on the other side of Fort Beacham, the divide between us and them substantial. The lines blurred at our shared schools, but the housing situation had always grossly skewed our way. Some raised issue with it over the years, unaware that the only reason this base existed *at all* was to cover for Cronus. They were our beard. As far as civilian locals knew, our surroundings all rolling hills and cash crop farmland, we didn't exist, and this base was like any run-of-the-mill military installation.

As soon as I hit the ground floor, I pivoted right, past the foyer corridor and straight into the kitchen. Pure white from the cabinets to the island and everything in between, the floors traditional kitchen checkered and the appliances pristine stainless steel, it combined with the breakfast nook to take up the full east wing of the house.

"Hey, Dad?"

His usual breakfast of thick-cut bacon, olive-oil fried eggs, and gluten-free toast hit like a brick to the face long before I breezed into the kitchen. All that paired with his aggressive organic coffee—black, of course—only made my morning tummy churn extra angry. Swallowing down the flood of saliva, I took a deep breath and rounded on him at the table in its pale Scandinavian wood, where I'd always find him at this hour, dwarfed behind the Fort Beacham daily newspaper.

How there was enough unclassified stuff to report on *every* day still astounded me, honestly.

Warm, soft sunlight filtered through the wall of windows, the round four-seater table bathed in light by day and lit by the wrought-iron chandelier by night. I waited, patience thinner than usual, until he finally fluttered the paper so it folded just enough to allow him to peer over the top.

"Selene..." Ah, yes, Disappoint in D-sharp. "Your hair."

"I—"

"You really think that will pass protocol?" he drawled, closing the paper over and zeroing in on my chaotic curls. Insecurity rocketed up to a twelve, followed by a prickle of anger in my chest that I shoved deep, deep down, I hastily made a slick ponytail with the hair tie that left grooves around my wrist, smoothing and smoothing and smoothing so my hair lay flat and taut against my skull.

He had always been a nitpicker. *Always.* First try was never good enough—unless someone else deemed it stellar before he had the chance to pick it apart.

But that was why he was head of general practice at Cronus, lording over his own top-secret department and responsible for the health and well-being of all three hundred employees and their families.

"And your shirt," he chided with a pointed nod at my waist. "Let's get that properly tucked, shall we?"

"I'm not leaving just yet—"

"Did you take your meds?"

"*Yes.*" Sighing, I gave my ponytail a few jerky tugs so it was as tight and slick and *professional* as possible, then went for my shirt, tucking the excess material in so it sat more to his liking. As frustrating as it was growing up with a dad who hovered, he had a reason.

That was what I always told myself, anyway.

I mean, I couldn't imagine being a parent to a kid with an unknown autoimmune disease, one that required strict management—one that didn't even have a *name*. He had been researching the symptoms all my life: the nausea, the fatigue, the sleepless nights, and the aches in my bones. The random weakness in my hands. My sensitivity to light, a symptom that came and went on a whim; wearing shades to class, indoors, pale as heck and struggling to gain weight—none of that had put me in the base's popular clique. He watched me operate on a consistent *blegh* for as long as I could remember. I saw what it did to him.

These days, I had just gotten really good at pretending it didn't exist.

That the meds were enough.

That I was *fine*.

So, whatever. Let him nitpick my hair and fuss over how I tucked my shirt: at least that was stuff we could fix.

Only when I knew I was up to his standards did I hold out my arms and do a little turntable spin. "Better?"

Dad flashed a toothy grin, those chompers big and white and straight. "Perfection."

Seriously, that word belonged on his tombstone, because *perfection* was the name of the game in his world.

As the morning shift started at Cronus HQ, email alerts pinged on my phone. Shoved in my left pocket, it chirped and rumbled until I reached in there to mute it, eyes on Dad as he went back to the paper, the lump in my throat back with a vengeance.

"Do you know anything about Sub-level Z?"

"Why?"

My blood ran as icy as his tone, but I played it off with a weak smile and a one-shouldered shrug. "Just, uh..."

Sighing, Dad closed the paper for good this time, everything about him hard. Scary how he could turn it on and off like that, warm and familiar one second, serious and intense the next. *Beacham Daily* set aside, half-drunk coffee still spiraling steam from its mug and breakfast about a quarter off from finished, he pinned his full attention on me —and it made me feel about two inches tall.

Like I'd done something wrong.

Said something I shouldn't.

Business as usual.

No one would ever mistake us for father and daughter in public. Where Dad was ashy blond with layered hazels, I was stuck with a mane of rebellious black curls and eyes so light blue they verged on horror-movie transparent. He was olive-toned and tanned in the summers; I was pale enough you could map my veins and had suffered blistering sunburns all my life. He had a few concerning moles; I had a smattering of weird, off-brand freckles on my cheeks and nose that didn't match the rest of me. The only thing we had in common was the tall, lean beanpole gene.

Which meant I got the rest from my mom.

Who was a persona non grata in this house, not because she had done anything wrong, but because Dad got all awkward and reclusive anytime I brought her up. He must have really loved her, and as far as I knew, she had died from the same mysterious illness that haunted *my* every waking hour.

As a kid, it hurt that this house lacked her presence. No memories. No photos. No old clothes that still smelled like her perfume. Asking about her in any respect was a huge trigger for the man staring me down from the table; I'd let it go a long time ago, but as I settled into my looks, sometimes...

Sometimes I wondered.

And sometimes I wished *we* looked more alike so people wouldn't ask if I was his student or girlfriend or niece or whatever.

"Selene, you know how I feel about *just* and *like* and *uh*—"

"I'm assigned there today, on Sub-level Z," I told him, so not in the mood for a lecture on colloquial slang. Didn't he realize those filler words represented necessary *pauses* in one's train of thought? Drove me nuts that he homed in on them like a heat-seeking missile anytime I let one slip.

Dad eased back in his chair, arms crossed and head cocked, assessing me in an almost painful silence as his breakfast wreaked havoc on my olfactory system.

"Well..." *Here it comes.* "That's a big compliment, isn't it?"

Oh.

I blinked back at him, mouth dry, the lump in my throat verging on strangulation territory.

Because... I mean, what was I supposed to make of that?

I'd braced for the standard verbal undressing—the speech about why *I* didn't belong on Sub-level Z.

That this was a mistake.

"I... guess," I said slowly, fiddling with my super-short nails—then immediately dropping my arms to my sides when Dad glared at the fidgety habit. "I'm surprised, and there was no indication of the species I'd be processing—"

"Do your best to wear your most professional face." He scrutinized me *again* from top to bottom, from my lack of makeup all the way down to my white ankle socks. If only I had head of department status: no one picked apart his cozy knits in the dark mustardy-yellow color family he loved so much. Heck, no one would *dare* tell him corduroys should have stayed in the seventies and the bell flare didn't go with how baggy he wore his sweaters.

But then lab coats covered all manner of fashion sin, so he got a pass.

That and most of his underlings were scared of him—and therefore nauseatingly respectful of me if we crossed paths.

Which was just... awkward.

"I mean, of course." Was it really necessary to tell me to be professional at my *job*? The one I was really good at? For real. "But I—"

"And don't ramble," he added like I hadn't said a word, grabbing the newspaper again and opening it, ruffling it flat. "Sometimes you ramble."

"I... *Dad*—"

"Just do your intake assessment and get out." He flipped to the sports section, photos of the base's high school football teams splashed everywhere after last weekend's homecoming game. "Nothing *good* ever gets housed that deep, and I've heard you can be a little overly... *friendly*."

Great. Nothing like my supervisors shooting the shit with my dad about my job performance. Palms cold and sweaty again, I abandoned the more probing questions I had about the deepest, darkest floor at Cronus—because somehow, anything I asked would get twisted back around to me. Instead, I drifted over, braced on the back of his chair, and kissed his sharp, clean-shaven cheek.

"Have a good day at work, Dad."

"You too, honey." He grinned up at me like the conversation had never happened. "Lunch is in the fridge."

I bit my tongue and smiled. Just once, I'd like to eat cafeteria food. Sad hamburgers and room-temperature pizza and tacos every Tuesday.

Dad had prepped my lunches since the first grade.

Same brown paper bag. Same weird health breads, salads, and snacks.

Same smoothies with my second dosage of medication hidden in the creamy fruit swirls.

But I shouldn't complain. What other dad made their adult kid's lunch for them? He *cared* enough to do it, to

15

make sure I took my meds with something healthy, balanced, and nutritious.

So, I grabbed the heavy paper bag and tucked it under my arm, then nudged the fridge shut with my hip.

"Good luck today, Selene."

I brightened, my confidence as wavering as my smile. "Best foot forward."

"That's my girl," Dad murmured, his affectionate nose crinkle the only thing I'd take from this conversation.

Sighing, I threw my shoulders back and headed for the front door to grab my coat, shoes, and purse, then left for the uncertain day ahead.

Nerves frayed and doubting myself every step of the way.

CHAPTER TWO

Species Classification: Shade (3)

"Uh..." I scanned the one-page fact sheet on the intake clipboard again, wondering if I'd missed something, and then lifted it. Nope. Same stuff as the first read-through—then the stack of blank lined paper underneath was for my notes. Most intake dossiers looked similar, but we usually went into a situation with more information. Name. Estimated age range. Species. Where they were from or how they had been captured. Volunteer or not. Previous crimes. Family lineages, clan associations, coven affiliation —*something*. This was... a species classification and today's date, all the other lines and boxes left blank, made official by the freshly inked department stamp in the bottom corner. "What's a shade?"

"Some sort of demon—maybe." The elevator doors whooshed shut, and I arched an eyebrow at Mavis, the junior psychiatry resident assigned to my intake, who shrugged and dug her phone out of her white coat's baggy pocket. "Don't read too much into it. Just a working theory for now. First encounter for Cronus."

A twiggy brunette with eagle eyes and a vicious intelligence, Mavis Bradwell's reputation preceded her everywhere she went around HQ. Like Dad, she could make you feel about an inch tall with nothing more than an up-and-down sweep of her judgy bright greens. She lived to work, which I kind of appreciated, and the three interns in ill-fitting scrubs cowering behind her as security swiped his key card and pressed the button for Sub-level Z seemed terrified.

Maybe of her, or the assignment, or whatever was waiting for us in the cells.

Probably a combo of all three.

Same, guys.

It always felt weird outranking interns when they had at least three years on me. But with the ID card and clearance badge hanging from my purple lanyard, I had the second-highest authority here after Mavis. Security was their own thing, the pair of burly dudes in black uniforms and strapped with weapons operating outside our jurisdiction.

Today, however, my clearance card had been specially modified to allow for Sub-level Z access for the next week. After, it would expire, the doors would stop opening, and the option to take the elevator into the deepest bowels of Cronus HQ would be out of reach.

Which was *beyond* fine.

Even if the ride was smooth, the elevator descending like silk, my gut still did its flip-flop thing, knotting and spinning and launching into my throat as we whizzed south from intake on the fourth floor.

"Scouts found these three in a demon trap we laid near a Hell gate just outside of Edmonton," Mavis mused, all the sharp, fae-like angles of her very human face illuminated by her phone as she scanned what I assumed was intel that went above my pay grade. "All the standard containment sigils seem to hold them, so we're operating on the hypothesis that they're just a class of demonkind we haven't documented before." She sniffed and flicked her long bob over her shoulder, the herd of interns at her back deathly quiet and getting paler by the floor. "Go about your usual procedures. It's just another day."

Uh-huh.

Before I could counter with something snarky but respectful, one of the guards—Dermott, according to the ID patch on his chest, his insignia indicating he only worked the lower levels—cleared his throat pointedly. As the elevator slowed, unleashing another wave of tummy churn, he and Mavis locked eyes, glaring, fighting for dominance.

Did they... have a thing?

Both midthirties. Both annoyingly attractive. Given the way Abrams, the second guard who worked intake with me regularly and was about a year out from retirement, rolled his eyes and sighed, maybe, but—

"Miss Abbott," Dermott started as the elevator came to a graceful halt, *Sub-Level Z* flashing on the teleprompter above the doors, "you should be aware that three other intake officers have been attacked by these *things* in as many days."

I flinched, cheeks prickling as the color drained away. That was news to me. Usually we got email memos about attacks, but no one had said a thing.

No one had even *warned* me until the doors were literally peeling open into the belly of the beast.

As Mavis huffed over my shoulder, I followed Dermott and Abrams out into the corridor, numb. My mind ought to be racing with the news, readjusting and reassessing, determining the appropriate strategy for violent detainees.

But it was just... blank.

Abrams slowed and steered me off to the side as the others exited the elevator. With one thick gloved hand on my shoulder, he ducked to meet my eyeline, his all warm and chocolatey, mine the exact opposite. All my life, people refused to hold my stare. We made a drinking game of it in high school, me and the other nerds; if someone could out-stare me, I'd have to finish my whole drink.

Never happened.

But Abrams with his Mediterranean warmth and silver-fox looks always did his best to look me in the eye.

To give me that respect.

"We're here to keep you safe," he reminded me gruffly. "Same as any other intake. First whiff of a threat and we're gone, understood?"

I nodded because I had to—because I had promised Dad to put my best foot forward.

Go about your usual procedures. It's just another day. Mavis's words echoed with the click of her heels, their crisp preciseness resonating in the sterile corridor. At long last, my working theory that the deeper you went, the colder and less hospitable Cronus became had officially been proven correct: Sub-level Z was metal and chrome from floor to ceiling. Empty nothingness in either direction, the odd door without a handle or a knob or even a card reader catching my eye. It was like stepping into a sad spaceship, one designed by aliens with no imagination or aesthetic flare. Matte black and reflective silver, floor panels that looked slippy in socks, doors that led to goodness only knew where —the largest of which loomed directly across from the elevator. Maybe ten-by-fifteen, the hulking metal panels wove together like a puzzle, arcing around each other where they met in the middle, demon containment sigils carved into every inch.

Right.

I guess the most *serious* demons—archdemons, maybe? —wound up down here. I'd dealt with tricksters and crossroads hellions on the upper floors, those levels visually warmer with more amenities if the beastie was on their best behavior, but the supreme badasses? Above my skill set.

Anyway, demons were kind of a nightmare to process. I always dreaded my shifts whenever I spotted one on my schedule. Give me a prickly shifter or a horny vampire literally any day of the week over one of those black-eyed psychos.

"Security has been such a fucking *nightmare* this week." I nearly jumped out of my skin when Mavis's husky whisper tickled my ears. Back on her phone, she loitered by me as Abrams and Dermott unlocked the containment doors, punching number codes I now had stored in my Cronus-issued phone and swiping their ID cards. Shaking her head, the junior resident who hadn't said more than two words to me before today glanced between the pair, then scoffed. "The attacks weren't *attacks*... The shades just seem to get a bit testy when you ask questions."

Oh, cool. They got annoyed when we did our job. Awesome. "And that means?"

"I seriously doubt it'll be an issue," Mavis remarked as she activated her phone's video recorder, then lifted it to the doors to focus the picture. "You're good, Selene. Just do your thing."

Right.

This day felt... odd.

And terrifying.

And like... a mistake. Still. Even if everyone kept pumping me up, insisting I could *do* this, being here seemed wrong.

I don't get it.

But there wasn't time to mull anything over. As soon as the doors untangled themselves and hissed open, we were off, moving as one, security at the helm, then me, then Mavis and her intern lambs bringing up the rear. Shoulders back, head held high, I strode in like I owned the place—like this really was just another day and shades weren't a completely foreign species.

Confidence went a long way with the supernatural.

As soon as they spotted a chink in your armor, you went from predator to prey like *that*.

I slowed once I crossed the threshold, however, taken aback by the state of the space. Usually creature containment on the upper levels was a long hall with individual cells, some glass, some titanium or silver, iron for the rare fae we had at this location. The vibe, no matter the wall color or number of potted plants, said prison or psych ward. *Maybe* two-star hotel for our volunteers.

This was just a huge brightly lit hangar housing three glass cubes—with walls ten inches thick, bulletproof, and *very* creature-proof. One to my left, right, and then dead ahead. In the center of the triad sat the security console with two monitors, a laptop, and panels of unfamiliar buttons. Inside the cubes, I *hoped* there was a light source somewhere.

Because I couldn't see it for the life of me.

Swirling smoke and darkness filled each glass square,

shapeless and flecked with grey. I staggered to a full halt, struggling to take in each cube, to process exactly *why* the black inside struck me as ancient and eternal. Maybe the assault from the overhead fluorescents had my sensitive eyes searching for relief. Maybe it was the newness of it all, the thrill of cataloguing a previously unknown resident of the underworld—solo, I might add. Maybe...

Interest piqued, I dug blindly in my pocket for my pen, then remembered I'd clipped it to my lanyard in the office. Moving on autopilot, unable to rip my gaze away from the cubes, I dragged it off and pumped the end, the *click* muted, the whispers behind me incoherent.

The *shadows*...

Fascinating.

Beguiling.

Soothing.

I'd taken three long strides left before I tapped back into reality, then firmly planted my feet and scribbled my initial reaction on the clipboard's second page, embarrassing as it was, my face tingling with an unfamiliar and very much unwelcome heat.

Pop culture, oblivious and unaware, made supernatural creatures out to be really *hot* these days. Just... sexy, shirtless, buff guys who swept the ladies off their feet. In my experience, the hot factor varied amongst the paranormal like it did with humans. Good looks only ran skin-deep. Even the most attractive wolf shifter could be an absolute dick.

And a lot of the shifters were.

Sexist, chauvinistic, patriarchal douchebags.

At least the ones who ended up at our Cronus HQ, *especially* the paid subjects.

What had started as gentle black mist, easy spirals and soft billows, sharpened as soon as the doors shut and bolted us inside with a few thunderous *clunks*. While Abrams tapped around the security console, eyes up and wandering, Dermott prowled between the three cubes, sporting a semiautomatic with antidemon sigils carved down the barrel—probably on the bullets, too, just for added security. Whether it was the doors closing or our presence intruding on the shades' space, the darkness moved faster, zipping around the cubes, slamming into the glass walls.

And not just in one spot either, but all over, like they were testing it, searching for weaknesses.

I made a note of that, ignoring how my hand trembled through the wonky letters. An especially loud *wham* from the cube directly across from the main doors made me flinch, but I held my ground with a deep, steadying breath. Intake teams took the most abuse right off the bat; we suffered the brunt of supernatural rage until med and research came up with a way to subdue whatever roared behind the metaphorical bars.

Only this didn't feel like anger.

That usual tension in the air just wasn't there. The hair on the back of my neck stood up like always, but it wasn't a fear response.

It...

It was like electricity.

Like a deep, beautiful bass thumping in your bones.

Just as I was about to ask the others for their observations, maybe check with Abrams and get his read on the way this hangar suddenly felt like one big dancing live wire—the darkness changed again. It centralized in each cube, spiraling like a tight tornado, drawing all the shadows to a singular point.

And shifting from floating matter to something *very,* very solid.

Scratch that.

Someth*ings.*

Humanoid.

I swallowed thickly, an inferno blasting through my insides. Not just humanoid—men.

Three outrageously beautiful *men.*

My arms went limp at my sides. My heart tripped over its own feet, again and again, erratic and frantic in its cage. My jaw—well, I caught that before it dropped, but barely.

To my left stood a tall and wiry creature, the kind of man who had a subtle strength about him, subdued and nowhere near braggy. Beneath an impeccably tailored black suit, black tie, black oxfords, he struck me as the sort drunk jerks might heckle in a bar, only to realize their mistake when he nailed them with a single, precise knockout punch. Broad shoulders. Long limbs. Hands hidden behind his back—pale as his face and neck, probably.

Blinking furiously, I catalogued him with what I hoped seemed like clinical fascination, breathless and weak-kneed. Oval face with a sharp jawline and a slightly pointed chin. Blush-pink lips, thin and quirked at the ends. Faint dimples. Pronounced cheekbones. Black brows, his hair like freshly spilled ink. Shoulder-length and slicked back like he'd just run his hand through it—or someone had finger-combed it out of his handsome face, a thought that triggered *jealousy* in me, bolting through my veins like lightning. A slight curl, his hair soft and layered, coiling artfully around his expressive features like the gods themselves had arranged it.

Black eyes.

Not black like the demons I'd met before—hollow and empty and soulless.

No, this was *layers* of darkness, the iris faintly lighter than the pupil.

Okay, okay, enough. Focus.

Difficult as it was, I turned my back on him to assess his fellow shades, only to jerk back at the figure in the cube to my right.

All limbs, he made long and willowy an art. Wearing black trousers and a black turtleneck, this one hugged the shadows to him. Leftie had banished the darkness—or absorbed it, or whatever. Rightie kept it swathed around him like a protective aura, the shadowy backdrop only making his skin *more* translucent. Unlike me, you couldn't map the blue veins twining under his flesh. Tall like his companion. Leaner. Spidery fingers and a heart-shaped face. Gaunt. Lips pale as diluted rosewater. Eyes black and vacant—but still not *quite* like the demons I'd processed. There was just... more to them.

Messy white-blond hair, shorter on the sides, longer on the top.

Stylish.

Like a twiggy aristocrat or a haute couture model.

A little scarier than his friend—but intriguing.

Curious. Alluring, his beauty ghostly and dangerous.

I lifted my clipboard and flipped a few pages deep, scribbling what might hopefully be useable first impressions of both shades for intake admin—only to notice *literal* scribbles.

Great.

Maybe the containment sigils painted along the tops of the cubes weren't cutting it with these guys, because no monster had ever done this to me before.

Get back in the game, Selene.

Right, and the final—

"*Oh.*" I reared back and looked sky-high the second I faced the cube behind the security console—because this one was naked.

Just...

Buck-ass-nude.

Face on fire, I risked a quick sweep—just a fast up-and-down glance, because, like the sun, I couldn't look at this one for long without him blinding me. Biggest of the three, he was all muscle, toned and defined, pure female fantasy with the broad, rippling shoulders and the olive skin tone, complexion like he'd just stepped off an Italian yacht where he tanned just as naked as he was now.

Braced against the glass, arms over his head and huge hands dangling, he wasn't exactly hiding the way black hairs peppered his chest and slanted down to a cut torso, that defined V so *tempting*—but I skipped it as fast as I could, noting strong thighs and calves, big feet.

Wild eyes.

Black like the rest, but pure predator in the way he watched me, square-jawed, the first with facial scruff that would probably *hurt* if it dragged over your—*my*—bare skin. Thick, stylishly short black hair. A roman nose. Straight, big teeth when he grinned at me, canines as noticeably sharp as mine.

Crazy. Chaotic.

Killer. A shiver sliced down my spine.

Number Three screamed trouble without saying a word.

"Hello, little one."

My head snapped to the left, drawn by a voice like the softest velvet, rich and deep, luxurious in a way that felt beyond my reach. Leftie had drifted up to the glass at some point, and he meandered down the wall now, his walk a glide and his movements almost feline. Sleek. Slow. Easy, like he owned the room, not stopping until he reached the vent in the corner and gently tipping his head back as if to speak through it.

Thank goodness the demon containment sigils seemed to be working, or these guys would probably just smoke through the grates—

Smoke.

I blinked.

Smoke and darkness and mist—now men.

Shapeshifters.

Gnawing on the insides of my cheeks, I flipped through the clipboard pages and hastily wrote that down, my scrawl sloppy and shaky, all over the place and barely following the lines.

"Uh, hi." Awesome. Solid start. *Way to assert your authority.* Clearing my throat, I rolled my shoulders back and looked pointedly between the cubes. "I'm sure you're all a little confused about what's happening and where you are—"

"*Cronus.*"

Leftie in his scrumptious suit, those exquisite cheekbones, his voice that of a tenor in an angelic choir—he purred the name of our secret society like a filthy prayer, and *want* flared between my thighs.

Followed by another explosion of heat across my face, my blushes always so obvious, my feelings out in the open— a giant, gaping weakness in a place like this. At this point, all eyes fell on me, monster and human alike, and I busied myself with the clipboard, scribbling literally nothing under the *shapeshifter* note in raggedy cursive.

"Yes, uh, that's right." *Get—it—together.* My gaze darted between Abrams and Dermott, drawing strength from their stern energy, their take-no-shit expressions. "So, I know this is unsettling—that's perfectly normal. My name is Selene, and I'm here to—"

Naked Hottie burst out laughing.

No, not laughing.

Howling.

And snarling.

And—

Ugh, what an unsettling sound, primal and deep, throaty and gruff. Angry, almost, despite the manic lift of his lips.

"Selene, Selene," he parroted back to me in such a delicious, terrifying rasp. He then pounded his huge fist against the glass and pushed off it, pacing. "What a *silly* name they've given you." Abrams and Dermott swarmed, zeroing in on the biggest threat in the room as he stalked about like a caged tiger, eyes fixed on me. "What a cruel *joke.*"

Trapped in place, I just watched him move, lost in the sinuous dance of muscle, the almost effortless way he dominated every male on this side of the glass with a glance and a sneer and a voice rough as sandpaper—

Rough but lyrical.

I couldn't...

I'd never...

Like driving by an especially bad car crash, I couldn't look away. Couldn't resist the impulse to gawk, to really surrender to the morbid curiosity that called to the dark, dirty thing in my chest, the monster I'd repressed since I had the good sense to realize it didn't belong in civilized society.

"Selene." And then there was the velvet again, a balm to this one's brutality. "*Here.*"

He summoned me through the vent, his voice carrying like an intimate whisper. Without meaning to, body totally out of my control, I staggered toward his cube, then pumped the brakes a few feet out and hugged the clipboard to my chest like a shield.

"My name is Arawn," he murmured with a hand to his heart. How... did his words travel all the way out here and still sound so seductively soft? Could the others hear? Was it a spell—or something innate about him? *Arawn*, a name that resonated in the core of my being, pointed to the still-cackling monster across the way. "He's Balor." He then looked *through* me, stabbing at the glass wall. "And that one's Draco."

I wrote the names down because I had to.

But this time, my writing was the neatest it had ever been during an assessment, my hand suddenly steady, my pulse finding its rhythm.

"Okay, thank you," I muttered, my sidelong glance hesitant and fleeting—or I'd get sucked into his affectionate smile, like he was *proud* of me or something. Instead, I pointed at the trio with my pen, committing their names to memory even though they suddenly felt like they'd lived in my marrow since birth. "Arawn. Balor. Draco."

Draco remained still and expressionless when I said his name, though the darkness around him shivered. Balor, meanwhile, went quiet—which, frankly, was almost scarier than the laughter. His pacing quickened, like he was trying to sidestep security at every turn, locked on me with this *look* that triggered all my internal alarm bells.

Self-preservation shrieked for me to *run*—because the thinning of his lips, the narrowing of his dark eyes, the flex and twist and tautness of his sculpted physique...

He either wanted to attack me—or screw me.

It wouldn't be the first time a beastie pulled that crap on an intake officer, but it *was* the first time I wanted to open the cage and see what happened.

"I work for Cronus intake," I said instead, lifting my chin a little higher and focusing on the containment runes in black over their cubes. No getting out. Hellspawn couldn't slither around that combination no matter what tricks they had up their sleeves. "I'm here to ask some questions and take a few samples for the lab. Nothing invasive, I promise."

As if to prove my point, I motioned back to Mavis and the interns. The woman herself was eyeballs-deep in her phone, thumbs tapping away, brows furrowed. One from her terrified herd held up the intake bag, roughly the size of a large leather purse, its contents clinking together inside.

Draco immediately withdrew, swathed in darkness, his haunting beauty hidden and only his outline visible through the black mist. Right—not starting with him.

Across the hangar, Balor had started mirroring Dermott's movements, taunting him with cruel grins and fluttery black lashes, beckoning him closer with a crooked finger and a wicked gleam in his eyes. All teeth. All monster. Huge and precise, his movements disturbingly graceful for a man nearing, oh, maybe seven feet.

Yeah, *definitely* not setting foot inside that cube.

Which left—

"Come here, Selene." Arawn tapped on the glass, oozing charm from head to toe as he beckoned me closer. This time, I didn't blindly follow the command, desperate as my body was to obey. Standing still felt like nails on a chalkboard, but I held my ground just long enough to write *Manipulative* next to his name. Then, with a deep breath that didn't clear my muddled thoughts in the slightest, I drifted toward his cube. Arawn tilted his head back again to speak through the vent, exposing his elegant throat, the bulge there a distraction. "You can always talk to me."

Goodness, how did a creature from Hell sound *so* sincere?

It had to be a ploy.

A disarming tactic.

Something to lull their prey—

"I heard you attacked other intake officers." And it worked, because my tone should have been accusatory, not conversational.

"I give you my word." He swept his middle finger over his heart, elegantly crossing it for me. "I'll be ever so good for you."

Fire licked across my cheeks again. *Ever so good* for *you* —the connotations were a little too endless for my liking. Before I could regroup, Mavis called me over with a sharp whisper, my name suddenly so jarring coming from anyone *but* the beasts in these cubes.

Still, I went, practically sprinting to safety.

"Do your questions while you take samples," she told me, snatching my dark blue intake bag with the Cronus serpent logo on its side from her intern. The hagless ones were taking notes—probably way more thorough and clearer than mine, so I might need to defer to them later. Mavis motioned toward Arawn with a jut of her chin and a scowl. "No formal interview. Just get the basics, and leave once you have your samples."

Right. Clearly I wasn't the only one here with trust issues. Nodding, I faced the leftmost cube again, pointedly ignoring the rest because Balor and Draco were just too distracting. Draco in twisting, twining, slinking shadows.

Balor tormenting Dermott and Abrams, baiting them—helicoptering his dick around.

Oi.

Arawn, meanwhile, had drifted to the center of his cube, then gestured side to side. Shadows misted from his fingertips, dark and thick, rolling off lean, elegant fingers and coiling into—

Chairs.

He had made chairs out of darkness, stable enough to hold him when he sat and crossed one long leg over the other. Prim and proper, beautifully regal, he unbuttoned his suit jacket and got himself situated, the second chair directly in front of him—for me. Flashing yet another charming grin, he gestured to it, an invitation to take a seat.

Ugh. He was... *way* too good-looking for me to go in there by myself, but here I was, headed for the seamless door on the opposite side of the cube. With a death grip on my intake bag and clipboard, I hesitated by the ID scanner, facing Arawn head-on from this angle. He tipped his head and threaded his hands on his lap, waiting, radiating pleasant and polite, calm and composed.

"Shut the *fuck* up."

Balor had started hissing my name, and Abrams saw fit to chastise him.

Draco's shadowy form had slithered up to the wall of his cube, mist spiraling along the panel, his black eyes crystallizing, utterly fixated on me.

Jittery like this was the first time I'd ever done this solo when it was, oh, maybe the three hundredth this year alone, I took a beat to compose myself, then held my ID card to the scanner.

Two chirpy beeps and the reader flashed green.

The door slid open, wide enough for just one person to

squish through sideways, my boobs and butt brushing over the thick glass on either side.

Then I was caged with the monster.

The door hissed shut.

And Arawn grinned, charm shifting to mischief, Balor most definitely not the only predator in here.

CHAPTER THREE

"Hello, Selene."

I'd read about *sharklike* grins in books over the years, and the sharp lift of Arawn's lips, the pearly whites—this had to be it.

Only there was more charm to this.

Like you'd willingly climb into the great white's mouth and die happy.

It should have scared me.

Instead, as the door bolted at my back, calm slithered down my spine and pooled in my core. Unlike the usual confident air that hit once I settled into the meat and potatoes of an intake appointment, there was a strange intimacy here, like a dark secret that made my cheeks hot and my womanhood pulse with interest.

Something kind of humiliating if the others caught on. While Mavis and her interns couldn't directly see me, cameras angled into the cube from every corner, Abrams, like any good flock guardian, had picked up the scent of supernatural trickery. Tough and seasoned, my favorite security guard hovered by the glass wall to my right, then prowled around to loiter at the door. His looming figure should have been a confidence boost.

Instead, a little part of me was... *annoyed* at his presence.

Annoyed at all of them.

Everyone but these shades.

Still grinning like the cat who'd caged the elusive canary, Arawn motioned to the shadowy black chair across from him, the gesture elegant, the flourish of his hand with those long, lean fingers almost regal. "Have a seat. I made it just for you."

Curious. I didn't bother making note of my thoughts: when I rewatched the footage somewhere private, locked in my office where no one could see me blush, I'd remember *exactly* what I was thinking.

Then I would type up some safe-for-work version and submit it.

Call it a day and try to forget.

For now, I lived in the moment, strolling across the cube and studying the seat this shade had conjured out of nothing. While it had the bare-bones look of a basic waiting room chair, thick like wood, no cushion but ample back support, inky black smoke coiled off it in wisps. Reminiscent of fog-machine smoke, my hand should have gone right through it.

Huh. Completely solid. Squaring my shoulders, my insides a cocktail of surprise and intrigue, I went from ghosting along the surface to grabbing it like I meant to pull it away.

Hard and cool and weighty—probably couldn't lift it one-handed.

Out of the corner of my eye, I caught Arawn lurch

forward, elbows on his knees, deftly easing into my personal space with his large frame—

I retreated, even as instinct *begged* me to move toward him, not away. Protocol dictated... Outside of the physical exam and sample collection, we shouldn't... *touch* any of them—

Arawn leaned back and lifted his hands as if to apologize, that sharklike grin softened to pure silk.

"Easy."

That rumble—like molten honey.

Focus, Selene.

Dad's voice slashed through the abrupt avalanche of racy thoughts, and I cleared my throat, schooled my expression, then dumped my intake bag on the shadowy chair.

"I'm going to take a hair and blood sample," I informed him, stamping down any natural warmth, aiming for professional indifference and failing miserably, "plus a saliva swab, temperature reading, and a fingernail scraping."

"Are you?" I looked up sharply at the challenge lobbed my way, cordial and unnervingly charming. Arawn crossed his long legs again, then his arms, beaming up at me, his features so ethereally beautiful that I had the almost violent urge to sketch him after giving up the, quote, *useless hobby* before senior year. The aristocratic features. The silky black waterfall of waves and loose curls swept back and falling to the tops of his shoulders, somehow both neat *and* wild, the juxtaposition a siren song to my fingers.

"Yes." *Damn it.* Stupid breathy voice. Another soft *ahem* sorted that out, and I busied myself with the hair test tube and the tweezers, one in each hand. When I faced him again, I focused on his forehead; just a millimeter lower and

I'd get lost in those stunning black eyes, and then this whole intake was a wash. "Please tell me if anything I do hurts."

His chuckles floated around the cube like satin butterflies. "I very much doubt you could—"

Pride—such a distraction. Arawn's thin lips snapped shut when I quickly seized a loose black flyaway with the tweezers, me and the ol' gal *very* practiced at snagging samples from unwilling subjects. The handsome shade stiffened, then leaned back in his own wispy shadow seat, appraising me through fresh eyes—like I'd gotten one over on him.

And I did.

Which, I guess, was a surprise?

A pleasant one, if anything, his scrutiny intensifying, *burning* across my skin as I set the sample in the tube and corked it safely inside. At this point, spelling his name was just a shot in the dark, as all three males came nameless on their initial paperwork. While it sounded like *Aaron*, there was more to it, the pronunciation pure old-world fantasy. Thin-tipped marker in hand, the chair and my open bag between us, I frowned at the test tube label. The *R* had more of a roll to it, then a yawning texture at the end. Ah-*rr*-awn.

Arawn.

The marker wobbled through his name—because it belonged on a prehistoric carving, not a test tube.

Which was just... weird.

We had centuries-old vampires come through Cronus from time to time, and never had I put their archaic names on a pedestal like this.

Was it *his* doing—or were these supernatural beasties my kryptonite? All humans in this building had one, a weakness, an off-limits species, some creature they were more susceptible to than others.

I had never felt it before.

I thought I was above it, *better* than my biology.

Guess not.

Now that I'd realized it, the logical thing to do was to step back, pack it in, and ask a colleague to finish the intake exam.

"Roll up your sleeve, please."

Instead, as Arawn unbuttoned his black suit jacket and peeled it from his strong shoulders, his every move sinfully compelling, I carried on like nothing was wrong.

"So, Arawn," I started, wishing I could have breezed by his name but tripping over it instead. Teeth gritted, I rummaged around my intake bag for a prepackaged syringe, then ripped the plastic open as the shade neatly folded his jacket and set it across his lap. "How old are you?"

"Old as time."

He smirked up at me while I readied the syringe, his initial scribbled on the label alongside today's date. Of course he was old as time. Of course. Most of the beings that crawled out of the pit liked to exaggerate: humans were toys to demonkind, silly and insignificant playthings to be used and discarded.

Apparently.

"Right." No matter how my insides squirmed all deliciously the nearer I got to him, I did my best to play it cool and skeptical on the outside. "You got a rough estimate, or...?"

"No." He tipped his head, assessing first the syringe with its newly exposed needlepoint, then my face. "Sorry to be difficult, Selene. How old are *you*?"

"This isn't a back-and-forth," I told him, pleasant and

professional while I pointed to his arm. Black dress shirt uncuffed and open, Arawn rolled the fabric up to reveal a pale forearm, lean but powerful.

Huh. No veins.

I blinked and went closer, hunched by his side for a visual inspection, followed by some light finger prodding along the tender underside of his wrist. Then a few taps. He complied when asked to make a tight fist and let go—all the usual tricks to coax shy bloodlines to the surface.

Nothing.

"Slight pinch," I warned, refusing to air my confusion out in the open. Instead, I acted on muscle memory alone, drawing from the usual place. Arawn's gaze locked squarely on mine, so unnervingly *bright* despite the inky black sheen. He didn't flinch or inhale or tense when I plunged in near the crook of his elbow.

"Twenty-five years," he rumbled suddenly, just on the verge of the actual draw. I stilled, suddenly *very* aware that I hadn't put on gloves, that I'd skipped procedures and looked sloppy, like I had no idea what the hell I was doing—and that this shade had correctly guessed my age with no visual indicators. Everyone always told me I looked younger; I'd be carded forever if I ever bothered to visit a bar more than once or twice a year. Swallowing hard, I glanced at Arawn's pleasant smile, the slight arch of his left brow. He then eased closer, a half inch feeling like a whole damn mile. "I *smell* it on you."

A shiver slicked over my skin like an icy finger, and I focused on easing the plunger back to fill the barrel—

Uh.

Okay.

Black wisps and nothing more, darkness filled the vial, thickening like a midnight sky just before a storm.

Arawn offered a shrug when I frowned at him.

"Do shades not bleed?"

For the first time, he appeared genuinely taken aback, and not pleasantly so like when I'd nabbed a hair off him—almost offended.

"Who said I was a shade?"

I applied pressure to the draw site—probably unnecessary—and removed the needle. "You're all classified as—"

"Shades roam the grounds of Hades, little one." He sat straighter when I backed off, coiling those long fingers into a fist, his scowl just as alluring as his smile. "We are not shades."

Awesome. Nothing like the desk jockeys tossing you in the deep end with inaccurate information. Back at my bag, I cracked the needle off at the syringe hub, sealing whatever I'd taken inside, and disposed of it in the proper biohazard container. Then, sample logged and sealed, I scrambled for gloves, hoping Mavis hadn't spotted me without them.

"So, what are you, then?"

"You know."

I sniffed softly, snapping the left glove into place, the latex already starting to make me itch. "I don't."

"You will." Calmer, cooler, and more collected than I could ever be, the mysterious creature who had let me poke and prod him without a fight rolled his sleeve down and buttoned the cuff. "You'll remember one day."

My gut bottomed out, and I threaded my fingers together under the guise of fitting the gloves properly—not to hide the way they suddenly shook. "That implies we've met before."

Arawn zeroed in on my eyes again as he slipped his jacket on. "In a way, we have—"

"No." I blurted it fast and furious. Demons lied. They played tricks. They made you think you were *special* to drop your guard and bare your throat. *Nope. Not taking the bait.* "We haven't."

Fumbling with the scraper packaging, I ignored him until the last possible moment. Wood stick with its sharpened end in one hand and a sample collection baggy in the other, I gestured toward him.

"Hold out your hand, please."

Same as before, he let me do my thing with zero hesitation. No arguments. No debates. No questions. Arawn offered his hand palm down, and I moved in for collection, noting that not only was his skin ivory-white, but it was also hairless. Nothing on his arm or his knuckles—unlike Balor, who had artful smatterings of coarse black hair to highlight muscle definition...

And, you know, whatever was dangling between his legs. Arawn's companion struck me as overt masculinity, whereas he was just... Arawn. Beautiful. Cool manliness that wasn't an obvious threat. The spider *and* the web, this guy.

Long, elegant fingers, his skin barely lukewarm but enticingly soft despite the strength contouring his forearm. Neat, pale nails.

Clean.

Very clean.

Too clean.

I scraped all five digits and got absolutely nothing. No smoky wisps. No black flakes. Gnawing on the insides of my cheeks, I tried his left hand after—same results. Ugh. Might need to do fingerprint scans for these guys.

Just as I started to pull back, he pounced, snapping one huge hand around my wrist and jerking me back to him.

"You have her eyes," he whispered as the door hissed open at my back, Abrams' footfalls storming into the cube and accented by the grunt he always made squishing through small containment doors. I waved him off frantically, lost in the black, in the intensity of the moment, Arawn's breath like arctic freshness as it brushed my lips. His grip was brutal, the exact opposite of his charming, unassuming demeanor. *Power* bloomed under his soft, smooth skin like steel below ice.

"Miss Abbott—"

"Who?" I murmured, blocking out Abrams completely. Even as fear tickled my ribs, making my heart dance and my palms sweat, I *needed* the answer—needed to hear him say it.

Because that dark, brooding part of my psyche, the monster I blocked out—it already knew.

"Your mother's," Arawn rasped. I let out a shaky breath and pulled away, teary-eyed without a clue *why*. He didn't fight my retreat, releasing me at the last second, my hand almost as pale as his before the blood surged again. Trembling, barely holding on to my scraper and sample bag, I stumbled back to the chair and shoved my tools inside, half-present, half-gone, everything blurred by an unwelcome damp. Numb static seared my veins, the disconnect dizzying, the impact of two stupid words deeper than I'd ever admit.

With Abrams loitering inside the cube now, door blocked with his body and sigil-encrusted firearm drawn, I took a temperature reading at a distance. Temp gun leveled at Arawn's crinkled forehead, his brows lifted with what *might* have been concern, I waited for the beep, then recorded the digits that popped up on the little screen at the end of the barrel.

Eighty-six degrees.

Okay. Sure. Whatever.

Temp gun stowed, I frantically ripped open a cheek swab packet, then grabbed it and a new sample tube, ready for this to be done—to get out of this cube, this room, and Sub-level Z so I could *breathe*.

"They're nearly identical," Arawn mused softly as I marched back to him. "Her eyes. Your eyes. Beautiful—"

"Open your mouth." I sucked in my cheeks, biting them hard just to feel something more than whatever was going on inside, and waited for him to comply. This non-shade just stared up at me, seated and composed, either totally unaware of what he had done to me—or *very* aware and planning how best to break *this* Cronus employee. Either way, I wasn't in the mood. "Please—and no biting."

The creature uttered a gentle sigh, one that barely made a sound but I *swore* made the obnoxious white lights flicker.

"Selene—"

I stabbed between his open lips, making him buck and rear back, but the chair only allowed an inch or two of wiggle room. Looming over him, slightly crouched and way too intense about a freakin' saliva swab, I brushed along his gums, uppers and lowers, everything on autopilot and the walls closing in.

Pressing on every side.

Suffocating—

His fingers suddenly brushed the end of my ponytail. High and tight and perky, smooth as this mane would ever be, it must have fallen over my shoulder at some point, and I stilled, swab stuffed back to his molars. Just a ghostly caress, he stroked my hair, back and forth, then *barely* coiled a curl around one finger.

"What have they done to you?"

I sucked in a harsh gasp and jerked out of reach. His lips... They hadn't moved when he spoke, that painfully beautiful whisper echoing inside my head. Our eyes met, his suddenly a glossy black, glistening like starlight beneath the fluorescents. One blink and the dams burst in mine, hot damp coursing down my cheeks, my heart aching, my stomach in knots, my breath coming hard and fast.

"That's enough."

A rough hand closed around my bicep, and before I knew it, Abrams had hauled me clear out of the cube. Dermott swept in a beat later, maybe to grab my abandoned intake bag, maybe to punish Arawn for... something.

I felt drunk.

It had never happened in my twenty-five years, but this was how I imagined it. Like my stare, none of my friends could ever keep up. It took a few *bottles* of hard liquor to get me slightly tipsy, but this was so much *more*, weightless and unsteady, stuck in perpetual free fall with the ground a million miles away.

As the main doors unlocked, the central configuration twisting free and the huge metal panels sliding open, Balor started to scream.

Violently.

Savagely.

Over my shoulder, I watched like I wasn't even here, like this was just some drama unfolding on a screen. Several ceiling lights exploded, raining glass and sparks on Mavis and her shrieking interns.

Who had been feverishly recording *everything*.

Draco burst into shadow, his lean silhouette gone, the shock of stark white hair swallowed whole in the bleak, black darkness. Naked and howling, Balor hurled himself at the walls of his cube, misty darkness pluming out his back like the scorched black wings of a fallen angel. Thumps and whumps and *screeches* thundered from Draco's box.

And Arawn sat in that chair, legs crossed, hands threaded on his thigh, suit immaculate and hair artfully swept off his divine features.

Eyes watery.

Sunken cheeks streaked with *feeling*, same as mine—

Then Abrams yanked me over the threshold, grunting like that required *effort*, and the doors sprinted shut.

My knees buckled.

I hit the floor hard and sobbed into my hands, lost and alone, only vaguely aware of Abrams bracing me and muttering under his breath, then ditching his gear to rub my back.

Darkness raked up my insides, sharp and brutal, slicing so deep that when I coughed, angry currant-red blood sprinkled the floor, its desperation pure *agony*.

Because that was it.

No clue what was happening to me, around me—but I knew that much. Like Arawn smelled my age, I smelled the desperation inside myself, the secret shadows I had shoved down all my life burning to life.

Desperate to claw their way back inside.

Desperate to crawl back to *them*.

Desperate, above all else, for *home*.

CHAPTER FOUR

Standing before these huge doors with their intricate locking system in the center, the demon containment runes branded into the metal—a few new ones added since that first day...

I had no idea why I came back.

But my modified ID access card expired tomorrow, and then Sub-level Z would be out of bounds for good.

So... Here I was.

Here, alone, the metallic corridor so empty in either direction the yawning silence tickled my ears, its itch like an especially bad bug bite, getting more and more obnoxious by the second.

I'd wanted to come back, to stand right *here*, for five days, but Dad had put his foot down and ordered me on bed rest for three after that mess of an intake. Then, after doping me with meds that were supposed to knock out an elephant but did the exact opposite, hovering in my personal space and nitpicking every little thing I did, he must have pulled strings in *my* department—because they'd stuck me on desk duty for the last two days. Nothing like mindless data entry for eight hours straight to really scramble your brain.

But the tactic failed.

Each night I crawled into bed more wired than ever. Even with the upped dosages on my standard medication. Even with the white noise machines. Even with the new blackout curtains and Dad bullying away my raven visitors at dawn.

Messy. The last five days had been *so* messy, and my nights weren't any better.

Because whenever I finally managed a few winks, my dreams were all *them*.

Arawn. Balor. Draco.

Their voices whispering my name—even Draco's, who I hadn't heard yet but somehow instinctively recognized that it belonged to him. Whispers and caresses, safe and comforting in the stormy aftermath of *it*.

The Incident.

You know, where I collapsed and wailed and hacked up blood on this very floor.

I toed at the spotless matte metal tiles now. Not a whiff of evidence anywhere.

Swallowing hard, I zeroed in on the door again, cheeks suddenly hot, my outfit stifling, at the memories of *them* in my dreams.

Dreams—not nightmares. I wasn't afraid, per se, but I still woke up in a panic, heart racing, sweaty and flustered and a little horny.

And above all else, frustrated.

Lack of sleep did that to you, and this wasn't the first time I'd struggled to regulate my body's needs and give it what it needed. The disease wreaking havoc on my immune system was a lifelong battle, and while for the most part I had accepted my fate, that didn't make the rough patches any easier.

And if these *monsters* made it worse, I shouldn't be here.

I...

My shift had ended fifteen minutes ago.

Dad would be expecting me in the main courtyard any second now so we could walk home for supper—some thick, highly nutritious, and totally flavorless stew that he would connect to the changing weather. Something that was supposed to be warm and cozy against the gloomy fall day, so much of the orange canopy fallen, but, like all my meals, it would taste like a prescription from my doctor.

Not my dad.

Sometimes that was the most frustrating part—that he didn't understand I craved comfort and support and maybe a little indulgence from someone not wearing a white lab coat.

Just turn around and get back on the elevator.

I fidgeted with my purple lanyard, with the laminated ID card that was my key to the lobby, where I could walk out the main doors and into the beautiful courtyard and—

I pushed forward and swiped it through the security scanner instead, then punched in the eight-digit codes required to open the doors. Same as before, the knotted center slowly unraveled, and then the immense panels peeled open, a gaping prison bay inside with three cubes and the center console.

Crossing the threshold ought to be nerve-racking.

It *shouldn't* feel like filling my lungs with crisp fresh air after being stuck indoors for weeks on end, really absorbing something good and wholesome and clean.

Next came the flood of *feeling*, my lips wobbling, my chest clenching, my eyes watering.

Not normal.

Not right.

But as I glanced between the three cubes filled with darkness, all black but somehow each so strikingly different, it definitely didn't feel wrong.

With a sniff, I noted most of the fluorescent ceiling bulbs had been blown out, way more than I remembered, and then tried my best to lock that tidal wave of emotion deep, deep inside.

I had always been good at that—tucking away what didn't fit with my surroundings, what seemed abnormal compared to those around me.

Shadows hugged the corners of the enormous underground hangar, but true darkness was in *there*, a cube for each of them. Shapeless and still, not a hint of the gorgeous men who'd greeted me last time—but I felt them. With every tentative step into their Cronus confinement, eyes raked my body, distinct and telling, scorching twisty paths from head to toe so intensely that I had to fight the urge to check under my collar or roll up my sleeves and confirm they hadn't actually burned me.

I made it all the way to the center security console before good ol' self-doubt and insecurity kicked in. A better actor would have fiddled with the buttons or checked the monitors—done *something* to give this impromptu visit an ounce of professional purpose.

"I don't know why I'm here."

Honesty won out in the end.

Honesty, a dash of bravery, and a whole lot of stupid.

This is nuts. No species had ever followed me home

before, and I'd met a whole whack of them over the years. Nobody stuck to me like this. Nobody...

No. Face hot, palms cold, fingers tingly, I turned on the spot and beelined for the open doorway.

"You know why, Selene."

Then stuttered to a halt. Arawn's velvet whisper stroked the inside of my skull, piercing through the containment sigils on his cube, and with a deep breath, I faced them again.

And there they were.

Men.

Not darkness—three impossibly beautiful men. Arawn in his tailored three-piece black suit, jacket buttoned and hands in his pockets, the divine angles in his face worthy of their own hall at the Louvre. Draco surrounded by shadowy mist, his hair stark white, his skin morbidly pale, his cheeks gaunt, and his black turtleneck stretched all the way up his throat to his chin.

And Balor...

Balor broke the mold in a white button-up dress shirt, sleeves scrunched to his elbows, forearms dusted with black hair, skin still sporting that Mediterranean glow and looking the most alive of the three—alive and *strong*, oozing vitality and, honestly, a little crazy, his black gaze manic compared to Arawn and Draco. While they stood still, Arawn right up at the glass of his cell and Draco in the center, darkness shimmering around him like a shield, Balor prowled back and forth, forever a caged beast desperate to break free.

Hungry to escape and maul the zoo guests, probably.

These... *men*, monsters, non-shades—*whatever*...

They made me *feel.*

They called to the shadows in me, this unwelcome tug

at my navel, this string around my heart willing me closer, its pressure *sharp* as I held my ground.

This mysterious trio radiated pure black darkness, but each a different aura.

I mean, Balor's was the most apparent, not a lot of nuance there: intimidating, the stuff of nightmares, the blackness at the end of a dark hallway at night that played tricks on you.

Draco struck me as a bottomless well, emotionless, expressionless, forever watching, so *hollow* despite his beauty.

Arawn was the cozy darkness in your bedroom just on the cusp of sleep, rain hammering the windows and thunder rumbling softly overhead.

Where that had come from and how my brain constructed any of it—no clue.

My fingers twitched, in need of a pen to record all these thoughts, old habits dying hard, intake protocol like muscle memory. Instead, I went for my hair, for the taut, slightly painful and perfectly arranged ballerina bun on top of my head. Not a strand out of place, sure, but I needed to *move*, needed to drain this energy, the buzz in my blood, as three sets of black eyes drilled into me from all sides.

We were quite the foursome, not a stitch of actual color between us. Them in black, plus Balor's white shirt, and then me in a crisp black blazer, its subtle layers like the patterns of a raven's wing. The white tank below. The tapered heather-grey slacks that cut off at the ankle above my faux-leather loafers. Dad wouldn't have approved of them for work attire, but I had managed to slip out of the house this morning before he saw. Comfy, well-worn, no heel—black.

Dark and moody, this collection.

I fit in with them—

Which was ridiculous.

Tugging at my purple lanyard strap—*hey*, a bit of color, even if it was more midnight plum than bright neon—I shook my head again and backpedaled a few steps. "I shouldn't be here."

"Enough?"

I slowed again, frowning as Arawn's voice whooshed around the hangar like a warm spring wind.

"Enough." And there was Draco, his voice as hoarse and croaky as in my dreams, unused and distant, like the lingering echo in a cave. Lost, I glanced between them, then flinched when Balor pounded both fists to the wall of his cube.

"*Enough!*" he bellowed, an animalistic howl ripping through the space and bursting a few more bulbs. Sparks sizzled down just as he shot *up*, suddenly engulfed in a tornado of shadows and black mist.

My blood ran cold as the smoky concoction spiraled out the cube's vent, then up, up, up to the circulation system crisscrossing the ceiling, vanishing into one of the long metal cylinders.

He...

Oh.

No.

The demon containment sigils hadn't—

Panicked, I ran for the system-wide alarm button near the main doors, then shrieked when a swarm of cozy darkness gathered in front of me, feet skidding across the floor as I tried to brake too soon. Arawn materialized in seconds, black mist to towering *man*, and I slammed into his steely chest with a yelp, then shoved off, fumbling backward, heart in my throat and stomach in knots.

What have you done, *Selene?*

I could already hear him, Dad shredding me to pieces, insisting he had always known something like this would happen, that I should have taken one of the mind-numbingly *dull* human resource jobs out of harm's way—

Wearing a pleasant smile, Arawn glided forward, tall and imposing, calm and meticulous as he backed me all the way to the security console—then reached over for something. My back bowed over the table with its clacky keyboard and thin monitor, arched and barely breathing, instinct *screaming* to touch him again and self-preservation insisting I put as much space between us as possible.

Two clicks and beeps later, Draco's cube opened, the door sliding and the monster escaping. Shadows clung to him, trailing after like a comet's tail, and he moved soundlessly, rigid and reserved, tall as Arawn but leaner.

Outnumbered.

Outgunned.

Those stupid sigils *failed.*

Because... maybe these three weren't demons.

Maybe—

I scrambled off the console and darted around Arawn, pushing my legs hard to get out the doors and bar them inside—if that was even an option. A ghostly caress fluttered down my arm, pooling in my palm like frost, and I ran faster, cardio *so* not my thing, footfalls booming in the cavernous room.

Catching the doorway, I flung myself around and slammed my access card to the security scanner, shakily pounding in the number code to seal the doors and bolt them tight. Blood whumped between my ears, adrenaline sky-high as I pushed off the wall and stumbled back, needing to confirm everything closed with *them* on the other side.

Only doors didn't seem to matter to these three: black smoke trickled through the openings, seeping through the slits long before the twisting panels locked into place, Arawn's *eyes*, his smile, shimmering in the darkness, his silhouette clawing to freedom.

Shit. I charged the elevator next, key card swiped and button stabbed again and again and *again* until the chrome doors peeled apart. Survival slingshotted me forward—but I stumbled *just* inside the cabin when a smoky black waterfall spilled from the overhead vent, quickly taking Draco's form, his hair such a shocking contrast, his skin ghostly and ethereal in the darkness. Shaking my head—*no, no, no, no*—I reeled back—

And right into Arawn again, who guided me into the elevator with a firm hand on my lower back and an enviable confidence. Trapped between them, I *almost* went on the offensive with an elbow to Arawn's ribs and a knee to Draco's groin, if that would even do anything, when a high-pitched alarm *screeched* through the corridors and blared out the speaker above the elevator button panel.

Building-wide alert.

Someone else had triggered it.

Something had gone so, so, *so* wrong.

Shrieking, I clamped my hands over my ears, the siren an assault, its shrillness seconds from rupturing my eardrums. While Draco's cheek twitched, nothing else about his expression said the noise bothered him—but he used *my* pain, my distraction, to pop open my lanyard clasp and peel the strap off my neck, then pass the whole thing over to Arawn.

Cool as a gorgeous cucumber, the black-haired god

strolled over to the buttons, swiped my card, and gently pushed the close-door option.

And as those treacherous panels sealed us inside together, he tapped the button for the lobby, then faced me with a wicked grin and a soft sigh.

CHAPTER FIVE

"Now, Selene, I think we need to set some ground rules—"

Nope. Nope, nope, nope, nope, hell *nope.*

Fight or flight on overdrive, I scrambled around Arawn and hastily took in the floor letters as they flashed on the overhead display, then stabbed the button that would cut this climb off three levels up. Neither moved to stop me, not even when the elevator jerked and the whole cabin bounced at the sudden halt. Draco remained impassive, hugged by shadow and watching me through beautifully hooded black eyes, while Arawn unleashed another of those *sighs* as the lift *dinged* and the doors opened and—

And chaos spilled in.

While the system-wide alarm had dropped to a dull roar on Sub-level E, a cacophony of sound blasted in like a bomb. Screams and howls, glass breaking and lights bursting and gunfire cracking. Eyes wide and chest tight, I shouldered in front of Arawn just as a massive red blur bounded by—Beatrice Witten, fox shifter, thirty years old and here for a six-month paid fertility study.

I liked her.

She kept to herself, never caused problems, and made art in her room.

Two of her charcoal sketches were tacked to my desk corkboard—

There and gone in a flash, a thick, dark river of blood creeping across the tile after her, slowly inching into view.

The elevator doors started to close, but I stumbled out, refusing to be caged with two monsters again—monsters who wanted to set *ground rules*.

But... maybe it was worse out here.

Yeah. No. Definitely worse.

Sub-level E still had a few menacing beasties, but the décor palettes were lighter, greige on the walls with black and taupe accents. Light wood and the odd motel art landscape. Hunter green for the cell doors—on the outside, anyway.

Blood streaked that lush green this evening. Blood on the floor in puddles and streams. Blood on the walls in dramatic crime-show sprays. Blood on the ceiling, dripping, reaching downward like gory stalactites—a few with... *pieces* attached.

Monsters on the floor, dead, heads blown open and eyes hollow.

Cronus security right alongside them, throats shredded and limbs torn off.

The storm of sound dulled as I absorbed every sickening detail—then pounded back into me like the tide, security in black uniforms with guns drawn screaming for creatures to return to their cells. Bodies sprinting, monsters in soft specimen scrubs—teal on this level, same as the three below and two above.

"*Selene.*"

Arawn waved me toward the elevator, holding the

doors, maybe even grinding his teeth given the way his jaw muscles flickered. Why was it so *hot* when men did that? The jaw flare and the intense stare and the sharp features—

A vampire zipped between us, racing down the hall and around the corner in seconds, just a *whoosh* of black and teal, greeted with gunfire that lit up the corridor.

Shaking, shock dosing my blood in cold bursts, I stumbled after him, searching for friendly faces—

Until security peeled around the corner, guns up, helmets on, and visors down like some SWAT team—and opened fire.

I shrieked and hit the deck, flat on my face, arms thrown over my head as bullets buried in walls and bounced off metal doors. A few dinged the elevator, and while Arawn huffed an annoyingly sexy little growl this time, I didn't twist back to check if he'd been hit.

Because I wasn't about to lose my life in friendly fire. No fucking way. I wasn't a target, but it looked like *every* creature on this level had busted out, all the doors open, all these bodies strewn about—no one would bat an eye if some random intake officer fell in the crossfire. Cronus had always been about the bigger picture—the needs of the many over the needs of the few—and right now, restoring order and returning literal monsters to their cells took top priority.

Did you do this?

Is it my fault?

As if someone was actually listening, a bullet ricocheted off *something* and slammed into the floor, whizzing over my head and landing by my left ear. The sizzle, the scent of gunpowder, and the *heat*. Yelping, I curled tighter—

A guttural roar flooded the hallway, the kind that shredded your throat and left your mouth bloody. Viewport windows on all the open doors shattered. The eardrum-bursting gunfire slowed, and when I hesitantly peeked up, darkness barreled by overhead, a great shadowy cloud with an aura straight from humanity's nightmares. Security got off a few shots, holding their ground—and that steadfastness was their downfall. The black cloud swallowed them whole, sweeping them off their feet, engulfing every last man.

Strength like a waning moon, I managed to push onto my elbows, then fought back a rush of bile as blood gushed from the cloud, coating the floor from one wall to another, the air tinted metallic. Screams clawed out of the darkness—followed shortly by an arm, a hand, a leg. Every limb landed with a sickeningly wet *whump*.

And then the darkness centered, swirling inward, tight and thick and *black* as the deepest pits—Balor. Mist spiraled off his bare forearms. Smoke steamed from his shoulders.

His smile—horrifying. Wide and toothy and *bloody*.

His button-up so red I suddenly second-guessed if it had *ever* been white and crisp and clean.

Struggling to pull enough air into my lungs, I scooted back, this stubborn busted body of mine refusing to just get up and *run*. Balor tipped his head to the side, not even the slightest bit winded, and let loose one of those haunting, howling laughs I felt in my bones—that touched deeper than I'd ever admit, the scarier parts of *my* being purring behind the wall I had built and fortified years ago.

"Wild things don't belong in cages, Selene," he rasped as footsteps whispered behind me. "And that includes you."

Flight finally kicked into high gear, and I managed to shoot up, stagger around—and slam into Arawn again. He caught me by my elbows the second my knees buckled, which prompted *fight* to take the reins, to try and escape him and his stupid ground rules.

Bare feet pounded the taupe tile, and we all glanced back at the mage who skidded around the corner, his hands aglow, his stay at our Cronus facility very much *not* voluntary. Fifteen, dangerous, he hated humans with a passion, firmly allying himself with supernatural camps who wanted to wipe us off the face of the earth. His eyes, wide and brilliant and almost neon they were so blue, flitted from Balor to Arawn to Draco by his side, then down to me.

He raised his right hand, fingertips red with *power*.

And Balor stepped between us, blocking me from him and him from me.

"*Balor*," Draco drawled when his companion lurched forward, darkness swirling, his huge frame already bleeding from a solid state to mist. The mage hastily backpedaled around the corner, and Balor slowed, his growl steeped with frustration.

"I want out of this festering pit," Draco insisted, his voice stronger and more assertive than it had been in the cube, yet still so rough and raspy.

Still so empty—and mildly annoyed, maybe, with that slight inflection, his sharper affect the first sign of any real *feeling* behind his ghostly good looks.

Balor twisted around, solidifying again, his legs distinct and his long, grotesque shadow talons shortening to the standard ten-digit human length. Bloody teeth bared, he rolled his eyes, then gestured back in the direction we came from.

No.

No, I wasn't about to just saunter into the elevator and—

Arawn whittled my options down to one when he ducked and tossed me over his shoulder, manhandling me like I weighed nothing while I squealed and flailed and shoved at his steely back and pounded my knees into an equally hard chest. It was time to show them that just because I was *human* didn't mean they could toss me around—do whatever they wanted. It was time for the fire in me to soar and burn so freakin' bright—

His hand snuffed the fire out in one simple stroke, his caress firm and overly familiar as it smoothed up my right thigh. Goose bumps had never hurt before, but they appeared so fast and furious my skin ached, heat twisting in my belly and the little hairs on the back of my neck out like I'd touched a live wire. I fisted the back of his jacket with a shaky breath, his steps smooth, almost like he was gliding, as he followed Draco down the main artery of Sub-level E. Balor trailed after us, kicking torn limbs aside with a twisted grin—eyeing *me*, my flushed cheeks and my fluttering lashes.

Arawn's thumb stroked my inner thigh, and despite my slacks, I *felt* him. Intimately. Like neither of us was wearing a stitch of clothing, and I suddenly craved his *tongue* in place of his thumb—

"It's dead."

They all paused at the open elevator, and, heart booming between my ears, I swallowed hard and pushed up, peeking back as far as Arawn's hold would allow—because not only had he slid a strong hand between my thighs, but his other arm hooked around my knees to keep me *right* there, over his shoulder no matter how I squirmed.

It's dead. Draco wasn't wrong, per se. The elevator had never been alive, but since I'd stumbled out, the power to it must have been cut and, oh, *shit*, was that a giant puddle of blood in the middle with... *stuff* smeared on the walls?

Bodily stuff.

Nope. *Nope.* I faced away and gulped down the flood of

saliva. Hello, nausea, my old friend—*come to screw with me again*.

"Stairs," Arawn rumbled thoughtfully. "There."

"But we could just—"

"She isn't ready for that yet." Never heard an argument sound like silk before, a vicious Balor cut off without Arawn ever breaking his stride. "Once we're outside—yes."

The trio sauntered down the hall as a collective unit. Not in a rush. Relaxed. Confident. Maybe even a little bored now. No one glanced around or checked the open—destroyed and bloody—cell doors in passing. They moved so effortlessly...

Like they *knew* they were apex predators.

After about six broken doors, I finally surrendered to shock. Numb, I bounced lightly with every long step, dangling over Arawn's shoulder, his hand creeping higher up my thigh, a breath away from my core.

No one had ever touched me there before.

Only me and my doctor and one pimply jerk in high school who spread rumors that we went all the way when he barely *grazed* it—and none of that felt like this.

Like... fire.

Like the inferno I had always wished for, its burn so bright and beautiful I'd finally be *happy* in the ashes.

Fire that I thought this sick body just didn't deserve.

Shouts and roars exploded up ahead, probably around the corner given the way none of my captors slowed, the chaos splintered by gunfire. I clamped my hands over my ears, wincing, then inhaled sharply when Balor snarled and twisted into a shadowy black tornado midstride. The darkness darted around us, over us, ruffling Arawn's silky black tresses, his laughter tearing through the corridor and smothering the next hail of bullets.

More screams.

More laughter.

Something in my chest twitched, the sensation like stretching stiff muscles.

I did my best to *breathe*, falling back on years of therapy, on lectures from Dad, on all the tiny text written on the sides of my medication bottles—

Crrrrreaaakkkk.

Heart in my throat, I watched in horror as a nearby door slowly edged open.

And a familiar face poked around it, hollow eye sockets boring straight into me.

Sub-level E was no Sub-level Z. It housed dangerous critters, sure, but we knew a lot about these guys. We knew what made them strong and, more importantly, what cut them off at the knees. Vampires. Shifters. Warlocks.

Ghouls.

I really, really, *really* hated ghouls.

Especially the one lifting his chin and scenting the air through its gaping nasal cavity.

Flesh-eaters.

They preferred the live stuff, but in a pinch, corpses would do.

They were a three-person intake—always.

Dull grey snapped around their bones, not an ounce of fat anywhere, flesh stretched thin and taut, ripping over the sharp bits like clavicles and hip bones. Peeling skin flayed open to expose their innards. This one was missing half his left cheek. No nose, just the big empty hole. Eyes *deep* in their sockets, red with a pinprick black pupil.

Clothes that hung in tatters.

Hair greasy and long and thin, sticking to them like it was always an especially sweaty day.

This one curved its long, bony fingers around the door, head cocked, and then lurched out of its cell. It folded onto all fours, then flipped its body over, back bowed at an unnatural angle, and crab-walked after us.

Slowly, the hunt on, its head twisted back around opposite the rest of its creeping body, neck bones snapping and popping throughout the rotation, mouth open, shredded tongue lolling over chapped lips—

"Ghoul," I choked out. The creature flashed its canines, then lunged after us in a demented gallop, skittering over the tile, and I slapped Arawn's back, finally finding the strength to *scream.* "Ghoul, ghoul, *ghoul!*"

Talons clacking and teeth snapping, the ghoul hurled that decrepit body forward, its beastly howl revving like an ancient engine sputtering, barely clinging to life—

Arawn slowed and half turned like he had no idea we were being stalked by a beast with zero finesse—ghouls were pure monster, and all that mattered to them was human flesh. Juicy or dead, bloody or flaky. It didn't matter. As its favorite meal, I scrambled up Arawn's back and fought harder to get free and bolt.

But then a shadow materialized between us like spring mist. It swirled, the darkness wispy, before eventually crystalizing into Draco.

Gaunt, lean, pale, willowy Draco.

Where the hell was Balor when you needed him?

Another howl filled the hallway—one of blinding agony.

Oh. Apparently, we didn't *need* Balor for this.

Not when Draco grabbed the ghoul at the neck and shoulder and literally *ripped* him right down the center. Tore him clean in half, one side of him on the floor, the other dangling from Draco's loose fist. Down the corridor, more ghouls slithered from their cells, but one long look at their broken comrade and they were off, crawling the walls, up on the ceiling, headed in the opposite direction while a few stragglers stayed back to lap at blood puddles or gnaw on the broken bodies—on the literal feast all this had left for them.

Arms limp at his sides, Draco unceremoniously dropped the ghoul's twitching other half, then cocked his head for a moment, still as stone, cold as ice.

Strong.

Way stronger than his physique implied.

And that made him far more dangerous than Arawn and Balor.

The ones you underestimated always came back to bite you in the end.

"What *are* you?" I murmured, transfixed on the nearest ghoul half as Draco marched around us. Arawn's velvet chuckles didn't belong in this sea of carnage, too silky and soft for all this blood, for the death starting to stink and sour my stomach. As he followed Draco, he caressed my inner thigh, his hand firm—a reminder that I wasn't going anywhere—but his thumb gentle, a barely there touch, the kind you leaned into and *craved* when it finally stopped.

Tender.

Soothing, my eyelids struggling the longer it went on, heavier with each step.

Until the stairwell door opened and the hellscape bleating inside blasted out. More screams. More howls. More bullets flying and Balor laughing.

Blood thick in the air.

Blood and shit and piss—and tears. I couldn't smell them like the rest, but folded over Arawn's shoulder, I... *felt* them. The suffering, the fear, the terror—it all danced across my skin, peeled my lips apart, and clawed down my throat so I'd never forget the taste.

And that was so, so wrong.

Gagging, dangling, helpless to stop the inevitable, I gawked down the gory corridor we left behind as Arawn climbed the nearest steps, my mouth gaping, fear mounting —until the stairwell door crashed shut, heavy and final, and forced me onto the next horror waiting just around the corner.

CHAPTER SIX

Cronus is a war zone.

Paralyzed in a daze, that was my only thought as we scaled the underground stairwell one brutal level at a time, then cut across a bloody, body-strewn lobby and out the main doors. Every creature, from every floor, every cell—out of containment. Volunteers and prisoners alike roamed the halls, fighting their way out as legions of black uniforms swept after them, guns set to kill, our secret world falling apart.

Cool autumn air struck as we exited into the main courtyard, a crisp freshness that zinged through my clothes straight down to the bone. Still dangling over Arawn's shoulder, my gut aching from the constant pressure of firm muscles and bones like marble, I gulped down one deep breath after another, shakily pushing off his back to straighten out a little and just *think*.

I loved the courtyard most days, but especially in the fall. Autumn blooms thrived in raised garden beds over the herringbone cobblestone patterns. Benches everywhere for outdoor lunch breaks. Wrought-iron streetlamps like we were somewhere fancy and European—not here. Not in middle-of-nowheresville Canada. Lobby windows wrapped around the perimeter, floor to ceiling and slightly tinted.

Usually, it was so beautiful. Peaceful. The calm before the storm when you arrived for a shift and the warm embrace of quiet when it was done.

Blood slicked the cobblestones today.

Men's voices shattered the quiet, a chorus of uniformed officers shouting and shooting, their symphony broken every now and again by a creature's roar. The *whump* of wings beating the night air, of monsters finally stretching them as they got the hell out of here, tickled my ears and fluffed the frizzed curls falling around my head, my bun a disaster.

No—that was just a bit messy.

This was a disaster of epic proportions.

And... it was my fault.

Balor had already gloated about opening the cage doors and, as he put it, setting the *inmates* free, and now—

I jerked upright, back aching and stomach dropping.

Dad.

On the other side of the windows—my dad in his white lab coat, surrounded by a heavy-duty security escort.

"*Dad!*"

My screech cut above the chaos, and Arawn stilled. Balor's huge hand stopped unbuttoning his blood-soaked dress shirt halfway down. Draco drifted closer, shrouded in mist that seemed more like a security blanket than an intimidation tactic.

By some miracle, he heard me.

Dad wheeled around, eyes wide, his sandy hair disheveled and his tie loose.

Our eyes met across the courtyard.

He then hurled himself against the window, bellowing my name.

Balor's lip curled. Draco's mists shivered. Arawn sneered.

And then the darkness came for me, closing in on every side, shadow and mist and fog blotting out the world until it was just me and the black. Weightless, floating, I lost sense of time and space, serenaded only by the shrill song of howling wind. Darkness flooded my nostrils when I inhaled sharply. It obscured my vision no matter how hard I blinked.

It should have felt claustrophobic.

Suffocating.

Instead, despite the sweaty sheen suddenly slicking my body from top to bottom, my tummy upset and my raw throat and my head spinning—it felt *liberating*.

Like I was flying.

Floating.

Coasting along, cradled in a beautiful bubble black as the midnight sky and in need of a few twinkling stars. Gone was the gunfire and the shrieks. The smell of blood and shit. The visions of cracked skulls and smeared brain matter.

Just... darkness, warm and cozy and safe.

The bubble burst when I eventually touched down on damp grass. Yelping, I crashed to my knees and folded forward, bracing on my hands, really *feeling* how lush and thick and wet the blades were, so *green* in the moonlight. With a few fast blinks, the darkness retreated, mists and shadows backing off and spiraling, twisting, and coiling into the three men again.

They... had taken me away.

They could fly.

Carry an object between them in *that* form—*fast*.

Oh.

Oh no.

No, no, no, *no.*

My chest shuddered as I fought the breakdown, *trying* to stay calm as I devoured my surroundings. We had landed in a forest—in an open clearing surrounded by trees, anyway, somewhere far from Fort Beacham.

No black maples at the base, but here they dominated my view to the north, west, east, and south. The ground slanted down to a pond, its banks thick with tall grasses and swaying cattails, and a creek cut north from the main body like a jagged wet ribbon through the grass and into the trees, disappearing into the darkness there.

Panic stroked my insides, then *fisted* my gut, and, resolve growing, I heaved a choked breath, then relied on pure adrenaline as I bolted down the hill. Track and field, cross-country—neither was my *thing* in high school. Recreational running was just a socially acceptable form of torture, frankly, but I used the slope to my advantage, barreling down at full speed and already choosing an entry point in the, admittedly, creepy forest on the other side of the pond. That creek had to go somewhere: follow it to *someone* and find a way home.

A pipe dream, I quickly realized, as hooves thundered after me. Literal horse hooves pounded the ground, kicking up grass, and I shrieked at the enormous body that galloped by me—

Clydesdale.

Oh, I *loved* Clydesdales. We kept them on base for parades, and this one was absolutely breathtaking, fully black and *clearly* a male with that enormous shaft dangling between his hind legs.

Balor.

I skidded to a halt, sliding a little over the grass, then pivoted and chose a new spot in the black maples to dash between—

But he galloped in front of me, snorting, hooves as big as my head, mane like a black comet's tail.

"Where are you going, Selene?"

Balor's rough baritone licked the walls of my skull, and I stumbled, brushing at my ear, the sensation oddly warm. The shadow horse circled me, herded me to flat ground, and trotted around and around, really driving home the fact that no matter how hard I pushed myself, no matter how fast I ran—they would always catch me.

Breath falling fast and furious, I spun around twice, taking in my surroundings again. Static nudged Balor's whisper aside, filling my brain with fluff, a hot, sticky panic kicking in.

Nowhere to go.

Nowhere to run.

"*Hello?*" My shout echoed around the clearing, but only the oppressive quiet answered, the black canopy so *still*— just watching. "Anyone?" A full white-white moon lorded over the scene as yet another passive observer, so bright it blotted out the stars. "*Help me!*"

Stupid to cry for help around paranormal predators, but hey—maybe there was a farmer's cottage nearby? A shepherd on a nighttime stroll, rounding up the last of his sheep? Campers? Hikers? Rangers? *Someone?*

Nothing and no one. Just me, the black maples—and *them.*

While geographically familiar, a little farther south than Fort Beacham, autumn just at the beginning stage here, was the best I could deduce. Sure, I'd lusted over faraway cities, historic Vienna and downtown Paris and riverside London. New York. Miami. Istanbul. Sydney. Hong Kong. Dubai.

It was just fantasy, a break in the monotony of work and school and meds. I'd never been anywhere. Never really *done* anything. Dad had only ever taken me away from Fort Beacham a few times, and that was to visit other Cronus specialists in nearby provinces.

No holidays. No trips. Outside the base walls was all business. *Deal with it, Selene: that's life.*

Only now I knew literally nothing about the world beyond those walls—so, really, I could be anywhere.

I clutched at my chest as Arawn and Draco strolled closer, really taking their time down the hillside, while Balor dissolved from enormous black Clydesdale to man in seconds, the last echoey round of my shouts fading away.

"What do you *want*?" I demanded, throat raw and tight, on the verge of tears but desperate to be strong.

"You."

Of course Arawn answered, and of course his response was like cool lotion on a fresh sunburn.

"W-why?" *Damn it.* Cheeks hot from my voice crack, I squared up and took a deep breath, really *looking* from man to man as they closed in around me, lingering on Balor as his strong fingers lazily undid the last of his shirt buttons, drifting down his ripped torso and peeling the bloodstained fabric open.

Arawn stopped directly in front of me, head tipped, black brows gently furrowed. "Can't you feel it yet?"

I felt... a lot.

Too much.

Too *fucking* much.

My lips wobbled, the floodwaters rising, the dams trembling. "Please don't hurt me."

While Arawn flinched like I'd slapped him, his expression fracturing and hurt shining through the cracks, Draco just inched closer and closer, expressionless, gaunt, his black gaze somehow so hollow but impossibly deep—and completely locked on me.

On my lips.

Which I licked, wilting a little under the pressure of his presence.

"Never," Balor said gruffly as he peeled his drenched shirt off those impressive shoulders, muscles dancing for me, seductive and powerful and overtly dangerous. Like some carnivorous bloom emitting a sweet scent to draw the critters close, then snapping them up when they dropped their guard.

That was Balor with his olive-toned complexion and his manic smile, his eyes hauntingly dark, his hair short and neat and crisp, the facial scuff so flattering along his strong jaw—

See?

Siren.

Only they weren't sirens. I'd met one before, and these creatures were just as alluring, just as beautiful—but infinitely more powerful. Something about the charge in the air around them, that ancient survival instinct begging for you to *run*.

Or freeze.

Don't draw their attention.

But I had it, and from the way all three gazes hounded me in the moonlight, I wasn't about to lose it anytime soon.

Okay.

Okay.

Think.

Balor and Draco had absolutely obliterated all kinds

back at base, from humans to monsters and everything in between. Anything that got in our way didn't stand a chance.

They could have done that to me. With every escape attempt, it was more about capture and contain than beating me into submission.

"You have to take me home." So, maybe they would be open to reason. I looked from one pair of black marbles to the next, all dark but different—all annoying obstinate. "You..." *Shit*. Not ideal to expose a vulnerability to the supernatural, but my weaknesses were all I had at this point if for some reason these three *cared* about my well-being. "I-I need my medication. I can't—"

"Why?" Draco rasped. I flinched with a sharp breath: at some point he'd drifted *right* into my personal space, only a few inches clear of my shoulder nudging into his chest. I shied away, head bowed, arms slowly crossing to hide the shakes and shivers.

"Because I'm sick."

Balor snorted—*actually* snorted, balling his bloody shirt up and tossing it on the ground as his cruel chuckles floated around the clearing. But then our eyes met, and I clearly wasn't laughing with him, so the gruff noises tapered off, and suddenly he was looking at me like I'd sprouted an extra head, same as Arawn and Draco.

"I-I'm really sick," I stressed, and this time, I played off the voice-crack with a lazy shrug. "I've been ill all my life, and I *need* my meds. Please."

Man, they so did not understand the gravity of this.

From their blank looks and swapped glances, these three just didn't believe me.

Medication had been a necessary evil for as long as I could remember, and if I could just *stop*, just toss them in the trash one day and go on living like normal, I would have done it already. Relying on the regiment sucked. A lot. Planning around the dosages, adjusting to changes and new additions—a constant waking nightmare. I hated the way they made food taste like nothing. I hated that I felt like hot garbage most of the time, forever just a little dizzy, a little nauseous, a little off.

But the alternative was worse.

Right? That was the point of doctors prescribing all these chemicals—because the pros outweighed the cons, and the side effects, whatever they were, paled in comparison to what you *could* experience day in and day out.

"You aren't... *ill*, Selene," Arawn said slowly, finally bursting that stunned bubble thickening around us. His tone, his expression—it was like the thought of me being sick was the most ridiculous thing he'd ever heard. I glowered up at him, the steel settling into my spine at last, and gritted my teeth.

Who the hell was he to judge?

I'd been suffering with this my whole life. From day one —disaster. Pain. A simmering queasiness that triggered hot flashes like I was menopausal in middle school, but I *did* it. I survived. Put one foot in front of the other because Dad created a regiment that made it so.

And to totally invalidate my experience, all of them radiating this dismissive aura—

No.

"I'm sick."

"Please." Arawn patted the air and eased down to my height. "Listen, you aren't—"

"Oh, are you a doctor now?" I snapped, to which this breathtaking creature licked his lips and *smiled*.

"No, of course not, but—"

"Then you don't get an opinion."

"You aren't sick," Balor interjected, and I rounded on him, temper rising at the way he just smirked and picked the dried blood out from under his nails. "Stop this. Choose a better manipulation."

My hands balled to fists. "I *am*, and I need—"

"You really cannot get sick," Arawn insisted, his gaze all soft and gooey and warm, just pleading for me to see *reason*. I whirled back to him, fuming, only for Draco to pile on as well.

"Your kind is immune."

While my knees managed not to buckle, my arms went limp, and I just blinked back at him a few times as my overloaded brain finally blew a fuse. "W-what?"

"Sweet Selene..."

Arawn moved in, and suddenly his finger was just *there*, under my chin and tipping my head up when I started to fold in on myself. As much as I craved his touch, the memory of his hand hot like a delicious burn on my inner thigh, I jerked away and crossed my arms again, and while he followed after me with a soft sigh, he didn't touch me.

And for some reason, that hurt.

"You aren't sick, little one." He towered over me like a dark god, beautiful and terrifying, powerful in stance alone. "You can't be... because you are a daughter of night."

CHAPTER SEVEN

At the dawn of time, *they* ruled the world—as above, so below, the skies their domain as was the deepest, darkest pits. Before titans. Before gods. *Them.*

First, there was Chaos, and from his void came Nyx, goddess of the night. So too came Erebus, lord of darkness. Deeply in love, forever entwined, Nyx and Erebus birthed many offspring, including Aether, the first brightness in the cosmos, and Hemera, the blessed dawn.

When the time came, powerful Nyx, whom even Zeus feared, danced with her beloved Erebus across the sky, painting it black with her veil of night and his cloak of darkness. Come morning, their daughter Hemera broke through the shadowy mists left in their wake, making way for the sun.

Over and over again, Nyx and Erebus draped the world in night, entwined in each other's arms, lovers until the end. By daylight, they slept in the pits of Tartarus, together, night and darkness, soulmates, *the* love story.

In the eons since the beginning, Erebus's cloak has frayed here and there. So worn, so thoroughly used, occasionally it tore, snagged on a star or a mountain peak. From his cloak came the shadows, creatures who roamed the earth, settling amongst humanity, feeding off all that darkness did to mankind. Shapeshifters. Primordial. Ancient. A piece of Erebus, a sliver of his darkness—*not* a demon.

They stood before me now, apparently, Arawn wrapping up his little history lesson with a soft smile.

Not demons...

Pieces of a primordial god's... cloak.

Alive?

Dead?

Somewhere in-between?

And then me—a daughter of night, of Nyx herself, whose name wasn't a total mystery, but to be associated with her by *any* degree was just... stupid.

Because...

No.

I gawked up at Arawn, still stuck in the center of these three ancient creatures, and then let out a halfhearted cackle. It died a few seconds later, any humor I might have found in this shriveling up in my throat, just another uncomfortable knot inside to ruin my day.

"That's..." What the hell was I supposed to say? How do you respond to some *thing* insisting you were the daughter of a goddess who was there when the cosmos began? "That's a really nice... story."

"You have her eyes," Balor remarked, positioned behind me and still picking the blood out from under his nails—there was just that much of it. To my right, Draco nodded, and a slithering breeze hissed through the nearby cattails.

"You are almost precisely her—"

"My dad—"

"Nyx birthed many of her offspring *alone*," Arawn remarked, bulldozing my argument so sweetly, so kindly, that it was tough to be annoyed at him. "We do not believe you have a father, per se. You are pure night, little one—"

What a load of crap. "My dad is my dad—"

"It's a lie." No matter how delicate his lightly accented tone, how gentle his expression, I still blanched at that—at the certainty in his words. Just spitting facts, this beautiful slip of darkness, this piece of primordial fabric in the shape of a man. "None of us wish to hurt you like this, Selene, but it's best to know outright. It's best to understand..."

Shaking my head, I peeled around him and stumbled across the grass. Ice in my veins, shock stilled my tongue— made my movements stilted and awkward, our surroundings blurring in and out of focus. I couldn't... *believe* any of this, right? Demons lie. That was the saying— they spouted all kinds of crap to claim what they most wanted: your immortal soul.

But...

Deep down, a part of me I'd always repressed, this jagged puzzle piece that never fit and found solace after nightfall, kinship among the monsters—all it felt was *relief*.

The lump in my throat thickened, and I closed my eyes, back to these three and face lifted to the night sky.

"You feel a pull to us." Sighing, I peeked over my shoulder as Arawn closed in, his black hair especially silky tonight, like he was in his element. He paused a good five feet away, hands behind his back, suit immaculate, cheekbones sharp and high with the way the moon's glow touched everything in the clearing—but cast shadows, too. "You, us... We are cleaved from the oldest, greatest love story in the cosmos."

Behind him, Draco held his ground, but that intense,

unblinking stare drilling straight into me made it seem like he was *here*, pressed in close, touching something deeper than flesh and bone. Balor, meanwhile, tipped to the right to peer around Arawn, involved but at a distance, picking his nails and flicking bits of dark, dried blood on the grass.

"There is no finer couple than Erebus and Nyx," Arawn insisted—another *fact*, his eyes like black hot springs in the middle of the arctic, a reprieve, a blessing, just *begging* me to see what they did. "It draws us together—"

"You came from Hell," I said flatly. Their intake forms had literally no useful information besides that: we had pulled these three from a Cronus demon trap in Alberta, one set directly at the mouth of an unsanctioned Hell gate. The only way to get stuck in its web was to slither out of Lucifer's realm, through the door, and *bam*. Trapped.

Bound by containment sigils—

Sigils that... hadn't contained these three when it mattered. At all.

"We were *found* in a demon trap," Balor countered with a raised finger. "One we intentionally put ourselves in—to reach *you*." With a flash of teeth and a glint of mania, he eased further around Arawn and went for his belt. "A very important distinction." The buckle rattled, followed by the slap of leather as he roughly peeled it open. "And don't get me wrong, I love Lucifer's kingdom. I've never sampled such sweet terror... He takes me on tasting tours every time we visit."

"Balor," Draco chided, and Arawn angled his body between us as Balor proceeded to just... strip. For some reason.

Clothes are a prison.

Face hot, I shook my head and focused on the soaring black maples up the hill. "N-no."

"We *felt* you." Arawn ambled a few steps closer, so casual in the way he stalked his prey. Calm. Collected. Unassuming—like he'd suddenly be at your throat, teeth and all, and it would make sense to find him there. Gulping, I countered his forward momentum, adding a few shaky steps back to maintain our distance, and he stilled with a slightly dejected huff. "Upon our return to the mortal realm, *we* felt *you*. Centuries have gone by visiting the darkness of Erebus, dwelling deep in Tartarus. We come and go as we please. Go where we wish, when we wish, my brothers and I—"

A sharp look from me nipped that story in the bud. Because, sorry, *brothers*?

"We three are tatters from the same corner of his cloak, little one," Arawn insisted, gesturing back, a hand for Balor and the other for Draco. "We are kin—deeper than mere friendship. We are brothers by design, not blood. Not in the way you perceive it."

Cool. Just another casual mindfuck for the night. Arms crossed, I twisted my body away from the three, nibbling my lower lip as I tried to *think*.

I'd never felt so small. Monsters, creatures, beasties—they had been my life at Cronus for years. But navigating the *cosmos*, face-to-face with beings that just happened to fray from a god who personified darkness itself...

Yeah, two inches tall ought to do it. Maybe one and a half.

The pull Arawn had mentioned, *feeling* each other: it had been there from the start, my body both resisting it with everything it had and desperately *needing* it so much I dreamed about them and only them for five nights straight.

"If you were not a daughter of Nyx, there would be nothing between us." Arawn strolled around in a wide arc, still the casual predator, still the hunter cornering his prey no matter how safe she *thought* she was with all this space between them. "No pull. No lure. No connection—in either direction."

"By that logic—" I cleared my throat, stupid voice box enemy number one tonight with all its embarrassing breaks. "—any, uh, cloak fragment could find me and say the same thing—"

A snarl ripped from Balor's mouth, this hulking mountain of raw *man* stripped down to nothing, bloody and bare and beautiful in the moonlight. He stalked back and forth, half-hard dick swinging, fists trembling, eyes so black it kicked my adrenaline into overdrive so I could get the hell out of here. His strong jaw worked, like he was searching for the right words to throw back at me.

Run, you idiot, while he's distracted.

"First come, first served." Draco cut the tension effortlessly. No clue if he'd blinked at all since we got here, but briefly, all eyes on him, the corners of his lips twitched —*barely*, the movement so subtle I thought I'd imagined it— and he then shrugged his lean shoulders. "Isn't that the common phrase this century?"

My eyebrows shot up, heart stumbling over itself at the flicker of humor in his black gaze.

"We're bonded, Selene." Emboldened by his brothers, Arawn marched into my personal sphere, close enough to graze the top of my hand, then ghost the backs of his knuckles along my jaw, so *achingly* tender my chest hurt. And I... let him. Closed my eyes and leaned into it. "One touch and we belong to you, and you to us." Another soft breath cooled my cheek. "I understand how overwhelming this is, but it's as old as time, our love—"

My eyes flew open as I slapped his hand away, fire finally nuking all the icy shock of tonight's fiasco.

"We don't have *love*," I snapped, stumbling back with another crazed laugh, the sound triggering a twisted leer from Balor. "I don't *know* you. I don't know any of you!"

A bitter wind cut across the clearing seemingly out of nowhere, slicing through my clothes, burning with every breath. The black maples whispered, their canopy full of laughter, and then it all went flat, the noise dead, the air still —except for the wispy ball of shadow Balor lobbed at the back of Arawn's head. It exploded on impact, black mist flaring around him like a warped halo.

"You might as well get the offspring bit out of the way now."

"*What?*" I hissed, eyes narrowing as Arawn waved the mist away with a sigh. Balor, meanwhile, seemed to have recovered from that mini-meltdown at the thought of another cloak fragment stealing me away, all goading smiles when his... *brother* twisted back to glare at him. He lifted one of those hulking shoulders, still totally naked, his sculpted chest bloodstained, the look in his eyes wicked.

Seriously, what was this guy's deal?

Pick a lane. Psycho, sadist, predator, friend, brother—or all of the above?

Clearing his throat, Arawn patted the air again, this time as if to settle Balor, his presence unleashing a frenetic charge that made the hairs on my arms stab up on high alert. Draco, meanwhile, suddenly appeared a little too interested in the nearby cattails, head cocked, black eyes tracking the fuzzy brown tips as they drooped over the surrounding long grass stalks.

"There are..." Arawn winced when my eyes narrowed, and that expression, the flicker of genuine concern, instantly softened me. And that sucked. Because *his* moods, his feelings, should have absolutely no impact on mine, but here we were, my temper at a simmer as he mulled over whatever he planned to tell me about, you know, *offspring*. It took another few long drumbeats of my heart for him to spill the beans—every last miserable one.

"There are so few daughters of Nyx unspoken for these days. She rarely procreates anymore—the dawn of time came with a proliferation of offspring. *They* have their lovers, their chosen mates. Most favor gods, others of their ilk and status. Some procreate alone, like their mother, but should *we* pieces of Erebus wish to bring new shadows into the world—"

"*Monsters*," Draco interjected, his voice a rough, slightly nasally whisper on the wind. He then abandoned the cattails and swiveled that unflinching stare around, boring directly into mine. "Our children are *monsters* by Cronus standards, Selene—shadows that haunt humanity."

"Er, yes." Arawn angled himself between us as my gut bottomed out for the millionth time, followed by a fresh burst of cold sweats and a sky-high adrenaline kick that nearly knocked me on my butt. As if sensing the physiological shift in me, Arawn went for my hand with both of his, then stilled when I flinched back, trembling. Another soft sigh, bringing with it a touch of warmth, a ghost of a kiss across my lips. "We can only create shadows with... someone like you."

Bingo.

There it was.

The meat of the issue, the real reason these three hauled me out of Cronus and not some other random intake officer. *Me*. A daughter of Nyx—supposedly.

I sucked in my cheeks, gnawing at them. *No*.

Yes, the darkness within rumbled in my voice. Not theirs—*mine*. Relief chipped away at the sea of less helpful emotions storming through me, and I crossed my arms, holding myself like I always had, needing a little support or I'd crumble.

This... isn't happening. It's a dream.

It isn't, the darkness crooned, unseen fingers stroking my rib cage, my spine, willing me to breathe—to let go. *And it is.*

Awesome.

Arawn crouched into my fallen eyeline, so hopeful and raw, so open and earnest. *Want.* I'd read about it in books, in filthy online smutfics I devoured as a teen in an incognito tab. I always thought it was a made-up thing because I'd never seen it before.

Never experienced *want* so vividly from another person.

Creature.

Cloak fragment.

But there it was, blazing up at me—a desperate want that made my left knee buckle, but the right held firm, stubbornness and self-preservation refusing to let me crash onto the grass in front of him.

Refusing to accept his touch no matter how viciously the darkness lusted after it.

"Your value to us, your worth, is immeasurable." *You're his—their—baby-making machine.* I closed my eyes with a shaky breath, trying and failing to block out Arawn's velvet-laced words. *That's it. You serve a purpose... Fill a need nobody else can meet.* "Selene, for you, we would—"

I raised a hand but kept my eyes closed, fully aware that if I opened them and tripped into Arawn's black pools of *want*, I'd lose it. "I-I need a minute."

More than that. I needed a goddamn lifetime to come to terms with all this—with the fact that the longer I stood in their presence, the deeper I *felt* these shadowy figures in my marrow, and I was starting to believe it.

All of it.

Footsteps padded softly away, and when I risked opening one eye, Arawn was gone. All that mounting relief whooshed out of me, and I staggered around, blindly fumbling my way across the grassy slope and eventually stopping at the pond. One more step and I'd be ankle-deep in muck and algae and questionably dark water; I plopped down instead, snapping the longer grass blades, the wood-like stalks of cattails. Still shivering, I made a little nest for myself amongst the weeds, then stared blankly at the still pond water. Mosquitos hovered above the surface, and tiny dark slips wiggled below, little fish preparing for the winter ahead.

All this time and space ought to be used to *think*, to use this big brain that had made me top of my high school class and really pick their story apart.

But my mind was just static, and whenever I tried to push through, it hurt. Slowly but surely, a familiar headache flared behind my eyes, and I pinched the bridge of my nose to alleviate the pressure, then hugged my folded knees and thunked my forehead into them with a groan.

Yeah, it might be cliché, but I could have sat there alone for minutes, seconds, or *hours* with no clue how much time had passed. The air around me was just a dense fog of confusion, thickening, swirling up my nostrils with every breath.

It lifted somewhat when a figure sat next to me, his approach quiet—but not silent, which I figured it would have been normally. If these *men* were just tatters of a primordial god's cloak, they could move without making a sound. Here, whoever it was, he approached with *just* enough noise that I didn't panic when he sank into the grass.

Sniffling, the static buzz inside my skull a little quieter, I peeked under my arm—and found Draco making himself at home. Not Arawn with his easy charm and gentle smile. Not Balor with his intensity and *presence*.

Draco.

Hollow and empty and vacant—*Draco*, his short on the sides, long on the top white hair messily tousled, his black turtleneck clawing up a thin neck and brushing the underbelly of a strong jawline and pointed chin.

Draco, now seated cross-legged in the grass like we were two kids at summer camp—and we'd just snuck out to smoke by the pond and watch the stars.

Not that I'd ever... done that.

But books and TV made you think you'd lived so much more than you ever had.

He kept a foot or so of space between us, and I straightened with a frown, both arms wrapped around my knees, watching him stare blankly at the pond, just as I had, expressionless and so very far away.

"You are not sick," he said lightly. While Balor was a gritty bass and Arawn a delicious tenor, Draco was a rough alto, always sounding like it strained him to speak above an intimate whisper. I scanned his sharp profile for a moment, a little surprised that I found the gaunt, alternative male model schtick so attractive, then refocused on the murky water, on the dark shapes darting near the surface.

"I don't know what to think right now."

"You are perfect," he muttered, unfazed by my scoff. His eyes narrowed and his jaw clenched, the dancing muscles much more prominent than they had been on Balor. Skin so pale it was almost translucent suddenly turned pink, Draco's version of a heated blush scattered and subtle—if you hadn't been cataloging every hauntingly beautiful detail, of course. His black eyes snagged on a mosquito, tracking it as it wafted in our direction, then catching it between his thumb and pointer, *smooshing* it so blood oozed over his skin. "You are *perfect*—and they have clipped your wings. All this time... That is why we were so *furious* the first day."

Tears pricked the backs of my eyes and stung inside my nose, but I refused to let them fall. Instead, I concentrated on not blinking, on studying the pond's perimeter and the spooky tree line beyond.

"You feel it." Draco tapped at the center of his chest. "Here. Maybe not as deeply as we do—"

"You *feel?*"

He finally faced me, long spidery fingers threaded together on his lap, and falling into his black gaze was like staring into a bottomless abyss.

"Yes," Draco admitted with a slight twitch of his white brows. "I feel."

Head bowed, I finally blinked the tears into my knees, preferring they drip straight onto my pants rather than stream tellingly down my cheeks. For some reason, questioning his ability to feel, hearing his answer—it made *me* feel guilty.

Like, what a stupid question to ask.

What a *rude* question, no matter how curious—

"No doubt you have sensed the differences in the darkness between us," Draco mused, back to staring down at the pond, his features smooth and even, relaxed and empty. "Balor is the terror of black night—the horror lurking in the corner of your eyes, the one that makes you terrified to close them, to fall asleep in his presence."

I pursed my lips and nodded, because, yeah, definitely picked up on that vibe—but that *didn't* mean I was a daughter of Nyx. Literally anyone *had* to sense that about Balor.

"Arawn is soft predawn darkness," Draco continued, his tone verging on affectionate when he glanced over his shoulder, presumably back to the silky-haired god who could drop me to my knees with one stunning smile. "Soothing, I imagine, rather than frightening."

I swallowed hard, waiting for him to elaborate on himself, and when he didn't, I toed at the damp shoreline with another sniff. "And you?"

"Surely you can guess."

"I'd rather you just tell me."

"I am hollow." He arched just the one eyebrow this time when our eyes met, almost daring me to argue. "I am the black depths of a bottomless ocean, the vast yawn of space."

Oh.

I'd read them all perfectly.

Another wave of tears blurred his dark beauty, and I swiped at my eyes, hating them—hating that I didn't understand why they were here or why the realization that I had tapped into each of their darkness made me feel so fucking lonely.

"But I *feel* as deep as they do." Draco motioned stiffly over his shoulder. "As deep as *you* do. Never question that."

Biting at the insides of my cheeks, willing the pain to center me like it always did and annoyed that it came up short tonight, I studied the black maples like they had all the answers. "I-I want to feel right now. I want to be able to think and... *reason* through all of this. Figure out if you're lying to me." The corner of his mouth twitched—subtle again and barely readable, but I assumed it happened because he found the notion... amusing? "But I can't. I can't f-feel anything, or think. It's just static and noise up there, and I can't—"

Draco grabbed my hand out of nowhere, snapping tight as a hunting snare around a rabbit's neck. I sucked in a ragged gasp; one touch and the floodgates shattered. One touch, one squeeze of his hand around mine, and it all hit like a fucking nuke.

Grief and sadness. Loneliness and longing. Aches and agony and emptiness. Feeling like the Other after a lifetime of tests and needles and *pain*. Exhaustion. Dad making my meals *and have you taken your meds today and let's try something new but there are some serious side effects. Be brave. It's just a needle. It's just a spinal tap. Stop crying in front of my colleagues. Brace yourself. It'll be worth it, Selene.* Uncertainty and darkness, and the vast brokenness that I could only smile away for so long—

Need oxygen.

I couldn't breathe.

Couldn't think—but I sure as hell could *feel*.

Everything.

Everything I had worked so hard to push down and suppress, to pretend wasn't there—to explain away like this was just life with a chronic disease.

That this was just the body I had and suck it up, buttercup, people have it so much *worse*.

Chest tight and aching, I gulped like a fish out of water—and then wailed. Tears careened down my cheeks like hot, wet fire, and I stabbed my fingers through Draco's, squeezing, squeezing, *squeezing* with all my might.

And he squeezed back, black mists coiling off him and

slithering up my arms, his grip so hard it was a miracle he didn't break me. Through the tears, I caught him shaking ever so slightly, fighting whatever was going on behind those black eyes.

I wanted to ask—

I wanted to *scream*.

I chose the latter, emptying my lungs again and again, ripping my throat raw. I gasped and wheezed. I ugly-cried into my knees. I ripped out grass and crushed it in my fist and sobbed like the world was about to end, like something inside, something cold and hollow, was plucking at my stitches and undoing a lifetime of trauma I'd just ignored night after night—

A firm arm snaked around my waist.

And just when I thought I'd pass out, Arawn's hand settled over my eyes, his skin cool against the pain of that damn headache raging behind them.

His lips on my neck and his touch so achingly kind.

Then sleep.

A dreamless sleep, safe in the darkness, swaddled in shadow, everything else just... gone.

CHAPTER EIGHT

The world greeted me with soft light behind my closed lids —and campfire smoke. Not huge gusts of the stuff, but the air was lightly scented against a backdrop of crackling wood and distant songbirds. My first deep breath dragged in the heat, followed by the cool damp of an autumn morning outdoors.

I clenched my eyes tighter; the slightest movement told me I'd been on my side for hours, because my shoulder was one cranky asshole right now, stiff and sore like I had slept on it very, very wrong. Throw in an achy hip and a grumpy lower back and we had a party.

But softness pillowed my head, and something like a weighted blanket stretched across my whole body. One gulp told me I'd screamed my throat bloody last night—or whenever. Still sore, it took a few tentative swallows to soothe the burn.

Unfortunately, all that goodness wasn't the only pain creeping into focus.

Expecting the worst, I cracked one eye, then the other, and quickly realized Arawn, Draco, and Balor had loaned out their clothes for the sake of my comfort. Arawn's jacket folded like a pillow under my head. Balor's huge pants draped diagonally across my torso. Draco's turtleneck tangled around my legs. Leaves and underbrush and shadowy black mists for a woodsy mattress—and a nearby fire ringed in dusty grey rocks for warmth.

Someone had even taken my hair out, bun gone, curls falling frizzy and free across my face. Dawn slipped through the canopy, a gentle breeze rustling the black maple leaves so the light was all dappled and mystical.

And it *hurt*.

Groaning, I shut my eyes tight against the onslaught as a stabby ache swelled behind them, a perfect pairing to the jackhammer slowly pounding away at the back of my skull. Fully aware that sleep did nothing for this kind of shit, that what I really needed was in my bathroom cabinet, I faced the bonfire head-on, squinting in the morning haze—and then found Arawn seated on the other side. Higher up, maybe on a rock or log, he watched me with a kind smile, his aura calm, his presence more reassuring than I cared to admit, looking dapper as hell in the black suit vest and dress shirt. Hands threaded, elbows on his knees, he eased closer to the low flames and cocked his head.

"How are you feeling?"

Like I'm made of pee.

Seriously, could bladders explode? Because mine was so full it *hurt* all the way up to my left kidney.

That combined with the full-body *ouch* like I'd been hit by a truck and I was just *peachy*.

With a deep breath that did nothing to slow the painstorm brewing inside, I grunted and pushed upright. *Ugh.* Hazy pinks and soft purples and gentle reds—this should have been a breathtaking sunrise, but it just *hurt*.

Feeling like an absolute dumpster fire had conditioned me from an early age to take my meds at the *exact* time, because hell no did I want to experience this on a daily basis.

And at this point, I'd officially missed one, maybe two doses.

Shit. This was going to be sheer, unadulterated *torture*.

They had no idea.

Even if I wasn't sick like they said, my body was used to its chemical cocktails.

It craved the elixir.

And, you know, maybe they were all wrong and my dad was right and I really was horribly ill because my immune system continuously freaked out and attacked itself until everything just stopped—

But before the inevitable mental and physical breakdown—bathroom. *Now*.

Difficult as it was, I eventually managed to get up on my own two feet. The world looped around me twice, and, arms out, I took a few more deep breaths to keep the inevitable dizzy spell at bay. Arawn watched me like a hawk, on his feet and tensed, looking seconds from leaping over the fire to catch me if I fell.

I stumbled off in the opposite direction instead, hair snagging on taller, pricklier brush than they ever showed on TV or movies as the heroine dashed dramatically through the forest. Not exactly picky but preferring Arawn didn't hear me empty my bladder, I went until the landscape slid to the left again, then the right, my eyes flicking through a few fun microsaccades. Body calling the shots, I finally braced on the nearest maple, caught my breath, and then shakily yanked my belt off, pants and underwear down, and squatted.

Sweet relief.

Even when it was over, skin prickling from the morning chill, I slumped against the bark for a few minutes, airing things out, staring, cataloguing the symptomatic influx even as my mind tried to just go numb and block it out. Once I was vertical again, I skipped tucking my button-up into my slacks and ditched the belt, so not in the mood for anything tight and restrictive around a body that was headed downhill fast, then scanned the surrounding forest.

A quick glance over my shoulders and around the thick maple.

Arawn hadn't followed me.

I could just... run.

But where?

They'd find me.

Catch me.

Lecture me—or worse. Maybe I just hadn't pushed the right buttons yet, no matter how poetically they waxed on about what I meant to them.

Daughter of night.

Daughter of Nyx.

I snorted weakly, then squinted up at the sound of talons clawing roughly over bark.

Two ravens peered back at me, perched on a thin branch above, watching, silent and beautiful.

Huh.

Apparently, I really couldn't go a morning without them there to greet me.

Weird.

But comforting.

Belt in hand, I studied the duo for a few moments, then mustered a frail smile and a pathetic wave. The one on the left croaked back at me, while the one to my right stayed silent, ruffling its big wings and assessing me with eyes almost as black as Draco's.

Wait.

Was that Draco? And Balor?

Were they creeping? Spying?

Rubbing the stabby throb at the base of my skull, I bailed and trudged back to the campsite, where Arawn had perched on his fireside rock again, perking up when our eyes met. Insides crashing, I dropped my belt on Draco's turtleneck, then collapsed onto the makeshift bed, kneeling by the fire. The heat felt good, but not quite as good as Arawn lurching off his rock, regal features twisted with concern. To his credit, he stilled when I raised a shaky hand, in no mood to be touched or fussed over.

At least he respected boundaries.

Sort of.

"If I'm late with my dose," I forced out, throat sore, words croaky and scratchy, "it hits r-right away."

Concern warped to *rage*, so visceral and sharp that it threw me, but then Arawn bowed his head, hands on hips, and when he lifted it again, there was that familiar calm.

"I'm sorry to hear that." While he looked cool and collected, his left hand clenched in a fist so tight his knuckles blanched bright white: my reality pissed him off. A lot. "That isn't fair, Selene. I'm sorry."

I shrugged and lost myself in the bonfire, which he'd fed while I was gone, fresh kindling and new logs coaxing the flames higher. Footsteps crunched my way, and suddenly Arawn dropped into my right peripheral, crouched and hunched but somehow still so much larger than me. I stiffened, wishing I could smell *him* like I could the fire, the crisp autumn air—like if he had a natural musk, if *any* of them did, I'd know them even better, be able to read them as *men* and not shadows. Because, after Draco's rundown of their distinct darkness, clearly I had no issue tapping into *that*.

And I would rather process them as a normal person might, using the same five senses everyone else in my life had and not some deep-seated darkness radar that made me such a... valuable member of Cronus intake.

Huh.

Never really considered that before...

That I was put on the tough cases... maybe because the monsters sensed the pitch-black in me that I always shoved down, down, down. Not because I was good at my job, but because—

Fingers brushed my hair, and I jerked out of that potentially huge downward spiral to Arawn gently wrestling a twig from my hair. As if to confirm he wasn't just pushing boundaries for nothing, he briefly held up his proof before tossing it in the fire.

He then stilled when I shuffled closer, inching down the shadowy bed of moss and dead crunchy leaves, and offered my head for further grooming. Because where there was one stage-five clinger, there had to be more, and Arawn's fingers felt so distractingly *good* in my hair, tender and careful as they picked through the thick black mane I'd wrestled with my whole life. He pulled out a few bits of broken leaves and another small twig, and I let him, eyes threatening to drift shut, willing my body to relax under his care.

It wouldn't.

It never did.

Especially not when nausea made its grand entrance to the party, booting some acid reflux up my esophagus, tummy suddenly in knots. I braced on the ground, hands spread and buried in the forest bed these three had made me, needing something sturdy to remind my brain that, no, we weren't spinning and we didn't have to feel dizzy.

We were just sitting here, minding our own business.

Pain soared from a dull three to a sharp six in no time, determined to hit the coveted ten out of ten if I didn't take something *soon*.

Still, silver lining in all this: it was tough to have a full-blown panic attack about being kidnapped by primordial cloak fragments when your body felt like it was being slowly dipped in hellfire.

With my hair officially twig-less, Arawn reached around me for his jacket, then draped it across my shoulders. He'd noticed my shivers escalating before I had, apparently, because only when he bundled the fabric tight at my chest, frowning, did I clue in to my chattering teeth and my visibly jittery hands. Awesome. Crouched in front of me, Arawn went for the buttons, his cozy black gaze glued to my face like he was searching for something.

Waiting for me to crack, more like.

A loud and sudden tromping through the underbrush behind him made me jump, while Arawn merely turned half around as Balor and Draco ambled through the maples. Once again totally naked, Balor approached with a slightly manic smile on his face—and a dead rabbit in his hand.

Draco had one too, but it hung limp by his side, bobbing along, same as his arms. While not naked, he had lent me his black turtleneck at some point, which left him shirtless now, and...

Wow. Apparently the hipster goth attire hid a toned torso and strong arms, the muscle definition less cut and sculpted than Balor's bulk but just as alluring, overtly masculine in his own way, his hair pale white in the dappled dawn light.

Full of surprises, that one.

They stopped on the other side of the fire, my two hunters, and Balor raised the—oh yeah—*very* dead rabbit by its back feet for my viewing pleasure.

"Hungry?"

Saliva flooded my mouth, and the landscape took a hard left. I gritted my nails into the ground, dizziness and nausea teaming up to take me down any second now.

Blissfully unaware of what he'd just walked into, Balor then *skinned* the entire rabbit in one fell swoop with his bare hands, stripping off the pelt from the bottom to the head, then the limp back feet, and tossed it all aside, leaving only the bloody carcass dripping over the fire.

"For your breakfast," he declared, sounding rather proud of himself as the pre-vom saliva sweats hit hard and fast. He swatted at Draco, who hoisted the second tawny rabbit up by the ears, his expression neutral and his eyes locked on mine as Balor babbled on.

"These two were the meatiest in the fluffle. Did you know that's what they call a rabbit colony these days? A *fluffle*. We can cook them over the fire for you—"

Hands up, *pleading* for him to just shut up and get that thing away from me, I heaved once, twice, three times—then emptied my guts all over the forest floor.

CHAPTER NINE

It only got worse from there.

That first upchuck was pure bile, my stomach basically empty at that point, and it really set the tone for the rest of the day.

The second my feet touched down on concrete, the shadowy bubble that had whisked me from the forest to wherever we'd ended up dispersed fast, from black lightening to varying shades of grey, until finally the mists twisted into familiar figures—into *men*.

Still adjusting to that.

Apparently going all mist and shadow and smoke was the easiest way to transport stuff, the trio coming together to carry me long distances. I should have objected harder, but given how much I'd already deteriorated, fatigue whittling into my bones, I let it go. Pick your battles and whatnot.

Besides, the black bubble was the only thing that didn't make my nausea worse; a lifetime of carsickness, whether I sat in the front, back, or middle, meant I walked most places. Buses sucked even harder, so, yeah, I skipped public transport on base from the start. Planes—total disaster.

Nothing like spending six miserable hours heaving over an airplane toilet while other passengers pounded on the door to really sour one's heart to travel in general.

But this...

Cradled between them was like floating in a sea of black nothing. Time had no meaning in the bubble. It was... a dream. A comfort. Paradise in its darkest form.

Bubble now burst and three gorgeous men solid matter again, everything came crashing down. One sharp, painful breath told me we had left the forest far, far behind, the air thick and warm and full of life. My knees buckled just as I started a quick scan of our new surroundings, but Arawn's strong arms caught me before I hit the ground.

More specifically, the dusty, unforgiving concrete.

Concrete *everywhere* and an open black but starless sky above.

We had landed on what looked like the top level of a metropolitan parking garage. Half-full, cars of varying make and quality scattered around, all the empty spaces suggested we were well past regular business hours. Breathing quality meh and the twinkling lights dizzying, a maze of towers and skyscrapers soared all around—yeah, we had left the forest *way* behind. Thick, smoggy air punctuated by *noise*. Screams and laughter. Car tires screeching and sirens wailing and motorcycle engines revving—everywhere. Hard to place. Hard to pinpoint the source. Oppressive.

Bright. Even in the dead of night, my eyes hurt. Stupid white-white bulbs used in the lot lights.

"The inn is there." Draco pointed to something behind me. "It is the most pristine in the city."

Groaning, limp and useless in Arawn's arms, I peeked around to see this *inn*, only to be met with the tallest tower in sight. Given the crisp, clean lines, the black glass exterior —what Draco considered an inn was most likely a luxury hotel.

No complaints, really. The linen quality, the mattress plushness—probably top-notch if books had taught me anything.

These three had promised me a safe, secure place to recover.

Because...

Detox was a bitch. So many of my high school friends had suggested at one point or another that I stop taking my medication. *Don't tell your dad. You feel like crap—stop taking them. Or just take a couple. He'll never know.* Sure. Like it was that easy.

Without the legion of white and pink tablets, I spent today either curled up on the ground or throwing up in the brush. All cried out, I still couldn't keep anything down, be it a cup of water or the cheeseburger Balor scrounged up from a fast-food joint somewhere, almost like an apology for the rabbit incident. Nothing stayed. Everything made a violent encore.

Pain had taken over, the aches, the agony, all one big fuck-you at this point. It wasn't just my head, just my shoulder, just my tummy—it was system-wide. They had joined forces to drown me, making it impossible to stumble more than a few feet without exhaustion knocking me back down.

Unconsciousness would be great.

That dreamless sleep Arawn gifted me last night—*bliss*.

But the fear that I might not wake up this time made me refuse his offer at every turn, determined to ride it out.

Determined to *survive*.

Arawn, Balor, Draco—they hovered. Back in the forest,

they were just *there*, always within reach. Watching, grimacing, scowling, occasionally stoking the fire and drying the sweat off my brow. When the afternoon hit, they were forced to basically mummify me in clothes and smoky blankets, fending off the more aggressive shivers and the chill in my blood, only to then frantically peel it all away once the fever sweats came crashing back.

All day, they had discussed *me* in a language that didn't sound remotely modern, harsh and guttural, full of hard consonants and yawning *W*'s like in Arawn's name. At one point, Draco disappeared, and when he returned, they pounced, surrounding me as shadows.

And now we were here.

The ravens hadn't followed.

The two in the black maple, my morning bathroom buddies, had posted sentry on a branch over the campfire. Sometimes I just watched them, lost in the beautiful shades of their black feathers. The guys, meanwhile, barely seemed to notice we had visitors, so focused on my every movement, my every expression, my every fucking shudder, that their intensity had started to grate on my already raw nerves.

I felt like death—probably looked it too, all pale with bruised bags under my bloodshot eyes, my tangled curls something those ravens would happily pluck out for a nest.

These men, however, looked like they belonged in the cityscape, what with Balor back in the white dress shirt and black slacks getup like some hot mafioso on his way to crack skulls. Then Arawn in his pristine black suit, reeking of old-world money, radiating aristocracy and power and backroom deals made with the slightest lift of his brow. Even Draco had thrown on a stylish swishy black trench, almost as if to hide the shadowy mists that hounded his every stiff step.

"Excellent," Arawn rumbled suddenly, hoisting me higher so I had to straighten my knees and *try* to stand on my own. "We'll take the most private suite." His face wandered into my left periphery, peering around to address me directly as he said, "How do we acquire a room?"

I blinked, exhaustion dragging my lids down, then side-eyed him with a breathy scoff. "You think... *I* know?"

Seriously, I seldom left Fort Beacham, and Dad was always with me on the rare occasion we did. Here, now, I was basically useless.

More than useless, given my current state.

I mean, most of the knowledge I had about how the normal human world worked came from TV, but even reality shows were proven fakes. What good were any of the dramatic narratives swirling around my brain? Double useless. All those years of devouring steamy, angsty breakups and makeups of the rich, elite, *fictional* teens we all wanted to be at one point or another—wasted.

"Right. Not a problem." Arawn gently retracted his arms, forcing me to knuckle down and stand on my own. "I'll get it sorted."

Just as the city started to sway, Balor swept in and scooped me into his arms, going full bride and groom on a dime, my feet dangling, my arms folded against my chest—and my face seconds from nuzzling into his, because, sure, it might be pure steel, but it also suddenly seemed like a *great* place to pass out against.

Balor managed two steps, then stopped with a low growl. "The *eyes*."

Sighing heavily, I frowned up at him, then followed his line of sight to the security cameras mounted on the light poles. One for each, and as he drifted around in a slow circle, I spotted a few more on the concrete structure off to the far left—probably for stairs or elevators to the lower levels.

Silent as ever, Draco glanced between *the eyes*, then dissolved into black mist. Just—poof. Gone. Man one second, darkness the next that scattered in every direction. Tough as it was to follow the dispersal, I managed to track him to a camera by the grungy metal doorway, his shadows settling over the lens.

Hiding us.

Maybe because they assumed Cronus was looking for me.

Or, more likely, hunting *them* down, these three by far the most dangerous monsters in recorded Cronus history. Supernatural alphas, top of the food chain, *real* predators, Arawn, Balor, and Draco were prized possessions for a secret organization that researched how best to outsmart the paranormal.

How to ensure humanity's survival if the supernatural population ever got tired of living in the metaphorical shadows and finally staged an uprising. Because, according to Dad, it wasn't a question of *if*—but when.

I used to care.

A lot.

I started at Cronus after my senior year ready to *hate* these beasts who were way more powerful than any human.

Time shaped perspective, I guess.

And pain soured *everything*. Right now, none of it mattered. Not the kidnapping. Not this daughter of Nyx shit. Not Cronus. Not Balor's burly chest calling me home as he carried me across the parking lot.

I just wanted a little fucking *relief*.

My eyes drifted shut as he set me down on the blocky cement divider between two empty spaces. Tears prickled to life, but when I peeled my lids open, nothing fell. All cried out, remember? No relief from *that* pain either, the sorrow lodged in my throat, my ducts swollen and dry.

Balor, meanwhile, seemed lost in his own little world. A few paces away, he stood there like a superhero—or a supervillain?—hands planted on his hips, head tossed back, eyes shut and nostrils flared. He just needed a fluttering cape to complete the look, his smile toothy and a bit deranged, but also oddly... peaceful?

Like he was drinking in the city.

Breathing it, filling his lungs and absorbing the visceral *energy* all around us.

Gripping the edge of the divider, I glanced over one shoulder, then the other. No Arawn. No Draco—not really, anyway. Just me and Balor, alone on top of a random parking garage, in the middle of a random city.

It should be ordinary.

A parking lot should be old news. People my age wouldn't think twice about using one, about sitting in the driver's seat and checking their socials after work, or leaving their car parked for a night in the city...

But instead of ruminating on my lack of life experience, all I could think about was—

"What do you eat?"

Seriously. I'd yet to see them consume a damn thing, either out here or at Cronus, and while I was falling apart at the seams, they all seemed so... fine. Healthy. Full and functional.

Balor's black lashes fluttered as they opened, and he sucked down one last gloriously deep breath before dipping his chin to his chest, lowering himself ever so slightly to look me dead in the eye.

"What do *I* eat or all of us in general? Be specific, little blackbird."

Warmth flared deep inside at the affection curling around his pet name. *Little blackbird* marked the second this trio had given me, and I should really put my foot down —stand up and be indignant. *I'm not your blackbird, Balor. I'm not your little one, Arawn.* It all implied a level of intimacy that *they* clearly felt, but I...

I...

I *hated* that something as simple as a name made me feel better.

Just a brief reprieve from the storm battering my crumbling defenses.

So, I rolled my shoulders back, as much as it hurt *everywhere*, and frowned. "Is there a difference?"

Best to breeze right by the name—not even acknowledge it. That spoke volumes, right?

Plus, I didn't have the energy for the back-and-forth bound to follow any objections.

"We feast on darkness," Balor mused as I teetered on the brink of collapse. His left eye narrowed, almost in a subtle assessment of my well-being, while the rest of him remained as dangerously handsome and upbeat as ever. "What we elicit from humanity..." He then pressed a hand to his chest with a little bow, the dramatic weirdo. "I eat *fear*, Selene." Oblivious to the twist in my gut, he pursed his full lips, eyes darting around the parking lot. "Draco... He..." Another pause, a careful consideration. "Draco favors the emptiness. He doesn't feast often."

Huh. That explained the physical differences between them, if anything. I assumed they chose these forms—that Balor's Greek god *thing* and Draco's gaunt, ghostly male model vibe had been products of their imagination. Maybe not. Maybe, like the old gods, they had humanoid features that were unique to them.

"Arawn is a nibbler," Balor carried on with a wicked little chuckle. "He lulls his prey—butters them all over, fattens them up for a long-term entanglement. He craves the delicacy of relaxation, the richness of pure calm."

Wait. I swallowed hard, body on fire, head throbbing, eyes getting so fucking heavy every blink was a fight. "Have y-you been eating... *me?*"

Was that why I felt extra gross on top of everything? I mean, this couldn't *just* be missing a couple doses of meds, right? This had to be something more.

Balor's howling laughter wasn't exactly encouraging, his manic rumbles echoing across the parking lot. The windshield on the nearest car *cracked*, faded white spiderwebs streaking the glass, the driver's-side window next—until the humor died and Balor cleared his throat. Once again, he just stared, waiting for me to join in on the joke, and when I didn't, he threw his hands up with a drama queen groan, then rubbed at his stupid, stubbly, gorgeous face.

"We can't *take* from you like that," he drawled, pinning me with an exasperated look that was all teeth. "You aren't human, blackbird. You're a—"

"Daughter of night," I finished for him, the sardonic tone and flippant head-bob my undoing. The skyscrapers buckled in the middle and lilted left, and I folded over, stabbing my toes at the concrete to ground myself, and took a deep breath. "Uh-huh. Sure."

Pain sharpened behind my eyes, seemingly in a competition with the stabbing nonsense in my lower back. *Who's gonna finally make me pass out? Come on now— place your bets.* Elbows on my knees, I clenched my eyes shut and massaged my temples, willing things to just *settle* for a little while. The lights, the sounds, the *air*—this city was too much.

And I wanted to scream again.

Rip my throat open and hurl my agony into the night sky. Spit the poison out. *Breathe*.

I kneaded my temples instead, really grinding my thumbs in there while my fingers worked my forehead, hunting for pressure points. No screaming for me. No pouring it out for the world to hear.

A lifetime of experience had taught me to just shut up and *take it*.

Adding to the sensory symphony, the door to the elevators and/or stairs creaked open shrilly, followed by an explosion of male voices. I whimpered at the onslaught, folding in on myself, bracing, lashes suddenly damp as a few bottom of the barrel tears squished out. Laughter and chatter and footsteps crashed across the rooftop lot, and I slowly pushed against my knees, locking my elbows to stay upright, and twisted around to take in the sights.

Guys—a whole herd of them, nowhere near as fancy as mine, but clearly they'd just had a boys night in the city. They prowled across the parking lot together, cackling and pushing and shouting, drenched in a beer cloud that made my acid reflux spike. Twentysomethings, maybe a bit older than me, all meandered down the lane, hopefully one or two of them designated drivers, and while most drifted by the empty parking space at my back, a straggler slowed to a complete stop, our gazes tangling.

"Are you... okay?"

Nerd-chic with the round glasses and beanpole frame. Caramel-blond hair that looked like he had tried to style it at some point, then just gave up. Eighties jean jacket with

Star Wars patches over a striped tee and too-tight pants, Converse at the bottom—just a normal guy.

Asking if a random girl was okay.

I blinked back at him, touched that he cared enough to ask—humiliated that he felt the need to, because obviously I radiated pure walking corpse vibes for him to stray from his buddies.

Before I could croak something back at him, he pulled his phone from his jacket pocket and held it up, beady browns darting between me and Balor.

"Do you, uh, need me to call someone?"

My lips parted—then snapped shut with a sharp inhale. Big hands, strong and warm, smoothed over my knees out of nowhere and nudged them apart, and suddenly there was Balor sidling between, making himself at home with my thighs. Stunned, I reared back, then grabbed at his shirt before I toppled off the other side of the cement block.

He said nothing, locked in a staring contest with a tipsy guy who didn't deserve it. His fingers coiled around my wrists, holding me there—either for balance or as a warning, his grip wasn't exactly clear. Black eyes cut into my would-be rescuer, unblinking, still and terrifying and so, so dark, all of Balor's casual snark and manic humor gone, his presence big as a mountain and just as hostile.

Too weak to fight him off, I tapped my heel against the back of his steely calf, once, twice, then as hard as I could the third time when it didn't even faze him. Balor merely tipped his head to the right, locked on target, and smiled.

Then the poor bastard behind me *screamed.*

Not a startled shout or a shocked cry, but a full-on, balls to the wall, *I'm going to die* screech.

And he wouldn't stop.

Footsteps pounded the pavement again, and over my

shoulder, I watched as his friends ran back and dragged him away, talking low, shaking him.

"What the fuck is *wrong* with you?"

I faced Balor's torso, trembling, unsure if that was directed at us or the screamer. A few moments later, a car beeped, doors slammed, and all the noise muffled. Rubber burned over concrete, and two vehicles—a dark blue sedan and a grey jeep—whizzed out of here as fast as they could swing it. Red brake lights flared briefly in the corner of my eye, the pair taking the ramp down at warp speed, and then nothing.

Just me and Balor and the chaos of a city after dark.

"Did you just—"

"*Yes*," Balor growled, rough and wild, his grip bruising my wrists as he glowered in the general direction the cars had taken. "I did."

Too exhausted to shout, to demand what the *fuck* was wrong with him, I flexed my fingers in the hopes to get the blood flowing again. "You really shouldn't—"

"I protect and *keep* what's mine." Balor finally released me, only to swap my wrists for my chin, one huge hand cupping it and forcing my head up. His eyes lured me in, trapping me in his dangerous thrall as he rumbled, "You should get used to it now, blackbird, because that's not going to change."

Crisp footfalls clipped across the parking lot, and Balor stroked my lower lip with his thumb, grinning, the inferno dampened and the mischief back, then eased away just in time for Arawn to replace him at my back.

"I've arranged for the penthouse suite," he announced like a velvety lullaby, his hand drifting up my spine to cuff the nape of my neck. Unlike Balor, he was pure silk, his hold firm but gentle, like protecting a baby bird in a loose fist. "Come along, little one." And then he was just *moving* me, easing me off the cement block and steadying me when I wobbled. "Time for a proper rest."

Mist swelled behind Balor's husky figure, swirling and gathering, shifting from translucent grey to inky black—to Draco in all his ghostly glory, the wispy shadows clinging to his trench coat. Much to my annoyance, he and Balor swapped glances, and while he was still the most expressionless creature I'd ever met, Draco's eyes said more than his face ever could.

He... *approved* of that toxic masculinity crap.

Balor's bullshit caveman performance—he seemed to agree with it.

Ugh. I was still too weak to call either of them out on it.

But I would.

Tomorrow.

"H-how did you pay for it?"

Seriously, some luxe penthouse in a tower like that must have cost a fortune. Did these guys have a credit history, or could Arawn make cash appear out of thin air like those chairs back in the cube?

"Pay?" Arawn's lips twitched as he walked me around the cement barrier, herding me into his arms. "Don't be ridiculous."

"We owe this world *nothing*," Draco insisted hoarsely. He and Balor drifted after us, all three males chuckling at some private joke that just made me groan and roll my eyes, beyond frustrated even after they engulfed me in the dark bubble again.

So *sick* of being out of the loop here.

But whatever.

It didn't matter. Not really. Not tonight, anyway,

surrounded by sweet darkness and soft shadow, carried away on a pillowy black cloud.

What mattered was finding somewhere safe to rest my head, preferably behind a locked door, so that I could *hopefully* get some real sleep with the illusion of privacy—and tomorrow, I might even feel a smidge better.

Or, more realistically, a whole hell of a lot worse.

CHAPTER TEN

If I was a child of night, some daughter of Nyx, did I really need air?

If I stayed under long enough, would I die?

Blinking heavy eyes, the water making my lashes drag, I was about to find out—one way or another. Pressure mounting in my lungs, I let a little air out of the balloon, exhaling another round of nostril-bubbles and watching them dance to the surface. Even with that, the tightness never let up, pressing in, strangling me, the answer *screaming* into focus as I braced on the sides of the claw-foot tub and held myself under, staring at the grey world outside this slightly too-warm bathwater, waiting for something to *happen*—

Arawn's wobbly head poked over the edge of the tub, blurred yet recognizable, his silhouette already a little too familiar for my liking. Pale skin. Fitted black suit across a lean, strong figure. Angular features. Black hair that fell in soft waves around his face and dusted the tops of his shoulders, reaching for me now as he tipped his head left, then right, his aura breaking the sensory deprivation down here, calm and soothing, coaxing me to rise.

And I did.

For him, I jolted up and broke the surface with a gasp.

I guess even the offspring of primordial goddesses needed to breathe. *Good to know*.

Arawn straightened at the side of the huge oval tub, white pillar candles in each hand, and grinned as bathwater cascaded down my face and slicked my black curls to my skull.

"You all right down there, little one?"

Cheeks warming, I nodded and breathed, still smoothing the water from my face, my eyes—then nearly jumped out of my skin at the next *boom* that rocked the skyscraper from top to bottom, followed by a brilliant flash of lightning that turned the luxury master en suite bright white. Heart in my throat, I scooted to the opposite side of the tub, gripping the curved porcelain lip and taking in the storm as though it hadn't been raging all morning—like that wasn't the first apocalyptic thunder and lightning strike to shake the tower to its foundations.

So high in the sky, it felt like we were really *in* it, the elements battering us from all sides. A floor-to-ceiling windowpane soared next to the tub, rain lashing the glass and drizzling down in racing rivulets. A smothering fog, deep and rich like charcoal, blanketed the surrounding cityscape, leaving nothing but the storm, the savagery pouring from the heavens like the start of some biblical flood.

Quite the view.

Unlike anything I'd ever seen before, that was for sure. We had storms around the base. Sometimes, the other Cronus kids and I—we theorized the monsters were doing it from their cages, bringing the chaos down, turning the skies dark and angry.

I knew better now.

Maybe.

I thought I did, anyway, but then three tatters of Erebus's cloak showed up and flipped my life on its head.

So...

Really, what the hell did I *actually* know?

Right now, only two things were certain: this was a doozy of a storm, and the agony in my bones felt marginally better this afternoon than last night.

Or this morning?

Whenever Arawn had charmed our way into one of two penthouses in this luxury tower comprised of upscale boutiques, swanky apartments, and pricey hotel suites. From my spotty recollection of the elevator map, there was also a spa, a gym, a pool, and a movie theater, plus an organic grocery on the ground floor.

Given how absolutely destroyed I'd felt yesterday, it was a miracle I had processed that much. After Arawn secured a key, he carried me into the tower, Balor and Draco at his heels, their black eyes forever on the prowl, and then the elevator brought us straight to the two-floor west penthouse. Today, vague snapshots peppered my memory of sitting on glittery tile in the shower, crouched under the hot water for a while, then hauling my broken body into the California king in the attached master suite.

Then a dreamless sleep, no doubt courtesy of Draco or Arawn or both.

Balor struck me as the type to gift you with nightmares.

I awoke to a thunderclap. Barely ate any of the room service breakfast despite Balor's impatient insistence. Weak, exhausted, sore, foggy, I'd stuck to juice, then eventually filled the tub with piping hot water to chase away the perpetual chill.

And here I was.

Naked in front of two shadowy creatures and feeling way too shitty to care about modesty, with Draco lurking in the doorway and Arawn sauntering around this kingdom of porcelain and marble, all gold and black accents against a majority white on white on white. Walls, floors, cabinets —*white*. Too white. So white I hadn't been able to leave the lights on because the glint and glare off all the very shiny, very clean, very reflective surfaces made the headache behind my eyes ten times worse.

"What's that?" I mumbled, turning my back on the dark and moody autumn storm to watch Arawn place thick pillar candles around the bathroom. Countertop. Back of the toilet. At the base of the claw-foot tub, the lion's feet below brass to match the rest of the bathroom hardware.

"We raided the spa," Arawn remarked pleasantly, way too overdressed in his suit but his expression soft and handsome, serene and easy. Exactly the energy my touchy five senses needed today, his velvety tenor the first noise that *wasn't* an affront since I climbed in the tub and willed the world to shut up.

As the black-haired god arranged the last pair of candles at the sink, Draco strode into the en suite clutching a clear plastic bag, his arm stiff and awkward by his side. Frowning, I drew my knees to my chest, no more soapy bubbles to hide me below the surface, and then wrapped my arms around them. So serious, Draco. So gaunt and ghostly and *gorgeous*.

So unintentionally hilarious when he stopped at the end of the tub, then thrust the crinkly bag full of what looked like dried rose petals over the water and flipped it around. The petals plopped unceremoniously onto the surface, and as my eyebrows shot up, his expression stayed the same: breathtakingly macabre and stunningly neutral. He then crumpled the plastic in one hand and leaned over the tub to disperse the clump with the other, fingers gliding soundlessly across the water, barely making a ripple.

My face lit up like the sun, but he seemed not to notice, hell-bent on spreading the petals far and wide. His black eyes eventually snagged on my legs, drifting up the slope to where my arms locked tight around my knees. Pink flared in his hollow cheeks, fast and furious, but vanished by the time he straightened and drifted back to the door without a word.

The hiss of a struck match snapped my attention back to Arawn, and, fiddling with a lone rose petal, pinching it and smooshing it and dragging it underwater, I watched him putter around the bathroom, lighting all the candles. Scentless—just what I needed. Pops of warm orange filled the otherwise storm-lit space.

"Beautiful," he rumbled as he knelt at the end of the tub, the porcelain underlit by flickering flames like some witch's cauldron. Face hot again, I glanced his way, half expecting him to be doing that swoony TV thing where the guy stares longingly at the girl and murmurs a compliment that could, in theory, apply to anything around them but is so *obviously* about her.

But Arawn was lost in a candle, holding it right in front of his face, eyes fixed on the flame as it shivered and found its strength. Shadows played across his regal features, and he tipped his head, his grin as warm as candlelight and brazenly affectionate.

"The way the light dances," he whispered. "Just beautiful."

Once again, my eyebrows launched up my forehead, because... I mean, was this tatter of pure shadow, this piece of the personification of darkness from the dawn of time—was he infatuated by *light*?

After slipping the small hotel matchbox inside his jacket, Arawn sauntered down the bathtub to crouch by me at the other end, bringing his beautiful candlelight with him.

"Remember, little one," he started, his voice like honey, his presence like home, "we are both creatures of darkness, but we are not *monsters*." With one crooked arm resting on the rim of the tub, Arawn eased closer and held the candle between us so we could both watch the fire dance. "Not evil, not good. We love shadow, my brothers and I, but Erebus loves Nyx more than life itself." He then swept his fingers through the flame, not so much as a twitch on his beautiful face to suggest the heat hurt him. No burns on his pale skin, fingers unharmed when they wiggled back at me.

"And Nyx..." Arawn pinned me with a strangely firm look, like I needed to really *hear* him, and I drifted closer—then planted a hand on the tub rim to stop from outright climbing onto him. The candle disappeared, back on the floor where it belonged, and Arawn leaned over the rose petals, over steadily cooling water. I stiffened. Lightning slashed the black sky behind me and cast his face in harsher, sharper shadows. With a sigh, he plucked a petal and stuck it to the top of my hand. "Selene, *you*, your lineage... You cannot have night without day. No dark without light."

I swallowed thickly. "Balance."

It came out of nowhere, the realization, and seemed to boost Arawn's spirits, his smile brightening and his eyes glinting even as the raging storm reflected back at me from the black.

"Yes." With a grin like heaven and a sigh like sin, Arawn stroked my cheek, his knuckle's kiss featherlight and torturous. "Balance. Your mother birthed dawn and light, not only night. We understand all this... Our world, the darkness, the shadows—it's frightening. But, I beg you, for your own sake..." He then tapped under my chin, gently nudging my head up even as I tried to hide behind my crossed arms. "Don't be afraid of your legacy."

I wasn't afraid.

Not really.

I kept waiting for the meltdown to hit. Three, two, one —panic attack. Mind lost forever after being ripped away from the only home I had ever known. Tatters of Erebus's cloak and primordial moms and legacies and the possibility of so many cruel lies designed by three handsome devils. Use *my* pain and anguish to hurt someone I loved. Dad. Cronus. *Something.*

But with Arawn, it was just... calm.

Quiet.

From all I'd read and heard, a world of darkness meant demons rising from the deep, crawling out of the pit and conquering the world.

But so far, darkness was... this.

A thunderstorm and candlelight.

Togetherness, the penthouse huge but Balor, Arawn, and Draco's combined presence always so very near, like a constant hum under my skin.

Our gazes tangled, mine translucent blue, his pure black. My heart skipped a beat and my breath hitched. Time stopped. The world stood still in his eyes, in the unexpected intensity burning behind the calm.

His jaw muscles flared through a clench, and then that ghostly touch was back, caressing my cheek—two knuckles this time, soft and cool and so *real* that I leaned into it with a sigh, eyelids heavy and threatening to close.

Until he cupped my chin.

Held me. Cradled me. Trapped me in his world of cozy darkness and infinite shadow—

Arawn went in for the kiss first, but I was the one who moaned. As soon as his lips gently brushed mine, the *want* simmering in my belly clawed to the surface. So soft. So tender. So innocent, our lips just grazing, our eyes hooded and the air heady with roses.

Somewhere deep down, self-preservation insisted I shove him away—splash him, hurt him, curse him, and demand they both get the hell out of the bathroom and leave me alone.

But the darkness in my chest, the slumbering creature that had been there my whole life, ignored and dismissed— she silenced the protests with a languid stretch and a molten sigh, one that carried up to my lips. They parted with a sharp inhale, and Arawn seized the chance to claim me *properly*. Mouths open, tongues meeting in the middle, no longer shy and tentative but curious and bold, I surrendered to the abyss.

Closed my eyes and breathed in the roses.

No one had ever kissed me like this before. All my past kisses were sloppy make-outs at high school dances and bonfires in the Fort Beacham woods. Throw in the odd drunken hookup at Cronus holiday parties, *him* shitfaced and me barely tipsy despite drinking so, so, so much more. After, that *him*—there had only been four over the years— stopped talking to me.

Rarely even looked at me again, like kissing the pasty, raven-haired girl in a supply closet was the gravest of sins.

Or, more likely, word had gotten out and Dad put his foot down.

Health and job first, frivolous relationships second.

But here, Arawn kissed me like he never wanted to stop, deep and passionate, his hand cradling my face. Slow and sensual, our noses nudging here and there, our tongues stroking—*pleasure* brewing low in my belly, untapped desire ready to spill over and drown the world.

Water sloshed and dribbled as I reached for him with both hands, my fingertips creeping along his jaw in a slow, intimate exploration. Despite the clean-shaven look, there was a whiff of stubble, a hint of roughness, and that paired with his groan the second I touched him, the kiss suddenly deeper, faster, like his self-control dangled by a frayed thread...

Hot.

Fucking *hot*.

Goose bumps rippled over me from top to bottom, even underwater, followed by a rush of *fire* when his cupped hand wandered lower. Down my neck first, stroking under my ear as our breaths fell faster and harder. His thumb kissed my collarbone, all the way across to the tender hollow of my throat, then delved lower. As soft and soothing as Arawn felt, his presence like crushed velvet on a cool autumn day, his touch below the surface, sleeve and all, was like his jawline: it had the appearance of smoothness, but look closer and it was *harsh*. Firm. Possessive in a way that made my heart jump and my back arch. Down, down, down he went, cupping the side of my breast, tickling my navel, smoothing around my hip.

It wasn't until those long, elegant fingers slipped between my thighs that I panicked.

I...

I'd kissed before.

Given the odd—sad—handjob.

But...

I mean, no one wanted to admit they were a twenty-five-year-old virgin—

I reared back with a gasp, bathwater slopping up to the rim, rose petals caught on tidal waves. Humiliation roiled in my gut as Arawn retreated—but not completely. He stayed pressed up against the claw-foot tub, eyes hungry, the black big and glossy, his smile more a predatory snarl than the gentle grins he'd lobbed my way since we landed in this suite.

Say something.

My mouth opened, but nothing came out, nothing but gasps as I chased my breath and used both hands to hide the embarrassed color aching in my cheeks.

Say anything.

"Did you..." *Not that.* "Did you three take me to..." *Stop. Pump the brakes.* "To..." *Swallow it down and forget it like you always do—* "Did you take me to breed me?"

"Yes."

Arawn and I both flinched at Draco's frank response from the doorway, his face as flushed as mine and his neutral expression verging on pained. Slowly, Arawn glowered over his shoulder, cozy warmth swapped for acidic annoyance.

"And no," he said in a soft hiss. Danger sparked in the air, followed by a great *booming* thunderclap. As a lightning strike lit up the sky milliseconds later, bright white spilling through the window onto the glaring pair, I sidled across the tub, naked and aroused and mortified. I then gathered all the nearby rose petals close and chomped down on the insides of my cheeks as Arawn twisted back to face me.

My lips...

Tingled.

Buzzed with the memory of his.

And, frankly, felt a little full. Not swollen, but almost. I glanced down with a gulp, half expecting to find my collarbone bruised.

"We took you, first and foremost, because you deserve to be free." With both arms resting on the tub rim, Arawn dragged a lone finger over the water's surface, occasionally flicking at a petal, his eyes never straying from my face. Even if I didn't meet them, I *felt* them. Not fiery, not a burn that left the cinders of wildfire in its wake, but an intensity impossible to ignore. Heavy. *Present.* Like nothing else deserved his attention. "You should let your feathers grow in and *fly*, Selene. They've clipped them all your life."

Wait. Literal feathers, or...? Because, seriously, who knew with these three.

"But—"

"*And* because we belong together," Arawn stressed, tossing another narrowed look Draco's way with a sigh. "Erebus and Nyx. You and us." He then nudged two floating petals toward me. "We are pieces of this great love. We deserve to revel in it, same as them."

"Our offspring fade." My gaze soared to Draco in the doorway, who neither leaned nor slumped on the frame but stood ramrod straight right in the middle of it, arms at his sides, expression blank but his eyes so terrifyingly *alive*. His cheek twitched when Arawn cleared his throat, but he refused to meet his eye—or mine, for that matter. Instead, he watched the storm rage, the next blast of white lightning to fill the bathroom making him even paler. "In time, the shadows we make disperse. Carried away on the wind. There are so few in the world today, and all of Nyx's female offspring are mated with others."

Right. I gnawed at my lower lip for a moment, pushing through the fog of exhaustion to dissect every word.

So...

Was I just what was available to them, or did they actually want *me*?

Draco paused, gaunt cheeks even hollower as his white brows knit, and then a firm nod came with the next violent *boom* of thunder.

"We were meant to find each other," he insisted. Tone firm, stance self-assured, I wasn't sure who he was trying to convince: him or me. "We three felt you the moment we set foot in this realm again. Centuries in the pit, basking in hellfire, and then *you*—"

"Draco, perhaps—"

"She asked, Arawn." The pair locked eyes for a moment before Arawn acquiesced with a subtle nod, toying with rose petals again as Draco stared holes into the back of his skull. "Balance, remember? Yes, we wish to create shadows, to bring our progeny back to mankind, and to do that, Selene, we require *you*, but... it is more than that." His black gaze cut to mine. "It is... deeper, this lure, the thrall we share in each other's presence."

Years from now, the trauma I suffered yesterday would feel like a fever dream. The blinding agony ripping apart my insides—a painful piece of history I'd rather forget.

But I could never forget our conversation by the pond when I'd asked if Draco was even capable of *feeling*—that wounded look, the hurt in his voice when he swore he did.

I saw it here, all that feeling. Stoic as he was at first glance, Draco burned bright in his own way, his eyes so expressive, his emotions turning the air stale and heavy.

Maybe even a little cold. A shiver ran through me as rain hammered the window, and I drew my knees back up to my chest, hugging them tight and settling my chin into the dip there with a huff.

"You," Arawn murmured as confusion and heartache and loss came trickling back in, internal mayhem on the rise. "Selene, we want *you* above all else. To free you. To watch you soar. To love as we deserve."

I closed my eyes and groaned. "This is... a lot."

Suddenly, the light behind my lids died, and then there was Arawn with a candle again, the wick black and smoking —every other candle in the room out.

"See?" he whispered, holding it higher with a dimpled smirk. "See what they've suppressed?"

The bathroom blurred at the sting of fresh tears. I sniffled and wiped my nose along my forearm; *I* didn't do that. There wasn't a pulse of energy or some internal intention. And if it *had* happened without my permission, if Draco and Arawn weren't messing with me just to sell their narrative, then that *sucked*. Lack of control? Not good.

"Don't be afraid, Selene." Arawn set the candle aside and stood, looming over me as he swiped a hand through his silky black waves. "Not of us, and most certainly not of yourself."

"You say that," I argued lightly, "but you won't let me leave."

"You can go anywhere you want—"

"But we will follow," Draco interjected, a sentiment that didn't earn a glare from Arawn this time. "Always."

When the intensity of *both* their stares threatened to set me ablaze, I sucked in a deep breath and sank below the surface, blowing nose-bubbles all the way down. Flustered and overwhelmed, I braced on the sides of the tub and stretched across the bottom, really pressing my back against the cool porcelain.

Where was the breakdown?

Where were the objections?

Why wasn't I losing my mind? This whole situation should trigger a million alarm bells. I should be screaming objections over what was a literal kidnapping. I should be trying to get to a phone *constantly*. I should fight them tooth and nail, insist they had no claim on me, that we weren't *destined* to love—that this was some demonic trick to hurt Dad or Cronus or humanity as a whole.

But my mind rebelled against *that* more than anything Arawn and the others had said so far.

Which made no sense.

I held myself under as long as I could. When I finally resurfaced, Arawn and Draco had left—but not without lighting all the candles again. A small metal tray of sealed bottled drinks and prepackaged sandwiches, cookies, and salads sat on the nearest counter, but the thought of eating made my stomach turn.

So, I went back to the storm. Hanging over the side of the tub, I tracked the rain on the glass, the way it slithered this way and that. Watched the fog roll over the city. Braced against the thunder and lightning that hit like bombs, the skyscraper shuddering and my bathwater rippling with each strike.

This wasn't the first time I had a symptom-flare hangover. Weak and wrecked, exhaustion in my bones, years of experience taught me how to survive until I eventually climbed out of the hole.

No meds yesterday. No dose today.

I felt like shit, but Dad had always led me to believe it would be *so* much worse.

That one pill forgotten meant catastrophe.

I frowned at my barely there reflection in the window, only then noticing—

My fingernails.

The bottoms—they were black.

Like a shadowy sun cresting the horizon, *black* nudged out from the nail beds.

Panicked, I shot up and tried to rub it away, but it stayed, all ten digits infected. Painless—hello, silver lining. For once, it didn't *hurt*.

But this time, I had to figure out what to do with the weird shit my body threw at me alone. Before, Dad or my doctors called the shots. I rarely had a say about what I did with or put into my own body. Medical assessments and treatment plans: I never had a voice. I did as I was told or suffered one of Dad's scathing lectures, maybe even lost a few privileges depending on how stubborn I was and who witnessed my tantrum.

This, the darkness creeping up my fingernails, what it meant for my well-being...

This was all me. My decision. My voice. My opinion. My consequences.

And as the storm raged, the penthouse silent, the candles flickering—I suddenly realized I had absolutely no idea what to do with all that power.

CHAPTER ELEVEN

One week after I left Cronus, I woke up from a twenty-five-year nap with a gasp, a sob, and a sigh.

Before today, drugged and complacent, I must have existed in a high-functioning daze, because the world had never looked this bright—so clear and crisp and *alive*. Naked and alert, pressed against one of three enormous windows in the master bedroom, I devoured the east coast metropolis of Dunston with a keen eye. In the distance, a moody Atlantic swallowed the sunshine, but here, much closer, golden beams bounced off glass towers with their sharp corners and sleek exteriors. Cars puttered like stop-and-go ants through midmorning traffic, pedestrians crowding sidewalks and intersections. From here, I saw the clouds for what they were, the nuances—they weren't just white. Oh no. No, there were layers and intricacy.

The *world* was suddenly so much more than I'd ever seen before. My bright blue gaze snapped up at the hum of an overhead airplane. Small craft, a two- or four-seater—maybe to monitor traffic? I noted the red detailing on the body, the matte baby blue finishing, the whirring propellers, the plume of grey exhaust in its wake.

Dunston wasn't even a blip on my memory's radar, but the landscape was full of clues. East coast, English the predominant language, somewhere north-*ish* given how the trees stitched an autumn canopy throughout the downtown streets.

And I could see the leaves. All the way up here, I could pick apart what was full orange and what was more yellow. The red versus the brown.

Seven days off base and the world looked different.

But so did I.

Pale hips, breasts, and forearms thrust against the glass, my nose and forehead leaving smudges, I glanced at my nails, then cocked my head, eyes narrowing.

All black now.

Every day a little blacker.

Draco, Balor, and Arawn had said nothing about them to suggest something was wrong. No one panicked as they got darker and darker. No one floated the idea of finding one or two of my old meds to keep the transition at bay. Hell, Balor even complimented them the other night, insisting they suited me.

Black and hard as diamonds, they edged slightly above my fingertips at this point. Smooth and glossy, I'd need a drill to trim them when they inevitably got too long, but that was a problem for another day.

Said mantra was how I had survived the week detoxing from a lifetime of medication: every new problem was one for future me. Not present me. Not the me who was just trying to get through the next minute, the next hour, the next TV episode.

Easing off the window, I lifted my right arm to assess the angry black hairs poking out of my skin. Barely a millimeter long, the hard texture reminded me of a bird's feather—that little bit at the end that, for a time, was a great writing utensil when dipped in ink. Three new hairs total near my armpit, then the familiar asshole who always came out around my boob.

This time, I didn't pluck it.

I left it, left all of them, for the fluffy white bathrobe at the end of the California king, then beelined for the door.

Two stories tall, the penthouse had served us well the last week. On the upper level, styled like a swanky loft with all the windows and glass dividers, sat three bedrooms with a bathroom for each. Lots of white and shiny surfaces, inoffensive wall art paired with thick, nondescript grey carpets. Fake plants that must have cost a fortune because they sure as hell looked real. Most of my time had been spent up here, sleeping off the pain, splish-splashing in the claw-foot tub, and forcing down room service. I'd fallen asleep in front of the bedroom TV more times than I could count, my body so empty, running on fumes, that staying awake during the day had been a pipe dream.

And throughout all that, three tatters of Erebus's dark cloak hovered. Sometimes they all piled into bed or around the master suite to watch a movie with me while I slumped on a mountain of pillows, looking and feeling like a zombie who had been repeatedly run over by the same truck. Balor usually handled food, sitting and staring until I choked down at least half a plate. Draco was my night creeper, always *there*, loitering in a shadowy corner when I jolted out of a nightmare, sweaty and panting and on the verge of tears, desperate for comfort and finding *him*.

Falling back asleep to him, this awkward, ghostly guard dog who kept the nightmares at bay afterward.

Arawn liked to talk, to lull me to sleep with his silky words and velvet tone while he stroked my hair.

They hovered and pampered and babied and complained when I kicked them out and locked the bedroom door, *very* aware that no lock could keep them out and *very* appreciative that they respected the telltale *click* of it sliding into place all the same.

Seven days of our strange routine—but I had yet to feel genuinely refreshed until this morning.

Looping the thick belt around my waist and tying it off, I slowly padded down the spiral glass staircase to the first floor. Three days ago, this thing made me crazy dizzy. Today, it was just a bunch of steps, round and round, that offered a full three-sixty view of the main floor. Totally open-concept, the penthouse provided its guests with a full working kitchen, island and all. Top-tier appliances—that was my read, anyway, given the sheer number of buttons and what you could do with them. Throw in a formal sitting area near the back by a window wall, then an informal lounge between the main door and the kitchen that the stairwell emptied into, plus a bar area made for parties, and I could spend the rest of my life here quite comfortably.

Minus all the cold mid-century modern furniture and the white on white on white, of course. Not exactly homey or comforting; not even the odd splash of black and gold, the wood and hemp accents, could make this place soft.

Nearly seven feet of Balor stood at the dining table arranging my room service breakfast, his back to me, but his ear angled my way as I stepped onto the light hardwood.

"Morning, blackbird."

Arawn sat on the too-hard couch to my right, one long leg crossed over the other and dressed to the nines in his full black suit, his upper half hidden behind a flimsy newspaper wall of *Dunston Today*. Meanwhile, Draco lurked in a dark corner by the door like he was trying to avoid the sunlight glaring through all the huge windows. Arawn ruffled the newspaper by way of greeting, a little too similar to Dad for my taste, while Draco just stared, the slight twitch of his white brow when our eyes met his version of *good morning*.

Without a word, I headed toward Balor and food, breathing deep, sucking it all down—every morsel, every rich scent in the air. Food had never called to me before. I didn't understand the fascination with chocolate or cookie dough ice cream, nor had I ever salivated when a friend cracked open a freshly delivered pizza in a grease-stained box or unpacked a bag of burgers and fries.

But this morning?

Different.

Everything—different.

Sounds sharper. Smells more pronounced. Sights...

I stopped at Balor's side just as he straightened by the head of the chic dining table, dusting his hands off and grinning like he was proud of the way he'd arranged my blueberry pancakes on china plates. The polite thing to do would be to take it all in, smile, and thank him for the effort.

I grabbed his face instead. Just slapped both hands to his scruffy cheeks and ripped him down to size, lost in his eyes, in the braided hues of black. So intense. So luscious. So darkly beautiful, gothic and dangerous, the complexity both a wonder and a horror, all the delicious contrasts tied up in a neat little bow.

And his *scruff*. Balor's black brows crinkled as I dragged my palms over his coarse facial hair, black and rough, the perfect accent to an oval face and strong jaw and statuesque nose. With a short, sharp breath, forcefully hunched to stay in my eyeline and our faces about an inch apart, he seemed more than a little taken aback as I mapped every detail, really absorbing his sinful elegance, the way he looked like a fallen angel who turned *bad* the second he hit Earth.

But then I caught a strong whiff of thick, dark, sugary syrup, and I was gone, thighs and hips pressed against the table as I surveyed this morning's spread. Fluffy blueberry pancakes stacked four high on the biggest plate, then a side of fresh blueberries in a teeny, cutesy little blue and white bowl. A glass syrup dispenser with a glittery diamond-cut lid and slender spout. Two slivers of crispy bacon on a separate plate.

Nostrils flared, I sucked it all down—and my mouth watered.

All week Balor had refused me my smoothies. I asked and asked and asked, arguing that I might do better with something familiar, but he wouldn't even entertain it: only solid foods while my body healed.

And now here we were, me reaching for a plump, round, taut blueberry and popping it in my mouth. I held it for a moment, gently nudging it around with my tongue, then bit down and—*oh*. An explosion of flavor, tart and sweet, another rush of saliva hitting my mouth, and I threw my head back with a *moan* that would make a call girl blush. My hands crested up my curves to my neck, then my cheeks, then my loose hair, more moans tumbling out, my body so *sensitive* to the touch.

Not because it hurt.

But because the pressure felt *wonderful*.

"Has it always tasted so *good?*" I demanded, my voice ragged and my mouth slick. The rustle of paper had me peeking over my shoulder, and there was Arawn, gawking, folded newspaper on his lap. Draco stepped out of the shadows and into the sunlight, backlit by fire, his gaunt features suddenly drenched in shadow. Balor, meanwhile, crouched back down to my height, white dress shirt sleeves scrunched to his elbows, the top button open and his smile beastly.

"Well, well, well," he rumbled as I went for the top pancake on the stack. "Isn't this interesting?"

Ignoring the predatory twinkle in his eyes, I ripped the thing down the middle and stuffed half a pancake in my mouth, dry and thick and ho-ly-*shit* so fucking *good*. Another chorus of moans fell out of me, one right after the other, unstoppable and wildly encouraged by the dance of flavor and texture and *fuck*.

"*More*," I grunted through a way-too-full mouth, barely swallowing it all down before shoving the second half in. Hands planted on the tabletop, Balor leaned closer, his smile bewildered and delighted and growing darker with every giant handful I crammed past my lips.

"Yes, Penthouse A," Arawn crooned smoothly after I'd demolished three pancakes in less than a minute, struggling for air but refusing to abandon this *feeling* for even a second. Popping blueberries in my mouth, I watched him on the penthouse phone, the cord spiraling up from the little glass table next to the couch, so *suave* just standing there with one hand in his pocket, effortlessly regal in his suit. Arawn smiled kindly and bobbed his head, black gaze on the floor for a moment before darting my way. "We'd like everything on the room service menu." A brief pause while I tilted the blueberry bowl back and tapped the last few holdouts into my mouth. "Yes, everything, that's what I said. Dinner items too if you can swing it—yes, I understand it's rather early."

Back to him, I went for the bacon as Balor chuckled and Draco crept across the room. Shit. *Shit*. No wonder Dad pitched a fit if we forget to grab a packet on the weekly food shop—it was so *good*. So salty and crackly and fucking phenomenal I needed it for every meal from here on out.

"As quick as you can," Arawn drawled, a strange tension stringing his words together. "No, whenever something's ready, bring it. Yes, yes, thank you."

The phone crashed back to its base just as I swallowed the last bit of actual food, already eyeing the syrup, belly howling, taste buds demanding I guzzle *that* too. Running on hard, ragged breaths, I reached for the crystal bottle— then stilled when Balor slipped his hand under my hair and lifted it. Just the left side, the curls frizzy and wild, splayed across his strong fingers, his huge palm. Stunned, I tracked him from the corner of my eye as he brought it closer, then ducked down to *sniff*.

Eyes shut, lips parted, he inhaled deep and long.

And I *liked* it, my skin prickling with want, desire tingling low in my core. The arm that lunged for the syrup just about fell limp at my side, but Arawn caught it at the last second. He dropped into a graceful kneel and nudged my thick white sleeve up to run his nose along my wrist, first the top, then the underside, the sensation tickly and hot and foreign.

Lust throbbed between my thighs in a single fiery *whump*.

My shoulders edged up when Draco's presence hummed behind me, and a lone finger ghosted down my spine, featherlight and barely there, stopping just shy of my ass before lazily drifting back up. With a gulp, I peeked over my shoulder again; Draco's eyes flashed to mine, so full of feeling, so rich with *emotion*.

His expression? Neutral. Distant. Empty. At first glance, he was all those things, but it was just a mask, a façade to hide the maelstrom within. I saw it clearer now than ever before, same as the sharp dip at his cheeks, the defined lines of his pale lips.

This morning, two of the three struck me as more... textured.

Pain twitched at my forearm, and I looked down with a sharp breath, heartbeat skyrocketing to discover Arawn—sweet, charming, soothing, calming *Arawn*—had nipped at the delicate skin there. Teeth bared, a predator in every sense, he stalked me, hunted me with his eyes, as he dragged his teeth along my bright blue veins. Gentle at first—then *rough*, seconds from breaking skin.

I jerked my arm back, but he held tight, blunting my escape. His sharp smile then jumped to my hip, landing there with a kiss that was nowhere near as sweet as our first, his beautiful hands undoing the fabric belt around my waist. While Draco's fingers expanded their tentative exploration from my back to the nape of my neck, Arawn delved under my housecoat, his tongue painting my thigh with *fire*.

Balor went deeper too, twining my hair around his fingers, tugging my head aside with a low, dangerous chuckle, exposing my neck properly. Draco jumped at the offering, suddenly pressed up behind me, lips just as light and torturous as his fingers while they grazed my skin right up to my ear.

Here, trapped between them, heat rising, my core a firestorm and my mind blissfully empty, I *saw* them. Yes, they looked the same: Balor huge and imposing, Arawn sleek and elegant, Draco sharp and gaunt. Black eyes for all three. Pale skin for two, sun-kissed for one. Well-dressed. Well-mannered. Well-groomed. Dangerous yet restrained. Wolves in tailored sheepskin.

But they were so much *harder* than I remembered.

For seven days, these three took care of me in their own ways. Carried me to bed when I passed out on a couch. Helped me out of the tub when my legs wobbled—*without* leering or insinuating or touching where they shouldn't. Dressed me when I was just too fucking tired to lift my arms. Dried my tears when I couldn't anymore. Sat through dumb movies just so I wouldn't be alone. Joined me for meals while I struggled to force even a few bites down, my tummy churn the gift that kept on giving, and their plates always empty, sustenance acquired elsewhere on their own time.

This was different.

In a flash, a single beat of my wild, dark heart, they were *men*. Not caregivers. Not protectors. Not concerned onlookers. Tangible. Real. *Present*. Hot and hard and wanting. Bold, Arawn's hands curving possessively along my inner thighs and prying them open, the gust of cool air followed by *suction* that would definitely bruise. Arrogant, Balor's grip in my hair like a master at the end of a leash, steering his beast this way and that. Tenuous, Draco's ghostly caress trembling like he just *couldn't* hold back anymore.

Squaring my shoulders, I shook off the shock of *them*, of how they really felt, and went in for the kill. A whispering caress for Draco, my hand smoothing up his sharp, clean-shaven jaw. A rough embrace for Arawn, my fingers twining in his silky hair, steering him even higher up my thighs than he dared climb. A challenging look for Balor, unblinking, unchecked, goading him to make a real *move* as he bared his teeth and growled.

All three faltered, Arawn and Draco pushing into my touch, Balor's domineering hold on my hair going slack.

Black flames snapped in their eyes, hot and hungry and ancient.

These three creatures—so strong. So masculine and otherworldly, but even if Arawn was the only one literally on his knees, Balor and Draco surrendered the second I finally responded to them. They softened, molding to me, fitted to my curves and mounds and dips like we were one big puzzle, all the pieces finally settling into place...

Like we were made for each other.

Like... they had been telling the truth from the start.

Erebus and Nyx, lovers old as time and deeply entwined—

Three knuckle raps at the main door jolted me out of the moment. My mouth watered, the scent of crispy bacon and fried cheese wafting around the doorframe. Food. *More* food. More explosions of flavor and taste and excitement—

I twisted and shuffled and shimmied around the trio, suddenly *ravenous*. They were good, those three. Great, actually. Possibly even *made* to sing to the darkness deep in my soul, to show me why I had suffered for so long and give all those years a *purpose*...

But *food*.

I'd gone twenty-five years hating just about everything I ever shoved past my lips.

Until today.

And I just—

Tying off my bathrobe again, I yanked the door open, the *whoosh* rustling my hair. Two hotel attendants in grey uniforms stood on the other side—men, probably around my age, conventionally attractive blonds with big white smiles. A week ago, I would have blushed so hard it hurt. This morning, I absently groped around behind me, desperate for the three shadows that set my body on fire, pretty-boy looks falling flat.

Arawn met me in a flash, sidling close behind and nudging something firm and long and thick into my backside.

Not now. Even the darkness in me agreed.

Taste buds already frothing, rabid and starved, I went for the bacon on the cart, barely clocking the lone rose in its crystal vase, the elegant silverware, the domed plates and breadbaskets and steaming coffee—

No, I shoved three pieces of crispy *perfection* in my mouth and moaned.

"Keep it coming, boys," Arawn remarked as his arm snaked around my waist. He then hauled me back inside and dragged the cart after, cutlery clinking and crystal rattling. "She woke up *famished*. You know how it is." A shiver cut down my back, falling like a missile and exploding on impact. As if sensing my body's response to him, this black-haired god, a shadow who possessed more elegance in his pinky than everyone in this entire skyscraper —he jerked me against him, my back to his hard chest, his grip, his touch, his lips brushing my ear with every word all screaming *mine*. "Repeat every order until we tell you to stop..."

Cheeks pink, body an inferno, I ignored their gawking and went for the four remaining bacon slices on the plate, each bite worthy of another orgasmic moan as Balor flung the door shut. Draco removed two dome lids and tossed them aside, the clatter of chrome on hardwood barely registering, the air soaked in flavor, a smorgasbord of scents unleashed, and all three shared triumphant grins when I grabbed the spinach and feta omelet with both hands and chowed down.

Not even a little self-conscious of my actions.

Of how I looked wearing nothing but a hotel robe, my hair mussed and my skin covered in goose bumps and cool saliva and faded bite marks and, oh, that hickey on my thigh actually smarted a little—

For the first time in as long as I could remember, I just existed. No thoughts. No fears. No pain. No nausea. No restrictions. I relished every moment, indulged every sense.

And had never felt more fucking alive.

CHAPTER TWELVE

"This feels... questionable."

"A moral grey area, that's all." Arawn glanced back at me as I hugged my would-be purchases to my chest, his grin pleasant as a spring morning and his eyes glittering with mischief. As soon as the woman at the cash register sashayed away with a few tiny bags in tow, the boutique's luxury brand scrawled across their glossy sides in cursive, he drifted forward and I followed after, trapped in his thrall—even if it didn't technically work on me. He then quirked one black brow, his grin sharpening. "*Balance*, remember."

I rolled my eyes and awkwardly dumped my armful of clothes on the counter, the woman behind it eyeing Arawn with the same uncertainty as the other shop assistants had throughout our visit. However, before she could get a word out, this tatter of some old god's cloak popped on his charming cap, leaned casually on the matte countertop, and gently tapped the top of her hand with one finger. The second he made contact, *poof*, the wariness disappeared, and this blond in black designer duds melted. Her dress might have been all fitted and severe, but she turned ooey-gooey in a heartbeat, her smile dopey and her lashes fluttering as she scanned my selections and removed the security tags, always in physical contact with Arawn.

And I just watched the numbers soar on the display screen, one item after the other, my palms sweaty and my incredulity climbing.

After this morning's room service feast, cooped up and antsy, I couldn't sit in the penthouse for another day. As if sensing my stir-crazy, Balor floated the idea that we explore downtown Dunston—get a feel for the place that had been our week-long hideout. So, dressed in the dry-cleaned outfit I'd been wearing when Cronus went to hell, plus one of Arawn's suit jackets with the sleeves rolled way up, I headed out alongside my three stylish captors.

The air had never smelled so good.

The sky had never looked so clear.

The world had never felt so *open*.

No walls closing in despite the cluttered skyscrapers and tight streets. While I still didn't have an exact location, Dunston was like the set of a teen drama at the start of a new year, what with the imposing architecture and the chaotic sidewalks, the chilly weather and the fall-kissed trees.

And best of all, no one gave two shits about us.

I mean, *yes*, we got a bit of attention, but I suspected it had more to do with the trio of breathtaking men than anything. Balor got the most sidelong glances from the ladies, looking like some Greek god, buff and tanned and tall, but Arawn and Draco were no strangers to the random appreciative glances.

Or maybe I was projecting. Maybe, like the boutique sales assistants, Dustonites were just trying to get a read on them—figure out what they were and why they radiated *power*.

Beyond that, no one stared at me. Top marks, Dunston. Sure, it got hellishly busy around the lunch hour, car and foot traffic swelling, the energy surge chaotic and busy and beautiful. But no one openly gawked. At the base, someone was always watching. Curious eyes. Judgy eyes. Unimpressed eyes. I'd experienced the full Fort Beacham gossip spectrum growing up, and anytime I found the courage to glare back, the starer would turn and pretend it had never happened.

Twenty-five years of gaslighting, of people pretending they *weren't* scrutinizing me.

Here, I was invisible.

Just another face in the crowd.

A face with only one outfit who realized her wardrobe for this absurd kidnapping was woefully lacking as soon as we hit Dunston Square. A village within the city, southwest of the more hectic core, the literal square neighborhood was stacked with restaurants and shops, clothing boutiques like this one and clubs gearing up for the Friday night crowds. With a gorgeous park at the heart of the borough, I could have stayed out there for hours on a bench just taking in all the *life* going on around me.

But sitting and watching and distancing myself from the real world *again*—that seemed kind of sad.

So, when Arawn swept me into this boutique three hours ago, I let him. No more living vicariously through a screen: time to just live.

Balor and Draco might have skipped my shopping montage, but Arawn milked every second of it. He followed me around the store with two shop assistants in tow, making suggestions and praising my picks, then settled on the white leather couch in the fancy changing rooms, waiting on the other side of the curtain for me to model clothes that felt softer, richer, and more delicate than anything I'd ever owned. Three hours of *that* and he didn't complain once. No tracking the clock. No impatient huffs. No bored or annoyed expressions: he genuinely seemed to enjoy himself.

Just as I genuinely enjoyed the way he shot up to smooth fabrics and straighten jackets and tug down pantlegs, meticulous and thoughtful, firm and assertive so that every garment hung just right.

In the end, we filled two medium-sized glossy black bags.

That was it.

And it cost a fortune. Like, a month's rent for a swanky apartment in the city, I bet.

But it was all free. One touch from Arawn, a charming little suggestion whispered in her ear, and the clerk gave us a one-hundred-percent discount. She stayed in a lovey-dovey daze, openly smitten with him, even after he disconnected and grabbed a bag in each hand, and I trailed after him with a frown.

"She's going to get in trouble for that," I muttered as I passed through the boutique doorway, Arawn holding the plexiglass open with the tip of his leather shoe. His shrug and breezy smile spoke volumes. It wasn't that he and his fellow cloak tatters openly despised humans, but they didn't go out of their way to make the world a better place either. They observed mankind with a neutral indifference. The charm, the schmooze, the smile that cut you off at the knees —a predatory advantage that he alone specialized in.

Not good. Not evil.

Grey.

These three were dark grey—until it came to me.

Which was... flattering, I guess?

With the sun inching toward the horizon again, warm amber bathed Dunston Square and all its pedestrians headed for happy hour. Shops lined this stretch of sidewalk, while restaurants dominated another, salons and nail bars directly opposite us, then pubs and nightclubs to my left. Two-lane streets boxed in the park, the mishmash of trees and flower beds only slightly dampening the chaotic city vibe. It offered a buffer, this big green square in the center, with a huge children's playground and a tennis court, then what seemed like a greenhouse newly decked out as a haunted house for the spooky season.

Stone walls roughly four feet high kept the two worlds separate, the green and the concrete, the floral and the chrome...

And I never wanted to leave.

Sauntering along behind Arawn, the moral ambiguity of our shopping escapade on the back burner for now, I craved the hum in the air, the electric undercurrent buzzing away. It made my heart beat faster and my smile spread wider—

Until I plowed face-first into Arawn's stiff back. My crash came with a humiliating grunt, and I stumbled back, rubbing my nose and frowning up at him. Arawn, meanwhile, stared across the street, head cocked to the left, then the right, just an elegant black Dutch shepherd trying to make sense of something.

"Arawn—"

"What d'you think he's doing?"

Still massaging the ache out of my nose, I followed the casual toss of his chin toward the park's main entrance—and spotted Draco standing in the center of it, people milling around him like he was invisible. Dressed in the familiar black turtleneck, slacks, and trench coat combo, nothing about him seemed off...

Until I clued in to the really intense staring contest he was having with a kid.

Arms crossed, I sidled up next to Arawn to better assess the situation as it unfolded, Draco staring, arms limp, that usually vacant expression bordering on confusion. The pint-sized human in his line of fire had to be nine, maybe ten, and stood directly in front of him, right in his personal space, with strawberry blond hair, jeans, and a sage-green jacket that looked two sizes too big.

"Uh." My eyebrows shot up when the kid offered Draco an open bag of chips. "You know him better than I do, but if I had to guess..."

Draco peered stiffly into the bag. His black gaze then darted down to the boy, back to the chips, boy, chips—and then he fished out a single yellow crisp. Oh, a curled one—apparently those were good luck. He held it aloft, expressionless, locked in his awkward staring match again, then slowly put it in his mouth.

His white lashes flapped like frantic butterfly wings until he finally chomped down.

Then, a sight I never thought I'd see: Draco smiled.

Barely.

Sort of.

One side of his mouth quirked in a halfhearted smirk, anyway, which made him look like he'd just had dental work done, the rest of his face still frozen in place.

A snort slipped out before I could stop it, and I clapped a hand over my mouth when Draco's gaze vaulted our way and the kid toddled into the park, their interaction officially over.

"Goodness, what a performance," Arawn rumbled,

steering me around and leading me to the nearby crosswalk. Once across, he pressed a firm hand to my lower back and nudged me in Draco's direction. "Make sure he doesn't frighten the villagers. I'll be right back."

I twisted around—but he was already headed down the sidewalk with my shopping bags, one swinging in each hand. Arms crossed, I watched him go for a moment, then followed a few steps after, curious, but quickly stilled when Draco's attention burned a hole in the back of my skull. For all his neutrality, the guy's stare really carried a wallop. So, sighing, I drifted his way, taking in the trees and the kids crawling all over the jungle gym, the gentle hills and dips inside the park.

"Did you acquire all the clothing you need?" Draco asked as soon as I was within earshot, and I refocused on him, on his ghostly pallor and sunken cheeks, the most physically out of place amongst my captors. My shrug wasn't answer enough, apparently, his eyes narrowing at my empty hands.

"Yes and no?"

"Explain."

His blunt approach to conversation actually worked for me. Over the years, the monsters at Cronus HQ had taught me that the supernatural *loved* tricks. They spoke in riddles. They talked down to humans. They hissed in ancient languages and sneered when you reminded them the interview was English-only, though we had translators on staff for *modern* dialects. They played games with words.

Draco did none of those things.

Neither did Arawn and Balor, mind you, but their tones had more nuance, leaving room for interpretation.

"I got a few really good pieces," I clarified. Three tops, two pairs of pants, a dress, a skirt, a bra, and a fresh packet of high-waisted underwear. "Kind of makes a wardrobe, I guess?"

He hummed softly, the slight head-bob acknowledgment enough.

"So," I started, changing gears in a flash—because I so didn't want to talk about clothes anymore, "what was that *almost* smile we saw with the kid? I had no idea your face possessed such range."

After a few blinks, like there was a lag in the snark processing department, Draco cleared his throat and zeroed in on the playground.

"Human children are less likely to cry if you appear friendly."

"Ah." I pursed my lips, nodding. "Do they usually cry when they look at you?"

"Sometimes."

Made sense, I guess. Not only did he give off a creepy horror vibe from a certain angle, but he said it himself: he was the emptiness of the deepest depths.

Not exactly warm and fuzzy.

"How was the chip?" That earned me a slight frown, his white brows barely furrowed, and I closed the distance between us with a grin. "The thing you put in your mouth..." Then, just to test the waters, I wiped his lips with my thumb. "You know, the thing that left the salt and grease here... It was a chip."

Draco stiffened, nostrils flared, eyes wide and alarmed, but he let me brush the evidence off without a fight. Then, just as I pulled back, his pale pink tongue swept over his lower lip, and he rubbed at both with his fingers, studying their tips for a moment—then mine.

"Too salty for my taste," he mumbled, cheeks speckled with color. My breath hitched when he reached for me—

maybe my hand, my wrist, my sleeve. No clue, but curiosity bolted me in place to find out—

A dogwalker ruined the moment before it could take off, lumbering way too close with a pack of sniffing, pulling, barking charges who had zero chill about the park. Black eyes narrowed and too-white teeth bared in a snarl, Draco leapt into action, hastily tucking me under his arm and marching me to a nearby bench. Without asking, he spun me around and urged me into it with an insistent press on my shoulders. Fighting back a grin so he didn't think I was laughing at him, I did as I was told.

Because...

He...

He had just... looked out for me.

Put himself between me and the dogs, then sat me somewhere safe and out of harm's way.

Strong protective instincts. Was that a shadow thing, something passed from Erebus to them, or was I a trigger for hypervigilance?

Either way—not a bad quality in a man, so long as they didn't take it too far. None of those dogs cared about me; they just wanted their off-leash time in the fenced dog run. Draco, however, stood right up against my knees, stiff and towering as he scanned the park for threats.

Kind of endearing.

Kind of intense and a little too much.

"Are you happy?"

I squinted up at him, the sun still a way's out from sinking behind the tallest building in the square. "What?"

"To be off the Cronus base," he said flatly. "It must be nice... breathing free air."

My gaze dropped to my hands, to the black diamond-hard nails that looked more like talons outside of the penthouse. The self-conscious Selene who had always struggled to find a place amongst her peers—she wanted to tug Arawn's jacket sleeves down and hide them. The darkness in my heart, the monster in my chest whose chains had loosened this past week—she wanted to rip his jacket off, toss it aside, and show off *everything*. The nails. The hard, feather-tipped hairs nudging out of my skin.

But wearing the same outfit now as the night everything went to shit on base, the pinstriped dress shirt and the grey slacks, the loafers, I struggled to detach completely. As good as these three had treated me during my meds detox, all their sweet words and thoughtful gestures, twenty-five years didn't disappear overnight.

"I don't know how to feel," I admitted after some quiet contemplation. "This morning, the food, you three..." *Touching me.* Nibbling at my skin. Breathing me in and circling like sharks. *Shit.* I'd never felt more desired over touches so innocent, all things considered. "It was... exciting. Physically, I'm different. Something's happening to my body, and I don't know what it is, but it feels good." For once in my life, this flesh prison was *happy*. "It feels strong. I'm not dizzy or nauseous. No headaches. No fatigue."

I thumbed at the black talon on my ring finger, the *click* of nail to nail louder now.

"Emotionally—" I hesitated, the cold, hard truth clogging my throat. "—I'm waiting for the crash."

"Well then," Arawn purred, sliding onto the bench out of nowhere. "Let's put that off a while longer, shall we?"

Shopping bags set neatly between our feet, he offered paradise in a cardboard box: street meat slathered in all the fixins. My mouth watered and my eyes rounded, belly roaring as I snatched the box and devoured everything first with sight and smell. A foot-long sausage on a slightly sad bun, doused in ketchup, mustard, relish, onions, and pickles, plus a mountain of crispy fried somethings on top. Salty. Meaty. Greasy. I moaned as I shoveled it into my mouth and took that first glorious bite.

I'd missed out.

The meds must have dulled my taste buds, or there was just something in the Dunston air—because food was so—fucking—*good*.

After another scandalous moan, I slumped into the bench with a happy sigh, savoring every morsel, every flavor, every texture. While Draco's concerned gaze flitted around, glowering at anyone who dared glance at his hot-dog-devouring freak show, Arawn grinned and stretched one long arm out along the back of the bench, content to watch me gorge.

And gorge I did, stuffing myself to the point of breathlessness, about three-quarters of the sausage gone in under a minute. At that point, I set the cardboard on my lap and threw my head back, bonking it on Arawn's arm, opening my airways to swallow that last bite and just *breathe*.

Breathe and think, all that blissful nothingness of this morning temporary.

"Not gonna lie," I started, tracking a stretch of grey fluff as it billowed across the sky, sunset purples and pinks and reds bleeding over the daytime baby blue. "I feel like you guys are... maybe buttering me up?"

"For what, pray tell?"

Draco's flat affect didn't exactly lend itself to open and honest communication. I shrugged and swiped a ketchup-mustard smear from the side of the street meat box.

"So I'll make shadow babies with you."

Neither said a word as I licked the combo off my finger, taste buds dancing at the mustardy tang and the ketchup's aroma. Draco went back to scanning the park, whereas Arawn shuffled a little closer, cloaking me deeper under his wing, but just as his lips parted with a soft breath, screams erupted behind us.

Heart in my throat, I whipped around, expecting the worst—and then spotted some teens racing out the back of what I'd guessed was a haunted house, suspicions now confirmed.

From this angle, I noted the rustic wood signage —*Dunston Hell Haus* in dripping fake blood—and the creepy masked faces behind the tinted windowpanes. Fabric ghosts dangled around the main entryway of what was probably a greenhouse or observatory during the rest of the year, all glass walls and gothic arches. Organizers had blacked out most of it, and a small line gathered by the front doors, mostly parents with elementary-aged kids, the real thrill seekers probably waiting until after sunset to pay for a few cheap scares.

More shrieks erupted from inside, and I leaned over for a better look, realization dawning as a pale-faced adult couple stumbled out clutching each other.

"I take it Balor found a way to entertain himself while we were gone?"

"He was hungry," Draco mused. "Terror is easy to find this time of year—when the daylight dwindles."

Right. Balor ate... terror. Arawn consumed cozy relaxation.

Draco feasted on depression.

Weird.

Weird, weird, weird.

Clearing my throat, I went back to eating with a frown, my bites small and distracted.

"Selene," Arawn murmured, "please don't think of it as us buttering you up." He then hooked his arm around my shoulders and knuckled under my chin. Despite two sets of eyes burning into me, I focused on the sausage, which resulted in another affectionate tap and a silky, rumbly, *yummy* chuckle. "Little one, think of it as *flirting*."

I swallowed my recent bite, then huffed a laugh, cardboard back in my lap and expression incredulous. "Flirting. Sure. So then I'll make shadow babies because I'm a smitten kitten, right? That's the end goal—"

"Shall we chain you to the bed instead?"

Heat exploded across my face, Draco's bluntness sparking something dark and dangerous in me.

"Draco lacks the inflection for sarcasm." Arawn to the rescue, as always, pleasant and conversational as he angled into me and let his hand dangle over my shoulder. "What he means is... You are *invaluable* to us."

I rolled my eyes. "Because you think I'm a daughter of—"

"What would be achieved if we beat you into submission?" he posed, a sandpapery quality coating his usual velvet. "If we forced you? Brutalized you? Raped you?" Arawn paused, as if to give me time to consider what this kidnapping *could* have been, his black brows raised as he toyed with a few locks of my hair. "Hatred, Selene. Loathing. Bitterness and anger."

"I mean..." My voice cracked, and I cleared my throat again, the thought of that grim reality turning my blood cold. "Yeah."

More horror shrieked from the haunted house, and a giddy group of preteens in pleated plaid school uniforms pointed in its direction as they hurried by us, oblivious to the literal monster hiding inside.

"What a misery," Arawn muttered. "What a farce of a love story."

He then stole a sliced pickle from the end of my sausage and chomped down on it with a noisy *crunch*, letting out a pleased rumble that warmed me from the inside out.

"I guess it still feels like I need to take anything you do for me with a grain of salt," I told him as he went for another pickle. "If all you want at the end of the day is to—"

"Have we not been clear enough?" While he didn't sound annoyed, passion blazed in Draco's eyes as he squared off with me, still at my knees, still soaring high above. "Offspring are a perk, not the prize."

The fire forever in my cheeks around these three cut south, and I glanced at Arawn, whose nod seemed so genuine, so earnest, that it made me want to swoon onto the bench and groan.

Because as desperate as I was to dive headfirst into the fantasy that *I* was an actual romantic prospect for someones, wanted and desired and coveted just for being me, the struggle was so fucking real. A lifetime of questioning my interactions, of being watched and studied, poked and prodded, Dad experimenting with my doses and hiding me away in my bedroom when the side effects got ugly—none of this registered as *true* in my detoxed brain.

The loudest screams so far suddenly exploded from the haunted house, and I twisted around, heart pounding, as a large group of parents and their kids rushed from the back exit, a few dads carrying wailing toddlers...

And then Balor strutting out behind them, suave as sin in his slacks and white button-up, the leather jacket a dangerous touch and his aviators popped up on his head now that the sun had set. Beaming like the cat who'd caught and tortured the canary, he abandoned the scene of the crime, hands in his pockets, and radiated pure *power* with every stride.

By the time he made it to us, the line of little ones had thinned considerably by the front entrance, parents peeling away and the haunt workers manning the doors frantically talking into walkie-talkies.

"*So...*" Balor squatted in front of my shopping bags and rooted through the swishy tissue paper. "What did we get?"

"Clothes," I told him. He didn't strike me as the type to want details, whereas Arawn would have pressed for the fabric and fit of every piece.

"Excellent." And just as I thought, Balor eased back on his haunches with the demonic grin, just teeth and hellfire, then clapped his huge hands and rubbed them together. "Where next?"

All three glanced around, covering every base, before coming back to me.

"Uh..." I wilted somewhat into the bench, the pressure slicking my palms. "I don't know? I've never socialized off base before. I don't..." *I don't know what to do with myself in the real world. Or what to do with any of you.*

Super embarrassing to admit any of that, of course. At twenty-five, I should have had more life experience, because there was way more to it than work and school and home and the odd house party with people I'd known since kindergarten.

Nibbling my lower lip, I swiveled around for a quick study of all four fall-dusted side streets—then settled on the building that called to me the loudest. With a nod, I pointed to the big black brick box with cursive red neon, lights flickering to life in the hazy twilight.

Ritual Nightclub

That name felt weirdly appropriate.

"I think I want to test a theory." Crossing one leg over the other, I noted the tinted windows, the bouncers in black setting up the red velvet ropes and rolling out a carpet along the front of the building under the neon sign, the long, steep steps leading up to brassy double doors. "I've always been able to drink and drink and drink... It's just never really hit me before. But maybe now I can... feel it, like everyone else—"

"Don't strive to be like *them*, blackbird," Balor said with a dismissive sniff. He then eyed the passing Dunstonites with a sneer. "The wolf has no desire to grow wool and live among the sheep."

Yeesh. I rolled my eyes. Had he forgotten I considered myself one of those sheep until a week ago?

Now? Not so sure.

"Yeah, well, getting drunk has always looked like fun." I swooped my hair behind both ears, street meat forgotten, eyes glued to the nightclub slowly unfurling like a nightshade in the moonlight. "I-I want to... have fun. I never have fun—not really."

No one said anything to that. Quiet blanketed our dark and moody quartet while the rest of the square came to life, the line at the haunted house about to fill out again as more teens in school uniforms headed in its direction.

Shit.

Had I made it awkward?

Wincing, I looked from one cloak tatter to the other, Draco, Arawn, Balor, but they seemed locked in a silent conversation far above my pay grade. Eyes so black they lost the pupils, bigger than usual, the pigment dominating the white, they stared at nothing, some random air pocket in the middle of their three eyelines, then broke apart, normal again.

Relatively speaking, anyway.

"Excellent," Balor drawled, sporting a great white's grin as he grabbed the last of my bun and sausage and held it to my mouth. "I love fun."

Something told me our definition of fun drastically varied, and while I was less than thrilled about him force-feeding me in public, as soon as the meat touched my lips, I was gone, demolishing the remainder and lightly grasping at his forearm. He held his fingers there as I swallowed the last of it down, like he wanted to see if I'd lick them clean.

Tempting.

The dark, deadly thing inside perked up like he'd issued a challenge she couldn't refuse. I, on the other hand, registered that we were like twenty feet from a kids' playground. So, I pulled away and wiped my lips clean on the back of my hand.

A hand Balor grabbed seconds later, pure steel circling my wrist and hauling me off the bench.

"Come on, blackbird," he urged, all singsongy and jazzed, practically prancing as he led me out the park's entrance, his back to the nightclub and his eyes alight with some of Arawn's good-natured mischief. "Let's have *fun*."

That devilish smile—*My, what big teeth you have, Grandmother*—was so fucking infectious, as was his silly little hop-skip thing. It made my heart happy, the world and all its problems lifting off my shoulders around Balor, so much so that I put some pep in my step, giggling instead of panicking when I lightly rolled my ankle tripping over a sidewalk crack.

Because a stumble here and there wasn't a disaster anymore.

Not in this body.

No, I just brushed it off and kept moving, Balor's thrall irresistible.

Meanwhile, behind us, Arawn and Draco followed with far less enthusiasm, the former carrying my shopping bags again and the latter eyeing Ritual Nightclub like it was his worst nightmare come to life.

CHAPTER THIRTEEN

"Are you feeling it?"

Balor's seductive bass licked up my bare arms, triggering a wave of goose bumps and a delicious shiver. I finally broke eye contact with the tequila sunrise on the table in front of me and looked up, the first-floor lounge of Ritual Nightclub glossy and twinkly and just a little different now.

And why shouldn't it be?

Three hours of sampling every cocktail on the menu would do that to a girl, right?

As soon as we checked our coats and my shopping bags, we claimed a less-than-comfortable black booth near one of the smaller bars and hunkered down. Arawn took care of the ongoing tab. Balor demanded a menu and handled the orders. Draco huddled in the corner, pressed against the wall and hating every second of it but game enough to try a spicy wing or deep-fried pickle or whiskey shot when I prompted him.

In those three hours, we'd conquered the whole menu, drinks *and* food, our waitress flitting by the booth every few minutes, probably expecting a stellar tip—unaware that the stunning creature in the black suit beside me would charm it all away once my new bottomless appetite finally called it quits.

Because, I mean, this had all been for me. Sure, the guys tried a few drinks here and there. Arawn and Balor were way more open to taste-testing fruity mixes with me, Balor still rocking the little blue and pink cocktail umbrella I'd tucked behind his ear about six drinks ago, all giggly and flirty and showering him with compliments. They poked at the bar food but always seemed more interested in my moans than the odd saucy wing or loaded nacho chip. They bobbed along to the music, muted enough for conversation but loud enough to muffle other clubgoers.

For the most part, however, this was very clearly for me.

Hesitant at first, I gingerly set my inhibitions aside, the monster in my chest locking them up for good after that third tequila shot. By now, I felt tipsier than ever before—but not drunk. Not *drunk*-drunk like it was on TV or how my high school friends always acted, falling all over themselves and slurring their words. Sure, the lounge suddenly had a soft, fuzzy glow to it. I couldn't stop smiling and chatting, eating and drinking. Buoyant. Light. Giddy—so much so that I shivered all over in the middle of especially heated discussions about... well, shit, about *anything*.

"I think so." Sitting back against the rigid booth, the faux leather barely padding the wood base, I nudged my latest cocktail aside and sniffed. "Wait, wait, lemme stand up..."

That was the real test, right? The one that confirmed just how tanked you really were?

Arawn shuffled out of the booth, just a simple table with high-backed benches on either side, a spot that felt too small, too claustrophobic, for Balor and Arawn but *just* right for me and Draco. As soon as he was out, I scooted after him, then staggered to my feet, waiting for the hurricane to hit.

Nothing.

Maybe a little shakier than I was a few hours ago, but unlike many of the stylish Dunston women I'd seen breeze by, I also wasn't sporting a pair of heels. Nope, just these work loafers. Zero regrets.

"I feel *good*," I trilled, throwing my arms up and spinning in place. Warmth pricked my cheeks when I lilted into Arawn's chest, but I found balance all by myself, thank you very much, quite capable of standing on my own two feet. Suddenly breathless, I swooped my curls behind my ears and grinned at the cloak tatters who had given me my first *real* adult bar night. "Really good."

Each stared back with his own brand of intensity, *hunger* chipping away at the protective caregiver personas they'd adopted for the last week. Maybe that was why it felt like someone was holding a lit match to my face: the way they branded me with their eyes, gazes lazily perusing my figure, devouring me on the spot and spitting me back out a much darker, hornier woman.

Or maybe that was the booze.

And maybe the brazen leering was because of this dress.

After skimming the dress code requirements posted just inside the main doors once the bouncers waved us through, I'd zipped into the bathroom to swap my boring business casual for a little black dress. Spaghetti-strap sleeves with a blunt, horizontal neckline that showed off just the crest of my cleavage, built-in bra a lifesaver, the stiff fabric clinging to my curves all the way down to my knees. Classy and sexy, black as a starless midnight in the dead of winter, it called to me.

I had almost put it back, almost refused to come out of the dressing room at the boutique, because, ugh, it was a little too rich for my blood.

But Arawn insisted I looked *divine*.

And some of his effortless charm had shattered in that moment, violent predator exposed, his elegant hands in tight fists and his angular jaw rippling through a clench.

So, I added it to the pile.

Here it was now, drawing three dangerous gazes my way.

For the first time in my life, I felt like a fucking bombshell.

Curves out. Showy but not too slinky. Designed for support and comfort, not once did I feel like a stuffed sausage despite shoveling down bar food and cocktails.

The loafers kind of ruined the look—shoe store tomorrow. Yeah. Plan.

Vibrations rumbled underfoot, followed by the muted cheer of goodness only knew how many clubgoers below. The club portion of Ritual had opened about a half hour ago, and since then, most new arrivals headed straight for the various stairwells leading down. The lounge population ebbed and flowed, but it was clear that the *real* party was down there.

Lower lip snagged between my teeth, I cocked my head and rode the beat once again, the deep bass pounding rhythmically before tapering off, then looked to the guys. Draco shrank further into his corner of the booth, but a few pleading eyelash flutters had Arawn flagging down our server and Balor drumming his hands on the tabletop.

"Let's roll out, boys," he barked. He then slapped at

Draco's sunken chest before *barely* squishing out of the booth, the table edge jutted into his torso, and I made space so he could wrestle that huge body through.

Bill sorted a few moments later and Draco begrudgingly bringing up the rear, I led my misfit gaggle of godly cloak fragments toward the nearest stairwell. We passed the women's bathroom I'd used recently, suddenly way busier than when I'd changed into my dress earlier. A line of bored, texting women stretched along the wall outside it now, but back then, Draco had stood in their place, *right* at the door and waiting for me to do my thing. When I'd toddled out, there was the club's indoor security urging him to back off—and Draco staring into the depths of his soul, unfazed, not moving until I sauntered by.

He had followed me back to the booth then, so up my butt we collided when I paused to fix my stupid shoe, but a quick glance back revealed a broken man. Forearm braced on the wall, the bouncer who had confronted Draco held himself up—barely—and shook, head dipped into his jacket lapels and fellow security hurrying over to check on him.

All from a *look*.

Draco wore the same look now, expression blank, gaze aloof and distant, but as I caught my slightly wobbly self on the doorframe, I noted he wasn't making eye contact with anyone. Maybe that was how it worked for him. With Arawn, it was a touch. Balor—his presence. Draco? The haunting nothingness that cut deep down, straight to the soul.

Anyway.

Not now.

Squaring my shoulders, I trudged down the staircase— the dark, sketchy, narrow staircase with steep steps and stone walls, twirling down, down, down underground.

"This seems a bit silly," Arawn remarked pleasantly. With Balor at my back, one huge hand hovering in case my loafers betrayed me, Arawn floated along behind him, hands in his pockets and silky waves fluttering with every step. "I can smell the blood."

I stumbled, catching myself on the rough stone wall just as Balor snagged my shoulder.

"Uh, *what?*"

We all squished aside as a trio of women hurried by in a symphony of clicking heels and a cloud of whiskey so strong it made me cough.

"Likely from the humans who've fallen on their face on these *ridiculous* steps," Arawn mused. He watched the women go, nodding, almost to himself, when he squinted at their shoes. "Not to worry, little one." He then grinned, black eyes warm and soft as I tentatively started down the stairs again. "Nothing sinister."

Uh-huh.

Right.

Shake it off. They all say the weirdest shit sometimes— this isn't new.

Frowning, I rushed the rest of the way down, eager to get out of the medieval spiral that apparently smelled like blood. Gross.

We emptied onto a balcony that lined the four walls of a mammoth underground warehouse. Whereas upstairs was all black tile and wood, faux leather and seduction, this was pure metal. Iron and steel dominated the grated flooring, the towering walls, the hollow ceilings. All black as far as the eye could see—except for the laser light show sweeping the dance floor below, splashing everything with red and white. Clubgoers milled around us up here, chatting, swaying, smiling, drinking—

"Oh, *shit*, okay."

Face hot, I bolted away from the couple seconds from having full-on sex against the wall next to the staircase doorway.

A few small bars peppered this upper level, but down the fleet of metal steps positioned around the balcony—there was the club's heart. Tiptoeing to the thin black railing, I peered over into a sea of writhing, jumping bodies, a good hundred or so down there in front of an insane DJ setup on the stage. A beanpole in a huge duck mask controlled the party, pumping his fist to the beat, the bass deep and rhythmic and eardrum-shattering. Infatuated with the sheer *energy* in the air, I wrapped my hands around the railing and sank into the moment, into the thick, rich aura so intoxicating it made my head spin.

To my right, Arawn studied the crowd with a cool disinterest, mouth quirked in one of his usual charming smiles that, for once, didn't reach his eyes. Balor popped up seconds later on my left, huge and impressive, bobbing along to the music. Draco, meanwhile, settled on the other side of Arawn, the usual emotional depth of his gaze gone—like he had retreated to his happy place and was waiting for it to be over.

I closed my eyes.

Breathed in the cacophony of scents: liquor and perfume and metal and BO and mint from someone's open-mouth gum-chomping as they drifted by behind us. For once, none of it made me want to hurl. Not even a little.

I timed the vibrations in my palms, the beat humming through the railing, the roar of the crowd and the pounding of hundreds of feet with every jump like a war drum.

Whump, whump, whump.

Followed by very *real* drums—

My eyes snapped open to Balor slamming one hand against the railing in time with the music, his whole body involved now, his eyes pure black, his irises huge, his smile positively feral.

And in a heartbeat, it all landed on me.

Our eyes met. His smile sharpened.

"Wait—"

He lunged before I could get the rest out, snatching me up in his strong arms and hauling me away from the railing toward the nearest staircase. Chuckling wickedly in my ear, he thundered down, plowing by—or through—anyone who stood in his way. Balor stood out above the music, his footsteps clanging like the *crack* of a continental split, and he didn't let go, didn't even loosen up, until he put a few long strides between us and the stairs. Nothing about him was gentle: not in the way he carried me, and definitely not how he set me down, practically tossing me and shoving me toward the crowd.

Barely anyone loitered under the upper balcony, the space empty and cool except for a few whispering pairs and the odd loner on his or her phone. Across the way, a neon toilet blazed over the entrance to a shadowy hallway. Huh. *Good to know.*

"Blackbird..."

His voice licked up the nape of my neck, around my throat, and under my chin, buzzing in my lips as his deep, guttural laughter tickled my ears. I swatted at the sensation, my movements big and clumsy and tipsy.

Turning on the balls of his feet, Balor moonwalked toward the crowd, which suddenly seemed way more imposing down here than it had up there. He beckoned me to follow with a demanding wave of his big hand, but I held my ground, fighting back a grin as I shook my head and crossed my arms.

"Why not?"

His lips hadn't moved, but his dark whisper rumbled in my ear.

"I-I..." *Shit, this is so stupid.* "I don't know how to dance to... this."

Nostalgic high school tunes? Sure. It was all for sillies back then, just teenagers fumbling around and trying to figure out what *sexy* really meant. Here? This wasn't my scene. Not my people, my crowd. Not my music, the poppy undertones sliced with heart-pounding bass and electronic fades.

Balor cocked his head, then pointed at his chest and scoffed.

He said nothing this time, not out loud and not in my head, but I *felt* the sentiment way over here.

Woman, do you think I know how to dance to this?

Right.

If they were to be believed, Arawn, Draco, and Balor had spent a few centuries anywhere *but* Earth. To their credit, they all did a stellar job reassimilating, and Balor proved it yet again when he faced the crowd. For a few moments, he stood still as stone, watching, calculating— then an explosion of movement. Jumping, pumping his arms, perfectly synced to the music and the crowd's heartbeat. Bouncing in place, he swiveled around to me and arched a black eyebrow.

I mean, if *he* could do it, I really had no excuse...

When he beckoned me forward this time, I came, an unconscious sway in my hips as his hungry gaze dipped lower. As soon as I was within reach, he snatched my forearm and ripped me the final few steps into madness, surging into a crowd that parted for him like the Red Sea. It didn't seem intentional on their part, more like the clubgoers sensed *him*, a tingle of fear on the back of their necks. Discomfort and panic flashed over faces at random as we passed, but Balor moved at such a steady clip that I didn't have time to take it all in.

He dragged me into the eye of the storm, not stopping until we reached the chaotic epicenter. If I'd come to a club like this for the first time without him or the others, just me and some Cronus work friends, I wouldn't *dream* of diving this deep. The crush felt so real here, the heat of their bodies, the constant movement in the corner of my eye beyond overwhelming. I almost kicked him in the shin—just to startle him enough that he'd loosen up so I could bail.

But he released me first, unprompted, his fingers peeling away slowly, seductively, and when Balor eased around, we were in the true core, the center of the center, a force field around us that no one else seemed to notice or intrude on. Clubbers kept dancing, jumping and writhing and throwing arms around each other. Friendly. Romantic. Drunk. Stable. It was like we weren't there—yet we hoarded prime real estate in direct eyeline of the DJ, a small circle around us so I could *breathe*.

And Balor could *move*.

So big. So powerful.

This intimidating creature who stalked haunted houses and made grown men weep—suddenly jumping to a ditzy techno beat, his arms up, his smile all teeth and madness.

Was he feeding?

Chaos was just another flavor of terror, right? Both were a loss of control...

But he only had eyes for me, tracking my hips as they

swayed tentatively at first, then my knees with the first bend.

And suddenly, *I* was jumping right along with him, embracing the music, the atmosphere, surrendering to his dark thrall, our grins identical, my pulse pounding—my heart so fucking happy. Head empty. Mind off, instinct on.

The music, the mood, the crowd—*Balor*. Over the next three songs, we drifted closer, our protective private bubble solid and my inhibitions weak. Our jumping and bouncing to the beat softened, bodies aligned, swaying, rocking, more attuned to *our* rhythm than the music.

Only a few inches apart, I locked onto his eyes—and the darkness in me stirred.

No, it didn't just *stir*.

It roared.

For Balor, this *thing* I had shoved down all my life, this animal who wanted to do and fight and sing and soar and *run*—she came alive. Her heat spiked my veins. She breathed *life* into me, and before I knew it, both my hands were on him, one to his broad chest, the other at his stubble. I caressed the rough hairs hesitantly at first, then surrendered to my thoughts when we first met, that gut instinct—

I rubbed my whole hand *hard* across his skin, embracing the pain, mapping the rugged planes of his cheeks and the sturdy line of his jaw.

Balor slowed to indulge me, his eye twitch a hint of his wavering resolve, his control precarious and his teeth bared like a *monster*.

Huge hands gritted into my waist, then down to my hips, curving to cup my ass and jerk me into him. A sharp breath shot past my lips—and I explored his cheek with my new black nails, as if to return the favor. Pain for pain.

He lifted me with a snarl, hoisting me high above the crowd and sitting me on his shoulder like I weighed nothing. Then, in a move that would have sent me slinking into the shadows a week ago, Balor paraded me around our invisible bubble—showing me off, bobbing to the beat while I threw my hands up at the DJ's phenomenal *drop*, the crowd roaring, so many hands in the air, the night electric with screams and whoops and muddled lyrics.

Way across the space, Arawn and Draco stood watching from the balcony, Arawn leaning on the railing, Draco ramrod straight by his side.

Despite the distance, I felt them, their eyes roving my body, their dark intentions *booming* louder than anything else.

Flushed, heartbeat thumping between my ears, I slid off Balor's shoulder—slow and intentional in the way I eased down this mountain of a man, my ass grazing pecs and abs and thighs like steely tree trunks. Hands in my hair, I stumbled away, then whipped around and dared him to *hunt* with just the quirk of my brow.

He obliged in spades, on me in a second, our bodies flush and our hips swaying. One huge hand splayed possessively across my lower back, the other slipped into his pocket; this was a mutual encounter, not some drunk dude at a club groping a girl. This cloak tatter, a shadow monster, he radiated effortless control and raw dominance. It wasn't an act or a display. Not a power move to scare off other men.

This was just Balor—conquering my body and making me think *I* called all the shots.

Maybe he needed a lesson, just a casual reminder...

Balor, tatter of Erebus, did *not* rule my world. Despite everything, *sometimes* the shots taken were one hundred percent *mine*.

Smirking, I seized his crisp white shirt collar and ripped him closer—and Balor fell like a meteor, his lips crashing to mine with the same intensity that wiped out the dinosaurs. The hand at my lower back gripped my hip, his arm crushing me to him, hoisting me off my feet for a kiss so wildly different from Arawn's tender passion that it made my head spin.

Where Arawn had been soft and gentle, deep and thorough, every sweep of his tongue tingling all the way down to my toes, Balor was pure violence and grit. He kissed hard and vicious, his brand of passion—or poison?—came with teeth and pressure and pain and a delicious, rough fucking of my mouth. My talons raked his jawline again, but his huge hand quickly tangled in my hair, his grip sharp and firm, possessive and declarative. He came at me so hard I arched backward over his arm, trapped and captured, a prisoner in his embrace even if I had been the one to start it.

And I never wanted it to stop.

Never—

Think of it as flirting.

My eyes snapped open, and I sucked in a harsh breath through my nostrils.

Shadow offspring might just be a perk for Draco, but he didn't speak for all of them.

And...

I...

You're a womb to be used.

Panicked, I slashed at his face and kneed his thigh, tactfully avoiding the iron shaft driving into my belly. Balor broke the kiss with a snarl, his forehead to mine, his eyes the black of Hell, Death on his pale horse charging me down. Trembling, I shoved again, keenly aware in that moment that the only reason I wiggled out of his hold and staggered into the crowd was because he *let* me.

Heart heavy, palms sweaty, mind a mess, and body on fire, I shoved my way through the crowd, eventually staggering out the other side a little worse for the wear.

"*Selene.*" Balor's heated whisper ripped up my spine, gunning for both ears and swarming the inside of my skull like a hive of furious bees. I whipped around just as he prowled from the depths, more than a full head taller than most and tracking me like *the* predator. Not just some random bloodthirsty creature, supernatural or otherwise, but the apex hunter. Top of the food chain. King of the jungle and the ocean and the land—

Headed straight for me like a missile.

"This... I-I... I can't," I stammered, backing up frantically, two or three of my steps no match for one of his. I motioned between us as soon as I passed under the metal balcony, the space empty, the shadows falling, the music deafening—but he seemed to hear me, despite the distance, despite the maelstrom of *sound*, and I barely spoke above a whisper. "You're *using* me. Because I-I'm Nyx's daughter, or whatever, you... I'm the only one who can give you shadows—"

Balor closed in on me in no time, dangerously fast for such a big man, aggressively graceful, his long, thick limbs fluid and beautiful and terrifying as he stalked me—and snapped a hand around my throat as soon as he was within reach. I squealed the moment he made contact, his fingertips bruising, then shoved uselessly at his burly chest as he yanked me against him, forced onto my toes as those black horrors bored deep into mine with none of Arawn's softness, none of his practiced patience and kindness.

"Why do you keep resisting this?" he demanded, more

monster than man, his words growly and rough. "Is it a test? You throw accusations out there—to catch us off guard? Hope we fail?"

He eased up on my windpipe when I smacked his forearm but didn't let go, marching us backward so subtly, so easily, that I hadn't realized we'd moved until my back hit the wall.

No, not just the wall.

A dark, empty corner, not a soul around to hear me gasp.

"I—"

"Are you waiting for someone to confirm it? Prove your suspicions?" His thumb swept roughly along my jaw, then up my chin to my lower lip, plucking it as he flashed his teeth and snarled. "Give you a reason to *hate* the monsters who pried open the bars of your cage and set you free?"

I blinked up at him, mouth gaping, mind whirring— struggling to *think* of something coherent and rational that would make this all make *sense*. Nothing. Just emptiness and longing, the monster in my chest a little too thrilled to be cuffed and conquered like this.

"Don't—"

"I understand, blackbird." His hand suddenly slid down to my chest, flat over my breastbone, fingertips ghosting my collarbone as Balor cocked his head and sighed. He moved closer, crowding me, trapping me in the corner, then brushed a few damp black curls from my forehead. "Hate is easier than love... Infinitely so."

Of course it was. I swallowed shakily and rubbed my throat, a twisted part of me hoping I'd find bruises in the shape of his hand tomorrow morning. *Love* was confronting. It exposed you. Flayed you alive. Peeled you apart, layer by layer, until there was nothing left—and the other person could inspect your bones, right down to the marrow, and still choose to walk away.

Hate *was* easier.

I tried not to dabble in it—because all the pain, the physical suffering, the visceral Otherness I'd endured with a shaky smile and a tepid laugh all my life...

It could have consumed me.

But I didn't hate them. I should have. Arawn, Draco, Balor. They stole me from my home, my family, and turned my life on its head.

"I-I just don't want to be *used*." My eyes watered, honesty turning my throat raw. It wasn't hate driving a wedge between us: it was fear. Fear that like Dad and all my doctors, I was just a *thing* to be studied and documented and molded to fit *their* hypothesis.

Balor brushed my tears away before they fell, then bared his canines with the next snarl, shadows rising off his skin, darkness swirling and thickening.

"We are not *them*," he hissed as he tipped my face up by my chin with a single knuckle. "Am I using you? Right now?" His free hand skimmed down my figure, first over the outer curves, the dip of my waist and the slight swell at my hips—but then he drifted inward, driving the base of his palm over the helm of my sex. Pleasure bloomed in my core, and Balor nudged my head back further, really forcing me to meet his eyes. "*Tell* me, blackbird. Say it."

"Balor—"

Darkness exploded all around us, first like the ragged wings of a demonic bat, ripping out his back and curving over like a dome. But then it solidified, thickened, blotted out the rest of the club in a wall of pure obsidian, just me and him on the other side. Sound trickled in, muffled as it might be, and my hammering heart beat just a little harder, a little faster, forcing short, sharp breaths from my lips.

"Tell me I'm fucking using you, Selene."

He kissed me again before I could get a word out. Not his name. Not *no* or *stop*. Just his mouth to mine, hungry and raging, powerful and masterful like he might just swallow me whole this time. Fear poked through the desire slick between my thighs, and I squirmed and squealed when he yanked my dress over my hips so it bunched at my waist. The fabric groaned, pliant to an extent, and a rush of electric air flooded my exposed thighs.

"*Wait...*" The word straddled the line between a sob and a gasp, and Balor flat-out ignored it, dragging his laughing mouth along my jaw and down my neck. Teeth grazed my collarbone, and my traitorous body arched into it, the fire of his touch so fucking *hot* after a lifetime in the cold.

"Tell me I'm using you," he demanded once more, only this time he fell to his knees as he said it, shoving my dress up higher—yanking my nude panties down my thighs, the cotton damp. "Here, now, *tell me...*"

My fingers twisted into his coarse black hair, so artfully sideswept, effortlessly hip and modern like he was some Italian aristocrat set to inherit the world. I meant to yank him back—put him in his place. He was on his knees, after all, at *my* feet.

But I just held him. Anchored myself as he shoved my legs apart and dove between them, brutal kisses slashed up my thighs, hoisting me onto my tiptoes the second he reached my center.

That first lick ignited my whole fucking galaxy.

My mouth tumbled open. My eyes clenched shut. Pleasure plumed low in my belly and turned my knees to jelly—but that didn't matter. All this week, Balor and his shadowy brothers had propped me up. Held my hand and steadied me every step of the way. Once again, Balor used himself for *my* benefit. He nestled deeper, manhandling me, arranging my legs over his shoulders as he licked my sex, stroked my clit with his firm tongue, and thrust deep inside.

I'd never...

Nothing more than some pathetic fingering in high school that just *hurt*—

Trapped in the darkness, shadows rising from him like heat waves off black pavement, I surrendered to the sheer *ecstasy* of whatever the hell he was doing down there. Because, *fuck*, never felt so *good*.

And his groans—his *groans* and growls and snarls, like a monster claiming his prey, relishing every last bite. His fingers bit into my ass, my hips, my thighs, Balor forever on the move, rough and enthusiastic while he played my body like a fiddle.

Serenaded by whumping bass and the distant roar of the crowd, I tentatively rocked my hips. Rolled them against his starving mouth. Twitched and twisted and turned, steering him where it felt *best*.

I might have been a virgin, but I'd had orgasms since I was thirteen.

Alone in my bedroom, grinding first into pillows, then using my fingers for an almost clinical experiment—learning fast that sometimes, on rare occasions, my body could be happy.

But I had never come like this before.

Throw in his ruthless thumb circling my clit while he tongue-fucked me, the tip stabbing that glorious spot along the inner walls again and again, the mechanics almost impossible—

I shattered in Balor's arms with a scream.

When it happened in romance novels or fanfic smut—the heroine shrieking through a climax—I usually just rolled my eyes and skimmed the rest. I mean, *I* had never screamed before—until now. Until the pleasure roasted me alive. Until my body went nuclear, every muscle and nerve aflame, the ecstasy tingling from my scalp to my toes, everything between caught in the riptide.

Never been a whole-body experience—

Never been more than the physical—

But this was a heart and brain orgasm too, *feelings* plucked raw and beautiful, mind blissfully empty.

Not numb.

Cozy and still.

No racing thoughts. No doubt—in them *or* me. Just instinct and *pleasure*.

I slumped into the corner the second Balor clawed out from between my thighs, sweaty and panting, a hand to my forehead and the darkness suddenly so beguiling I just couldn't look away.

Not until he soared up my body and nipped at my neck, marking me hard and insistent, the pain cutting through the hazy aftermath sharp enough to ground me in reality again.

"*Tell me.*" His harsh whisper echoed inside my head, that talented mouth still at my throat, still nibbling and sucking and claiming me. Balor then grabbed my left hand and dragged it down, forcing me to cup his very prominent —very *big*—erection. I'd seen him naked before. This *thing* wasn't new, but feeling it was something else entirely. "Tell me I'm using you, Selene. Say it, out loud." He yanked my hand away and pinned it to the wall, rising like an ancient beast from the deep, suddenly towering over me, pure power and darkness. "Say it, or I'll fucking do it *again*."

Was...

Was that a *threat*?

I inhaled sharply, coming back to a part of myself the monster hated, and then shouldered around him. Stumbling into the darkness, the shadows circling, caressing, I tugged my underwear up and my dress down, terrified of just how *intensely* I craved him back on his knees, mouth doing its dark work, hands possessing me, conquering me—

Arawn's eyes blazed in the shadows, invisible hands smoothing over my hips and up my back. Startled, I reeled and pivoted, groping around until suddenly I was in the nightclub again, the world carrying on like normal. No one stared. No one noticed me stumbling from a shadowy back corner, predators at my heels. Flushed and flustered, I beelined for the neon toilet above a dark hallway, then yelped when I just about plowed into Draco around the corner.

He said nothing.

Did nothing

But his *eyes*.

Oh, his eyes—their depth could drown the world.

Needing just a few minutes alone, preferably unsupervised behind a locked door, I scrambled around him, and his nostrils flared as he tracked me, rotating on the spot, locked on target and unbreakable.

Overwhelmed, seconds from losing it, I skipped the line and crashed through the women's bathroom door. Protests bounced right off me. Insults. *Bitch!*

Hazy, barely aware of what *I* was doing let alone what anyone else was saying, I darted into a stall the second it opened and nearly knocked the woman exiting on her ass. She swore at me too, her words so incoherent and the lights, no matter how artfully muted in the crowded space, so fucking bright I wanted to *scream*.

Suddenly peak overstimulated, I slammed the door in her face, then collapsed on the can, dress and all, and buried my face in my hands.

A soft exhale gusted the nape of my neck. Smoke trickled through the overhead vent in the ceiling.

I closed my eyes, plugged my ears, and focused on my breath.

On the in and the out. In and out. In and out.

Unable to ignore the fact that despite the inner turmoil, the chaos and the darkness in my wild heart, the creeping self-doubt and lingering uncertainty—all I really wanted in that moment... was *them*.

CHAPTER FOURTEEN

The bathroom never cleared out.

I kept waiting and waiting, ignoring the knocks on the stall door, needing just a few quiet minutes to process, you know, everything.

Everything everything.

From being assigned to Sub-level Z that fateful day to the abduction—because kidnapping usually implied a ransom request, and as it stood, my captors didn't seem like they planned on ever selling me back to Dad *or* Cronus—to Arawn's kiss in the tub and Draco's half-smile at the park and Balor doing that *thing* with his tongue...

My nails. My senses.

My confidence.

My place in the world outside of Fort Beacham.

My... mom. My history. My truth.

Seriously, my brain wasn't designed to tackle all this shit at once—and definitely not in a cramped bathroom stall at some random nightclub.

Eventually, circuits way too overloaded for critical thinking, I just stood up, flushed the toilet I hadn't used, and left. A woman shouldered by me and slammed the metal door, and I drifted to the sinks, on autopilot as I waited for one to open up and thrusting my hands under the faucet sensor as soon as it did. Lukewarm water with solid pressure pummeled my skin, my new nails, and I went through the motions of a deep clean, getting every finger, every inch, like I was due in a sterile containment cell any minute now.

An expressionless Selene stared back at me in the mirror, and I narrowed my translucent blues, expecting so much more. Fear. Anger. Grief. I ought to be planning an escape—*something*.

But fight or flight had died a week ago, my body too weak for either, and now that it was strong enough to actually do something, I just stood there and numbly washed my hands.

I'd grown paler in the last week, a feat old friends used to joke was impossible. Paler, but also somehow fuller? I tipped my head side to side, assessing the healthy glow in my cheeks, some of the sharper angles dulled. All the consistent meals Balor made me eat. All the rich, heavy, hearty foods that would have turned my stomach on the meds... Maybe. Maybe my body had always needed this, but the drugs made it impossible to choke much down.

My black lashes flickered when I refocused on my eyes.

What did Arawn, Draco, and Balor see when they peered into them?

Because I saw so much in theirs, layers and strata I'd never gleaned from anyone before, centuries of life and experience, depth and emotion untouched by time.

"Selene?"

A soft whisper jolted me out of the scrutiny spiral, and I flinched when the woman beside me locked onto my gaze in the mirror, our reflections meeting as she too spent way too long washing her hands.

"My name is Audrey," she murmured. Red hair cropped in a pixie cut. Black septum ring that looked a bit off, like it wasn't a real piercing. Slightly shorter than me, with a straight build and an olive complexion. Hazels that should have been warm but... weren't. Not when she lifted a knowing eyebrow in the mirror, and definitely not when she pulled her hands out of the sink, shook the water off, and then cracked open the little black clutch hanging off her shoulder, revealing an ID card. "I'm with Cronus."

I blinked down at the security badge, then up at her, surprised that this willowy woman in tight leather pants, low heels, a semi-sheer white tee, and a paint-splattered jean jacket had made it onto Cronus security. Such a boys' club at HQ—

I then frowned, suddenly more surprised that it wasn't relief sweeping through me... but disappointment. It flooded my veins and gave me a breath of fight or flight, feeling like vacation just ended and I hadn't made the most of it.

"I'm here to take you home," she insisted, snapping the clutch shut and wiping her hands dry on her jacket. I finally pulled mine away from the faucet sensor, then went for the closest paper towel dispenser, drying them just as aimlessly as I'd washed them.

"Uh, I—"

"It's okay." She grabbed my arm hard and steered me to a trash can, huffing when I didn't immediately ditch the paper towel clump. "I'm sure this has been nuts, but you're safe now—we just need to move *quick*."

I...

I didn't want to move *quick*.

I wanted my feet to grow roots and stay *right* here.

"H-how did you find me?" I managed as she hauled me through the bathroom crowd, charging headfirst like the littlest bull ever.

"Cronus has quite the reach," she insisted, her voice luxe and faintly accented like she'd been born an English rose but then grew up somewhere glamorous on the west coast. Audrey glanced back just as we reached the door, pausing for an influx of women in short, tight dresses, all of them smiling and laughing and chatting, oblivious to what went on in their world behind the curtain. "But I'm sure you already knew that."

Then, rather than plowing straight through the door when she had the chance, Audrey lifted my arm and scowled at my new nails, at the sharp points and the opaque black.

"Shit, do these hurt?" Before I could answer, she shook her head and wrinkled her nose. "Those fucking monsters... What did they do to you?"

An eerily familiar line of questioning to what I'd heard from three tatters of a god's cloak the first day we met—only theirs hadn't insulted me.

Because as far as I knew, the nails, the color and strength—that was all me. Not them. *Me.*

Audrey slipped out the door without another word, her hold on my arm bruising, and then took a hard left down the dark, noisy corridor. She kept pushing, dragging me away from the heart of Ritual, away from where I'd last seen my captors, not stopping until the clubgoers thinned nonexistent and we were face-to-face with a matte metal door, bland and knobless.

Like many, many, *many* doors at Cronus HQ.

Too many.

And its familiarity didn't trigger fond nostalgia, work

memories suddenly so bland and lifeless, dull and hollow compared to the new ones I'd made today alone.

After digging a sleek cell phone out of her pocket, Audrey held the back of it to the touchscreen lockbox. A digital hourglass flashed on the screen, sand sprinkling from the top to the bottom. The lockbox beeped angrily, then flashed green. Seconds later, the door nudged open, and Audrey raced through, yanking me after her. It shut on its own, bolting in place, and a part of me wondered just how far Cronus's influence stretched around the world—because knowing it was a global organization was one thing. *Seeing* it in action, right at the thick of it, was another.

This moment—I'd seen it, *felt* it, a thousand times before. Doors opening with secret passcodes and number combinations, then bolting with a bang, sealing you inside a too-bright hallway. I squinted at the onslaught of white-white light, the service corridor lacking any of the nightclub's dark, rich touches. Grey concrete and humming fluorescents on the ceiling, broken only by the odd metal vent. Ugly black garbage containers and blue recycling bins sat on either side of this particular door, and then it was just vast nothingness ahead.

A nothingness that Audrey raced headlong into, picking up the pace, almost at a full gallop by the time we both caught it: smoke trickling from a ceiling vent about ten feet ahead.

Audrey slowed.

I planted my feet, mesmerized. Darkness fell like a silky waterfall, pluming, thickening, expanding to fill the hallway's width.

Phone tucked away, Audrey dug into her jacket again, this time coming out with a small handgun etched with demonic containment runes. Her fingertips gritted deeper into my bicep, nails and all, and the shadows spiraled, twisting inward like a tornado, eventually solidifying into a form I'd recognize anywhere.

Draco's bright white hair pushed through the maelstrom first, followed by his pale skin, his gaunt features. He emerged from the darkness like the most exquisite creature, his beauty haunting, his expression bored, and his eyes an inferno.

"Where are you taking her?" Darkness slashed around him, a lightning strike from the devil himself, his shadows keeping close like a divine suit of armor.

I wanted him.

Him.

Them.

Not her. Not Cronus.

"*Home*, where Selene belongs," Audrey said firmly as she leveled her gun at his throat, right where the turtleneck stopped and his ice-white flesh started again. "She belongs with her family—"

"We are her family." His darkness swelled, the slashes like whips now, cracking against the walls, the floor— reaching for me like an extension of his hand. "Since the dawn of time, we would burn the world for her." My heart soared, the monster inside *purring* at the thought. Draco's nostrils flared briefly, his tone even, his black eyes raging. "Would you?"

Audrey motioned to the left with her gun. "Step aside, shade—"

"They aren't shades," I muttered, locked on Draco as a pleasant calmness washed over me. Warmth blossomed in my belly and tingled up my back, cradling me with invisible arms. "Not even close."

"That place is not her home," Draco remarked, his flat

affect finally getting to Audrey. She held me harder and yanked me back, as if to put herself between us. Arms limp, he just stared, eyes slowly drifting to mine, all the *feeling*, all his emotion, blazing there instead. "It was her cage. Selene is a long-standing Cronus prisoner, and we believe it is time to—"

Latin filled the corridor, Audrey's recitation of a demon binding spell flawless, her pronunciation natural and easy. How many demons had she taken down before tonight? Was this just business as usual? Just another job for her— when it was *everything* to me?

Nothing happened. She rattled off her pretty speech in her flowery Latin twice, and in that time, Draco's shadows receded—like they sensed she wasn't a threat. Black mist shrouded the hallway behind him, thin enough to see through now, while bolts of pure obsidian still slashed around his body, electric and vibrant, a warning to keep her distance.

To let go of his... girl.

His mate?

"We're not demons," Arawn drawled from behind us when the last of Audrey's echoes finally faded. She whirled us around, gun still raised, eyes wider and grip punishing. Arawn, meanwhile, held his ground, suit jacket open and casual, hands in his pockets while my shopping bags dangled at his sides, one around each wrist. He glanced my way and winked. "And we're most certainly not from Hell."

Behind him, Balor stalked down the service corridor, huge and menacing, looking especially murderous.

"But I rather enjoy vacationing there," he snarled. He then stretched out both arms, darkness surging violently from his fingertips to the wall, dragging, slicing deep, and tearing the concrete apart in five long, brutal grooves on either side.

"You've made a valiant effort, but enough now." Arawn offered his hand, shopping bag swaying. His charm sharpened when Audrey didn't immediately comply with his unspoken demand, the glint in his eyes dangerous, his smile yet another warning. "Let her go and we—"

In a flash, Audrey yanked me in front of her, threw an arm around my shoulders—and shoved the gun under my chin.

Time stood still. I dipped my chin slightly to confirm that yes, she had turned her gun on me, that one pull of the trigger would blow my head clean open.

She...

This was a *rescue*.

And now—

The seething darkness in my chest *screamed* betrayal.

"You'd burn the world for her, huh?" Audrey mused as the wildfire spread, my blood boiling but my heart beating so eerily slow. "Pro tip for the future: don't blab your biggest weakness to the person holding the gun." She then shoved it harder into my chin and dragged me in Draco's general direction, as if she really thought he would just step aside and let us pass. "Let's go, Selene."

What.

The.

Fuck.

The inferno in my veins leapt to the others. Smoke coiled off Arawn's aristocratic features, shopping bags abandoned, his hands as black as his suit, his elegant fingers like raptor talons. Draco's darkness slithered around our feet, visceral and thick, somehow both fog and quicksand, slowing Audrey to a shuffle as she tried to push through.

And Balor...

Balor. His mouth dropped in a silent roar, elongating way down his broad chest, a forked tongue lolled over steadily sharpening teeth, onyx mist oozing from his depths. The air turned electric with his contorting limbs, his arms long and spindly, two more sprouting from his back as he dropped onto all fours, slowly transforming into a literal monster before our eyes.

I should have been terrified.

But the rage...

The *fury* overtook everything, followed only by an unholy fascination as gnarled branches burst from Balor's sides, his nails now claws, his feet deadly cloven hooves, this new shape a mishmash of haggard werewolf and flesh-starved ghoul—with a pinch of killer tarantula. All black. Pure shadow. Nightmare fuel.

Gotta admire Audrey for not instantly bolting: anyone else would be long gone by now. She did, however, suck down a few panicked breaths with his first clicky-clacky step toward us.

Enough.

My arm still ached from where she'd grabbed me, and then the gun jabbed under my chin—her rescue attempt actually hurt.

And I'd suffered enough hurt to last ten lifetimes.

Scowling, I snatched her wrist and *twisted*. The gun jerked away, and bone *snapped* in my ear, the crunch making my mouth water and Audrey screech. She stumbled off, her weapon clattering to the concrete at our feet, and I slowly faced her, darkness enveloping my heart.

"It's all true, isn't it?" I studied my black nails with a thoughtful frown. "I'm just like them."

Shadows swirled, warm and soothing, Arawn's

influence cloaking me, settling along my limbs like a second skin. But I didn't want his calm. I wanted *my* fire. Audrey's frantic movements blurred as hot, angry tears stung the backs of my eyes, and no one moved to stop her as she lunged for the gun with her good hand.

"Are you taking me back to my house?" I hissed, trembling as my fury, my hurt, my darkness scorched down my cheeks in fiery rivers. "Or was the plan to put me in a *cell?*"

Audrey rolled onto her back, lifted the gun, and fired.

Right at me.

Arms coiled around my waist and yanked me aside, shadow taking over, black mists circling and blotting out the horrors, same as the night they carried me away from Cronus HQ.

Only here, now, I still heard the screams.

Audrey's terror filled the corridor as I leaned into the dark embrace, and I closed my eyes at the burst of fresh blood in the air.

Then, blissful nothingness, floating, flying, fleeing into the night.

Just me, the shadows—and my rage.

CHAPTER FIFTEEN

We swapped black and red for white and blue, Ritual Nightclub way in our rearview mirror, replaced by an empty beach on some island in the Mediterranean.

That was my best guess on the location, anyway. While I sank into powdery soft sand and heard the *whoosh* of the tide first, it wasn't until the opaque darkness dissipated that I got a good look around. White sand. Crystalline blue waters, even at night. A clear sky dotted with millions of stars and a new moon. The soaring beige escarpment up the beach smeared with scraggy brownish-green foliage.

My old high school clique went to Sicily for their senior grad trip. Dad wouldn't let me go, but the photos I obsessed over through a screen, alone in my room, wearing the same pajamas I'd had since freshman year with the covers up to my chin and eyes full of unshed tears, jealousy and want burning bright where no one could see—the beaches looked a lot like this.

Shaky and weak, I staggered toward the surf, absolutely *fuming*, this anger a scorched-earth wildfire. One hard gulp and I still felt it, the gun under my chin, the barrel cold and unfeeling. One furious glare down my body and I remembered it—all of it, every painful fucking moment of my miserable existence on the base thinking I had some horrific unknown autoimmune disease. Swallowing pills throughout the day. Wishing it—life—would just stop. Pretending everything was *fine*.

When, really, it could have been supernatural all along.

Maybe *I* was the normal one, and those fucking meds—

I yanked my loafers off with a strangled gasp, tossing them out of sight and staring at my toes in the sand. As I clamped down on the insides of my cheeks, raging, I wiggled them.

Burying my feet in sand like this had been on my bucket list since I was eleven. Now I could score it off the list, but holy *shit*, it was nothing like I'd imagined. *Ruined*. A lifelong dream totally destroyed because someone with a security badge that I once looked to for protection at Cronus pulled a fucking gun on me.

And *fired*.

Was it a *Wanted: dead or alive* situation, or...?

Flexing my hands in and out of fists, I ambled toward the creeping surf, so lost in anger that I barely processed the fact that we had hopped across the world in no time at all. In the shadowy bubble of three cloak tatters, time had no meaning. Cradled between them, their auras prickly and staticky after the fight, the ride was still smooth as silk and, above all, *safe*. I mean, I'd landed without a scratch, the lingering aches all courtesy of Audrey.

Mist and shadow swirled in my periphery, some of it reaching for me, the rest whirling, gathering, three figures crystallizing on the beach. The air thickened as their presence turned to solid matter, and before I knew it, three sets of intense, penetrating eyes zeroed in on me. The hairs on the nape of my neck rose. My thighs clenched, memories of Balor's tongue between them still so fresh that every step came with a damp reminder of exactly what he could do to my body.

Arms crossed, head down, I barreled into the surging tide, right up to my ankles. Huh. Still warm-*ish*, the east coast's October chill absent. Here, summer's humidity lingered, the air temperate and pleasant, the wind gentle, the black sky clear and starry.

The scenery should have been my chillax pill.

But nope.

No matter how I breathed, falling back on anxiety exercises from therapy—breathe in for four, breathe out for eight as you picture a fucking *box*—it didn't matter. Rhythm escaped me, that even tempo out of reach. I dropped my arms to my sides, then clasped them behind my back and stretched, hoping opening up my chest might do the trick.

Again—nope.

Down the coastline, a dilapidated lighthouse slouched into the rocks. No roof, but the walls were in pretty decent shape, the white stone bathed in unfettered moonlight.

Light and dark.

Balance.

I sucked in my cheeks and scanned the horizon. Nothing for miles but choppy waters and stars. No other islands. No ships. *Nothing.*

My new nails clenched into my palms.

My throat burned the longer I held it in—so I fucking let it out, my scream a roar as I exorcised the rage in my heart. I pushed and pushed until my lungs about collapsed, vision blurred and the world on its head.

Darkness drifted in at my right. Feet sloshed through

the surf. A shock of white—deathly pale flesh covered by a familiar turtleneck.

Draco offered his hand without a word, expressionless but never, never emotionless, but this time, I shook my head.

"I don't want to *cry*..." Not like I did at the pond, where one touch, our hands clasped and fingers desperate to entwine, ripped a lifetime of sorrow clean out. "I just want it to—"

Stop. Draco snatched my hand without a word, his long, spidery fingers wrapped around mine, his grip pure steel, cold and merciless.

I closed my eyes. My head tipped back. My nostrils flared through a deep, glorious breath.

He'd done it again.

One touch and he gave me everything I needed—and that was *nothing*.

Nothing but my pulse slowing between my ears, racing thoughts extinguished, body sinking into the black abyss. Eventually, my eyes fluttered open, and I refocused on the surf, lost in the tide as it swept up and down the beach, splashing at my bare calves—and Draco's pants, his leather shoes goners and his slacks slick to thin but strong legs.

As the storm inside calmed, my hand numb from both of us gripping a little too hard, I peeked at the man beside me. The soft breeze fussed with his hair, white flicking all over the place, and his thousand-yard stare to the horizon had an oddly endearing quality about it. If I looked and found him gawking at me, brows knit with concern, eyes alive with *feeling* that all fell on my shoulders, I wouldn't have been able to breathe as deeply as I did now.

He was just... there.

Eyes misty again, I yanked him into a hug, catching him off guard enough that he stumbled in the wet, sinky sand underfoot and crashed into me like a falling marble star. As I flexed my fingers behind his back, blood flowing again, arms locked tight around his neck, I pushed onto my toes, struggling, the Mediterranean floor swallowing the few inches gained.

"Thank you," I whispered as his spindly arms snaked around me—mid-back, not lower back like Balor or a firm hand between my shoulders like Arawn. Somewhere in the awkward middle, like he didn't know where to put them... or how to accept a hug that he hadn't already thought through.

I expected the silence.

I didn't anticipate the shaking.

Draco trembled against me in seconds, all rigid and jittery, and I pulled back, worried I'd overstepped my bounds with him. Maybe Balor and Arawn were the touchy ones—maybe his love language, his flirtations, was all eye contact and shadow lurking.

"Hey?" Hands on his shoulders, I leaned back a little more, taking in his rigid features. "Draco, what's wrong?"

His black eyes blazed brighter than the night sky as they fell to my lips, and his hands finally found their purpose, dragging roughly down to my waist, fingers really *pressing*. The cheek twitch, the locked stare, the possessive crush of his strength around me—

Like he was trying to hold back what he *really* wanted to do.

How he really wanted to touch me.

I swallowed hard and tentatively brushed my fingertips up his stiff jaw, then across the hollow planes of his right cheek. The jutted cheekbone. The pale pink lips, so thin and tenuous, fighting for neutrality. He was so hauntingly beautiful—

And he went after me.

Back at the nightclub, he found me before Audrey could haul me back to Cronus.

All of them did.

I glanced up the beach to find the others nearby, Arawn with his hands in his pockets, his posture perfect, and Balor, this hulking monster, huge and terrifying and *stunning*...

Watching.

Eyes on me, on my face and my mouth and my figure.

Draco had called me *family*.

We would burn the world for her.

"Did you mean that?" I asked in the smallest, most hesitant whisper ever, a part of me dreading either answer. Truth. Lie. Both had implications that would change my entire life from this moment onward. "What you said back there about family and burning the—"

He answered with a stiff nod. An inferno blinked down at me, ancient and primal, and I looked to the others, expecting the same.

They didn't disappoint.

They hadn't yet, not once.

With my head turned, neck stretched and throat exposed, Draco's control seemed to finally *snap*. He pounced with a raspy groan, crashing like a fiery meteor, his mouth on my skin shockingly *hot*. His teeth grazed my throat, and his hands gripped harder, all the while breathing me in so deeply his inhale drowned out the surf. My lips parted just enough for a surprised gasp, which made Balor and Arawn visibly perk up, both striding toward us as Draco hoisted me out of the water.

This time, however, *I* pounced.

If all this was true, my entire life a lie—they weren't the only predators on this beach tonight.

As he carried me away from the tide, want sizzling between my thighs and his desire already nudging at my leg, I grabbed his face and yanked it up. He resisted at first, his features sharp and angry, but my determination won out: the second he set me down in fluffy dry sand again, I claimed my prize.

A kiss.

Nothing more.

Nothing less.

A kiss from a creature who went stiff the moment our lips crashed together. Kissing Draco was hard and brutal and, just like him, ran deep on the *inside*. No tongue. No dancing mouths and harsh gasps. He moved slowly, his hands claiming my body one curve at a time, stroking rough and cautious, while I cupped his face and caged him in place, his kiss so *centering*—so different from the others, yet so perfectly him.

Salty air suddenly heady, the sea turned up the volume as a second pair of hands found my body. Waves crashing louder, tide surging higher, fingers worked under my hemline and dragged my dress up, up, up, until a decision had to be made: put my foot down or throw my arms up. End it or embrace the start of something *new*.

I lifted my arms, the kiss with Draco broken just long enough for Arawn to drag the fabric over my head and toss it into the sand. Hair fluffed and frizzed as it fell back to my shoulders, black curls thriving in the coastal humidity, I blinked a few wayward strands out of my eyes, a little unsure where to put my hands as Draco attacked my shoulder, nibbling a path across and down to my collarbone —and Arawn stroked the curve of my backside with his knuckle. Shivers streaked through me at the gentle caress, goose bumps prickling, and I peeked over my shoulder at him.

His smile could change the world.

Really, it could.

So beautiful and regal. So thoughtful and nuanced.

And here, now, it was all for me.

His arm circled my waist, the fabric of his jacket sleeve cool enough to pearl my nipples tight, and Draco cupped my left breast with a growl, planting firm, sharp kisses down my center as he sank to his knees. Arawn, meanwhile, nuzzled into my neck with a contented rumble, his voice warm and lush like honeyed wine.

He controlled me with one finger under my chin, a new flesh memory to replace the cold barrel of a gun. I submitted to the pressure, tipping my head back for him, lips parted, and melted into his kiss with a moan. Arawn kissed like the finest silk, fluid and deep, *passionate* suddenly too dull an adjective for how his mouth moved against mine.

Darkness drifted across my closed lids, and when they snapped open, I found Balor by my side.

Our side.

Arawn at my back, Draco at my feet...

This virgin should have shoved them all away to take stock of what the hell she was getting herself into.

Instead, as Draco stroked my calves and Arawn's tantalizing mouth grazed the other side of my neck, Balor swooped in for the kill. He kissed to claim, to conquer, to *win* no matter how savagely I kissed back. My fingers wove into his short hair and *ripped*, which only earned me a growl from the primordial beast dominating my mouth—followed by a sharp snap of Draco's teeth behind my knee and a chastising chuckle from Arawn as he licked the shell of my ear.

Fire raged between us, around us, unseen and scorching. It felt natural as breathing to touch all three, to kiss them one right after the other and still crave *more*.

As Draco retreated, Balor fell to his knees and took his brother's place, then yanked my legs apart and tore my damp cotton panties right along the seams, shredding them in seconds. Arawn cupped both my breasts from behind, delicately pinching my nipples between two fingers, rolling them as an electric charge splintered down my core and made me squeal.

Thunder rumbled in the distance.

Balor licked roughly up my right thigh, delving in with a snarl and cupping my ass the second his monstrous mouth closed over my clit.

I threw my head back with a much higher, much more embarrassing squeak, up on my toes and nowhere to run.

The stars—

Where had all the stars gone?

Like their god had tossed his obsidian cloak across the sky, darkness descended. Waves crashed and hissed up the shoreline. The air, charged and heavy, thickened as I looped an arm back around Arawn's neck for support, my thighs trembling, pleasure soaring. My free hand tangled in Balor's hair, his head bobbing at the crest of my legs, his tongue plunging into me again and stroking my inner walls.

And Draco—he circled like a hawk, prowling, trudging a protective ring in the sand around us. I tracked his slow perusal whenever I had the chance, but when Balor did that beautiful *thing* with his tongue, a tongue that had to be distorted and elongated or *something*, because holy *fuck* there was no way a standard tongue could do *that*—

But he wasn't standard.

None of them were.

I cried out when, in his ferocity, Balor scooped me off the ground and really tucked in—like I was his last and final meal before the sweet release of death. My toes wiggled, and I realized *this* should have been on my bucket list. Not toes in the sand at some random beach, but the feeling of being taken and worshipped at the same time, surrounded by monsters who promised to burn the world for me.

"*Fuck.*"

Here I'd been, thinking the first climax of the night was the best I had ever had.

Then this one hit out of nowhere, gale force winds and all, and my shriek echoed down the beach and over the whitecaps. Pleasure scorched me alive from the inside, my core exquisitely taut, my body slick with sweat and my heels driving into Balor's back while my hands yanked at both his and Arawn's hair.

As the second wave hit, another torturous surge of fiery pleasure stealing my breath away, lightning split the sky.

Planted directly ahead, intense as ever, Draco zeroed in on me—until a cool rain misted the beach. Then, as I gasped and arched, my nipples pebbled harder at the shock and my skin covered in goose bumps, he tipped his head back and closed his eyes, letting the wet wash over him.

Another lightning strike backlit the relaxation, the slight parting of his lips, the droplets clinging to his lashes—it was one of the most beautiful things I'd ever seen.

Followed by *thunder*, booming, crackling, raging drumbeats directly over us, one right after the other, so sudden and so violent that they must have felt it in Hell.

Orgasms before tonight were seldom a full-body experience. That gorgeous light-as-air sensation, my brain floating in a happy daze—all firsts. But the rain brought me back to earth, cool and damp, sprinkling my bare skin like a shot of adrenaline. By the time I folded forward, weak-kneed but coming back to myself, Balor had shifted from feasting between my thighs to kneeling in front of me, ready to catch me, brace me, my body slumped across his chest and over his left shoulder. Huge hands massaged up my calves to the backs of my thighs, and as he settled back on his heels, he brought me with him, lifting me onto my tiptoes—

I stiffened with a sharp breath when Arawn nudged against my entrance. Not a finger. Not his tongue. *Him*, the head of his cock thick and firm and so fucking present as he gently pushed into me—

"I-I..." Panicked, I jerked upright, one hand fisted around Balor's damp shirt, the other swatting back at Arawn. Heart racing, eyes wide—probably made wider and more terrified with the next apocalyptic flash of lightning. "I've n-never done *it*."

Shit.

What a mood killer.

All three stiffened, Balor beneath me and Arawn behind me, the silky smooth head still nuzzled at my slickness, just *waiting* to plunge in. Draco always looked still as stone, but the way he lifted his chin and appraised me, a sentry reporting for duty—this felt different. Concern turned the air soft, and I craved the crackle of desire, the thick, heady mixture of lust and fear and uncertainty as we all figured each other out...

And I'd ruined it.

"I've never... I haven't, with anyone, I—" Shit, shit, shit, *shit*. I licked the rain from my lips with a frustrated huff. If my voice could go back to normal, or even that dopey post-climax rasp, that would be *fan*tastic. "Not that I haven't, uh, like, given, you know, with my hands..." I pushed up on

Balor's shoulder and peeked back at Arawn, shame burning my cheeks. "But I just—"

His smile made me melt like butter on a hot pan. Tender fingers swooped my hair behind my ear, gathering the wet curls and smoothing them flat. A beat later, he pressed his forehead to my temple with a sweet sigh, then a shaky rumble—like he had tried to temper a harsher, more brutal sound with one that wouldn't startle the doe.

Wouldn't send her sprinting into the forest with a wolf on her heels.

"Slow and easy, little one," he murmured. Thunder pounded the sky overhead. Balor massaged the tension from my upper thighs, his strong hands working up to my backside as a lovely warmth washed over me. Arawn's influence touched down like the first breath of spring after an especially brutal winter. Then, out of nowhere, he eased the first inch or two of his cock into me, and I hissed instinctively, clenching, eyes snapping shut.

Not because it hurt, really.

I mean, yeah, *it* was larger than the fumbling fingers of the past. Thicker and firmer than Balor's tongue. It stung a little—but nowhere near as much as I'd expected.

"You tell me when to stop," Arawn rumbled through an openmouthed kiss, one he dragged lazily from my temple to my ear, then down my throat as I shivered. "You tell me anytime. Now or then—and I will stop. You're in control, Selene." Another inch dragged a whimper from me, the sting sharper the deeper he went, and Arawn stilled with another flood of heat, sunshine blooming across my skin in the middle of a worsening storm. "Little one..." His rakish whisper made my core clench pleasurably. "Tell me, and I'll worship between your thighs instead, hmm?"

I shook my head without thinking. All things

considered, at twenty-five and only *just* losing my virginity —in front of three godly beings on a random beach, no less— I ought to be embarrassed as hell. But with Arawn's soothing touch, his soft murmurs, the barrage of velvety compliments inked across my skin... I wouldn't have wanted my first time with anyone else.

Then Balor in front, supporting me in more ways than one, solid as a rock with one big hand between my thighs, his thumb with its rough pad circling my clit—it was like I'd never stumble and fall again. Briefly, he proved he could switch off his default setting—Balor could be *gentle*.

For me.

And Draco...

Draco drifted closer, watching, arms at his sides. When I stole a glimpse at the next flash of blinding white, the next cacophony of divine war drums, I caught him scanning the perimeter, on guard, protective of me and the others while we lost ourselves in this moment.

Selfless.

He stepped back to let Balor and Arawn take charge, almost like he sensed I needed *them* right now.

But I craved him too. The depth in his gaze. The solid assurance of his presence.

All of them...

My eyes drifted shut again as pleasure licked up my center, my clit the belle of the ball, my sex relaxing just enough for Arawn to thrust another inch deeper.

I need all of you.

Please don't leave me when it's over.

No matter how turned on, no matter how hot and wet and aroused, it hurt.

A deep, throbbing ache in my core that made my eyes water and Draco growl and Balor pay more attention to my clit. But Arawn was so thoughtful. So gentle. So slow and careful in how he worked me, easing in and then waiting for my body to adjust, until finally his hips collided with my ass. The pain dulled with every kiss, every sweetly whispered word, every sweep of Balor's rough thumb, every moment of blazing eye contact with Draco. Even as the storm moved closer, the rain pelting harder and the lightning snapping brighter, hotter, angrier—I came down from the high under their care.

Only for Arawn to punt me back up, just a few feet, with his first pump.

"*Oh.*" I bit my lower lip, shy when Balor's lips twisted into a devilish smirk. "Oh, I..."

Another buck of Arawn's hips, and I inhaled sharply, struggling to process the sensation, the line between pain and pleasure blurred. Filled, claimed, stretched wide—my body *loved* the movement, the grind and the thrust. Same as before, Arawn started slow, until eventually it was so fucking *easy*, so sublime to bend over Balor's shoulder and let him *take* me.

"Wow, I just—" I gritted my teeth and squealed at the first sizzle of white-hot bliss slashing up my core, timed perfectly with the next lightning strike.

"There you are, blackbird," Balor growled. With a manic grin, his black gaze chaotic and wild, he stopped supporting my leg and instead closed that hand around my throat. Panic flashed in my chest, followed by an embarrassing moan that made Arawn rock faster. Balor, meanwhile, tipped his head, his eyes darting between where Arawn and I met and my expression—probably full-on bewildered, looking drunk on lust and lost in the climb. He squeezed just enough to force my gaze to his, and he flashed his canines with every word as he drawled,

"What a good girl—taking a cock like *that* on your first try."

I latched onto his wrist with both hands, whimpering through the next barrage of thunder, my sputter pure nonsense that only made his grin wider and his laughter wicked. Meanwhile, Arawn maintained a firm grip around my waist as he bucked into me—but one hand, a hand usually so poised and elegant, suddenly worked into my slick curls.

Twisted and gripped and nudged my head back so that out of the corner of my eye, I could see him watching me, his eyes hooded and his lips parted, his breath harsh, his presence intense.

Shaking, rocking, my body awash with *feeling*, I glanced down at Balor, then Draco, briefly wondering if we should involve them—

"Now, now, little one," Arawn chided, pounding into me a few times so that my jaw went slack and my eyes rolled back in my head. "We have all eternity... No need to rush anything."

Balor zeroed in on that one *spot* at my clit, really stoking the inferno, the hand on my throat gripping tighter.

"What d'you think?" His voice plunged into beast territory, so rough and sandpapery, dangerous and terrifying —to anyone else. "She wants two of us fucking her?" Suddenly, his hand slid up my throat, gliding over the raindrops, and he smooshed my cheeks. "Blackbird, is *that* where your filthy mind's wandered?"

Shit, *maybe*. As I strangled his forearm and whined, trapped in place, toes barely grazing the sand as Arawn quickened his pace, I wondered...

No.

One was enough—for tonight.

The hand in my hair eased up, stroking my curls, brushing them, finger-combing it all to one side—only for Arawn to wrap it around his fist and use it like an anchor, jerking my head back again and pounding into me.

My eyelids fluttered open to the stormy sky, to the grey wall of rain and the fireworks of lightning on the horizon. Suddenly, Draco loomed over me, right at Balor's back and forcing himself into my limited line of sight. My muscles tightened. My core clenched. Pleasure reached that point of no return, where your brain shut off and your nerves fired on overdrive. I gasped, stuck at the door of the plane, seconds from free fall and questioning it—

Draco cocked his head to the side, expression passive and eyes like hellfire. A slight quirk of his white brow—like a silent command to climax. *Now.*

And I obeyed with a strangled wail, letting go *just* enough for my third orgasm to tear clean through me. Veins on fire, heart open and vulnerable. It wasn't just me spiraling out of control between Balor and Arawn, but the storm too, suddenly so violently alive, so full of color and light and sound. It felt like the end of days and the start of something *new*, an ancient power tearing across the sky, lightning pulsing against the black in time with my pleasure.

"A-are we doing that?" I babbled, riding the ecstasy in my blood, only half-aware that my words sounded more coherent than I actually felt. Draco looked up, studying the sky, mapping the chaos, and then shook his head.

"I think that would be *you*, Selene."

I snorted, my head dropping, ready to argue that there wasn't a chance in hell that I could control something as powerful as *this*—but then Arawn shed his pretty exterior, his charm cast aside and replaced with this fierce, primordial *monster* I had only seen in Balor when he went full shadow and tore his enemies apart. The arm around my waist vanished, and suddenly we were both clawing at Balor, using him for support as Arawn claimed me for good. The beast at my back was still so fucking beautiful, physically my fallen angel, a dark god who could rule the world with just his smile.

Kindest of the group. Gentlest of the brothers.

Violently divine in his climax.

He stilled with a choked growl, fisting at my hair and driving into me one last time hard enough that his hip bones might just leave permanent scars.

But then he was back, my sweet, charming creature who showered me with hushed praise and arranged my body like I was made of glass. As soon as he eased out of me, Balor caught me long before I hit the sand, scooping me into his arms, cradling me to his burly chest as he stood and towered high above the beach.

Without a word, the trio drifted toward the dilapidated lighthouse down the shoreline, black mists trailing after them, clinging to their backs and shoulders, dragged away on the wind. Spent and sore, I couldn't put words together. Couldn't really process what had just happened or what was to come.

Because all around me, the storm ramping up, the sea furious and the sky devastating, light and dark ruled the world.

And all I could think about in that moment, what I could truly, deeply understand for the first time in my life... was *balance*.

CHAPTER SIXTEEN

Last night, I crashed at the peak of a cataclysmic storm. Light and dark. Balance.

Today, I came to under similar conditions, light and dark ruling the world—but the storm had passed. Muted sunshine was the light, and the dark...

Well, the dark was all around me, filling the base of this old lighthouse, the concrete floor just inside the entrance blanketed in shadow. With a deep breath, I pushed up on my elbow in the middle of it all, achy and stiff and sore in a weirdly satisfying way, surrounded by mist and smoke.

And men.

My men, apparently, all three arranged around me, dozing in the translucent black fog, their solid forms faded and blurred. To keep out last night's rain, Draco had conjured a thick black cloud to plug the open ceiling, our own shadowy tarp that hadn't let a drop through. At some point after I'd fallen asleep, one of them crafted a bed—or a mattress, maybe a platform. *Something.* It kept me off the floor at the very least, the thick circular swath of darkness below firm and *real*, just like the chair Arawn had made in his Cronus cube a little over a week and a half ago.

Might as well have been a lifetime ago—that was how distant the memory felt.

Sitting up fully, I scrubbed the sleep from my eyes and the dried drool from the corners of my mouth. Strange. I'd never seen them sleep; all this time, I assumed they just... didn't. But there was Draco, flat on his back, stiff as a board, full-on Egyptian mummy with his eyes shut and jaw locked. Sprawled across him, Balor took up the most space, limbs everywhere, spread-eagle with his head on Draco's chest, mouth open, snores getting louder and more obnoxious the more sleep I shook off.

And Arawn...

My face flashed hot when I found him on the opposite side of his fellow cloak tatters, slumped against the wall, head hanging down to his chest and long legs fully outstretched—he made sure to fall asleep touching me. I poked the tips of his oxfords, but rather than snapping to, shooting awake and crawling to my side, he snuffled, handsome face curtained by his black waves, feet falling to the sides and disrupting the lazily swirling mists.

Adorable.

While I was stark naked and draped in a blanket of onyx smoke, they were fully clothed—and dead to the world. Nibbling my lower lip, I shifted onto my hands and knees, then winced when my bladder screamed bloody murder; I needed a spot to squat *stat*.

Careful not to jostle anyone—seriously, these three deserved some sleep after waiting on me hand and foot for seven days while *I* slept like the dead—I stood and tiptoed over to a busted window, the glass long gone and Arawn's suit jacket folded neatly on top of the stone frame. It drowned me, sure, but this wasn't the first time I had borrowed it, and buttoning it provided just enough coverage that at a distance, if you didn't look all that hard, it *might* pass for a dress. Rolling the sleeves to my wrists, I padded out, picking my way through the dogpile of men and mist, eventually slipping out the arched door, the wooden panel in pieces just outside, and onto the beach.

A beach that had been absolutely hammered by the storm last night. While it looked a little worse for the wear, the sand damp and smooth, the scraggly foliage battered and bent, there were no real casualties anywhere. With a dry chill in the air, the tide swept in and out like always, dragging bits of wood and debris back to the sea, the water dark teal and choppy. Hazy browns and greys streaked the sky, this afternoon's overcast somehow bright *and* cloudy. Honestly, the *worst* combination.

After debating between sea or scrub to relieve myself, I hurried down to the surf. With Arawn's jacket hiked up to my boobs, I waded hip-deep into the aquamarine waves, the water cooler after the storm. Then, bladder empty, I sloshed my way out, graceless on the shifting sands, and strolled along the beach to dry off.

All things considered, my captors knew how to pick the most peaceful hiding spots. Quiet. Empty. Serene, serenaded by the whooshing tide and the odd bird call. When my lower half felt dry enough, I let the jacket hang like a dress again, the material luxe and soft, armor forged of silk and cashmere.

Then stilled when black mist spiraled off the cuffs.

Frowning, I blinked down at it, at the way the shadowy darkness moved like it had a mind of its own. Not aimless. Not meaningless. Hands raised, I watched it dance for me, twining and twisting, braiding the shades of black together, the splayed ends flicking at my nose.

"Uh, hi."

Shit, that felt really stupid—

The mist surged, braid broken as the trio wove up my arms and around my neck, snuggling in like a scarf, warmer than the outside air.

Soft. Gentle. Soothing.

Arawn.

Was a piece of him clinging to the jacket? I brushed my fingers through the mist with a grin, suddenly feeling safer at the thought of him out here with me.

A raven's throaty cry split the serenity.

I whipped around, eyes wide, and scanned the escarpment for a familiar little pervy face and snappy beak —because that sounded *exactly* like the raven who greeted me every morning after my shower.

But...

No.

No.

The quiet had a way of playing tricks on you, and as I scrutinized the beige-y cliffside, the thorny brush staggered down its face—no ravens anywhere.

No mists either, the darkness dispersed, my neck exposed and the shadows gone.

Great.

Scowling, I wheeled back around to continue my aimless wandering down a vacant beach—

"*Fuck.*"

Only the beach wasn't so vacant anymore. Ten feet out, directly in front of me, stood two dangerously attractive men, one with tousled blond hair, the other a spiky redhead with the shaved sides of his head tattooed like a skull, the ink tapering all the way down to bony blackwork cheekbones and a detailed mouth cavity.

And beside him: a fiery hole in the sand hastily sealing itself shut.

Pulse pounding crazier than last night's storm, I stumbled backward, mouth gaping while theirs quirked into sharp, cruel smirks. Throw in the leather jackets, the black jeans, the bone-crushing steel-tipped boots—the gun in the blond's hand...

All that *plus* the severe beauty and the supple lips—

They both blinked, eyes snapping from sort of human to completely black, whites and all, and their smirks bloomed into full-blown demonic leers.

Demons.

Fucking demons.

"Where are your guard dogs?" Blondie drawled. From the slight lift of his chin, I figured his gaze had snapped up the beach to the lone set of footprints behind me—but how could you ever tell where demons were actually looking when their eyes went full black? No iris. No pupil. Just the forlorn emptiness of a damned soul.

Nothing like the black of Arawn, Draco, and Balor's eyes. My boys had *depth*.

"Seems risky," Ginger Skull mused, "letting their quarry wander off so far."

Say something. I gulped when Blondie's black eyes narrowed. *Be a snarky badass heroine for once in your miserable life.*

"Ho-lee *shit*." Blondie snickered as he pointed at me with a gun that had all the makings of a standard pistol, plus a few modifications reminiscent of Cronus security hardware. "Look at her fucking eyes."

"More of a whore than Daddy led us to believe, eh?"

Ginger Skull added, his booming laughter startling a flock of birds from the wispy underbrush along the escarpment. I, meanwhile, resisted the urge to look away, to turn my head and hide in my hair. Seriously though, what the *shit* was that supposed to mean?

It all happened so fast.

Demons clawing out a transportable Hell gate on *my* beach.

Sneering about my eyes.

Blondie leveling his gun at my chest and pulling the trigger.

It fired with a whispery *sput*. Shock locked me in place, and I braced for impact.

Never cower in front of a demon. Never turn your back. Never run. Three rules intake officers lived by, and having heard the horror stories, I'd committed them to memory my first month.

At the last millisecond, however, I closed my eyes—but the hit never landed. I cracked one eye open again, then the other with a shuddery exhale, relief making my knees weak. I wasn't alone out here. At least ten feet tall and fifteen wide, billowy black smoke had absorbed the shot, now spiraling inward, centralizing, twisting and lashing, swiftly shifting into Arawn.

Arawn with a tranq dart between his elegant fingers.

"Now, now, gentlemen," he started, voice smooth as silk and cold as ice, "no need to be *rude.*"

I slowly scoped his back, this towering figure that managed to be lean but *strong*, his shoulders nowhere near Balor's girth but just broad and powerful enough for me. Peel away the outer layer of his suit and he was left in a dress shirt and a snug vest, slacks that clung perfectly to his legs, his *ass* deliciously perky.

Heat bloomed in my cheeks, demons temporarily forgotten for the sake of *this* fine specimen.

How was a man like *this* my first?

A creature utterly divine and staunchly protective—someone who declared our love story one of the greats, willing to take a bullet for me.

Or, more precisely, a Cronus-issued tranquilizer dart, the make and model one we used on aggressive alpha shifters.

Was I...?

Was that how they saw me now? Something that needed a knockout punch, the serum strong enough to send a male bear shifter to dreamland for two days? *Really?*

"Look, Selene—Miss Abbott... We don't *have* to dart you," Blondie admitted with a shrug, weirdly civil now that a stronger predator had entered the game. While I didn't cower, I still edged closer to Arawn—not exactly hiding, but not stupid enough to ignore the world's best shield either. The blond demon then holstered his gun with a huff and offered me his open hand, gaudy iron rings on each finger. "I'd just come home if I were you. We can keep it clean and professional, all aboveboard. They don't want you dead, and *we* want to get paid. Simple."

"Picking *them* over your family is a... choice," his tattooed companion added, that snort and dismissive up and down of Arawn making me bristle. "What, you think these fuckers will stick around now that they've nutted in you?"

I grabbed at the back of Arawn's vest as the color bled from my face in great prickling rivers. "*Excuse* me?"

One hand reaching around for my arm, for a touch that should have been more comforting than it was, Arawn tossed the tranq dart aside with the other. "Look at that... *Rude.*" His fingers coiled snug around my forearm, and he jerked me closer without warning. "Really living up to your filthy namesake."

Blondie's lips peeled into a sneer, but just as they parted, some seething insult locked and loaded, a warning growl rumbled from my left. Scooting around to Arawn's right, I gasped as a pair of shadowy dogs stalked out of the grasses way up the beach. Roughly the size of border collies at first, they weren't exactly a threat—but that changed with every prowling step. Slowly, Balor and Draco blossomed into huge hounds, all sharp teeth and deadly claws, giant paws and rippling muscle. Black and chaotic as last night's storm, their fur glistened in the muted sunshine as they swelled to the size of male grizzlies.

While these weren't the physical forms that got me all hot and bothered, I could tell them apart now, their differences nuanced and complex, their individual quirks obvious... even as monsters. Balor at the front, his brutal muzzle open, teeth bared, saliva dripping in smoky plumes. Draco flanked to the left, sleek and silent, padding along with murder in his black gaze, violence in the subtle heat waves rising from the grooves his enormous paws left in the sand.

They stilled suddenly, locked on the demonic duo.

Blondie cleared his throat. "So—"

Balor snapped his jaws and lunged, Draco hot behind, both growing meaner and louder and angrier with each massive stride.

"*Fuck.*"

An echo of my earlier sentiment, Ginger Skull's shout blasted down the beach, his voice impossibly deep, guttural and grating, his inner demon crawling out to protect him. Horns sprouted from both their skulls as they bolted in the opposite direction. Blondie hurled a smooth silver stone that burst into flames as soon as it hit the sand: their key to Hell's ethereal crossroads, pathways that cut from our realm to theirs, invisible, untouchable unless you were the right species.

Angels. Fallen. Reapers. Hellhounds. Dragons. Gods. Demons.

These ones didn't make it.

Balor and Draco caught them *just* on the cusp of the fiery opening, ripping their prey back and slamming them to the ground. I watched, stomach in knots, as the portal slowly sizzled shut...

And as two gnarled shadow hounds shredded those demons to nothing, tearing open their chests, devouring their hearts, peeling flesh from bone—consuming their heads whole. Black blood painted the sand, the screeches and cries long gone, replaced only by the hiss of the tide.

Nausea tickled the back of my palate, and I twisted away from Arawn, stumbling off in a daze.

"Selene, wait—"

"What..." I scrubbed at my cheeks, then rooted around Arawn's empty jacket pockets for a mirror or a spare button. Nothing. Panic knotted in my throat, making my words all squeaky and tight. "W-what's wrong with my eyes? What did he mean?"

Effortlessly graceful as always, Arawn glided around and cut off my escape from the snarls and the *crunch* of broken bones. With a soft sigh, he cupped and stroked my face, his smile so brazenly affectionate that I *almost* swooned.

Almost.

"Your eyes are stunning as always," he insisted, brushing a few frizzy curls from my forehead. "They're fully black today—"

"*What?*"

I flailed, panic at a twelve and climbing by the second, but Arawn held firm and guided me back to him.

"Selene, there's darkness in you." When I just stared blankly up at him, he sighed again, that gust of cool air nothing like Dad's patronizing huffs, and pressed his forehead to mine. "*Our* darkness."

Wait. Wait. *Our...*

Oh.

Oh *no*.

Suddenly cold all over, I shook my head. No, no, no, he couldn't mean—

"If you want to get technical about it..." Arawn pressed a quick kiss on my forehead, his grin like spring sunshine, his eyes so warm and comforting despite every internal alarm bell in my body starting to shriek. "Little one, you're pregnant."

CHAPTER SEVENTEEN

I have sex one time, and boom—pregnant.

This is such bullshit.

Having glared at the sea long enough, tracking the sun sinking behind a murky horizon over the last hour or so, I finally turned and stalked back up the beach. In that time, Arawn, Balor, and Draco had been busy: they'd built a bonfire surrounded by shadow benches and pillows, topped by a misty, wispy gazebo-thing, darkness spiraling skyward from its pointed roof. Then, stockpiled around Arawn and Draco, food for my empty belly, while Balor tended some sort of thick, fatty, dripping piece of meat over the fire.

They all stilled when I marched under the gazebo's shadowy gothic archway, hands in fists, heart pounding, fear eating me alive—but *rage* keeping me going.

"So, pregnant, huh?" I snapped, gesturing from Arawn to my abdomen, because, *technically*, this was his fault. Unless, you know, one of these other assholes could impregnate me with a kiss, but that felt like a stretch. "Pregnant. That's... That's... *great*."

Groaning, I stabbed my fingers into my hair, then

roughly picked the knots apart, a scowl for each of the three cloak fragments, these primordial brothers who butchered two demons for me without a second thought. While Arawn and Draco remained seated on two separate cushions, legs crossed, the image comically casual given the circumstances, Balor slowly backpedaled to a bench beside them, offering more of the space I had demanded when the news first broke.

"You know, my period has always been the *worst*," I told them with a deadpan chuckle. "Like, just a total shitshow... Never consistent. Never all that much. Nothing like my friends. And I figured, you know, fuck *me*, my fertility is probably a nightmare too because why the hell would *I* get a functioning reproductive system in this broken body?"

Pretty depressing, actually, to realize I'd been thinking that exact sentiment since the first time I woke up to a pale red stain in my underwear at thirteen. My periods came and went at random, usually three or four months apart, and lasted about a day. No doctor could explain it; after a while, they stopped trying, and I eventually stopped asking. Frankly, there was so much other medical bullshit to deal with that an absentee period that never caused cramps and barely bled was kind of a blessing.

"My *immune issues*"—I finally found the nerve to add air quotes, because clearly that was a fucking lie—"and all the meds and their side effects and *Dad...*" Shaking my head, I gave up on my tangled curls with a frustrated cry, tossing the bits of torn hair into the fire. This close, I barely felt its heat, the flames dull and sad compared to the wildfire that had blazed between me and these three silent, staring *men* last night. "And now, I guess, it's all been a lie. Off the meds, I'm *fine*. I'm fucking fine. I'm not sick. I'm not an outlier. So, you know, what the fuck? Seriously. What—the—fucking *fuck? Pregnant?*"

Balor pursed his lips when my glare landed on him like a screeching missile, then swiped a pebble from the sand to fiddle with. He wasn't the only fidgety one: Arawn kept readjusting his position throughout my ranting, uncrossing and recrossing his legs, stretching them out, throwing one ankle over the other. Draco, meanwhile, just stared at the fire, at the roasting spit with its hunk of dripping meat.

Please don't be a chunk of demon.

Please just be normal, run-of-the-mill cow or pig or something.

"Well?" I motioned to all three with a dramatic flourish of both arms, voice cracking, head full of static again after barely forty-eight hours of blissful clarity. "What's... What's the deal? You three have been weirdly quiet and *not* hovering suddenly, so, like, what can I expect?"

Not that I could be annoyed with them for respecting my wishes.

Hell, after I'd told them to screw off—in kinder, more frantic, squeaky words—they had built a bonfire but made it cute with the benches and cushy pillows, then found me enough dinner to last a month, and, judging by the plastic bags full of fabric, even rustled up some clothes.

I...

They didn't deserve my anger, but I was fucking terrified. I'd only *just* had sex for the first time, and now I had to deal with some supernatural pregnancy *shit?*

No. No. This warranted a major freak-out until I had all the facts.

However, rather than Balor spitting said facts or Arawn launching into some eloquent, poetic, albeit rambling story about our shared history, they all just sat there.

Sat there and avoided eye contact.

My temper inched a little higher. Uh-uh. *Unacceptable.* Before I could rip them a new one for leaving me in the literal and metaphorical dark, Draco dug into one of the food boxes between him and Arawn—then offered me a chocolate bar.

Fully wrapped, the plastic exterior a shiny purple.

Chocolate.

To soothe the hysterical woman.

I closed my eyes and took a deep breath, held it for as long as I could, then let it all go at once.

"I—do not—want—*chocolate!*"

Panic flashed in his eyes as he tossed the bar over his shoulder, then stuffed his empty hands in his lap, still as a statue and studying me—leaning back ever so slightly—like I was a bomb on the cusp of *boom.*

"I want... information." And for my head to stop spinning and my heart to stop racing and my adrenaline to stop climbing. But, you know, one disaster at a time. "Like, do I get an epidural? Are there trimesters? Should I practice breathing? Is there a, uh, doula or whatever?" Silence. Uncharacteristically quiet, all three offered their own versions of pained expressions, and I threw my hands up with another frustrated cry. "Give me *something.*"

"We don't..." Arawn licked his lips, then glanced between Draco and Balor. "I'm afraid we don't exactly... have a lot of information for you—"

"*What?*" Boom. It happened: detonation. Run for cover, boys. "What?" I charged around the bonfire, headed straight for the one that did this to me. "*What?*"

Only Balor stepped in before my clenched fists made contact, his arm hooked around my middle as he hauled me back to the other side of the fire—as if I could actually *do* anything to hurt them. Right? These three were top of the top. They shredded demons like they were nothing. Ripped ghouls in half like they were made of paper. One little punch to the nose wouldn't do anything—

Just let me fucking hit something.

"But we do know it will be over fast," Arawn insisted, patting the air as if that might calm me. "From what I've heard, it never lasts more than a day, little one—"

"*Don't*," I jabbed a finger at him over the crackling flames, dangling on Balor's arm, toes *just* touching the ground, "you—*little one*—me."

Smacking at the thick forearm of steel cutting into my gut, I squirmed free and stumbled away, then paced. Back and forth, just a few steps in either direction, hoping that the movement would get my brain working again.

Pregnant.

Pregnant for only a day, apparently.

With *their* offspring.

That's been the goal from the start.

I glowered at my forehead, urging the darkness within me *there*, to that place where the nasally symphony of insecurity, anxiety, and self-doubt lived in my brain. Because I so didn't need the twisted sisters chiming in right now, not when, once again, something was happening to my body that was out of my control. All my life, everyone else called the shots with my physical health, the mental and emotional stuff literally just forgotten, scorched to a crisp on the back burner nobody bothered to turn off. One week of detox, and suddenly I had this *strength*, my senses heightened, the world brighter, food delicious and music exquisite no matter how loud.

And now...

One week of suffering, a few days of functionality, one *really* good one minus the Audrey hiccup...

And now I was back here, back where I *never* wanted to be.

My lower lip wobbled, and I pressed both together, refusing to cry no matter how sharp frustration and sadness needled at me.

"You *did this*"—I pointed at my stomach as I paced toward the bonfire—"to me, and you don't even know what happens—"

"It varies amongst the daughters of Nyx," Draco remarked, his raspy voice tapering to a whisper when our eyes met. "That... is my understanding."

I ground my back teeth and crossed my arms. "Awesome."

My tone, my body language—it looked and sounded childish, like a preteen mid-tantrum, but...

No, I had every fucking right to hold their feet to the fire. They had centuries on me and came directly from this world of monsters and magic.

They should have realized what could happen last night.

They should have prepared for this eventuality.

Unfortunately, it didn't seem like I'd get anything else from them, still so unusually somber and quiet.

"Why did you pick me?" So, time to revisit a previous topic that I still wasn't completely clear on. If anything, I needed the distraction—and I needed to know for *sure* that they hadn't ripped me from my life *just* because I was Nyx's daughter. Three mouths opened at once, brows all knit and creased and indignant, collective annoyance flaring, and I raised my hand to cut them off. "No, no, besides the Nyx and Erebus stuff. Me. You didn't know a thing about me. I could have been, you know, the worst—just a horrible person, but you all seemed to... *decide* immediately."

"Selene," Arawn started, shuffling to the edge of his shadowy cushion with a gentle sigh, the air warming with his influence. "The *feeling* we experienced that day—"

"Is this a serious question?" Balor interjected. Across the fire, turning the spit and scowling, he cocked his head and waited. I blinked back at him. Was *that* a serious question?

"Uh, obviously."

"Why *wouldn't* we choose you?" His voice deepened, weighted with a harsh blend of bass timbres, and shadow wafted from his temples like horns. "How is this still a discussion? Have you seen yourself? Blackbird, have you ever looked in a fucking mirror and really *seen* yourself?"

I sucked in my cheeks, gnawing at them as I mulled over the sentiment. "So, physically, I—"

"Deductions were made in a heartbeat," Arawn drawled. "First, the feeling. The spark." He snapped his fingers, the sound so crisp I flinched. "We sensed you long before Cronus. Then, inside, an assessment of you, as you were—in *seconds*, we knew."

More of the same. *We just knew.* Nausea plucked at my insides, acid nudging up my esophagus, and I knuckled where the hurt was angriest, hating it. "That's... not enough of an answer for me."

"Intelligence." All eyes snapped to Draco as he watched the fire, slowly folding his knobby knees to his chest and winding his willowy arms around them. In that moment, he seemed so small compared to his brothers, dwarfed by their height and breadth. But his voice—as always, Draco had an inner strength unmatched by anyone I had ever met. "You work for a secret society and have a heavy hand in creature management and care." He lifted one finger, then another, his feathery white lashes orange in the firelight. "So, not only intellect, but without ever speaking to you, I saw compassion, organization, and mental fortitude."

I gulped, not sure how to respond to that. No one had ever showered me in positives like these three, which was yet another depressing realization, made even sadder by the fact that I struggled to just *take* the compliments—to not argue against them or downplay my abilities.

"Oh" was all I could muster.

"We sensed they'd done something to you," Balor growled as he lifted the meat stick onto a higher rung, easing what I assumed was tonight's dinner away from the direct heat, the meat brown and juicy. "Likely with your medications, they dulled your mother's gifts." He wiped his hands on his slacks, then looked me dead in the eye, mouth quirked. That black gaze, even in an argument, was lethal and lovely, a combination that *shouldn't* exist, shouldn't make sense, but called to my heart like a siren's song. "And as her daughter, you are *fire* and rage and darkness. You are peace and solitude. You are eternal. You are magnificent, blackbird."

"Beauty unparalleled," Arawn added softly.

"Brave," Draco pressed as the bonfire's heat leapt from the dugout to my face, cheeks hot and lips trembling. They wanted to both lift in a grateful smile and cave in a trembling arc, so unaccustomed to a goddamn compliment that in the end, the confusion and the uncertainty and the disbelief—I just wanted to cry.

But Draco had called me brave.

"It takes courage to face monsters *you* thought could kill you in an instant," he continued, entranced by the flames, unaware of what his words did to me, how the emotions stormed across my face. Arawn caught it, his features softening, his body inching my way. Balor too, his huge hands fisted, his jaw clenched and flared—like he craved a *fight*. Draco cleared his throat and toed at the sand, lost in his own thoughts. "Not just the other beasties in their cages... but us. You proved your mettle from the start against three creatures who terrified everyone else."

"I saw your desk," Balor blurted, the rage melting away, replaced with an impish grin as he bounced on the balls of his feet. "In the chaos, I sniffed you out, Selene Abbott. The drawings—handmade from a prisoner?"

Beatrice's charcoal pieces. That fox shifter made them for me, no one else on the intake crew, and I tacked them up next to my computer monitor so I could always see them. "Technically, she was... a volunteer, not a prisoner."

While Draco rolled his eyes, Balor snorted. "Of course, blackbird. You tell yourself that."

"I—"

"You had other photos too," he carried on. "Pictures of friends—you looked quite young. Your false family. Your coworkers. Trinkets and collectibles. All gifts, I assume?"

Your false family. I barely heard what came after that.

They had been right about so much since they took me. Maybe Dad—

"You value what is *worthy* of it," Balor remarked, poking at the spitted meat chunk with a frown. "Friendship, family, personal touches—thoughtful and grounded."

Huh. I fidgeted with my ever-sharpening black talons, faded obsidian bleeding into the tops of my fingers today. No one had ever put that much time into considering *me* before. Sure, under Dad's long-term management plan, doctors and Cronus researchers were all about my body— bloodwork, hormone levels, bone marrow, symptoms and pain scale and how long can you run on a treadmill at varying speeds before you finally collapse. Not when you ask to stop, beg and cry and gasp for air—when your body fully gives out.

Nothing like this.

"You were *ours*." Charm mixed with unwavering *possession*, Arawn's voice licked up my inner thighs and wringed pleasure from my core. He stood slowly, his stature tall and imposing, bonfire smoke coiling around him. "There wasn't anything else to know, little one." He spread his arms, daring me to argue, but anything I might have come up with before this conversation fell flat. The little nod he lobbed my way told me he understood perfectly. "The rest will come in time."

I opened my mouth because I figured I had to. Seriously, I couldn't give in this fast. What had felt like years had, in reality, only been a week and a half. It... *No*. Love didn't work like this, right? You had to, you know, hear each other fart and get in a real fight over something dumb and see if they left the dishes to soak or put them straight in the dishwasher—all that boring stuff.

"But—"

"Why did you choose *us*?"

We all rounded on Draco again, still seated in a compact ball, knees to his chest, the tips of his shoes dusted with sand. His jaw flickered through a clench, as if the attention ruffled his feathers.

"This is mutual," he insisted. Despite the flat tone, the slight eyebrow quirk spoke volumes. "The kiss is always returned. *Why*, Selene? Can you even answer yet?"

I sucked in my cheeks, face on fire as the scrutiny swung back around to me. So, this was how it felt to be put on the spot, huh? Slit yourself open and bare your soul. Spill your guts all over the floor.

Maybe not the most tactful approach. Maybe I owed them a little more credit for coming up with everything they had.

"I-I..." How to put my feelings into words. How to take every wayward thought, every dream, every absent study of their bodies, every goose bump raised by their voices, every tear shed from their kindness—and cram it all into a few coherent sentences.

Before I could stammer a single syllable, however, an intense wave of nausea pounded into me. My knees buckled and my muscles seized, and I frantically staggered for the gazebo arch, catching myself on it with a strangled wail. Fire blazed up my throat, worse than any backbreaking acid reflux I'd suffered in the past, stronger than any painful heave and gag before I emptied my guts in the toilet, so angry and downright *mean*—

"Selene—"

"*Shit.*"

I stumbled out under the starless sky, clutching my gut and tumbling into the sand. As footsteps raced after me, I folded over, expecting to vomit a whole lot of nothing, to dry-heave until my throat bled and I couldn't see through the tears—

But then a violent scream sprinted up my throat, hellfire gone nuclear, and the force ripped my head back. The noise that tore out and cracked like thunder down the beach didn't *sound* like me—more a string of female voices, a chorus of screechy sopranos and flat altos, their harmonies ugly. Figures fell into the sand around me, but I barely saw them, barely felt Arawn's strong embrace from behind or

Balor grabbing my face as if to stop my head from wrenching all the way back and snapping my neck.

A few seconds later, *darkness* shot from my mouth, barreling over my lips and out my nostrils, shadow and mist and smoke hurdling skyward. In my mind, it dragged on for an eternity, my eyes tearing, my throat burning—but then it stopped.

The voices, the smoke, the contortion of my spine.

A black cloud splashed with electric purple hovered over us for a moment as I collapsed onto Arawn, then zipped out over the water like an arrow, vanishing into the night.

Gone.

Just like that.

A brutal birth—and that was that. No more nausea or heartburn. Exhaustion trickled through my limbs, cool and calm, soothing like aloe vera on a burn. I blinked the tears away, gulping down shaky breaths, broken in the sand and relying solely on Arawn to stay vertical.

"Blackbird..." Balor shuffled closer, crouched but still looming over me, his massive frame obscuring my view of the sea. "You've got your eyes back."

I blinked up at him, then Draco as he leaned into view. Given the grooves around us, the trench in the sand, he must have marched another protective circle around me, Balor, and Arawn while all *that* happened.

Not exactly the most cuddly-feely of the three, but knowing for sure now that he'd stand guard while the rest of us were busy suddenly made me breathe easier.

And with Arawn cradling me to his chest, I finally found the strength to lift my arms again, clumsily smearing the damp off my face, tears on my cheeks and saliva around my mouth.

"W-was that it?"

Draco turned back to the sea, then to me. Sea, me, sea, me. Then, after a long study of the horizon, he shrugged one shoulder. "It would appear so."

"Oh." Well, it happened fast, if anything. Exhaustion settled in deeper, followed by an emptiness that took my breath away. "I, uh..." Fresh tears stung the backs of my eyes. "I don't feel like a mom."

"Oh, sweet thing," Arawn murmured, bundling me up in both arms, his borrowed jacket suddenly feeling so big compared to his embrace. "Our offspring don't need to be nurtured... Try not to think of the process like that."

An hour ago, I found out I was pregnant for the first time.

And then it was over.

I'd been so upset, so uncertain, and now I was just... lost, unsure if I should feel devastated or relieved. Broken or grateful. I... I couldn't decide.

Rather than hiding them behind my curls, I let the tears fall, wetness trailing down my cheeks with one hard blink. Balor was on them in a second, roughly brushing the streams away with his thumbs.

"I-is there some sort of, uh, birth control I can take for this?" I managed. While the thought of *more* medication made my skin crawl, I had to ask.

"Not that I am aware of," came Draco's monotone response, and I nodded weakly, pleased I didn't need to explain women's birth control options to three primordial beings.

"I don't want to go through *that* every time we have sex," I blurted, *instantly* regretting it, snapping my lips together and hiding my flushed face behind my hands. While Arawn chuckled and nuzzled my curls, I caught

Balor perking up through my fingers, leering at me, his smile pure sin, so much darker and devious than the literal demons I'd faced down earlier.

"Are you saying you're hungry for more, blackbird?" He sidled closer, his heat a thrill, his presence domineering and powerful and—

"*Enough.*" Arawn kept the monster at bay, slapping a hand over Balor's smirking face and shoving him back. He then refocused on me, both arms wrapped in a protective embrace, his influence soft and cozy. "Little one, there is *much* more to intimacy than penetrative sex. Much, much more."

I swallowed hard, hating that I, at twenty-five, needed to be reminded of that.

Because, honestly, I figured they'd only want sex. The *more* hadn't even factored in, no matter how many smutty books and online fics I'd devoured and fantasized about over the years.

"Besides," he drawled, smoothing my hair over my shoulder, then tucking a few wayward frizzies behind my ear, "we can't drown the world in shadow." When I peeked back, hiding beneath my damp lashes, he offered a gentle grin that didn't quite reach his eyes. Instead, the black rebelled against his cozy nature, burning molten, hot and fiery and full of want, just like last night. "We *all*—" Arawn side-eyed Balor. "—have to control ourselves now that we've found each other."

"Speak for yourself, brother." Balor pressed a huge hand to his chest in mock disappointment. "*I*, for one, am a paragon of control and virtue."

A snort slipped out before I could catch it, one of those big, obnoxious, embarrassing, full-on little piggy snorts that made *everyone* turn on you. Once they did, I buried my face in my hands again and groaned, the flirtatious energy flatlining fast, reality such a fucking buzzkill.

"Are you hurt, Selene?"

What a question, Draco. "Uh..." I peeked at him over my fingertips. *"Yeah."*

They were all on me in a flash, searching for the wound, working my limbs, manhandling my arms and fingers and feet and toes—

"Stop, stop... Not physically." I wriggled out of the pile and crawled for freedom, scrambling to my feet to search the horizon for *our* darkness. Nothing. It was long gone by now. Gnawing at the insides of my cheeks, I then whipped around, wishing they could just *see.* Know. They read me so well before, and I didn't want to share what really hurt the most now.

I mean, yes, the birth of literal darkness scared the shit out of me. In hindsight, however, it wasn't... horrible. Jarring. Abrupt. Barely long enough of an ordeal to connect to or invest in anything on an emotional level. And, sure, it hurt when it happened, and my throat ached now from the scream, my back sore from the forced bend—but I'd had worse. For days and weeks on end, I had struggled through symptom flares that felt like literal torture, day and night, on and on and on until I just wanted to *die.*

I could handle a flash-bang like this in my sleep.

"I'm hurt because..." It felt like a betrayal to say it out loud, but what was the point of hiding it anymore? "Because he..." Dad's face flashed across my mind's eye, hawkish and unimpressed, dour and judgmental, annoyed and tense and secretive and selective and such a fucking *liar* —and rage detonated inside like a nuke. "Because he *crippled* me—on purpose!"

CHAPTER EIGHTEEN

"He didn't prepare me for this. I don't know how to do *anything*." An icy numbness set in at the thought. "My dad... He always put me in things to keep me busy, and I thought it was good because then I wasn't so focused on how shitty I felt. But he... He..." *For years, he got away with it.* "He was the one who did it to me—with the meds, with my meals, *everything*."

I rounded on my trio again, silent as the grave and eyeing me like they'd never blink again. A week ago, I would have folded under that kind of attention. Now, I stood taller —even when everything inside wanted to shrivel up and die.

"First he shoved me into daycare at Cronus, then school and activities and only friends *he* approved of..." Never had a choice. *He* selected my friends from the first day, and I stayed with them, my nerdy academic clique, until graduation twelve years later. "Then working at *his* job, where he calls the shots, and I... I just..." I threw my hands up, my next words so pathetic, so full of ache and want, so pitchy and frantic. "I've never *lived*. I never considered a relationship with anyone before. I never thought about *my* needs, because... because *surviving* day to day was good enough. I never... I don't even know how to take the fucking *bus* by myself."

While Draco just stared and Balor cracked his knuckles, his neck, his jaw, Arawn glided closer, all soft and gooey in the way he made himself smaller, ducking down to my level with a warm smile.

"Little one, I think you're being rather harsh on yourself." His elegant fingers wrapped around my forearms, then gently pried my wringing hands apart. "You know a great deal more about the *real* world than most of this planet." He flicked his gaze between Balor and Draco, then back to me as he kissed the tops of my hands.

"But that's..." Sure, I knew the supernatural existed, and after years on the intake crew, I could, in theory, handle myself with most species. Not that I had ever been trained to fight, or anything, but the mental vault full of strengths and weaknesses was there if I ever really desperately needed it. But that wasn't what bothered me. People my age —the independence they'd had, all this life they'd been allowed to live, the opportunity to learn and grow and make mistakes... "That's just not—"

"The shackles are gone," Balor said gruffly. After a kiss to each of my palms, Arawn swept aside, as if to allow his brothers proper access to me again. The largest of the three raised one massive fist and *snapped* his fingers, the sound cracking down the beach and making the bonfire flare. "Chains broken. It's time to learn—let your curiosities soar. Wouldn't you like that, little raven?"

Little raven. I swallowed hard. That was new, but maybe more appropriate with the way the black on my fingers had trickled down to the top knuckle, nails like raven talons, skin obsidian, darker than all their eyes combined.

Would it swallow my whole hand?

My arm?

All of me?

Fun. A new thing about my body to feel annoyed and helpless about.

"I've never had a boyfriend," I admitted, only partially aware that I'd let this specific train of thought run off the rails. "Last night was the first time I've had sex, and I'm fucking twenty-five years old. Guys have always seemed so... so put off by me, and I barely... I've never..." I gestured to Balor, low enough on his huge frame to make a point. A blush exploded across my face when his lips quirked, something dark and dangerous taking over, lusty and unmistakable. Shaking my head, I looked to the starless sky with a huff. "It's pathetic. And he did it to me. He said he loved me, and he did it anyway."

Dad hadn't just clipped my wings all these years.

He ripped them out, over and over again, so I would *never* fly.

Now, did he do it because he wanted to help, or because he had no problem hurting me, treating me like one big science experiment?

That was the question.

"Give yourself credit, little one," Arawn drawled, absently brushing the sand from my legs, starting at my thighs and working his way down. "You're a clever girl—highly adaptable. You pick up fast, and the rest... We'll teach you."

"Great." I rolled my eyes, fully aware that I still sounded like a toddler throwing another tantrum, but, shit, I'd earned this one too. Despite the pain, the symptoms, the constant doctor visits and the finagling with my dosages, the rarely ever going out on weekends like the rest of my friends —I never complained. Never. Not where *he* could see, anyway. Tears were for after dark, alone in my bed or in the shower.

"Oh, cheer up." Balor dissolved into black mist, which then zipped over the sand and twisted into a man again behind me in a flash. His burly arms circled my waist, and despite my mood, I let out a little squeal-giggle when he jerked me back onto my toes. Nose to my throat, he rumbled through a rich, deep inhale, adding a hint of teeth at my ear as he whispered, "Lessons with us will be *fun*."

I sucked in my cheeks, fighting a smile that broke through when he snapped at my earlobe. "Oh yeah?"

A gentle breeze gusted down the shoreline, carrying with it the scent of fatty, salty meat left to simmer high above the bonfire. Saliva filled my mouth, tummy gurgling, interest piqued—and then plunged inward when something hard and obvious nudged at my lower back.

"Tell me," Balor urged in a heated whisper, his hands suddenly delving lower, smoothing possessively down to my thighs, "has any male ever had the *privilege* of your exquisite mouth around their cock?"

Fire blasted across my face, and, embarrassed as hell, I tried to squirm away, only for Balor to hold tighter and angle me in Draco's direction. The palest of the bunch stiffened, our gazes crashing together.

"N-no," I managed, breath coming a little faster as Balor forced me one step at a time closer to Draco. "But I've... touched... you know, over pants—"

"Perfect." He squeezed my thighs, his purr stoking the darkness in my chest, and then scooped me up to carry me a few paces closer. "Lesson number one..." He then planted me in the sand and eased off, leaving me there on my own two feet, heat swelling between my thighs, nipples painfully hard under Arawn's jacket. One playful swat at my backside earned him a glare over my shoulder, but Balor just grinned, as wickedly handsome as all the old texts claimed Lucifer to be, and then clapped his hands together, their collision like the *crack* of an avalanche. "Remember this, little raven: you can bring the most powerful creatures in this realm to heel with your gorgeous mouth."

"By words," Arawn added, seeming to float *over* the sand toward Draco, his chuckles silky smooth, "or by touch."

As if sensing he had suddenly become prey in a pack of apex predators, Draco's thin mouth turned in a beautiful downward arc—but he only managed one half step back before Arawn's shadowy wisps materialized behind him. In solid form, the sweetest of the three, the one I always looked to for comfort, flashed a devilish grin, clamped his hands on Draco's shoulders, then cut him off at the knees. One good kick and he went down, crashing to the sand, on his back and flailing, effortlessly pinned by Arawn.

All I needed was the gentlest of pressure on *my* shoulders and I folded, Balor crouched alongside me as I settled on my hands and knees.

"Do you feel his eyes on you?" His harsh baritone slithered around my skull, and I knew if I looked back, I'd find that sinful smile and nothing more, his words for me and me alone. Balor nudged my thighs, hand big enough to press against both, and I crawled forward. "The way he hunts you, craves you..." I stilled at Draco's once polished shoes, now dusty like the rest of him, and when Balor spoke this time, his words touched all of us. "That is *power*, little raven."

"W-what happened to blackbird?" I choked out,

mapping the sharp bend of Draco's knees, his long, spidery limbs all stiff and tense.

"It's time to scale up the predatory hierarchy." Balor's knuckles ghosted down my thighs and along my calves, his voice like sandpaper—and how I *needed* its bite. "With strides gained, perspective changes."

Had I leveled up now that I'd unleashed a new shadow monster on the world?

Or was all this one big distraction?

Just like Dad.

I closed my eyes tight, jaw clenched, and lit a match under anxiety's tinny whisper.

Because these three—they were *nothing* like him.

Sure, that was still an assumption at this point, but as their captive I had seen more of the world, *done* more as a person, as a grown-up woman with her own wants and needs and desires, than I'd ever accomplished under my dad's strict roof.

So, with a gulp and a deep breath, I inched forward, carefully crawling through the sand—and between Draco's long legs. His knees opened somewhat to make room, but he stayed stiff and expressionless, locked on me, his muddled gaze totally unreadable. Behind him, Arawn loomed tall and powerful, matching Draco's intensity stride for stride, though his ravenous eyes danced between me, Balor, and Draco, as if utterly enthralled by the show.

My first gentle caress along Draco's right calf made him hiss, his head lolling back, so I rolled with it, surrendering to the distraction, to the distance this moment put between *me* and what happened tonight and twenty-five long years of bullshit. Both hands whispered up his legs to his inner thighs, and I exhaled shakily, smitten with how he responded to my touch. For a creature with no outer emotions, expressions few and far between, *this*, his jaw tightening and his hands fisting and his eyes hooded—this might be my new addiction. A thrill to chase and conquer, the others watching on, their interest spurring the pleasurable tightness in my core.

But, really, did anyone need a lesson on how to give a blowjob?

Male anatomy struck me as *very* straightforward, Draco's shaft already rock-solid beneath his slacks from the most basic touch.

"I don't think I need to be taught how to—"

"Unbuckle his belt," Balor urged, his hand delving between my thighs to cup me. I drew in another trembling breath, his hand warm and firm—and way too still. No rubbing. No stroking my slick folds. Not teasing my clit. He just palmed me, the promise of more pluming between us. Once I did as I was told, undoing Draco's belt, he gave me the *slightest* movement.

Not enough.

"Good girl," he rasped. *Never enough.* "Now the zipper..." His free hand walked up my back as I complied, each dig of his fingertips firm, not stopping until he reached my shoulder. "Free him, but no need to fully undress."

Draco's hiss surpassed the roar of the tide this time. As soon as I delved under his briefs, his head fell back again, hanging heavy at Arawn's chest, his hips bucking ever so slightly in my loose fist. Control bristled off me, already starting to understand what Balor meant about bringing a creature *this* powerful to heel.

"Silky, isn't it?" he mused as I cupped the head of Draco's cock, the skin so soft yet so taut. "But it needs slickness."

Duh. No one wanted a dry handjob. Clearing my

throat, I lowered my head, then yelped when Balor pinched my clit out of nowhere, brusque and punishing.

"Just the head to start," he added when I glared back at him. Smoke spiraled off his shoulders. Dimples poked through all that rough facial hair, his smile a mile wide and bright as a full midsummer moon. Black mist tousled his hair, like he was slowly losing his physical form to the darkness, succumbing to his base self. With another gulp, I checked on Arawn, and while his eyes read blacker than usual, his focus singular now—*me*—he seemed more in control.

Until I eased down again. His nostrils flared, black skittering up his neck in beautiful ribbons beneath his skin, veins finally showing themselves. My tongue flicked over my front teeth, imagining what it might be like to trace those shadowy spiderwebs, how he would taste.

Faintly salty, maybe, just like Draco. He jerked in place at my soft exhale, then groaned when I took the silky head into my mouth, the beaded pearl at its tip salty and thick. Desire threaded through my limbs, twisting into beautiful, intricate knots in my belly.

Selene.

Above the crashing surf, the choppy waters, Arawn and Balor's chuckles—there was Draco. Strained and pained, my name offered like a prayer inside my own head, his voice choked when I swirled my tongue around the tip. Braced on his thighs, I proved what an excellent student I had always been and would always be, suckling, saliva leaking down his pale shaft, working him carefully and gently, *very* aware of just how sensitive this area was for men.

My gaze snapped up, darting between Draco and Arawn, and it was then Balor *finally* started to move, stroking my sex, smearing the slick want around, toying ever so slightly with my clit between his two fingers. I moaned, eyes threatening to roll back, and took Draco's cock two inches deeper, my lower back arching of its own volition, exposing more of me to the monster at my back.

In another life, I'd be annoyed that they had found such a simple way to distract me, a game I fell into fully aware that, on some level, it was just a tactic to make me feel better.

Maybe even to make me forget, for a little while anyway, all the baggage I dragged through this world, tonight's *"birth,"* if I could even call it that, just another suitcase added to the load.

And maybe in that other life, I'd be indignant.

Irate.

Pissed off enough to climb out of this cluster of hotness and storm up the beach.

Here, in *this* life, in this moment, I melted.

Putty in Balor's hands—and puppet master pulling all of Draco's strings, Arawn our eager audience.

"Now, spread the wet with your fist," Balor ordered, all rumbly and rich, deep and rough, any semblance of the gorgeous Mediterranean trust fund baby disguise falling away. I didn't need to look to *feel* the monster emerging, his presence swelling, dominating the shoreline, turning the surging water in the corner of my eye inky black and violent. He caressed me with more purpose now, no longer just lazy strokes between my thighs. No, he found the spots that made my hips twitch and my thighs quiver, massaging them, slipping his thumb inside me with ease and anchoring me to him.

Blinking hard, determined to focus on the task at hand, I spread the damp down Draco's cock, up and down, my fist firm but not too tight, every stroke making his hands clench deeper in the sand.

"Your mouth is a *gift*," Balor insisted, his words kind, the sentiment empowering—but his tone delightfully vicious, "one that you choose to share, when and *if* he deserves it. Just like the rest of you—mind, body, heart, and soul. It's yours." He thumbed my inner walls, zeroing in on my G-spot with a vengeance, chuckling when I squealed and tightened around him. "*You* decide what to do with all of it, and who has the right to touch it."

"As if you guys would let anyone else touch me." It came out before I could stop it, a dare, an unspoken promise these three had already delivered on in spades. Draco stilled. Arawn inhaled sharply, visible black veins twining up to his jaw and splitting like lightning into his cheeks. Balor snarled and rubbed me faster, toying with me, tormenting me with his control over *my* pleasure.

Even if none of these ancient beings would heed Balor's sentiment, it resonated with *me*—loud and clear.

I called the shots.

I decided who touched me, when and how. No more strangers. No more men in lab coats and nurses in scrubs. No more strangers examining me with my legs in stirrups. No more insane blood draws and clanky MRI scans.

Mind, body, heart, and soul.

In that moment, it was all *mine*. Finally. For the first time in my life, mine, mine, mine, *mine*.

And I wanted to give it to them.

Bits and pieces, of course. At the end of the day, the only person who had a right to all of me... was me.

I fisted Draco from tip to base with more pressure this time, power storming through my veins, autonomy making my heart *soar*—and he groaned, head tipped back, legs open, fists in the sand, his strangled noises music to my ears.

"I'd say he enjoys you, little one," Arawn mused, he and Balor swapping devious glances, almost as if they found pleasure in Draco's forced surrender, in his tense submission to *me*. Bolder by the minute, I gripped the base of his cock and took the rest as deep as I could in my mouth, only stopping when he hit the back of my throat and made me cough.

Selene scraped along the inside of my skull, over and over again, Draco's voice shredded as he whispered my name like a hymn.

"Oh, the name suits you—bold little raven," the predator at my back growled. Balor sunk his fingers into my hair, catching my head just as it started to bob, slowing everything down to an agonizing pace. "Yes, easy... Slow to start." His grip loosened, and I mirrored his languid up and down, adding extra suction at the head. "Like that. Make him feel like he's going to *die*."

A tremor shuddered down Draco's thighs, followed by a tightening in his core, tendons flaring in his neck as he held himself up, braced on his elbows, to *watch*. Our eyes locked again, a challenge in mine, daring him to stop me, to cut the lesson short if he couldn't take it. His hands eased out of the sand, then plunged back in, a telling lip twitch the only visual of his wavering restraint.

And it made me feel *alive*. To tease a piece of an old god, to master him with something so simple—it was glorious.

Intimate.

Precious.

I might have embraced Balor and Arawn's teasing, their chuckles cruel as they walled me and Draco into this one-act performance together—but I wouldn't take advantage of it.

Him.

I wouldn't take advantage of the gaunt figure on his back, beautiful and divine in his own way, who let me experiment and *learn* with such a sensitive part of him.

Is this trust? Pure and uncut?

Focusing on the task at hand, I varied my pace, head bobbing, drool dribbling, jaw already a little sore but my spirit beyond determined to please both my victim *and* my teacher. Balor continued to stroke between my thighs, caressing me, palming my clit, sweeping his thumb over it with the same rhythm I sucked Draco.

Until he thrust two fingers into me out of nowhere, both sliding in *way* too easily, heat coiling tighter in my belly and pleasure throbbing from my clit. I whimpered and jolted up, lips open, brain off, submitting to the way he claimed me, pumping, caressing my inner walls with more precision and tact than with his thumb.

He had a goal in mind here.

To make me scream all over Draco's cock, pulling the strings inside tighter and tighter, hoping to make them *snap*—

"Focus, Selene," Arawn purred, his cozy chastisement paired with a knuckle at my chin. He tapped me back to the present, tsking. "Stay with *him*."

Which him?

Balor, his fingers demanding my full attention, my complete and utter submission.

Or Draco splayed beneath me, cock hard and proud with a slight blush at its tip.

Nibbling my lower lip for a moment, I went back to Draco. *He* was the lesson—Balor was the distraction.

And what a sublime distraction, my next hapless moan muffled, my mouth full and my fist pumping—but that *sound* harmonized so beautifully with Draco's raspy groan. As my hips started to rock back onto Balor's hand, my rhythm a mess up here, Draco moved too, bucking into my mouth to set his own tempo.

"You stop him," Balor ordered gruffly. "So impudent, this one."

Mind slowly drowning in hazy pleasure, I clamped both hands to Draco's narrow hips and shoved him into the sand, which unleashed a chorus of laughter from Arawn and Balor. Our gazes tangled, me and Draco, his on fire and mine just struggling to stay open.

"He's usually quite the dominant lover," Arawn insisted, patting Draco's cheek—then rearing back with a snort when Draco *snapped* at his fingers, teeth clacking hard. My eyes widened and shot Arawn's way, and he grinned, ruffling Draco's white hair before planting that hand on his chest, both of us pinning him down. "Yes, I know, hard to imagine given all *this*."

"Draco fucks like he wants to obliterate," Balor added, his pace quickening, fingers working me on the inside while his free arm twisted around my waist and, oh, *shit*, gave my clit some attention. "I promise, when he gets his hands on you, little raven, you won't be able to walk until the next morning."

I took Draco deeper, whimpering at the visual.

"And that was with lovers who didn't *matter*." Arawn beamed down at me, the brazen affection contrasting sharply with the way he slammed his other hand to Draco's chest, really forcing him to stay still. "With you, little one—he'll wreck you, and you'll sob your gratitude while I kiss it all better. Would you like that?"

"*Enough*," Draco growled, twitching when I nearly took all of him in my mouth this time, tongue dragging along the underside of his shaft. "Leave her be, both of you."

"It's part of the lesson," Arawn said gruffly, casually clamping down Draco's throat instead while his free hand swept through his black waves. "Selene, remember that submission is a *choice*. It's trust and respect. It's ownership and love. Draco offers it to *you* and only you—in exchange for what *you* give him. Never forget, a give-and-take—"

"Balance," I finished for him with a grin, the word wet and thick. Arawn hesitated for a moment, as if taken aback —or maybe he'd finally heard the way Balor's fingers made a slick sound with every thrust into me. Either way, a smile soon bloomed across his face, and he nodded slowly as I got back to the task at hand.

"Yes," he purred, pure velvet, the black under his skin snaking across his powerful hands now too. "*Balance*. Good girl."

See. I pay attention.

More than they knew, all three shaping into separate individuals in my mind's eye, unique and different and glorious in their own ways. Not a pack. Not just a trio. Not tatters of a cloak—Balor, Arawn, Draco.

Combining my mouth and my fist, I moved faster, encouraged by Draco's voice in my head and the groans he made aloud. Balor mirrored my pace, really driving into me, circling my clit with his free hand, dragging me closer and closer to the edge—

Draco beat me to it, tumbling into the black first. His cock shuddered, then stiffened, hot spurts of salty liquid coating my mouth. It came out of nowhere, which meant I barely had time to swallow it down. I did my best, using his hips for balance now as his sandy hands fisted in my hair, his hips bucking through a climax that made the sky darken and the sea sing.

My orgasm landed just as abruptly, trickling like a slow-burn volcano. Not the ones with some dramatic eruption, lava shooting into the sky—but hot, molten, *thick* magma rippling down the side of the black rock, creeping like fog, slow and steady. I squealed at the flutter in my core, the pulse of heat and pleasure in my chest, then pulled back from Draco at last.

And only because he let me, loosening that punishing hold on my hair so I could bolt up and writhe through the storm of heat and pleasure and bliss. Way, way out across the water, thunder rumbled. Nothing like last night—but still.

Two for two. Maybe I had more sway in the world than I thought.

"Well done," Balor rumbled, patting my ass when I finally eased back on my heels, his hand sticky with *me*. As warmth coursed through my body, relaxation kicking in, I expected him to grab me and fling me over.

Take what *he* wanted. Relieve that huge erection straining against his slacks.

"Lesson learned, I think," he added, and while he brushed a few random curls off my forehead, then wiped the sweat away with his shirtsleeve, he didn't try anything else. Arawn neither, his posture relaxed as he settled in the sand, lounging like a Roman emperor on his elbow.

"Like I said," he drawled. "A clever girl. She'll conquer the world before you know it."

I snorted weakly. Sure. *Sure.* Compliments were great, but keep it realistic.

Draco sat up wordlessly, emotionless as he tucked himself away with one hand—while the other threaded with mine. Our gazes met one last time, and I ignored the rest of his face, the severe features and the ghostly pallor, focusing on the blazing warmth there instead.

He squeezed my hand.

I squeezed back.

And there, just for a moment, I swore he smiled with his eyes.

Said *thanks* with the slight quirk of his white brows.

I offered a long, purposeful blink in return. *You're welcome.*

A part of me yearned to crawl in his lap, maybe keep this intimacy party going with a good snuggle.

Only Draco wasn't touchy-feely, and I respected that.

Arawn was.

Always *great* for a cuddle, my Arawn.

But then the winds changed, hurling the scent of seasoned meat my way, the bonfire still burning in the shadowy gazebo. Tummy roaring, food a pleasure and no longer a chore, I crawled out of our huddle and toddled across the sand, ready to stuff my face and regroup for a brand-new day, with a brand-new perspective, tomorrow.

CHAPTER NINETEEN

"Why didn't she ever look for me?" Eyes heavy, brain stuffed with enough Greek mythology to last a lifetime, I gently closed yet another Classics tome and slumped in this less than supportive wood chair with a huff. "I mean... She had to have known I was out there."

When no one answered, my gaze cut directly across the book-strewn table to Arawn, then Draco in the shadowy mouth of the nearby stacks. Darkness slanted across his sharp features, and for once, he didn't meet my eye, hiding whatever he actually felt and offering that blank mask instead.

Another squeak echoed across the second floor, followed by a *gasp* and a crash and then the heavy door to the back stairwell slamming shut. Unlike the rest of us, Balor was having the time of his life, feasting on terror in all the dark corners this old college library provided. At the first sign that our day was about to take a turn for the academic, he bailed, leaving the heavy lifting to Arawn and Draco.

After another night spent on an empty Mediterranean

beach, Arawn showed up at dawn with new bags of clothes for me to root through, these a near perfect match for what I had chosen originally from the Dunston boutique. I'd swapped his sandy suit jacket for a black pair of pinstriped slacks and a comfy apricot knit, really leaning into the October vibes. Top that off with a long charcoal trench, pockets oh so deep, and feet in brown women's oxfords, and I *almost* felt stylish when we touched down somewhere in the UK.

Once again, Arawn, Draco, and Balor ferried me around the world in a black cloud, settling this time for a blustery English village. Or—city? It didn't strike me as big and hectic enough to be a booming metropolis, but what did I know? The tidy high streets eventually brought us to this three-story library, cathedral-esque in style and gothic in mood. Given most of the patrons looked roughly my age or younger, I figured it was part of the small college up the road and around the corner.

What it lacked in modern tech beyond the basic communal desktops, the first two floors all bookshelves and grey stonework, the third just couches and study nooks, and the underground archives *very* off-limits—to everyone but creatures who could dissolve into mist and slip through a crack in the door, of course—it made up for in old-world charm. Coat on the back of my chair, I'd hunkered down at an empty table shortly after arrival and watched Arawn and Draco place book after book in front of me, determined that I learn about my mom, goddess of the freakin' night Nyx, through first-edition sources.

Secondary sources were only accepted after I'd griped about not being able to read ancient Greek or Latin. The first hour here had consisted of Arawn translating and Draco correcting him, then the pair devolving into nitpicky snits over grammar and syntax. The three that followed were all me, nose-deep in old and new books, devouring and learning and processing all I could.

Nyx had a lot of kids, apparently.

And they all seemed a hell of a lot more powerful and important than little ol' me.

I mean, the literal *dawn* was said to be her daughter. Light, nightmares—the Fates. Gods Thanatos and Hypnos. One source claimed she had one thousand daughters, then one thousand sons, some *just* from her, many more created with her beloved husband Erebus.

Was I... included in that list?

With so many offspring, did I even matter?

"Nyx has always been lauded as an exceptional mother," Arawn told me after a few moments of careful consideration, his cozy aura briefly dampened by his furrowed brows and handsome frown. "However, Hesiod named her a *protogenoi*—a firstborn deity. She is primordial and ancient, older than dawn and dusk themselves." He reached out for me, but given the width of the obnoxious square table I'd picked on a whim, he needed a few extra inches to take my hand. Dark, lush shadows cleared the divide, curling sweetly around my fingers and up to my wrist, their caress warm and soft. "Little one, your mother is a goddess whose existence extends far, *far* beyond our reach or understanding."

"Oh." I fluttered my fingers through the darkness, smiling weakly when it plumed into mist for me to disperse. "Right. Duh."

"If she has never connected with you, which I consider unlikely," Draco mused from the shadows across the aisle, all tall, gaunt, and creepy in the darkness, "then perhaps she is unaware of your existence."

I turned my hand over, some of Arawn's mist gathering over my palm, and scoffed. "But she's my *mom*, right? She birthed me but has no idea that I—"

"Are you aware of your offspring?"

Yeesh, low blow. I blinked fast, face immediately hot and prickly, and crushed Arawn's mists in a fist. No. I had literally no idea what happened to the *thing* that ripped out of me last night—but the darkness in my heart yearned for it today.

"Not to be cruel," Draco continued, ignoring Arawn's lethal side-eye. "Just to prove a point."

"Parentage works differently amongst the gods and monsters of old," Arawn said gently. A hazy onyx tendril clipped my chin, synchronized with his hand's movement through the air. "We are not shifters who guard our young with our lives, nor are we vampires whose sire bonds bind for all eternity. We are as different from them as night is from day."

I batted his black mists away with another huff, then crossed my arms. *Fair enough.* All things considered, I understood—kind of. Unfair to paint every supernatural entity with the same broad brush, after all. It'd be like getting upset that the porcupine you just rooted out of its den didn't curl up on your lap like the family dog. Life had always been about tempering expectations, and this was no different.

Still, a *little* maternal kindness would have gone a long way.

But that felt like an issue for another day.

Along with figuring out my dad's role in all this—and if he even deserved that title anymore.

Sighing, I stretched my stiff muscles this way and that, arching in the chair and cracking my neck, my jaw, and all ten fingers. Four hours spent under mediocre light in a dusty college library wasn't exactly the most thrilling thing we'd done so far, but the free coffee from the cart downstairs had been supporting me from book to book to—

Damn it.

I tapped the empty paper cup on the table, then appraised what was left of my to-read pile.

"I'm going to grab another coffee." Crowning the remaining two hardbacks with my cup, I pushed the chair back and stretched my legs, really rolling my ankles to get the blood flowing. "After I finish these, can we get lunch?"

Hands threaded and darkness rescinded, Arawn settled into his seat with a nod. "Of course, little one. Anything you want."

Huh. Food had never been optional before. My reborn taste buds craved anything and everything, but today especially, they longed for melted cheese and crusty bread and smoked meats and *grease—*

"Pizza," I said as I fluffed out my slouchy sweater and subtly unwedgied the cotton creeping up my butt. "Let's do pizza."

I then left Arawn and Draco to swap furrowed brows, *pizza* in all its plebian glory seeming like a mystery, then headed through the stacks to the main staircase. Big and wide, made of heavy dark wood and layered with a weathered plum carpet, it had three sets of creaky stairs and two landings to work around to reach the first floor.

Halfway down, the hairs on the back of my neck lifted.

Hello, shadow.

Not *my* shadow, and not my guys, all three of whom were more than welcome to creep after me at this point.

No, this was a flesh-and-blood *dude*, the same one who had dumped his bookbag on a table near ours about two hours ago. He might have clacked away on a laptop, earbuds in and shoulders hunched, radiating pure dork energy that called to the girl I once was—but he didn't fit.

I caught him as I rounded the second landing, stealing a quick glance from the corner of my eye as he sauntered down the staircase after me. Fitted jeans. Blue-and-green checkered button-up, cottony and crinkled. Round glasses and a black beanie. A baby face and a *very* English complexion.

It was a tailored façade.

Beyond that, I'd caught him staring at me over his laptop more than once.

Six times, to be exact. Either he was a straight-up weirdo who wanted to shoot his shot despite the gorgeous men *I* kept making eyes at throughout my study session—or he was yet another Cronus agent sent to bring me back.

Both made my skin crawl.

Scrunching my sleeves up to my elbows, I wove through the library shelves, taking the long way around to the coffee station in the middle of the first floor. Situated next to a small information desk, manned by a baggy-eyed librarian in tweed, it had all the essentials for a quick caffeine fix.

Or so I assumed, anyway. Coffee had never been a part of my vocabulary before today, but once you got around the bitterness and seasoned it just right, it wasn't half-bad.

And, you know what, *fuck it*—given coffee was a pop culture staple and a running joke with people my age, you bet your ass I'd drink as much as I could just to be *normal*.

This time, however, as I grabbed a cup from the stack, I ignored the milk and sugar and cinnamon. Instead, I filled my cup to the brim with piping-hot black coffee, then grabbed a lid. As I capped it, steam pluming out the mouthpiece and making my palm sweat, I looked up.

And there he was.

Directly across the table, copying me exactly, adding a lid to his drink and staring. Our gazes clashed, his a harmless chocolate brown behind glasses with no actual lenses, and I dropped mine fast—like I was embarrassed we'd made eye contact.

Like I was still shy and useless, just a helpless prisoner to three brutal monsters.

For the most part, I *was* still useless—but this wasn't my first rodeo with some Cronus grunt violating my space and bulldozing my boundaries.

It had been happening longer than I could remember.

Enough already.

The darkness in me stirred, interest piqued, the sensation like a cold dread—not for my well-being, but for his. Definitely not human, this creep, but with the coffee table between us, I couldn't get a proper read on what he might be. Not a vampire with the sad but present sunlight trying to breach the cloud cover. Not a fae—those eyes were too plain. A pretty mask, sure.

It was just too *clean*.

Head down, I beelined for the main doors, plan percolating along the way. A few swishy steps down to the cobblestone high street, my curly ponytail bouncing, and I ducked to the immediate right, following the signs for parking in the library's rear lot. A dusty alley stretched ahead, a towering building on either side, the sounds of noonday traffic ricocheting off grey walls and back at me.

But the slap of loafers on cobblestone—that stood out the most. All that cold dread in my chest solidified, fire sparking, the sensation morphing into something *more*. Something dark and deadly, something worthy of the three men upstairs.

The footsteps hastened around the corner, and I slowed, popping off my coffee lid and allowing him to catch up, head cocked, listening, waiting until he was *right* there—

I then whipped around and flung my coffee at him. The scalding liquid nailed him right in the face, and my new shadow stumbled back with a shout, those ridiculous velvet shoes snagging over each other. He careened into the library wall, frantically wiping the steaming black wet out of his eyes, sputtering furiously in a language too harsh to be from this world.

"Hi." Pulse pounding between my ears, adrenaline finally an asset, I crumpled my cup and chucked it at him just as he yanked off those fake glasses. "I don't know *what* you are, exactly, but I'm not interested in going back to Cronus."

Not yet, anyway.

Not until I understood *everything*. Not until I had all the answers.

And unlike Cronus HQ, unlike Dad, my captors seemed hell-bent on me finding every last one of them, no matter where they had to fly.

Beanie soon on the ground next to the glasses, my would-be attacker rounded on me with bared teeth and black eyes.

Demon.

Again.

Fear nipped at my heels, instinct whispering for me to *go*, slow and steady—back away to a spot with more escape routes.

But then there was Draco at the mouth of the alley.

Just standing there.

Neutral, arms dangling by his sides, head tipped—eyes molten.

His presence bolstered me. Someone—three of them—finally had my back. Anytime I fumbled, there they were, waiting, ready to catch me so I finally stopped splitting my head open on the ground. No more humiliating metaphorical face-plants, not with Arawn, Balor, and Draco by my side.

So, dumb as it was to goad a demon, I smirked and nodded in Draco's direction, then waited, arms crossed, for this black-eyed shit to twist around—

And realize he was outgunned.

His shoulders stiffened, and when he faced me again, he ground his teeth, the two rows no longer pearly white and straight but jaundice-yellow and sharp, like he had filed every single tip by hand. He lurched two menacing steps closer, but this time I held my ground. My muscles tensed. My *fight* alarm dinged.

No flight. No fear, Selene. You're not alone anymore.

The demon skittered to a halt, head snapping up, full black gaze suddenly fixed somewhere on the library's exterior. Knowing full well what he saw, I still glanced over my shoulder—then up to the vents, from which black smoke spilled like raging floodwaters.

"You can try your luck," I told him, "but I'd take the out and run if I were you. My boys have a taste for demon flesh."

Snarling, he spun on his toes, as if to launch into a sprint, then crashed into Draco.

Draco, who looked like a strong breeze might snap him in half.

Draco, who grabbed the demon's mouth and pried it open, one hand for the upper jaw, the other for the lower. One sharp jerk and the demon howled, his cheeks split down the middle, black blood oozing, his limbs flailing—

talons slashing blindly at Draco's face. My heart skipped a beat, but they only left four faint pink lines on his skin, the damage minimal.

Minimized even further as a roaring black tornado engulfed the pair, Balor's influence shattering windows somewhere nearby, his wrath trembling down the alley and shivering underfoot.

"Are you all right, little one?"

"Yeah." I nodded, focused on the ball of shadowy carnage as Arawn solidified in my periphery. "I guess."

It was over in less than a minute, but for the demon who lay in pieces at Draco and Balor's feet, his black eyes gone and only empty sockets left, his jaw locked in a tortured wail—his death must have felt like it lasted *years*.

"How do they keep finding me?" I muttered as Arawn wrapped an arm around my shoulders. I nestled closer, safe and supported under his wing while Balor and Draco gathered what was left of my most short-lived shadow— hands and feet, limbless torso and decapitated head—and then haphazardly tossed everything between the row of trash bins along the other building. Black demonic blood streaked their faces, their hands, but their natural mists hopped to, skimming their flesh like suckerfish on a shark, tidying the leftovers after a feast.

Usually, these three had something to say no matter what I asked.

Here, now, they swapped glances and kept me out of the loop.

"*What?*" My cheeks heated as I scooted out from under Arawn's arm, glaring from one to the next to the next. After a few tense moments of silence, Arawn sighed—of course he did—and steepled his hands at his lips, scrutinizing me with one eye narrowed.

"We have... a theory."

"Okay," I said with a flourish between us. "Please share it with the rest of the class."

Balor snorted, using his thumb to pick at his teeth. "You're really not going to like it."

"At all," Draco added as my scowl deepened, his back to me as he returned all the lids to their proper bins. *Awesome.* I closed my eyes and took a deep breath, blocking out the hubbub of village life beyond this alleyway, the stench of dead demon ripening by the second, foul and rotten and heavy on the sulfur.

"I don't like most things that are *theorized* about me," I stressed. "Just..." Head back, studying the steadily darkening overcast, I braced for the next wave of bullshit. "Just, you know, say it now so we can get ahead of it."

And stop playing catch-up already.

No more surprises.

"Right, Selene..." Arawn took my hand, and I blanched at the distinct lack of *little one*—at the tension stringing together words that were supposed to sound like velvet and honey and silk and *calm*. "Here's the thing..."

CHAPTER TWENTY

The *thing* sucked.

A lot.

And it sucked a whole lot more when it stopped being just a theory. Not a hypothesis, not a guess, not a shot in the dark—but cold, hard, painful *fact*.

"The building is clear," Balor announced, striding through a doorway so trim it forced him to duck and turn to the side just to fit. Behind him, Draco had to lower his head somewhat, but his sleek build had no issues passing through the unfinished frame, nails stuck in the wood at random, nocks and marks left for future construction.

Fiddling with my fingers, I just nodded, coated in a full-body sweat and emotions all over the place. Not exactly a surprise that the building was empty: this town teetered on abandoned, stores boarded up, fast-food joints closed, streets littered with foreclosure and seizure signs. We had swapped a cozy English hamlet with stunning old-world architecture for a dying town somewhere in the American Midwest.

This building in particular probably hadn't seen life in

years, the dust insane, the corners full of cigarettes and trash from squatters long gone. Shredded tarps hung from doorways, empty window sockets, even half-finished walls. At some point, there were grand plans for a mid-rise just off Main Street.

Now, it sat empty, forgotten and disheveled. The floor supports were questionable. Exposed insulation aplenty. The roof leaked on the top floor, and any windows that *had* been set were just busted shards on the frame now.

We eventually settled on this third-floor suite with the walls painted—at least primed—and the floors finished. It might have looked nice at some point, maybe even ready for showings, but visitors had graffitied the paint job and chewed up the laminate years ago.

But unlike the rest of the building, it felt moderately stable. Unfinished, sure, but the best of the worst by far.

Arms crossed, Arawn scowled down at me after some heated back-and-forth with his fellow cloak tatters, their conversation silent and all eyes.

"Little one," he started, his calm tenuous and his control wavering, "I think you're being a bit brash about this—"

"No medication. No drugs." I stabbed a finger between us for emphasis, then looked to Balor and Draco for backup —but from their terse expressions, I might be on my own here. "I don't want any *ever* again."

"This will be painful—"

"I can take *pain*," I argued, cutting Draco off, the crack in my voice a cry for help—a plea for them to understand why I never, ever, *ever* wanted to be drugged and doped up again, even in circumstances when, logically, I should have been out cold.

Balor clicked his tongue at me, his beastly gaze sweeping across what was probably going to be a combined living and dining space. "No one is asking you to be a martyr."

"I know." And no one ever would again. "I'm making the choice for myself."

Huh. Definitely a lot of clenched fists and jaws in here tonight, the air electric, their feelings stormy and *very* out in the open. They didn't approve. Not one bit. Not Arawn, who usually had my back. Not Draco, always ready to offer a hand and make the world go quiet. And definitely not Balor, shrouded in shadow, who had been ready to level the entire town when we realized their theory held weight.

I flinched when Arawn reached for me. While my body craved his, desperate to climb into his soothing embrace and ride out the incoming hellstorm in his arms, he moved just as Balor prowled closer and Draco positioned himself almost strategically at one of my obvious exits.

As much as these three catered to my wants and needs, there was always the chance that they might finally overpower me and force my hand. Do what *they* thought was best—what they thought I deserved.

"I can give you a pleasant sleep," Arawn murmured, his eyes glossy and his words clipped. "Little one, I can make it comfortable—"

"*No.*" If my tone didn't drive the point home, then hopefully my stomp, literally putting my foot down, would. "No, guys, *please.* It's my body. I want to know what's happening to it... even if it sucks."

Even if it sucks.

What a fucking understatement.

The unspoken sentiment glared back at me in their eyes, in their tight mouths and stiff postures. We all knew this would more than suck, but I could take it.

Anyway, I was all cried and raged out at this point, just needing this to be over.

Arawn, Balor, and Draco had a theory about why demons always found us: I had been marked. At some point in my life, I must have been branded with a demonic rune, my flesh scorched with the sigil of some demon house allied with Cronus so they could always find me.

When they first floated it, I'd laughed in their faces.

No way.

No way in *hell* would Dad allow that. Besides, they had seen my naked body, and if there had been some scar with tiny runes and a house symbol, surely that would have caught their eye.

And, realistically, they then all would have lost their shit and gone after the demon.

A possessive bunch, my shadow monsters.

Trackers—brandings, scars, whatever—were old news to a Cronus agent, especially someone who worked intake. While not every demon dealt specifically in soul deals and debts, they were *all* extremely controlling over their belongings, and that included any human who entered into a contract with them. Arawn had therefore theorized, given Cronus's involvement in the supernatural world, that before doctors found a way to temper my innate abilities, they had used the ancient power of demonic runes to bind me.

Like a choke chain with a long, long, *long* leash, the brand would not only cull my earliest gifts, but it meant that should I ever escape, any demon from that specific house would always be able to find me.

Bring me back—for a steep fee, no doubt.

Again, I'd laughed.

Dad wouldn't let anyone do that to me, whether I was a

lab experiment or not. I had to believe that—had to think that he wasn't *that* awful a human being.

After our run-in with the library lurker, we bailed on England, grabbed some food and supplies in New York City, then landed here. I ate, stomach in knots. I relieved myself in a hole that was meant for a toilet one day. I kept putting off the strip search, refusing to believe it.

But in the end, they found three.

Three binding runes on my scalp, under my hair where no one could see unless they shaved me bald.

Three *fucking* demonic brands that they had scorched into my *head* as a baby.

Animals.

Cowards.

Monsters.

And after my breakdown, betrayal forever a bitter pill to swallow, the darkness in my soul howling so long and so vicious that eventually her agony shredded up *my* throat and emptied its grief into the night sky—after all that, we discussed how to get rid of them.

As Arawn held me and Balor buried his fist in the walls again and again and Draco circled us all in shadow, I knew the answer.

The only way to break a demon's hold on you was to cut off the brand.

Right down to the bone—excise it and burn it.

And that was what we were going to do.

Before we left this decrepit building in this fading town, one of them was going to slice the runes off so I could watch *fire* consume the last of my chains.

For now, I watched a stiff Arawn wrench off his suit jacket, toss it aside, and get to work in the shadows. Like a master conductor, he drew darkness from the corners of the room, through the shattered windows open to a starry night sky. Mist and smoke coiled from his hands. Black veins scattered violently under his skin. He painted with elegant fingers, slowly creating a bed in the center of the space big enough for four. Black and billowy, misty and weeping shadows, he stacked the mattress high with pillows and blankets, all from *him*, his power. All black, yet every piece unique and discernable.

Beautiful.

A marriage bed.

Arms crossed, I swallowed hard as he jerked his sleeves down and buttoned the cuffs, still tense, still too quiet for my liking. Presentable again, he stalked around his latest creation, right to my side, and swept a hand through his silky waves.

Then frowned at me.

I arched an eyebrow, bracing for the next round of objections.

"For goodness' *sake*, Selene, at least let me take care of you while it happens," he gritted out, and I rolled my lips together, fighting back a grin. For some reason, Arawn as a grumpy Gus, all concerned and rumpled, this moment—*me* —out of his control... *Adorable*. He could pout all he wanted. Balor could prowl back and forth, snarl and flash his teeth, his eyes bleeding from man to monster by the minute. Draco could suck the life out of the room, his emotions a maelstrom playing out in his eyes.

All that—and I still called the shots.

Snagging Arawn's hand in both of mine, I tugged him to the bed, then clambered up.

Not too firm, but nowhere near soft.

Just the way I liked my mattresses.

Draco and Balor followed, and while Draco hung back

out of sight, his presence swelling behind me, Balor pounced on the bed, his eyes glinting with unseen flames. My dad's betrayal, Cronus's tactics with these tracking runes—he'd lost it when they found the first one. Gone was the breathtaking fallen angel crawling toward me now, tanned and toned, big and burly and *mine*. In his place, a shadow beast with wings ripping from his back, claws two feet long and brutally sharp. Since then, he had managed to reel in the chaos and the terror, the nightmares in his core, but I could still see all of it *fighting* to break free again.

We would burn the world for her.

I saw it now, what they could have done with all their feelings had I not needed them right here beside me. Because, brave as I tried to be, determined as I was to make the tough call and stick with it—deep down, below the darkness and the wrath and the devastation, that little girl who was terrified of the procedure room, of the operating theater, of the men in white coats and masks who promised it wouldn't hurt but it *always* did, so, so bad...

She was still in there, clinging to me, begging me not to leave her alone.

So they stayed, Arawn seated at the edge of the bed, Balor at my knees as I got cross-legged and pulled the blankets close. I motioned weakly to the nearest pillow, which Arawn passed over in a flash, and I squeezed it to my chest.

"Okay." With a firm nod, I scooted to the very end of the mattress. "I can do this. Let's go."

Draco's staticky presence closed in at my back, and over my shoulder, I watched him shape his right pointer finger into a shadowy scalpel. My tummy churned and my eyes watered, but at least his hand was steady. Of the three, he was always the most steadfast.

Balor could have lost it—slashed me to ribbons, his rage getting the better of him.

Arawn seemed like he didn't have the heart to make a single cut.

It needed to be Draco.

I hate this.

I closed my eyes tight, the shadows in my soul swirling, stirring, warm and present—like the monster sensed I needed comfort and strength from within. It wasn't enough that these three were here to hold my hand; *I* had to be brave too.

Tears spilled down my cheeks, and I let them.

This would *suck*, but it always did.

The final chain, the last hurt—and then I'd see, feel, taste, *experience* the real me...

Right?

Everything *they* did to me without my consent had to go.

"Tell me to stop and I will," Draco whispered, the dusty old construction lamps we'd placed around the room flickering. Shaking my head, I twisted back just enough to meet his eyes, but I couldn't hold that fierce stare for long, or I'd buckle.

"Don't stop." He couldn't. No matter what, my last link to Cronus needed to *die*. "Even if I scream and cry." My lips wobbled, and I wiped the next batch of tears on the shadowy pillowcase. "Even if I ask you to—*beg* you to... Just get rid of them. Please, Draco." He looked away, and I grabbed his wrist, squeezing, squeezing, *squeezing* until he faced me again. "I need you to do this."

Strong arms wove around me, Arawn coaxing me back around, and Balor eased closer. At first, I wondered if he might cuddle me too—but that thought was a fleeting fancy.

The meanest of the group, the most monster in the pack, he grabbed my forearms, then braced his knees on top of my legs.

Restraints.

He turned wispy and shadowy, his weight only temporarily crushing. While still a stunning male, he faded somewhat, his fingers longer, his teeth sharper. Half-ghost, half-man—all wild. Pure power in the way he trapped me in place, his hold savage. Arawn countered it with sweet murmurs and gentle kisses up my arm, but the second Draco parted my hair down the middle and fluffed it over my shoulders, I couldn't feel either anymore. The hard and the soft—gone.

Icy anticipation took their place. I sucked in a shallow breath, then forced it out, trying to remember to just *breathe*.

It'll be over soon.

That was what they always said—even when it was a lie.

"I will need to remove some of your curls," Draco told me, his flat affect weirdly comforting in the charged moment. "Selectively—only a few."

"That's fine," I whispered, trying to keep my head as still as possible while featherlight fingers picked through my hair. Arawn brushed a tear from my cheek, catching it with his knuckle.

"Close your eyes, little one."

"No." My vision blurred, and once again, I needed to remember bodily functions—*blink. And again. Blink. Breathe. Blink. Breathe.* "No, I'm fine."

Draco's soft exhale lined up with my ragged one, and then I felt and heard the slash of a blade through my hair. One, two, three pieces sacrificed for my freedom. Like a hairdresser hacking off a ponytail for charity, Draco deposited the curls on the bed, just within my line of sight. Not exactly a primo distraction, especially with Balor in my face, Arawn in my periphery, the construction lights just a little too white for my—

Pain.

Searing, blinding, soul-crushing *agony* burned through me at the first cut. A shriek burst out before I could stop it, then another, and another, Arawn and Balor forced to really lock on as I thrashed. Self-preservation seized control, limbs flailing, desperate to escape this *pain* trying to gobble me up and spit me back out a shell of myself.

No. Get it together.

I thought I knew pain in all its gory shades.

I thought I could handle *anything*.

So, so, so, so wrong.

"*Stop*, Draco, stop, stop, stop, *stop!*"

He didn't.

He cut and carved in silence, occasionally clipping my skull with the shadow scalpel's razor-sharp point. Not a lot of skin to work with. No fat. Just nerves and bone—they made it as painful as possible to remove.

Fuck them.

I closed my eyes and clenched my teeth.

Fuck them so hard.

They didn't get to win.

One last wail sliced up my throat—and then it was over. Bulbs burst and darkness fell. Glass broke and stone cracked. The building groaned and the sky *boomed*.

But it was done. No doubt Draco made the removal as swift and precise as possible, yet as I slouched into the pillow, Balor bracing my shoulders and the world so very *black* behind my closed lids, I felt like I'd gone twelve rounds with a titan.

"Almost finished, little one." Velvet stroked my damp cheek. Warm honey caressed my ear and trickled down my throat. Arawn's lips brushed my throat, his arm around my waist. "You've done so well. I'm going to close the wounds now."

His silk was a mask, a form of personal protection—because he shook when he touched me. Trembles and quivers in his hands and in his words, the strain obvious, the cord one frayed thread from snapping. Clearing his throat softly, Arawn delicately cupped the back of my head. I hissed, the horrible sting old news, then exhaled roughly when his influence smothered all that pain.

Stronger than his usual comforting warmth, *heat* blazed over my skull, and only when his hand drifted down to clutch at my neck did I pry my waterlogged lashes apart. Numb, I absorbed our surroundings: Balor in solid form again, staring like he expected me to disappear, fear and anger souring everything beautiful about him. I went for his strong jaw, but my arm fell back to the bed, weak and spent—

But growing stronger.

I'd knocked out all the construction lamps, their bulbs broken, their light gone. Cracks spiderwebbed the walls. What had been left of the jagged windowpanes was gone, the glass obliterated, the frames cracked.

And I...

I could see it. In the black of night, my new world came into focus. All of it, every little thing—including three painfully neat excisions in Draco's palm. Three bloody, fleshy perfect circles with the ram's head insignia of a demonic house.

They had found a way to track me long before I could ever run.

Had Dad done it?

Had he wielded the branding iron—jabbed it at a baby's skull and listened to the skin sizzle?

Had Nyx handed me over to Cronus in the first place?

Questions burning, I tried to squirm off the bed, but Arawn body-blocked me, herding me like a lost lamb.

"Wait a moment—"

"No."

Balor inhaled sharply. Arawn stilled. Draco's arm dropped to his side.

Was that me?

I sounded—different. My voice... *Richer*. Deeper. Complex, just like their eyes.

Powerful might have been an adjective too far, but their response to this new melody, me and the monster perfectly entwined, gave me the strength to climb off the bed and stand on my own two feet. No swaying. No dizziness. No nausea. No lingering aches. My walk to the window felt more like gliding, black mists clinging to my shoulders and the backs of my arms.

Sucking down the deepest of breaths, I looked to the night sky, to the millions of stars suddenly so *bright*, so big and beautiful. So many more than I had ever seen before. Light and dark. Balance.

Down in the abandoned construction lot, a raven perched on a vandalized *Men at Work* sign. I tipped my head to the side, and he did the same. When I went the other way, he mimicked, the two of us connected.

A croaky cry echoed from above, followed by the rush of wings, and there they were—his conspiracy. Thirty strong at least, circling the decrepit building like a black vortex.

The sight made my heart happy.

Their sounds made my soul sing.

I reached for them, desperate for one to land on my outstretched hand—

Darkness swirled around my fingers. Soft, delicate, gentle black shadows. Frowning, I watched the way they danced with even the slightest movement, then turned back to my captors—my *liberators*.

"Which of you...?"

A glossy-eyed Arawn shook his head, his smile so exquisite in the dark, so full and warm, openly colored with love. Beside him, Draco lost himself in my eyes, a dull pink flush in his hollow cheeks.

"Not us," Balor insisted, rough and wild, black mists rising from his shoulders like singed wings. "*You*, Selene."

Me.

Deep down, I already knew that.

I turned my palm over and curled my fingers inward. The darkness *obeyed*, gathering over my faded life and love lines, over flesh pale as Draco's, over once blue veins that were just... gone. I waited for the shadows to coil into a ball, then caged them in a gentle fist.

Then a harder one, black talons stabbing at my skin, a tear careening down my cheek.

Something bit into my palm. Not my new nails. Something... else.

My fingers peeled back.

A small diamond replaced the shadows, sparkly and new, glittering like a star.

Calm flooded my veins, and I looked to Balor, Arawn, and Draco, so fucking *smitten* with their kindness and affection, with their rough hands and conquering kisses and their brazen love. So viscerally taken with them it hurt—and for once, I welcomed the pain. The stab of love and longing. The ache of want. The siren song of darkness. The fear of absolute loss.

"Show me?" I whispered. Draco's white brows knit. Balor prowled to the edge of the bed, eager as ever.

"Show you what?" Arawn whispered back, his warmth faltering.

No need to be scared, love. I'm not going anywhere.

I held out my hand, diamond catching the darkness of this world, shining its brightest in the night. "*Everything.*"

CHAPTER TWENTY-ONE

I asked for everything.

They gave me the world.

For one beautiful month, Earth was our oyster. Arawn would conjure a shadowy black globe, as big or as small as necessary and so detailed it made my head spin. Countries and rivers lined in gold, he'd offer it to me so I could choose our next destination with a simple point of my finger. All the major cities I dreamed about as a teenager were first on the list. A day in London, a night in Paris, a weekend in Rome and Milan. A few hours in Bangkok, then a straight shot to Beijing. New York. LA. Seattle. Yellowknife. Miami. Dubai. Istanbul. Nairobi. Cairo. The beaches of Buenos Aires and the mountains of Kathmandu. Tasmania, just because.

Once I touched all the places on my Pinterest travel boards, we went off the beaten path. Historical monuments and national parks. Uninhabited islands in Fiji and vast plains in Mongolia. We hit every continent. We island-hopped around the Caribbean in a single day because we *could.*

While most of the time we traveled as a group, occasionally we ventured off for solo outings, just me and one of the guys. Arawn preferred *cultural* experiences, full of sightseeing and landmarks, museums and restaurants. Draco craved quiet, the peace of sunrise and sunset, not another soul around for miles, just us and nature. He had an affinity for water, much to my surprise, and if he could squeeze a waterfall or a tide pool or a bottomless black pit into our trip, he made it work.

Balor had proven time and time again that he was up for anything. Impulsive and creative, sometimes we were crushed by people, sometimes it was just us and the polar bears. He thrived no matter where we were, either as a group or just the two of us.

But he shone brightest in the dark, just like my diamonds.

Slowing my breath, I pressed back against the massive redwood tree, its brethren stretching like literal giants toward an inky black night sky. California redwoods—they'd popped up in a bunch of movies I loved as a kid, but there was no comparison to the real thing. Trunks so wide Balor needed to go full shadow creature to reach around their base. Trees so tall they could tickle the gods way up in the clouds. Thin underbrush—perfect for sprinting through with a predator at your heels.

Unnerving, probably, for humans to find themselves lost in the forest this time of night.

Exquisite for us, for monsters who thrived in the shadows.

A sharp sniff sounded from the other side of my tree, and I stilled, heart tripping over itself at that delicious *growl*. Desire thrummed between my thighs, like the strings of a harp *plucked* by skilled fingers. He knew just how to play me.

But I also knew how to make him *work* for it.

I tapped my bare toes on the forest floor, head cocked, listening, hands twisted in the fabric of my knee-length dress. Sleeves to my elbows. Scoop neckline. Fitted to the waist and swishy the rest of the way down. Black as Balor's eyes—I selected the sheen myself.

Hell, I *made* the whole garment myself, adept at weaving darkness into solid form after a month of practice, taught and encouraged and loved by the best.

His boot pressed into the earth to my right.

I sprinted left, shrouded in shadow, the night gathered like a cloak around me, and took cover behind another giant tree trunk. Then, lower lip snagged between my teeth, I peeked around—and there he was, forsaking the breathtaking *man* for something exquisitely *monster*. Balor prowled around the last trunk, sniffing the bark, his hands deadly shadow claws, his teeth pointed and black. Mists flitted around him, a vague pair of batlike wings slowly taking shape.

In the last month, we all found our rhythm, both as a group and individual pairs. Arawn was all conversation and innuendo and desperate kisses in the rain. Draco was hand-holding and silent contemplation, intense eye contact and frantic undressing.

Balor and I played more than the others, our games vast and varied.

At the top of the list, however, was *this*.

He loved to hunt me.

Chase me through abandoned castles and stalk me in crowded bazaars.

The me of old, with binding and tracking sigils burned

into her skull, so drugged and chained she had no idea *who* she really was—to be hunted by a monster as intense as Balor would have brought her to her knees.

Here, it made my heart race and my sex wet.

Here, now, I let him stalk and chase and capture and fuck to his heart's content—

Because here, now, I too was a predator. A daughter of night and a creature of the abyss.

In our games, there was no prey.

Only two alphas determined to outsmart the other until someone finally folded.

Until one of us—usually me—*needed* the other so badly the game died on the spot.

I always called it a tie.

Balor would just smile, dark and dangerous, sharp and violent, and say, *"Of course, little raven. Whatever you want."*

And then that would start another game, our cycle endless.

With a deep breath, I pulled the night in tighter, masking me from the beast as he skulked around this new tree, sniffing and growling, tasting the air with a shadowy forked tongue. For a few seconds, I thought he scented me, but then he stalked on, raking his nails over another tree, scarring the bark with a snarl.

One month after Draco sliced those demon sigils off my skull, the full weight of *me* was still settling. My cloak tatters taught me what they could, but I tackled the rest on my own, experimenting, trying something new every day just to get a feel for what this body, finally strong and able, could really do.

I still didn't know how it worked: I thought the thing and the thing happened. I stuck to shadow manipulation, to toying with darkness and tempering the night sky, blotting out stars one moment and making them scream bright the next. It had taken about two weeks to stop accidentally inking *power* in front of humans, just a little squid spurting at random, but I almost had a grip on it now.

Besides, Balor, Arawn, and Draco never let me struggle alone.

Never.

One month and no Cronus agents. No demons. Nothing.

Thirty days into late November, this was the first time in my life I was well and truly *free*.

And I planned to make the most of it for however long it lasted, a teeny, tiny sliver of the old me still waiting for the fall.

Hugging the darkness close, blanketed from head to toe, I padded after Balor, choosing my steps carefully, determined not to make a sound—

A throaty raven's cry cut through the silent forest.

Damn it.

We both stilled, my cover blown.

One month of ravens. Everywhere I went, a conspiracy of black-feathered friends followed. They were there when I woke up, when I fell asleep, when I dined on buckets of mussels at a Parisian café. Sometimes they came close enough for a few gentle pets. Sometimes they pecked at Balor for being too familiar, but they pestered Draco the most. Like cats, they seemed to sense who was the least interested in them, which suddenly made my white-haired weirdo the belle of the ball.

To hear one cry out for me now—a dead giveaway.

Balor lilted around, nine feet tall but shrinking by the second.

"Is that you, little raven?" he whispered, staring into my black bubble, his more attractive features sharpening into focus again. His claws shortened—but just enough to match mine, which had found their preferred length, the black down to my second knuckle by now with no signs of stopping.

Our eyes clashed, whether he realized it or not, and I weighed my options. Then, just as he went for me, that reaching hand about to rip my blanket aside, I hurled the darkness at him. One shove and the black barrier slammed into him, knocking him flat on his ass as I sprinted through the trees, the layered laughter, the chorus of me and the monster, just *daring* him to keep up.

Hooves thundered after me, and there was my gorgeous black Clydesdale in hot pursuit, his shadows drenching the bark, bigger and badder with every gallop. Even though I might have been able to lose him in the tighter groves, I wheeled around and charged straight for him, then ducked under his massive front legs, his stomping hooves and snorting nostrils, and darted around another tree.

The monstrous horse vanished, his shape *popped* like a pinpricked balloon, shadow and mist spreading, the darkness suddenly an obsidian fog hurdling over the forest floor. As hard as I ran, pushing until my lungs *ached*, I was no match for his speed. The black mist crashed into my calves like the tide, and brutish hands latched onto my ankles, rooting me in place as I squealed and wheeled my arms for balance. As soon as I shook my left leg free, extra hands smoothed around the right, followed by three more on my left, slithering up my skin and under my dress, stroking my inner thighs with the same loving bite as Balor's scruff.

Pleasure plumed in my chest, and I braced myself as he

rose from the darkness, emerging like a monster from the deep, this fallen angel who oozed sin in his smile and vice in his laugh. Before I could put Plan E into motion, Balor seized my forearms and marched me back into the brutal redwood bark, pinning me to the trunk and kissing me like the world was about to end.

In *fire*, of course.

Always fire—never ice.

Not with him.

He kissed to possess, to claim, planting his flag on me with a cruel grin and sharp teeth. At this point, anyone who dared try to take me from them was absolutely and unequivocally *fucked*.

Because my shadow monsters would never let me go.

And I would never let them consider it.

Here, bodies flush and mouths at war, Balor and I could properly tangle, the air electric and hot, our moans and snarls, the shred of cloth and the yank of hair—we were the perfect pair. Give and take. Submit and dominate. Kiss and control. We were all that and more, and as I slashed at his cheeks and ripped at his hair, one leg hooked around him while I ground my center along his stiff cock, I couldn't imagine it any other way.

One month of intimacy, of learning what it really meant. It wasn't just sex—though sex was a pretty awesome part of it. Arawn had been right that first time: we couldn't drown the world in shadow. Two more clawed their way up my throat in the last thirty days, but my trio taught me *plenty* about physical intimacy, about emotional connection and togetherness. We touched and tasted, licked and nipped, knelt between each other's thighs and worshipped at *many* altars.

Sometimes as a group.

Sometimes on little trips like these, just me and one of them, exploring and learning and setting *our* tone.

I enjoyed both. Spending alone time with each of them was like finding different parts of my being. Coming back to the group—we were whole.

Pain bloomed in my neck, Balor's teeth relentless and on the verge of breaking skin, his monstrous black shadow claws tearing my panties to pieces in a single swipe. He groaned against my skin when he cupped me and felt the wet heat there, the *need* that had started its slow-burn build from the moment he took my hand and stole me away from our oceanfront suite in LA.

I dragged a single brutal talon down his throat, then stabbed under his chin, forcing his head back, our savagery colliding, all bared teeth and wild eyes.

"*Fuck* me, Balor."

He snatched my wrist and slammed it to the tree. "*Scream* for me, Selene."

His torn clothes, that lovely button-up and pressed slacks, fell away like fading mists, leaving only a heaving, sweaty, sculpted *man* bearing down on me, one who hoisted the leg that I relied on for balance and plunged deep inside.

I gave him that scream, *all* of him still a shock, thickest and biggest of my trio. Every time, stretched and dominated, he *took* my body with a single savage thrust, filling me up, merging more than just our dark spirits. My cry ripped across the redwoods, and the ravens croaked a throaty serenade from all sides, accented by Balor's dark laughter.

Laughter I strangled when I tightened around his shaft, the pain of his claim melting to molten pleasure, then yanked at his hair and drove my ankles hard into his back. Our gazes clashed, words unspoken hurled between us. *You got your scream. Fair's fair.*

"Such a brave creature," he hissed as he kissed me, his guttural rasp echoing inside my head. "Such a foolish thing."

Balor had once told me Draco fucked like he wanted to obliterate a lover. One month later, I knew that to be true—but Balor was no gentler. He had restraint at first; they all did. Patience and understanding, care and concern for *me*, my well-being and comfort.

It got old fast.

I wanted all of them, every dark facet, and that included their ferocity.

Ferocity Balor always delivered in spades, pounding me into the redwood from the start, his fingers bruising into my thighs as he propped me up. At some point, when my own savagery wrenched a genuine snarl from him, he grabbed the hand that was causing all the problems, slashing at his neck and ripping at his hair, and slammed it against the bark.

I made sure the other hand worked double time in its absence, tormenting him even as he drove me to sweeter and sweeter heights.

Thunder rumbled in the distance. The night grew darker—we grew louder.

Right on the brink of explosion, fire sizzling down the last of the dynamite wick, Balor stopped. Fucking *stopped*. Propping me up with his hips, trapping my wrist against the bark, his free hand went for my throat—and then the other finally dropped to my clit, plunging down to where we met and stroking it hard enough to make me *sing*. Moans and mewls offered to the night sky, I tipped my head back and squeezed my eyes shut—

"No, no..." His voice all singsongy and wicked, Balor tightened his hold on my throat. "Give me those *eyes*." He pinched my clit, a brash chastisement, and clucked his tongue. "Those eyes are *mine*, and you'll *look* at me when I make you come."

"Pretty words," I stammered, the pleasure rising, the heat scorching. "For a second, I thought you were Arawn—"

Balor cut me off by palming my clit and stroking my swollen lower lips with his fingers, caressing his cock still buried deep in the process. I hissed his name. He squeezed harder, rubbed more intentionally.

I held off for as long as I could, clenching my eyes tighter, refusing to lose *this* game of all games—but the explosion rattled me to my core. Pleasure detonated deep in my soul, wildfire untamed, unchecked, burning up and out. My eyes snapped open, falling directly into his, and his laughter harmonized beautifully with my cries, his cruel fingers continuing to work me even as my muscles twitched and my core danced and my mind went hazy with color and light.

And then he went right back to it, his pace instantly punishing, his body pounding against mine—like this little pause for another earthshattering orgasm had never happened. Every vicious thrust spiked the ecstasy in my veins, dragging it out, making me *suffer*. It felt so fucking good I thought I'd die in his arms, screaming, with a smile on my face as the darkness circled and thickened and devoured the world.

Their climaxes were *way* less theatrical, but there was something so ridiculously *hot* about the stiffening of their bodies, the trembles and the shakes, the gritted teeth and clenched jaws. The way all three whispered my name like a prayer inside my head, their pleasure private and personal and deeply intimate, just for us.

It was the only time Balor let go. The wild and crazy,

the cruel and devious, the impulsive monster who consumed terror like some divine glutton—gone. When he came, he held me tight, face buried in my neck, a hand in my hair and my name his hymn. It was a moment of calm, peace and tranquility when our outings were usually anything but. In the aftermath, a blissful heaviness settled across us, in our bones and on our faces. Long but gentle kisses and sweet caresses of cheeks and hair and swollen lips.

I loved it almost as much as the act itself, these quiet moments with him.

They were short-lived, of course.

It wouldn't be a Balor date night if we cuddled and whispered and held each other for hours—

That was for Arawn and me. When the fancy dinners and the fireworks and the museum tours ended, we were romance and passion and slow, sweet desperation under a midnight moon.

So, grinning, I squirmed out of his arms and winced when he pulled that enormous shaft out of me, still half-hard and ready to go again. Rarely could I manage two rounds with Balor *or* Draco—not the way they had me. Still, with time, maybe my endurance would increase.

Maybe, one night, I'd surprise them.

For now, I tiptoed away, head tilted to the distant redwood canopy, *breathing* the delicious aches and twinges away. Then, as Balor planted a hand on the tree trunk and chased his breath, more man than monster, I pounced.

Jumped on his back.

Hooked both arms around his neck and bit his ear —*hard*.

"Show me the trees, Balor," I teased, my best impression of his psychotic snarl making him snort. After all, we were here for the historic redwoods, famous around the world, but as usual, after a few minutes of oohing and ahhing, we found more interesting ways to entertain ourselves.

He reached around, snagging my hair in a steely fist, and dragged me into a kiss that made my toes curl and my heart race. But he had won too many rounds already. So, when he slowed down at my whimper, his black brows furrowed, his gaze flecked with concern, I snapped at his lower lip and springboarded off his back. The force shoved him into the redwood and me a few feet behind, my landing not even a little graceful. Knowing I only had seconds to either move or lose, I rolled over and took off like a sprinter blasting from the starting block, swathed in night.

My giggles echoed through the redwoods as I ran, starlight slanting bright and beautiful between the leaves—and monstrous hooves soon pounded after me, the chase on once again.

Our game far from over.

CHAPTER TWENTY-TWO

"Oh, look!" The arctic wind stole my gasp, but I still elbowed Draco and pointed as if he couldn't see the stunning natural phenomena unfolding above. Nestled together in a snowy plain just north of Yukon's Whitehorse, cradled in shadow and night, thick black blankety mists keeping us cozy, we had watched the northern lights strengthen over time, but there was nothing more beautiful in the whole wide world than when they reached their peak.

Light and color slashed the sky like a watercolor abstract, the brushstrokes fanciful and free. Green, blue, purple, and pink ran in zigzagging rivers against a starry black, and for the longest time, I couldn't look away. Arms hooked around my knees, I just basked in it, the perfect balance of light and dark. Wind gusted across the empty field ahead, ruffling the freshly fallen snow, blowing away the animal tracks. Earlier in the night, we listened to wolves howl somewhere down south, their melody glorious, their togetherness enviable.

Now, the arctic called us north, the landscape wild, the sky the most open and raw I had ever seen.

And the lights. Oh, the *lights*.

Cheeks sore from my gaping smile, I glanced at Draco, and while he wore the same neutral expression as always, he too seemed enraptured by the display, awestruck by the color reflecting in his black gaze, with the way the polar lights danced together, twisting and twining but never fully losing themselves. They stood alone, the pinks and greens, the blues and purples, separate yet moving as one. A love for all eternity.

Like Nyx and Erebus.

Smitten, I shuffled closer under the blankets we had conjured together, scooting across the pillows below until I was *right* at his bony side. Tonight was all ours; I awoke this morning with black eyes, darkness percolating inside after me and Balor's games in the redwoods. Rather than asking, Draco just *took*, grabbing my hand and whirling us off for a day alone.

A day of quiet solitude on the west coast, dipping our toes in the Atlantic and sampling fresh fish at a coastal pub. Then north for the night, counting down the minutes, maybe seconds at this point, until I unleashed another monstrous shadow on the world.

The nausea hadn't hit yet. No burning in my throat or churning in my tummy. Just... this. The crisp icy wind and the northern lights. Outside of our black bubble, the frost should have bothered me, but after ditching the demon sigils, extreme temperatures ceased to matter.

I mean, not quite. I still *felt* the heat, the cold—everything. But it didn't hit as hard anymore, my new body strong, enduring, capable of so much more. In fact, most of my sensory issues had gone, except for my dislike of intense white light. No, with haunting memories of ORs and doctor's offices with blinding spotlights that made me feel less than human—that one was a stage-five clinger.

Still, even if I could have sat comfortably here in my sweater and slacks, maybe with a hat and some thin gloves for the wintry aesthetic, what was a date night under the stars, under these exquisite brushstrokes, without a bunch of blankets and cuddling for warmth?

Tucking my head onto Draco's shoulder, I nuzzled closer. He cleared his throat and dropped his shoulder, his soft inhale reading loud and clear. *Sorry it is so uncomfortable.* My white-haired tatter was all secret strength and sinew, bony all over without any real fat for padding—and I loved it. So, I grabbed his arm with both hands and squeezed, a silent reminder he didn't *need* to apologize for anything about himself. I chose to snuggle. I decided where to rest my head, and it was very, very, very happy to touch down here, eyes to the sky, his shoulder bones digging into my cheek and temple and forehead.

I *liked* that.

It told me I was with him—that he was real and here and mine.

"Draco?" I whispered a little while later, the light show everlasting, temperatures on a sharp decline and falling fast.

"Hmm?" He carried on stiffly rearranging our shadow blankets, awkwardly kicking and moving things around with his free hand when his feet couldn't get the job done fast enough. His other arm pressed against me like stone, almost purposefully frozen in place while I hugged it with both of mine.

"What does love feel like to you?"

Of my three tatters, Draco's perspective on such an elusive concept had always interested me the most.

However, as soon as the question dropped and detonated between us, he went quiet. Too quiet. Just my racing heart and the howling winds up here now, until I eventually pulled away and frowned at him. At some point, he had closed his eyes and bowed his head, and that tableau, hair as white as snow, skin pale as ice, folded in on himself as his personal darkness misted around his head like a halo—

Not good, right?

Arawn had been the first to profess that this was a love story as old as time. We were part of the greatest love the cosmos had ever seen, in fact, and falling for each other, being *together*, was as natural as breathing. It got easier after the detox. It got infinitely better once demons stopped randomly showing up everywhere.

But a small part of me still worried I wasn't good enough for any of them—that they had such grand expectations when they sensed Nyx's unmated and unclaimed daughter, and I had failed to meet every single one of them.

The old me wasn't enough.

The new me wasn't enough.

And as fast and furious as I fell for them, they would leave. Sojourn in Hell for another century or two, sleeping and feasting on damned souls, and then crawl back out hoping Nyx had birthed another thing like me at some point over the years—try again with someone better.

But then Draco's head snapped up with a sharp breath, and, blinking furiously, he brought me back to our shadowy fold with an arm around my shoulders. While my frown stayed put, I cuddled in under his chin, holding a metaphorical breath, waiting for the second bomb to drop.

"It feels warm," he rasped. Strands of want laced through his words, his voice harsh and more strained than usual. His icy hand, meanwhile, searched for mine under the blankets, not stopping until it found both of mine and pressed them to his chest. "And safe."

That tense breath whooshed out of me, and I nodded, tears stinging the back of my throat. "Yeah. I get that."

"I cannot speak for the others—"

"I would never ask you to." While we were all a team, pieces of a whole, my boys were their own monsters. I'd never yearn for anything but their truest selves.

With a soft sigh that didn't fog in the cold, Draco kissed my forehead. "To me, love feels like the bottom of the pit."

I took a few beats to digest that, then cleared my throat. "Uh, sorry—what?"

"The abyss," Draco whispered, thin lips brushing the top of my head with every hoarse word, "the vastness of space, the endless of the endless—time itself. It goes on and on. Hollow and empty, but enduring. That is me. That is my lot, Selene."

Right, right, hollow and empty and bottomless, feeding on depression—none of that was new. But this? His analogy? Yeah, didn't quite stick the landing. My frown deepened. Was our love... the bottom of a pit?

What?

"Love makes it stop." His fingertips ghosted under my chin, tipping my head just enough so our eyes could meet. I ignored the blank expression and focused on the inferno staring down at me, at the hooded firestorm of want and feeling that made him so fucking beautiful. Draco blinked once, twice, then brushed his thumb along my bottom lip, his other hand pressing mine harder to his chest. "Love proves there is a bottom, an end, a destination." His white brows twitched. "Love is *you*, Selene. You are my stop, my end, my destination. Love is peace. It is *meaning* in the abyss." His face blurred with the flood of tears, and, a little oblivious, Draco twisted one of my black curls around his finger, the edges of his mouth ever so slightly lifted. "Do you understand?"

I forced my eyes open, refusing to blink, refusing to let a single tear fall and ruin the moment. "Yeah."

But my croaky response made him abandon my curls for my gaze, cradling my face without actually touching it. "Oh. Have I upset you?"

"No. *No.*" I sniffled and wiped my runny nose on my shoulder, then cupped his face in both hands. "Not even a little. Your love is so beautiful, Draco."

He stiffened when I pushed into a kiss, firm and closed-lipped, and then melted—by Draco standards, anyway—against me with a rumbly groan. I watched his white lashes dance shut before I closed mine, surrendering to the darkness, to the chaste peck that was *us*. Unless things were about to take a violent, steamy turn, the air electrified, words few and far between, our kisses were just this. Comfortable. Familiar. Never pushy or showy. Confident. Secure. *Together*.

Kissing Draco made me feel safe.

Just like his love.

More happy tears clung to my eyelashes when they peeled apart, and I beamed up at him, delighted with the way the northern lights twinkled in his eyes.

"I—" Oh, *shit*. The churn and burn hit out of nowhere, darkness on the way. No stopping this runaway train. No holding it in no matter how hard I tried. Shaking my head, I flailed backward and crab-walked over the blankets. "H-hold that thought."

Scrambling from conjured night and darkness to snow that was fluffy on top and compact below was a sloppy mess. I stumbled and staggered, snow flying in my face, but the outfit I made myself—a cozy sweater, loose slacks, and fuzzy boots—held its own in the chaos. Hair wild and free, I shoved my curls back and crashed to my knees when the burn jumped from acid reflux to hellfire, then screamed my throat raw and bloody through the birth of our latest dark darling.

Still not exactly in love with the process of bringing darkness into the world, but when the last of it ripped over my lips, I was still *here*. It was doable. The sore throat usually went away in a few minutes, fading with every tentative swallow, but the exhaustion, the spent and empty feeling, took a little longer to shake.

Despite it all, not once had I done this alone. One or all of my boys had been there to hold me, and Draco was no exception. While he wasn't as cuddly as Arawn or as intense as Balor, the former all sweet words and warm embraces, the latter unbridled excitement and crushing hugs, he never faltered. My shaky body could have folded into the snow, but Draco drew me back into him, his form sturdy and hard, his hold steadfast. Unlike the others, however, he let *me* set the tone. If I needed more, he held tighter. If I needed less, he crouched by my side, waiting for the storm to pass.

Tonight, I collapsed into him and wrapped his spindly arms tight around me. Kneeling there in the snow, Draco kissed my temple as darkness swelled around us again, blankets creeping closer, crawling across the barren white wastes to engulf its creators in toasty onyx.

Above, my newly birthed shadow hovered—then mimicked the zigzag shape of the northern lights. *Love* crushed my chest, maternal yearning always strongest right after they left me. It would have been nice if they stayed, if we could have more than this fleeting moment with our offspring before they disappeared into the great wide world.

But this was what we were.

Me, Draco, Balor, and Arawn—this was how we made new life. Maybe one day I could scream out the darkness without missing a beat, immediately back to whatever I was doing beforehand with none of this longing and desperation.

For now, I let myself feel.

The monster in my chest didn't seem to mind. In fact, she felt the brunt of it, starving for connection with her children.

For her sake, I reached out this time, and while most of the dark cloud stayed put in the air, a sliver trickled down like mist off a waterfall. It eventually slithered around my reaching fingers, the caress cool and familiar.

And then it was gone, dissolving on the wind, lost in the bleak blackness of the arctic north.

"What kind of darkness do you think it'll be?" I asked, hoarse and sore, my voice a croaky disaster that only made Draco nuzzle closer, his stabby chin on my shoulder and the shadow blankets piled high.

"Knowing Balor, nothing pleasant."

I snorted and slumped against him. The shift in angles allowed for a few stolen kisses, until eventually we found ourselves flat on our backs, the night pulled close, cloaked in Draco's mists and shadows. Side by side, hands entwined under the covers, we watched the northern lights dance above in blissful quiet.

A little more of *our* darkness out there—and, in my opinion, the world better for it.

CHAPTER TWENTY-THREE

"Okay, enough suspense." They had kept this huge secret from me all day, a united front against my innocent but probing questions, and nothing about the landscape now got me any closer to an answer. "Where are we, and why are we here?"

Strolling through a fairy-tale forest of snow-dusted Douglas firs and spruces, I suspected northern hemisphere, but Europe, Canada, Russia, Scandinavia—no clue where we had touched down twenty minutes ago, all three of my smirking cloak tatters annoyingly tight-lipped.

While chilly, winter well underway and snow slicking up my calves, it was nothing this new body couldn't take. Still, I'd managed to glean *just* enough intel beforehand to know we weren't headed to the tropics, which led me to the starry black shawl draped around my shoulders, followed by the thick, durable brocade black gown below. Not exactly my usual style, but considering my old fashion sense spawned from the asshole I *thought* was my dad, it was time to explore what made my heart race.

And I could officially be as couture as I wanted, another

two weeks of practice under my belt, all my clothes forged of night and straight from my imagination. The laced bodice, the dense, flowy skirt that dragged across the white landscape and smoothed over my boot prints in the snow—devised out of thin air. *Way* too outrageous for anything but the Met Gala, probably, the darkness dotted with all my favorite star constellations, but as usual, the three men at my back had been overly complimentary, infatuated with anything I made.

With the sun set, I tugged the night closer, turning my silky shawl into a proper wool shrug, frowning as I took in the soaring pines, their needles lush and evergreen, the snow at our feet fluffy and untouched. Once again, they had brought me to the brink of civilization—just a matter of fine-tuning the exact dot on the globe.

"You'll see soon, little raven," Balor drawled, his smile all teeth and sharp humor when I glared back at him. He grabbed a branch in passing and gave it a shake, rustling the collected snow onto Draco.

"Ah, yes, very ominous," I muttered as Draco's mists plumed into a translucent black dome to protect him. "Awesome."

Before I could toss out my theories, adept enough by now at reading their facial expressions to sense when I'd landed close to the mark, Arawn snagged my hand and tugged me forward. Ever my charming prince, my cozy dawn god, he ducked into an elegant bow to kiss the top, his lips cool and tingly against my skin, and then swept me under his wing. With a hand on my lower back, he steered me away from the others, along a twisting, winding route through the trees, until we reached a clearing.

Perfectly round and open to the starry sky, it sat in the middle of nowhere at the edge of the world. In its center was an onyx altar, the rectangle perfect and smooth and massive. Stone seats surrounded it, the rows arranged like a Celtic knot, and then, way on the other side of the clearing, loomed a slate wall with a crescent moon and twinkly stars carved into it, the shapes white, almost glowing in the night.

Moon-kissed. Throat thick, heart full, I stumbled into the clearing, locked on the symbols. Amateurish as they were, they stirred something in me, the white of tonight's full moon glinting off them, the glow preternatural. Ancient and mystical. *Divine.*

Mine.

I swallowed hard, tears blurring the stone seats and the black altar, holding myself in a solo hug as the monster in my soul purred.

Home.

We... were finally home. It didn't matter where exactly that was on the planet. Which country, which continent —*who cares?*

Here, now, I felt—

"Little one, this is a site of worship... for Nyx." Arawn closed in behind me, his presence a welcome reprieve from the emotional surge, the night air suddenly charged as I took it all in. His arms curved around my waist, and I sucked in a wet, ragged breath, blinking the tears back as he nuzzled my neck with a delicious rumble, the smile I loved so much echoing in his words. "It's modern, of course. Perhaps one or two centuries old—"

"Ah, yes," I managed, struggling to get a grip, to ground myself in the moment. "One or two *hundred* years—very modern."

He nipped at my neck with a chastising huff, and I giggled, the sensation tickling and prickling down to my core, then tried to squeeze him off with my shoulder and chin. The pushback earned me a sharper bite, canines raking over my pulse, his fingers gritting into my thighs, working their way inward, almost in spite of my thick dress.

"We thought you might like to see it," Arawn growled, that rough rasp like he was falling deeper and deeper into *this*, just the two of us alone in the wilderness. However, a soft breath and a beat later, silk dripped from his tongue again, all honeyed and rich. "We thought... you should *feel* her. I believe your mother touched this sacred place personally."

I cut the teasing loose, flirtations on pause, and drifted forward. Arawn let me go without a word, and something whispered behind me. No longer a shoulder shrug or a wooly shawl, a veil now trailed down my back, night-kissed and beautiful, dragging like a bridal train over the snow. Head held high, eyes misty, I threaded around the stones, not stopping until I reached the altar.

"Hello, Mom," I murmured, running my hands over the smooth onyx. While snow piled around it, not a single flake stayed *on* it. Warmth flared throughout the clearing, a comfy familiarity settling in as I studied the carvings, the moon and the stars, a permanent offering to *the* goddess of night.

Darkness coiled off my black fingers, rising like steam from a kettle, and the next time I pressed both hands to the onyx, it *shocked* me. I peeled back with a yelp and a laugh, the sensation a sharp reminder to be *present*—that I wasn't out here alone.

That I'd never be alone again.

After another minute of study, I faced the three men who had brought me to the ends of the earth—who celebrated my curiosity, my connection to the wild in my marrow...

And found them besieged by butterflies. Little black critters with star-flecked wings fluttered by the dozens around the clearing, their bodies' soft white glow like the moon to a firefly's sun. A handful landed on Balor's enormous shoulders. Others gracefully settled on Arawn's upturned hands, flexing their wings, almost grateful for the safe haven.

One and only one went for Draco, perched on his nose, wings extended over his gaunt cheeks like a masquerade mask, his eyes crossed and locked in a new staring contest.

Me.

They came from me, these gorgeous night pearls, and went straight to *them*. Never more than one could handle, Balor taking the lion's share, Draco content with his one, Arawn reveling in quality and not quantity.

"Thank you," I whispered, a lump in my throat and my belly in knots. "Thank you all for *everything*." Misty-eyed, I blinked up at the night veil suddenly descending over my face, the monster inside, my sheer *will*, determined to go full bridal. Shaking my head, I lifted it back and off my face, three pieces of my soul watching me through the butterflies. "You said we were part of the greatest love story... and I couldn't see it at first. But I do now. I can't imagine life without you."

Each stopped fussing with their butterflies, and in a flash, my creations dissolved, spiraling to the real stars, on their way home. Three intense stares settled on me, on whatever had become of my outside, a bride of shadows and night waiting for them at the altar.

"Draco once asked why I chose you." Back then on the beach, panicked about my first birth, I had no idea. Now, it made all the sense in the world. "He... He said every kiss was always returned—*why*? Why do I love you..."

I stole a beat for myself, admiring the black under my skin, every finger engulfed, the talons at their tips lethal. "I love you all because you *see* me." Sniffling, I looked up with a trembling smile, the night peeling apart for what might read as a provocative neckline. But no. The darkness split down my front to expose my heart, pounding for them and only them, now until the end of time. "You *feel* me. Accept me. Love me. You make me laugh. You dry my tears. You protect me and ask for nothing in return.

"You breathed *life* into me. I was dead at Cronus, rotting a little day by day, this walking, talking, miserable corpse. You put the beat back in my heart."

There was nothing before them.

Life hadn't started until them.

"So, thank you." My gaze cut to Balor. "Thank you for your fire." Then to Arawn. "For your kindness." And finally, over to Draco, his eyes blazing bright as the sun. "And your quiet."

I held out my arms, suddenly draped in bridal lace, in silks and shadows, in feathery wisps at my shoulders and three starry diamonds embedded in a half-moon on my chest, my *love* in every word. "You are my family, now and always, and I would burn the world for—"

Balor broke rank first, charging for me with a snarl and dragging me into a kiss so fiery Hell itself would *weep* with jealousy. I tossed an arm around his neck, molding to him with a moan, taking every whiff of brutality, savoring the flash of teeth, the thrust of his tongue—the *monster* coming undone against me like it was the first time, the last time, the only time. He kissed like he couldn't restrain himself anymore, like every kiss before had been so restrained and gentle. Heat swelled between us, darkness gathering, the moonlit clearing somehow brighter, the stars like little spotlights to the main event.

Hands caressed me from all sides: Balor's at my hips, my ass, and Arawn's possessive hold at the nape of my neck while Draco delicately plucked the sheer black veil from my hair. Full to bursting with love, with want and need and passion, I took all their savagery, all their tenderness, praying to whoever might be listening that it would imprint on my soul and stay with me forever.

Tearing my mouth from Balor's, I fisted Arawn's jacket with one hand, then slapped the other at my most savage monster's shoulder. Already black mists plumed from his forehead like ram horns, Balor's eyes blacker than the blackest pits, his tongue forked as it swept the blood from his lower lip. My blood. I sucked my lip between my teeth, confirming the metallic tang, the flicker of pain. Breath rising, the clearing assaulted with soft rumbles and beastly growls, I pushed on his shoulder, pleasure pulsing between my thighs when Balor dropped without question. Kneeling in the snow, he shot me a wolfish grin, then dug through my skirts, through layers of night and shadow turned into silks and tulle, eventually diving under.

"*Oh.*" My cry cracked across the clearing, the first sweep of his forked tongue between my thighs like a lit match to gasoline. As easy as it was to get lost in one of them, these moments as a group were about sharing— connecting and growing and loving. So, I surrendered to Arawn's kiss, leaning into him so he could claim my mouth from behind, his elegant fingers brushing under my chin, tipping me back. He conquered like the most polite invader, a Viking with manners, somehow both filthy and sweet. His tongue was kind, his teeth sheathed—but his words in my head, his promises... Pure sin.

While Arawn possessed me, slow and passionate and deep, Draco made quick work of my cloak, peeling it from my shoulders and unfurling it over the black altar. Even with my eyes shut, I knew those spidery fingers, their work always swift and succinct, soon gently plucking the back clasps of my dress open one by one.

But then his teeth found my bare throat just as Balor licked between my thighs, and I arched, body no longer my own, as hot, twisty pleasure coiled up my core. They loved to make me squeal and contort—make me scream and wail with a climax that tore at my seams. Then, in the cozy aftermath, each would stitch me back together, tender and protective, sweet and teasing. I adored both. The fire and the ice, the burn and the frost.

What I couldn't do anymore, however, was sit back and let *them* call all the shots. So, as Balor spread my legs wider and really tucked in, feasting on me, fucking me with that forked tongue while his thumb assaulted my swollen clit, I settled on a target.

My first victim.

Draco was easy prey in the group, the first to fold and submit when the others pressed him.

It was something we all enjoyed—watching this emotionless creature fracture and split, his control gone and his deepest self bared.

Still lip-locked with Arawn, I grabbed at Draco's belt— ripped it open, followed by the buckle, the button, the zipper. He stiffened, still undressing me, so focused on *that* that I managed to catch him off guard.

Another victory.

I found him hard as rock and straining against cotton briefs that belonged on a man, not a primordial god, a tatter of our world's origins. Offensive, this thing—I snapped the waistband with a frustrated huff, but before he could appease me, I slipped my hand below and stroked his silky head. Draco jerked in my grasp, inhaling sharply as I smeared his arousal around, the beaded pearl so hot on his icy skin, so pliant and workable beneath my fingers.

Arawn let me break our kiss with a soft snarl, his black gaze hooded and tracking my every move. Just for a moment, I needed to watch Draco, see him struggle with self-control as I stroked him. Stiff arms fell to his sides, and he gulped, throat bobbing noticeably beneath that turtleneck. His eyes drifted shut, white lashes twitching, fighting submission every step of the way.

Lost in my win, I tuned out Balor for a *second*—and, as if sensing my distraction even under all those layers of night, the monster between my thighs *snapped* at my sensitive skin, then plunged two fingers into me, viciously stroking my inner wall as I shot onto my toes and yelped, eyes wide, heart on fire, pleasure like lightning in my veins.

With Balor on a personal mission to make me screech, my rhythm faltered with Draco, all that ground gained fading by the second. In need of balance, I groped around for Arawn, fisting his jacket and tipping my head back against his shoulder, blinking up at a starry sky, mouth open, heat soaring. He nipped at my shoulder, my neck, my jaw, the snap of his teeth featherlight and torturous.

But when our eyes met, mine watered, a surge of fresh tears to match the shimmer in his, emotion raw, my kindest monster the most vulnerable. His little nod told me he understood—all that talk of burning the world, of family and acceptance...

Arawn always heard me, no matter what nonsense *actually* came out my mouth.

Finding strength in that moment, I braced on his taut

abdomen and pushed up, then tugged insistently at his jacket. No words necessary: a demanding lift of my eyebrows turned his grin sharp, and he retreated slowly while I pumped Draco's cock and Balor lapped between my thighs. With our eyes locked, Arawn peeled off his jacket, then his vest, black fabric of the finest pedigree falling to the snow one layer at a time. Black twined across his body, his darkness rich and opaque under his skin, an intricate spiderweb that only showed itself when we were lost in the moment. One piece at a time—and then that sculpted body was all mine, that work of art, my marble god who designed this form to my tastes.

They all did.

I mean, they were tatters of Erebus's cloak—darkness incarnate, shadow and mist and fog. But they possessed a fraction of their maker's gifts, allowing them to shift and transform. Anything they set their mind to, just like me and the night... And they chose to live on two legs, beautiful men who made my knees weak.

They could be monsters.

But they reined it all in, composed themselves, for a daughter of night who loved their bodies as much as their minds and spirits.

The thought left a lump of *feeling* in my throat, but just before I could get it out, thank them again and again and again, Balor broke me. Tongue working my clit, strong fingers massaging that delicious spot along my inner walls, he ripped me apart and burned me alive, a climactic *surge* shredding my body so suddenly, so violently, that I gave him the shriek he craved. My body flailed and arched, totally out of control as pleasure rocked through it. A second swarm of night-touched butterflies exploded from my fingertips, spiraling out of Draco's pants from the one hand, fluttering through Arawn's hair with the other, circling above us like a tornado on their quest for the stars.

Balor's laughter—seductive, cruel, victorious chuckles —made the ground tremble, and he crawled out from under my dress, lips stained with my orgasm, eyes starving for more. Without his support, my knees buckled, but Draco caught me before I hit the ground, my handjob way off the rails, head too fuzzy to focus on much at this point. As he stood, Balor dragged my dress with him, peeling the night away strip by strip, the last of it trailing over my head. It too floated off, chasing the butterflies, morphing from a dress to a starry blanket, one with the sky in no time.

With me and Arawn stripped down to nothing, Balor glanced between us, sharklike in his assessment, and I tensed, half expecting an attack. Instead, he undid the top button of his dress shirt, painfully slow, like he wanted to put on a show, draw out the anticipation—

"Just get on with it," Draco muttered, rolling his eyes as I snorted and Balor cackled. Then, in a flash, the rest of his clothes—slacks that clung to strong thighs and cupped his sculpted ass, the shirt that made him so refined when he was anything but—melted away, literally dissolving to mist and sprinkling the snow.

Smitten with the rugged peaks and valleys of his gods-carved body, I reached for him, content to trace and tug at the black hairs littered down his chest—but hard hands and bruising fingers dug into my waist, and suddenly I was out of the snow, hoisted up and dumped unceremoniously on the altar. The only one of us still fully dressed, Draco hopped on behind me, jaw set, eyes my beloved inferno, and then rolled me onto my belly. I smoothed my hands across the bridal cloak draped over the onyx, so soft and smooth, then yelped when his punishing strength found my hips and yanked them up.

Draco pierced me to the hilt with a single brutal thrust, both plunging into me and dragging my hips back to feel the full brunt of his dominance. While he usually folded first, my white-haired shadow loved to remind *me* most of all that he *let* us torment him, and if he had the choice, he fucked to destroy. For all his quiet, his lurking in dark corners and endless staring, he was a conqueror unlike any other. He weaved pain and pleasure together like a pro, fluent in orgasm denial, confident in his ability to edge until you wanted to rip your hair out—masterful in the way he made me feel both inherently safe and forever at risk.

Tonight seemed less about that, however, and more about frenzied togetherness, Draco frantic, almost unhinged, in the way he pounded into me. With my hips trapped in a bruising cage, he set the pace, dragging me back into him just as he slammed forward to meet me. Rough and brutal, he claimed me on the altar while the others circled like hawks, watching, smirking, both the bastards chuckling every time I yelped or mewled or cried out. Fisting the veil below, I had no choice but to submit, braced on my elbows and knees, Draco driving us forward at a punishing pace, the slap of skin to skin cataclysmic, *booming* over the silent pine forest.

At one point, another set of gruff fingers took hold, Balor working his fist into my hair as my head hung low, jerking and bobbing, my breasts bouncing painfully with every harsh thrust. While Draco did his dark work from behind, Balor hoisted me up just enough to put me at eye level with a thick, veiny erection. High on endorphins and adrenaline, on Draco's savagery and Arawn's velvet voice and Balor's twisted grin, I acted without thought: I opened my mouth and poked my tongue over my lips, ready for him.

And Balor hesitated. His brows furrowed and his fist tightened, the silken head *right* at my lips—but not quite taking the plunge just yet.

"Not sure I trust that smile," he growled, his shadowy horns huge and twisted over his skull, his free hand sporting a set of talons very similar to mine. I quirked my lips more, smile dangerous enough to keep all of them on their toes, and barely managed a shrug.

"I-it's a r-risk you'll h-have to take," I stuttered with every harsh slam of Draco's hips, his cock deep and his pace shoving me back up the mountain. Fluttering my lashes at Balor, I opened my mouth again, waiting, offering him what he wanted—*daring* him to take that risk. Maybe he'd get some teeth. Maybe he'd find something hot and pliant.

With a flash of his canines, Balor arched my neck and plunged between my lips, burying half his substantial shaft in my mouth before it hit the back of my throat. His groan made the trees shiver, and once again, I had to brace on the altar. All my bravado—gone, dominated by two of the great loves of my life, both of them fucking me with a wild abandon I'd never tasted before.

They were always chaotic, these two, but this, *love* thick in the air, really drove us to new heights.

Around Balor's thrusting hips, even as my eyes threatened to roll right back in my head, I caught Arawn prowling onto the altar from the far end. Gloriously naked and streaked with black, he crawled toward us with the elegance of a sleek panther, every press of his paws unleashing a gust of shadow. Darkness pooled around his big hands, his knees, his feet, while black mists shrouded him like armor. I couldn't look away, not when his easy smile turned sharp and deadly, and definitely not when he slowly—so fucking *slowly*—eased over onto his back, then scooted backward across the veil.

Without a single word shared, Balor made space for him. After one last rough push between my lips, he reared back and lifted me by my throat. One strong hand raised me, bared me to an approaching Arawn. If he squeezed just right, he'd snap my neck. Instead, he *barely* cut off my breathing, the pressure on my windpipe gentle, the press on the sides more apparent. The goal was a lightheaded euphoria—not strangulation.

Despite the position shifts, Draco didn't let up. He continued dragging me back, spearing me again and again, violent in the way he loved me. Arawn, meanwhile, shuffled right into the thick of things, his graceful fingers stroking my quivering inner thighs, then my clit, such a cool balm compared to the others, gentle but just as torturous. With Balor's hand around my throat, Arawn dead set on breaking me all over again, and Draco merciless, I didn't stand a chance.

This second climax struck like hot syrup, a slow burn that oozed all over. Whatever sounds I made flew right over my head, tongue thick and mewls incoherent. My body clenched around Draco almost in reverent thanks, and he finally let up, jerking and stuttering, collapsing over me with a choked groan as he spilled himself inside, filling me with new darkness to unleash upon the world.

The moment Draco withdrew, however, there was Arawn to take his place, his fingers pumping gently inside, his influence blossoming like a wildflower under the sun. Brutal lovemaking came with a price, and in Draco's case, it was a sore pinch that made me wince—soothed fast by the divine creature between my thighs, his free hand massaging my taut inner thighs, his tongue occasionally flicking out to taste me. Braced on a plane of defined abs, I soon arched and whimpered, riding him, relaxing under his touch, the fires in my core wanting for his attention.

Attention that soon drifted elsewhere, the thick wet from my pussy smeared back. He circled the puckered hole there, then tentatively nudged inside, one finger at a time, readying me for more to come. Eventually, he speared me with three digits, and I knew right then and there it wasn't Arawn who'd reap the rewards of all this hard work, but a monster with a way bigger dick.

Grinning like the cat who'd skinned the canary, Balor guided me down to said cock, easing it between my lips, coaxing me without words to pay him a little attention. And I did—barely, drawing the bulbous head between my lips and nothing more, making him *suffer* because I knew exactly how he'd take me in a few minutes.

Meanwhile, Draco prowled in his usual circle, prim and proper and fully dressed, not a hair out of place, like he hadn't just fucked me into oblivion and left me destroyed on top of an altar. *Shit*, why did that just *do it* for me? I moaned anytime we made eye contact, his full of heady mirth, mine desperate for more.

Never a pair to leave me wanting, Balor and Arawn hopped to when my last whimper sounded just a little too pathetic. Retreating from my mouth, Balor scooped me up in his big arms and flung me around, manhandling me until I straddled Arawn, who caught my hips, almost under the guise of steadying me, and then pushed me back onto his cock.

"*Ah*, fuck," I hissed, sliding all the way down, pussy full, a pleasurable shudder zipping through me, bursting from my center like a firework. Looking a little too smug on his back, Arawn bucked up with a smirk, all his charm laced with mischief now. Then, just as I braced on his chest again, ready to ride him hard so I could watch that smugness shrivel and die, he cupped my face and dragged me into such an achingly tender kiss that my eyes watered and my heart swooned. Slowly, he eased back down, taking me with him, his hands questing over my curves like he owned them, not stopping until they hit my thighs—and spread them wider.

My eyes snapped open. *Tricks*. Tricks and distractions. We all liked to one-up each other in these moments, no need for words or teasing, our actions speaking way louder. Watching someone powerful fracture—there was no better high out there.

And here, now, Arawn had lulled me into surrender—just so Balor could crawl up behind me and claim my ass. You know, really tighten the noose so I had *zero* hope of escape.

I squealed and clenched at the first inch, like I always did, but there was Arawn to soothe me, the game briefly set aside so he could calm my alarmed body. After all, Balor was the biggest of the three, and taking him *there* had always been a challenge. From a twenty-five-year-old virgin to taking two men at once, the last month and a half had been an adventure, full of all sorts of lessons that were, as Balor had promised on the beach, *really* fun.

By now, I just needed to relax.

Submit to the moment, to Balor filling me an inch at a time, kisses and caresses and soft murmurs from the coziest darkness in my life easing things along.

Once Balor sank home, however, all bets were off.

Arawn rocked first. Balor ground just a little harder.

And suddenly it was a competition between them. Who

could make me squeal louder. Who could make me shake harder. Who could make me come first. Who could steal my attention the longest.

Fuck if I knew. Stuck in the middle of their games, pleasure burning and body no longer my own, the best I could do was hang on and try not to pass out. At one point, trapped between two thrusting, writhing, grinding bodies, hands everywhere, mouths marking me, bruising me, Draco grabbed my chin.

His white hand, those spidery fingers, shot out of the dark and held tight.

"All this talk of love," he whispered, his voice a dozen or more, hisses and snarls, growls and rumbles, nasally and impossibly deep. He then tipped his head as Arawn and Balor slowed to a torturous grind, really working my clit as I lay helpless between them. Hellfire flared in Draco's eyes, and he cocked an eyebrow, really gritting into my chin. "Do you know what I love, Selene?"

I blinked heavily, only vaguely aware that he expected —no, *demanded*—an answer. "W-what?"

"Watching them destroy you," Draco mused, releasing my chin so casually as Balor laughed, tossing me back to the wolves with a dismissive sniff, his blasé attitude *almost* enough to hurl me into the abyss. "Your cunt and ass filled and taken... There is nothing more exquisite in the entire fucking cosmos than what I see before me, here and now."

Oh. My eyes rolled back when, right on cue, Balor and Arawn resumed their pace, driving into me from the front and the back, four hands and two mouths marking me, claiming me, bruising me—*making* me theirs for all to see. As much as I loved *that*, my body so primed to explode it *hurt*, hearing filth drip from Draco's lips was almost better. Almost. So rare, to hear him whisper dirty sweet nothings.

So beautiful, like a bard reciting poetry, that I lost myself in the words, in the fire, in the final spark that burned us all alive.

I came this time with a hoarse screech, grabbing at Arawn's shoulder and Balor's pumping hips. The world went completely black for a moment, but I wasn't scared anymore. Darkness was home now. Darkness was where we belonged. I could live in it forever, but the two creatures driving into me dragged me to new heights, and suddenly, light erupted behind my clenched lids. Light and color and beauty unparalleled, my body's bliss playing out in my mind's eye like the last firework show before the end. A final hurrah and then *darkness*.

Balor broke shortly after, stuttering and grinding against my ass, his shadowy mists blanketing us, pinning we three to the altar. Arawn—he held out the longest, his teeth gritted and bared, his cozy charm all hard and tense, until finally his name murmured in my shaky rasp was his undoing.

And then it was done. Breaths racing, hearts pounding, fingers entwined and bodies sweaty, we peeled apart, then rearranged ourselves on the altar. Draco climbed on, extending the sides to accommodate for four bodies, at least two of which barely fit side by side on the onyx block to start with. When that was sorted, I pulled the night close, covering my boys, dousing us in black and stars, then curled into Arawn's side, finding the most comfort in his sweet embrace.

"In case it wasn't abundantly clear from the start," he murmured, stroking the side of my face, brushing a few curls from my temple, "we love you too, little one. Deeply. Forever and always."

I nodded, body pleasantly sore and spent, drowsiness

settling as the blanket of night across all of us turned weighted and warm.

"I know," I whispered back, heart so wonderfully full as Balor snuggled up against my back, burrowing his face into the dip between my shoulder blades with a contented rumble. Then, over Arawn's sculpted chest, I caught Draco's sleepy gaze and grinned. "Forever and always…"

He offered a slow blink in reply.

I meant to give one back, but when my eyes closed, they stayed shut, sleep taking over so I could play with these three monsters in my dreams instead.

Forever and always, beneath a starry night sky.

CHAPTER TWENTY-FOUR

Selene.

I woke with a start, heart jerking and gut dropping, the echoes of a woman's whisper still ringing around my skull. Dazed and more than a little groggy, I bolted up—only for Arawn's deadweight arm to drag me right back down. Mists whooshed when I hit the onyx altar again, and I blinked hard at a starry sky, at the swaying tips of the surrounding pine forest.

Oh.

Right.

The clearing—the altar, the declarations of love and fantastic sex.

Yeah.

After picking the crusts from my lashes, awareness trickling in, focus sharpening, I tried again, wiggling around Arawn's arm with a grunt. The night I had drawn close before we all crashed slithered down my body, a silky blanket that still fluttered over the extended altar. Balor snoozed away to my right, almost completely dissolved into shadow, just a black silhouette with snores like dull tiger roars revving somewhere deep within.

As if sensing something amiss, even in a sleep so deep his eyelids danced and black twisted under his skin, Arawn curled inward, nestling into my lower back with a warning rumble. After a few delicate strokes of his forehead, smoothing the worry lines flat, I turned and flinched, startled by Draco's back facing me from the far end of the altar, his hair like starlight in the darkness, his frame solid as the onyx below.

"Did you hear that?" I barely whispered, not wanting to wake the others but also unsure if Draco was actually with me—or had he just fallen asleep sitting up? It wouldn't be the first time. A silent beat passed, the wind dead, the pines suddenly much too still and the snow muffling everything. Arawn cozied a little closer, his long arms coiling around my waist, the tip of his nose icy against my bare lower back.

Mystery voice briefly set aside, I twisted back just enough to readjust the starry blanket over his shoulders.

"No," came Draco's scratchy reply. I straightened, frowning while he swiveled around, rigid and stiff like winter had frozen him down to the marrow. Hollow black eyes swept across me, Arawn, and then Balor, giving nothing away—and yet somehow that spoke volumes. My heart skipped another few beats, and I tugged the blankets up to my chin with a shiver.

"I heard—"

Selene. Come.

The blood drained from my face in prickly waterfalls, and I bit the insides of my cheeks, terrified. A stranger's voice had found a way inside my head. Womanly and rich. Powerful and commanding. Alluring too, my legs already swinging through Balor's misty form, adrenaline and interest and fear piqued.

Only Draco didn't seem worried. In fact, he gave me his back again with a nasally hum, head tipped, eyes to the sky.

"She feels different now that we found you," he admitted as I pushed forward and started to crawl toward him. "Still extraordinary... but she isn't ours."

Frown deepening, I changed course and climbed off the side of the altar, beckoning night in, using my darkness and shadows, *my* connection to the black sky above, to make a simple sheath dress. Straight up and down cut. Long, loose sleeves. Neckline a horizontal slash from collarbone to collarbone. Black and star-dusted. Warm, above all else, same as the fuzzy boots I added to my feet.

Without another word, I trudged through the snow across the clearing and into the trees. No clue where I was headed or why, but my body seemed to know. I let it do its thing, feet guiding me around the flared skirts of bushy pines, downwind and downhill, on and on until there was literally nowhere else to go. The trail flattened, then dropped off into a snowy crevice, the forest looming tall, bleak, and silent on the other side of the abyss.

Well then.

Kind of anticlimactic—

Darkness swelled from the ravine, blotting out the snow, soaring wide and curved like the top of a hot air balloon.

Only it wasn't smooth like a balloon.

No, the darkness had familiar dips and arcs—curls, almost, black and unruly and—

I shrieked and scrambled back when the darkness gave way to the top of a pale forehead, enormous, a giant suddenly crawling out from the depths of our world. A third eye in the dead center blinked at me, then two more in a translucent blue, followed by rich, deep, womanly laughter when my frantic backpedaling knocked me flat on my ass.

The ground shivered and the pines quaked, spurred by that *noise*, that voice so familiar—like one of the screams in the chorus that shredded my throat every time I birthed new darkness. Still, the familiarity didn't diminish the what-the-fuckery of the moment, and I held my breath, tensed in the snow, ready for fight or flight if necessary. Only when the head started to shrink did I let that stifling inhale out. Smaller and smaller, it closed in on itself, until finally it disappeared below the ridge. The laughter stopped. The forest stilled. I leaned closer—

And yelped when a pale, willowy arm flung over the edge, plunging into the snow, followed shortly by a second— *please, don't let there be a third*. Together, they hauled a woman up, a stunning creature with black curls and pale skin and bright, light blue eyes and holy shit it was like looking into a mirror.

I gawked at her, at this beauty in night silks, her dress cut seductively over curves way more generous than mine. But the rest—her high cheekbones and the freckles over the bridge of her nose that glowed like stars... I had those. Even her lips matched mine, dull pink and full. Her hair and her hands and those *talons*—

"M-Mom?"

She blinked back at me, all three eyes narrowed, until the one in the middle of her forehead disappeared—almost reabsorbed into her skin, which was... something.

"Hello, Selene." Her smile stretched a little too wide, too many pearly whites exposed behind those full lips. Ancient predator. Divine monster. *Nyx.* "What a title they've given you. Perhaps they thought it clever, to name you after a moon goddess—but it suits you all the same."

She headed straight for me, gliding over the snow, not through it, and it felt like she dragged all the cosmos with her. I wilted, the walls of this world closing in on every side, her presence all-consuming. The nearer she got, the more my brain reasoned that while we looked alike, this creature, *protogenoi*, was so much *more* than I could ever be.

Some teeny bit of the old me tried to use that flood of adrenaline—*run*. Shell-shocked, I pushed back a little when she finally stopped in front of me, then fluttered into a graceful kneel at my feet. But the night dipped with her, mists and wisps and starry darkness spiraling off her skin, her hair, more lovely than any of the night skies I had experienced over the last month.

When she offered her hand, I took it.

Because that hand—

Full black, the same tint as mine, but the shading shifted at her wrist, the darkness haphazard up her delicate forearm like watercolor brush strokes. Our nails almost matched. Mine were sharp enough to cut flesh and bone. Hers with their slight hooked ends were made to slash souls.

Still, I placed both my hands into one of hers, and she held them so sweetly it brought tears to my eyes.

"I am pleased you found each other," Nyx insisted with a thoughtful glance up the hill behind me. "We belong with our Erebus, and he to us."

The new thick and achy lump in my throat wouldn't budge no matter how hard I gulped, and, worse still, no matter how I steeled myself, my lower lip still wobbled and my words came out a strangled whine. "W-why did you leave me? Am I your... daughter?"

A gentle breeze gusted through the trees as she scrutinized me, starting with my hands, my arms, then up to my face.

"You are a part of me," she said eventually. I sucked in my cheeks, her response flat and vague enough to feed the fire that started the night we left Cronus.

"Is that a yes?"

Oh. Oh shit. No, no, no—*do not snark your primordial mom.* Nyx tipped her head to the side, and the whole world went with her, my head spinning and my belly looping.

"Sorry," I muttered, eyes down and head bowed. Her fingers coiled tighter around both my hands, and when I chanced looking up again, I came face-to-face with that great white grin, *so* many teeth in that mouth of hers, maybe more than a single row.

"You are a feather from my wings." Nyx then rolled her shoulders, and out flared two enormous wings on either side, feathery like depictions of angels.

Black as night.

Coarse and complex, streaked with undertones of dark, dark blues and purples and—

Raven wings. I gaped at them, the last of my reluctance just smoldering ruins as a strange kinship ignited inside me, a painful yearning that didn't *stop* until she let me brush one finger across one silky feather. As I retreated, settling cross-legged in the snow, night and mist billowing around us, it was like the final few puzzle pieces just clicked into place.

"This place was built by deceivers." Wings tucked but relaxed at her back, Nyx gave another pointed glance up the hillside. "A site of worship, yes, with most of the proper rites and procedures—so long after the world stopped their prayers." Her grin faltered, a faraway look taking over. "I made them wait. I made them prove themselves. For two centuries, *Cronus* left offerings to me on the same altar you did."

My head snapped up at that *name*, and Nyx flicked a muted pink tongue over her teeth, grimacing like she was trying to get rid of a bad taste.

"I blessed them with the sight of me... once. They tried to take me... once." There was that horrifying smile again, all those teeth on display, her eyes alive and bright as the North Star. "None survived the *once*."

Haunting laughter galloped through the forest, sounding like her but not coming *from* her. Not in the way you'd expect, anyway, but almost like the trees remembered —like the horrors she inflicted on those poor dumb fuckers still sparked joy so long after the fact.

"I flew home to my love, of course, but lost a feather or two on the way," she continued, permitting me to finally withdraw from her claw. I flexed my fingers under my loose sleeve to get the blood going again, then stuffed both hands into my lap as the great goddess Nyx sighed, staring at me like she could still see that feather. "I always lose a few in flight... but when the humans arrived to clear what was left of their dead, they took that feather."

Batshit crazy as all this sounded, nothing in me rebelled against it.

My body, my heart, my mind—with all systems online after a lifetime in limbo, I knew the truth when I heard it.

"Put the feather in a lab," she carried on, her lofty soprano side making the hairs on my arms rise. "And in their birth chambers—" An incubator, probably. "—with their *base* knowledge of those who once ruled the world, they grew *you*."

Like a baby chick under a heat lamp.

What the actual fuck.

Just as my insecurities flared, Nyx eased closer and cupped my cheek, the wet in her eyes glistening like diamonds. "A piece of *me*, my daughter. A little feather who became so beautiful."

She swept my hair aside and traced my face, and I fell into her caress with a strangled whine, nuzzling at her palm and clutching her wrist.

"My whole life h-has been *them*," I choked out. "Why didn't you come for me?"

She pinched my chin and sighed again, mists and snow whooshing around us in a gentle whirlwind. "In suffering, there is strength. In sadness, there is hope. How strong you are, Selene. How brave. You didn't need me—"

"But I *did*!" My shout cracked in the sky, displeasure and pain and *sorrow* chilling the air and setting off a drumline of thunder. Logic gone, I grabbed harder at this ancient being, this monstress from the dawn of time, and held on so tight she'd never leave again. "I-I needed my *mom*!"

"Hush, hush," Nyx whispered, the thunder rolling away and the frost receding. "She's here."

Here and on the move. One moment she knelt in front of me, and the next, she crawled behind me, bundling me in night and lifting me into her lap. We were roughly the same size for a while, but now it was like nestling into a ten-foot giantess. Eyes closed, I curled into the softness of her stomach, arms folded at my chest, and then *breathed* the clearest, freshest air, scented like morning dew on grass. I had never felt so small in my life, literally and figuratively, but as Nyx cradled me and stroked my hair, my back, my arms, humming softly, it was exactly what I had always needed.

What I'd been missing since my first squalling gasp under bright lights, surrounded by doctors and researchers and *humans*—

"But she has many sons and daughters, your mother," Nyx murmured, her words inside my head, firm but kind. *What I say goes.* That was the vibe, no room for argument or compromise. "Thousands of children—and she cannot be with them all, not when the night calls as it does, neediest of my creations."

While it wasn't what I had always craved from a mom, it... made sense.

Arawn had already popped this exact bubble back in that library. My mom was a busy lady, a primordial monster with a duty to our world and a husband who was *her* whole world.

"I don't think I really stack up to the rest of your sons and daughters." *My brothers and sisters.* Yikes. I'd gone from an only child to quite possibly the youngest of a thousand siblings. Kind of overwhelming, actually. My weak chuckle did nothing to lift my spirits, the feeling of worthlessness slinking in, trying to make itself at home even as my inner darkness barked it back. "I mean, they're all goddesses and gods and furies and—"

"And you are a piece of me. That is more than enough," Nyx crooned, tipping my head up with one enormous black talon under my chin. She fluttered her long lashes, her third eye back and only marginally less unsettling than it was before. "Shall I gift you a formal title? Would that ease your concerns?"

In the face of true godliness, eternity in all her glory, I really wished my brain could figure out how to be just a *little* articulate. "I-I, uh..." Instead, I gawked up at Nyx, at a complete and utter loss. *Formal title?* Like—was she offering to make me a goddess of something? Someone? A city? A patron?

What.

My mom proved she could, in fact, be merciful. After a story about the horrors of divine wrath, she grinned extra wide again, and her third eye trembled as it probed deep inside me, right down to the nitty-gritty stuff that made my heart lurch and my mouth dry.

"Ah," she mused, her whisper like a soothing west wind, "I see you've chosen your calling already."

"What? No, I—"

"Selene, daughter of Nyx..." She tapped my nose with a sharp, scary talon, then crinkled *her* nose down at me like she was cooing over a newborn. "Guardian of ravens, bats, and lost black cats."

Nyx then pressed her whole hand to the middle of my chest and *pushed*, crushing my ribs inward, a *whump* pounding through me like one of those TV defibrillator shocks. I sucked in a harsh gasp, eyes squeezed shut, lightning in my veins and thunder in my soul.

Boom. Purpose in my heart.

The world behind my eyelids went very, very dark for a few moments, followed by the flutter of feathery wings and wind so violent it hurled me up the hill into a fresh pile of snow. Cold splashed under my dress, and I came back to the forest with another gasp, only this time, it was like gulping fresh air *right* after you breached the surface, seconds from drowning: not exactly refreshing, but life-giving all the same.

And Nyx was gone.

No feathers left behind.

No chance to grow a sibling, I guess.

Weird.

My life had gotten so *weird* in such a short period of time—

"Frustrating creatures, aren't they?" Arawn stood at the

crest of the hill, hands in his pockets, casual as sin, and flanked by Draco and Balor. He shook his head, his smile thin. "The highest of the high... I'm afraid they forget how the rest of us exist most of the time. You know, with thoughts, feelings, fate."

As I brushed the snow off my legs, he looked to the sky with a tsk, a silent chastisement for the mom who had blessed me and left me just like that. The emotional whiplash might have dragged me under had Balor not jogged back a few paces, then went sprinting over the hilltop, flinging himself into the air and skidding all the way down to me, heralded by a tidal wave of white. I braced with a squeal-giggle, arms up and head ducked against the onslaught.

"Ravens, bats, and lost black cats!" he boomed, almost giddy as he shimmied to my side. Then, still very naked, his toned physique snow-dappled and *yummy*, he rolled onto his belly and propped himself up on his elbows, chin on his fists, feet kicking behind and lashes fluttering up front. "What a charge for all eternity, huh?"

Pride twisted in my chest, the sensation unfamiliar but not unpleasant. In fact, the monster it now shared space with *purred*, her interest in the black cat side of things especially apparent.

Which... wasn't bad at all.

I liked ravens.

Bats were pretty cute.

And nobody treated black cats as nicely as they should —so why shouldn't *I* be their guardian? A feather from Nyx's wing, a piece of the ancients and hopefully immortal like her: it was the least I could do with her gifts.

Arawn and Draco followed in Balor's massive body slide, padding down the compressed snow and eventually each offering me a hand. I took them both so they could heave me up, preening a little while all three brushed snow off the starry night hugging my figure. Then, Draco at the helm, Arawn by my side with a hand on my lower back and a bouncy Balor bringing up the rear, we climbed the snowy hillside together, headed for the clearing with its fake Cronus altar in a cozy quiet.

And I realized right then and there: as much as I had wanted *a* mom growing up, I didn't need this one now. My actual mom could do as she pleased—and would, no matter what I said. She would usher in the night as she had done for all time, her husband by her side, king of darkness who had inadvertently gifted me the three greatest treasures of all.

I wasn't alone anymore. Like Nyx, I had my darkness.

I had my family.

Balor, Draco, and Arawn—they were more than enough.

I... *I* was more than enough.

Selene, daughter of Nyx, guardian of ravens, bats, and lost black cats—is enough, just as she is.

For the first time in my life, I finally believed it.

CHAPTER TWENTY-FIVE

Tonight, I birthed darkness into the world alone.

And this one stayed.

Shy and sweet, we played in the trees for ages, shadow and mist twirling around me, ruffling my curls and slithering between my fingers. Nervous of hooting owls and skittering squirrels, it hid beneath my cloak, close to my heart, quivering, until I shooed the intruders away.

This one tugged at my heartstrings the most—almost like it *needed* me.

Until a horrible screechy howl shattered the night.

Then it was gone.

Just like that, *poof*, it rocketed straight up and vanished above the pines, never to be seen again.

Heart in my throat, I stilled and listened, eyes watery, soul on *fire* at that awful, awful sound.

To celebrate my new title, guardian of all Nyx decreed, Arawn had disappeared a little over an hour ago, zipping around the world to collect a feast so we could party in style. Given literal food wasn't really Balor's preference, he'd stepped away from the clearing too, temporarily gone to hunt terror in the nearby villages. Only Draco stayed behind, my silent sentry, but kept his distance when I asked, so inspired by Nyx's visit that I wanted to do this one solo— just like her.

While not thrilled about me wandering around the forest alone, Draco had waited in the clearing as I birthed *our* darkness all by myself, still close enough to summon with a whisper if I needed him.

But suddenly it sounded like *he* needed *me*.

Ice in my veins and terror in my heart, I sprinted as fast as these stupid self-made boots could carry me, dress and cloak all whimsical romantic fantasy at first glance but a pain in the ass in a crisis. Dragging the night with me, I whipped around the final fir, stumbling into the clearing, and then staggered to a stop, the sight ahead cutting me off at the knees.

Draco, flat on his back, stretched on the altar, legs flailing—and a *new* tatter of Erebus's cloak ripping him apart. Throat slit, thick black mist spilled from his gaping, jagged wound, and the humanoid shape lording over him had the same consistency, faded and dull, just two ghosts battling in the woods. Darkness collided, fighting, tearing into each other as snarls and more scratchy, nasally howls cleaved from *my* Draco.

"*Stop!*"

His attacker wheeled around, one hand still violently buried in Draco's wound, and he quickly sharpened into a spindly man with bowl-cut black hair and a Victorian suit, complete with dramatic coattails and a silky black ascot. An ivory walking stick leaned against the end of Nyx's fake Cronus altar, the air between us scented with chimney soot.

"Sweet Selene," he drawled, tearing at Draco without ever taking his eyes off me. That accent—vaguely English with a whole lot of other European lilts thrown in there. Another creature from the dawn of time... Here to *take*. "You are even more magnificent in the flesh."

"Get your hands off him," I ordered as I stalked into the rows of stone benches. "*Now.*"

Night swelled around me, thick and suffocating, the black aura sizzling and snapping in a stormy rage. Lightning lashed the clearing from the corner of my eye, my wrath made physical—my warning ignored.

"Call me Adam, sweet one," this new monster insisted, effortlessly batting Draco's clawed hand away when it swiped at his face, "and I shall call you Eve."

"You can fuck right off with *that.*"

My dismissive snort made his black gaze harden, and in a flash, he had Draco up in front of him, just like Audrey once used *me* with a gun under my chin for leverage in a fight, and I stilled, hands raised, silently begging him not to—

He plunged into the slice on Draco's neck and *ripped.*

"It pains me to do this to a brother," *Adam* declared over Draco's howls, "but for you, I would destroy them all. Every last one." His left hand ripped through shadowy tendon and flesh, splattering mists across the nearest stones, the pines groaning, their boughs cracking and twisting into gnarled silhouettes as Draco's agony flooded beyond the clearing. "There is only Erebus and Nyx, not..." He sneered down at my Draco, my beloved, his substantial nose wrinkled and lips peeled. "Not Erebus*es* and Nyx, after all. They're hogging you all to themselves."

I'm going to obliterate you.

One way or another, I would make this fucker *suffer*, and then I'd dance on his corpse.

But not now.

Not when he had the power to make Draco *scream* like that, a horror to haunt my nightmares until the end of days. Screechy and broken, nails on a million chalkboards, he bled sheer agony, his anguish, his destruction—he couldn't stop it, the floodgates blown to pieces.

"*Enough.*" I brushed some of the night away, the storm settling to a rumble, just a staticky plume of black cloud and mist around me. With feigned surrender, I added some bend to my knees, adopting all the submissiveness I could stomach, even as the monster in me craved that *thing's* head on a spike. "Stop, please. Just tell me what you want..."

"*You,* my love," Adam whined. Unlike Arawn, Balor, and Draco's early declarations of love and desire, his made me feel nothing but *fire.* "I want to bring you home so we can be together."

Of course he—

Wait.

Home.

I ground my teeth, the darkness around me shivering, the air sizzling with another blast of lightning. *Cronus.*

The only thing out there in Balor, Arawn, and Draco's weight class was one of their own—and clearly Cronus had found one, dangled me as bait, and sicced him on us like a mad dog. *Bring her home and she's yours forever.* I could hear it now, over the roar in my skull and the war cry in my heart. Those exact words—in Dad's voice.

No. I closed my eyes and took a deep breath. Not Dad.

Never again would that man be my father.

Another of Draco's screechy groans brought me back to the present, and a quick sweep around the clearing confirmed we were being watched.

By a fucking camera.

Right there, mounted in one of the pines, plain as day when you actually looked for it.

But who would think to root through the needles?

"Let h-him end me," Draco rasped, sagging in Adam's grasp, his strength waning, his throat gushing shadow. "F-fly, Selene, like you d-deserve—"

I raised my hand. Silence fell like a guillotine, night drawing closer and molding to me like armor. Gone was the fanciful gown and cloak, in its place sleek black trousers, a rigid dress shirt, and a fluttering trench backlit by stars.

"Adam," I called, rolling my shoulders back with a stiff smile, "I've birthed enough darkness with these three." My grin sharpened when he perked up like a wolf who'd scented blood on the wind. "Take me home."

The bastard tossed Draco aside like trash, my beloved's body crashing onto a nearby bench and sliding limp into the snow. He then hurried over to me and invaded my personal space without a thought, his arms outstretched, his teeth vampire-sharp. Before he could sweep me into a hug that would make my gut roil and my monster snap her own dangerously sharp teeth, I caught him with a hand to his chest. This Adam character melted, features softening, fuzzy darkness pluming from the top of his head like smoke from a lit candle. Solid, this body of his—but breakable.

With his guard down, he was just a lovesick pup.

And Nyx's fallen feather would snap his neck like a fucking twig.

Fluttering my lashes, I patted his chest—such a *good boy* —then dragged a black talon across it as I sauntered by, weaving around the stones to Draco. Hands clasped behind my back, I stood over him with a look that I hoped read as a cold, dismissive disinterest. My features did as they were told, lips thinned and nose crinkled, everything about me tight and distanced—everything but my eyes.

My eyes could never lie to him, to *any* of them.

Draco reached for me, his fingers crooked and warped, as if Adam had taken the time to break every knuckle. "S-Selene—"

Our gazes locked. I lifted my chin and sneered down at him. Draco shrank into the snow.

I love you. I love them. I thought the words as loud and clear as I could, repeating them over and over again until realization dawned in Draco's black eyes. They were all so adept at whispering inside *my* head. Over the last few weeks, I'd tried my hand at it, my efforts halfhearted and scrambled, lazy enough to make them laugh and fuss over me. Here, now, when it really mattered, I put my all into it. Darkness wobbled around me. Thunder rumbled in the distance. *I would burn the world for you too—and I will. Tonight. It ends tonight.*

Enough of this.

Finally free, I deserved to live my life as *I* chose, with the darkness *I* loved.

No more Cronus nipping at our heels.

I was a feather from Nyx's wings. Not a human. Not a hybrid. A piece of a protogenoi, a goddess who touched the skies at the dawn of time.

Enough.

Draco's voice, weak and fading, exhaled my name like a death rattle inside my skull—and it nearly broke me. Pain clogged my throat. Tears stung the backs of my eyes. Maybe that was all he could muster, maybe this was the end, but I shook my head, refusing to break character if it was just a hiccup in our love story, and pressed a finger to my lips.

Save your strength. Come back to me. Tell Arawn and Balor…

He reached those deformed fingers after me when I turned away, Adam's laughter whirling around us like a hailstorm. With a disgusted sniff, I paused, my back to Draco, and did my best to shoot one last glare over my shoulder.

You know where to find me, beloved.

Home was *them*, not Cronus HQ at Fort Beacham.

But there, the place I had called home for twenty-five years, was where it would all finally *end*.

Adam offered his hand as I glided back to him, his smile smug and his chest puffed and his fucking fingernails black like he'd changed them to match mine. Venom scorched up my throat. Hatred flared in my heart—but I kept my traitorous eyes down, all that loathing hidden behind demure lashes and a shy smile. I accepted his offer delicately, sliding my hand into his and suffering his bone-crushing grip as the darkness consumed us.

And as the shadows carried me back, I, a nightmare on the west wind, a monster of my own design, plotted how I'd make all of them reap exactly what they sowed.

CHAPTER TWENTY-SIX

This *Adam* jerk really needed to practice his landings, because, *ooof*, that was a rough one.

We slammed into the courtyard of the Fort Beacham Cronus HQ hard enough that the stonework buckled, and I stumbled out of his arms, wincing, walking off the twinge in both ankles. Darkness blanketed the familiar space, soft and gentle, the time zone planting us squarely in the late hours of night on the brink of morning. Snow dusted shrubbery and benches. Salt peppered the walkways. Blacked-out windows circled the space.

If you didn't know better, you'd have no idea that almost two months ago, just about every creature in the bowels of this place made a break for freedom.

Floodlights *screamed* to life suddenly, drenching the courtyard in bright white, and I ducked my head with a yelp. Eyes shut, the assault flickered behind my lids—and that was probably the point. As boots crunched over salt and cobblestone, on a slow but steady approach, closing in on all sides, the point of the theatrics was to throw me off.

Make me an easy target.

The monster in my chest roared, hungry for blood and pain, desperate to fill the courtyard with the same howls Adam wrenched from Draco.

Give it a second, girl.

With a deep breath, I straightened and rolled my shoulders back. While the light still made me squint, I masked it as best I could, sweeping the courtyard in silence, taking in every armed, masked Cronus security officer in their familiar black uniforms and body armor. They looked ready for war.

But they weren't my target.

Just good soldiers following orders—

"Not to worry, sweet Eve," Adam crooned, his hand slithering around my waist and crumpling my trench coat when he pressed closer. "It's just a precaution."

False pretenses dropped, I pinned him with a look that promised bloody, violent murder. His thick black brows furrowed as he blanched and loosened up on my hip.

"*Selene!*"

The floodlights dimmed a few settings—but strategically, meant to guide me, *tell* me where to focus without force. A new group burst from the building's main doors, the man who raised me leading the charge.

Albert Abbott.

Professor Abbott to some. Doctor Abbott to others. *Sir* to all the masked security, their helmets like matte-black mushroom caps.

Dad to me, all my life. Just Dad.

I went rigid, staring him down from the middle of the courtyard. Still in corduroy bell bottoms and shaggy dirty-blond hair, unassuming without his lab coat, without the various degree lettering stitched above the breast pocket. In this light, with a legion of fellow white coats at his back, his minions hunting me with their eyes as security swarmed to protect these *very* well-paid assets, he reminded me of a predatory bird now more than ever. Sharp, sleek features. Thin lips. Dismissive—even when he tried to look relieved.

"I'm so happy you're home—"

"Happy *I'm* home?" He stumbled, his mask cracking. Hearing *his* voice should have triggered the absolute shit out of me, every nitpicky, unimpressed, bored, apathetic thing he'd ever said blaring inside like a foghorn. Instead, I marveled at how *my* new voice must have sounded to him, deeper and richer, intricate and mature, me and the monster entwined and emboldened after our visit with Nyx.

Not only that, but I must have looked different the closer he got, my face fuller after finally eating *real* meals, my skin paler without all the drugs and demon marks. I raised my hands for good measure, a sick thrill tightening in my chest when the black talons and obsidian ink down my knuckles caught his eye. "Or are you just *happy* your longest-running experiment is back?"

"Now, beloved, family is so important," Adam murmured, wrapping his arms around me again like a deadweight sloth, violating my personal space in front of all these people, all these raised guns. "Go give your dad a hug, and then let's have a sit-down talk—"

"Get"—I turned in his embrace, seething up at him—"your hands"—I latched onto his throat with just one of mine, stabbing my talons in deep—"*off me!*"

His black mists flailed like a panicked rattlesnake's tail, but before he could scramble backward, I screamed. Out poured my hatred, my anger, my grief at being torn away from the darkness I so loved, my song a chorus of raging female voices. Sharp sopranos and flat altos. The monster and me and Nyx. Her daughters and their daughters after.

We all shrieked our fury, hurled it onto *Adam*—until he exploded.

Poof.

From a man to a shroud of lost black mist, he shattered right before my eyes. Instead of escaping into the beyond, disappearing on the wind like so many of my offspring, I sucked him back to me, gathering his remains as I did the night, dragging the mist close, hoarding every last fleck. It slipped through my lips and up my nose, into my skin and down to my soul.

Consumed.

Taken.

Destroyed.

Not exactly sure how, but the destruction had been instinctive; for the first time in my life, I trusted my body, my spirit, to do its thing.

Neither had failed me yet.

Energy thrummed in my veins, dark but placid, and when I straightened up again, alone in the middle of the circling wolves, security three rows deep was a hell of a lot closer. Guns up, they surveyed me behind opaque goggles and black masks, silent as the grave.

Once, it might have been intimidating.

Once, I would have crashed to my knees and cried, shaky hands raised.

I stood taller now, scanning the crowd, wondering if I knew any of them by name, before settling on Albert fucking Abbott.

"I'm not a fox you can sic the hounds on," I told him. "Don't ever send one of them after me again." I then tipped my head, appraising the man I used to think was so big, so powerful. Compared to the masculine energies I'd contended with since I left this place, *he* finally seemed about two inches tall, frail and painfully human. Intelligent but ordinary. "How do you hope to contain me, *Dad*? You know what I am."

He patted the air stiffly, never great at the whole empathy thing, at calming me down when the emotional toll got too high. "We can discuss this—"

"You should have left the feather alone." Sure, I wouldn't be here if they hadn't grabbed it and tossed it in an incubator, Nyx's magic nurtured and babied and poked and prodded until it morphed into something else entirely. "What a headache for you—for Cronus."

Starry night rolled off me in gentle waves, billowing like a fog toward the first line of defense. Security shifted their feet, a few looking down as twinkling black swept over their boots.

"*Selene.*" Ah, yes, there it was: chastisement in C-sharp, accented by a threatening undertone that always made the backs of my knees sweaty as a kid. "Stop that."

"No."

A guard yelped when my night coiled around his ankles and yanked him off-balance. One second he was upright, and the next, with me perfectly still, he was flat on his back, darkness surging over him like the tide.

"No, you need to understand who I am." Then, ever the merciful fallen feather, I urged the night to retreat, the starry black plumes rescinding just past the first line's boots. It settled there, billowing, roiling, choppy and silent in a huge circle around me. "Who I've *always* been."

Something sharp pricked my back, cutting through my conjured trench and dress shirt and twinging like a beesting. Frowning, I twisted around and awkwardly plucked the tranq dart from my mid-left back. No wooziness. No blurred vision or thick tongue. My frown deepened, the liquid inside half-drained and the color of sickly snot green. Not a bad play, all things considered.

I crushed the dart between my fingers and tossed its remains to the night.

"Wrong dose, Daddy Dearest," I announced, flicking the glass bits off my fingers. "That was the aim all along, right? Cronus tried to capture Nyx first, only that failed. But you had a piece of her to experiment on—make sure you didn't fail next time you tried to contain a goddess from the dawn of time. Big reach there, guys. Maybe stay in your lane—"

"You are my *daughter*," Albert snapped. His lips thinned and his jaw flared, that furious tooth grind painfully familiar. "No matter what, you—"

"No, I'm not." My chuckles shivered the night around me, and a beat later, the wrath I'd kept at a low simmer shattered one of the floodlights. The Cronus crowd flinched, a few of the lab coats behind my lifelong warden yelping and huddling together as glass and sparks sprinkled the cobblestone—and I just smiled as a dull pink awareness prickled in his cheeks. "Albert Abbot, you are a *shit* dad. Handlers in the hybrid program treat their wards better than you've *ever* treated me. No more. It's done."

A savage roar split the night sky wide open, Balor's war cry in all its brutal glory music to my ears. Tremors rumbled underfoot as shadows crashed into the courtyard like falling stars, like world-ending meteors, tinted windows shattering and white coats screaming, their cries drowned out by another raspy howl. *Draco.* He whipped around the courtyard like a black hurricane, plowing through security and knocking over anyone in his path. Arawn's delicious rumble followed, like a titan humming through his options of how best to crush the ants under his giant thumb and really make it *hurt*.

Gunfire rang out suddenly, but it died just as fast, maybe when they realized it was a waste of bullets.

Darkness swelled in my periphery, right and left, their presence thickening and sparking in the air. Heart full, I held my ground and waited until my dark gods took solid form. Arawn at my back, right behind me and scowling over my shoulder. He was the most human of the three, black lightning under his skin, his cozy comfort tucked aside for raw rage, his nails like my talons—ready for a fight. Draco, meanwhile, appeared less solid to my left, skin paler than usual, swollen bags under his eyes and the darkness around him like a raggedy, tattered security blanket this time. He was the only one I reached for, tentatively brushing his throat, pleased to find the wound sealed.

Closed but not gone. No, the faded pink slash across his neck stood as a reminder that one of his own had tried to butcher him tonight on my behalf.

For Cronus.

Our eyes tangled briefly, and he eased out of reach with a subtle nod.

I'm fine. He didn't say it, not out loud nor in my head, but I heard it all the same.

Just like I heard the cacophony of snarls and growls, the click-clack of claws over cobblestone to my right. Balor had gone full monster, naked and shrouded in shadow, enormous bat wings split from his back. Gargoyle legs and claws made for disemboweling. Face like a wolf, misty saliva spilled over three rows of razor-sharp teeth and a forked tongue.

"Don't you look handsome," I whispered, lobbing a smirk toward his monstrous face as Arawn's warmth bloomed in my core. While I had *despised* Adam's invasion of my personal bubble, I just about grabbed Arawn's arms and knotted them around me.

"Selene," my former father snapped when I leaned back against his chest instead, eyes shut as he kissed my temple, "these *things*—"

"I'm a thing too, technically." My eyes flew open, and the night at our feet darkened, stars culled, replaced by lightning that sizzled and *cracked* as far as my influence reached. Security on the front lines hesitated, and then as a group took a collective two steps back, weapons leveled at my head.

I barely noticed.

I only had eyes for *him*.

"I'm a feather, right?" Still weird. Still hard to wrap my brain around. It almost made Nyx less my mom and more... a piece of me. Or, really, I was a piece of her. But if she wanted to treat me like a daughter, I had zero complaints. "A feather you found—a feather nurtured in a lab. A feather *you* drugged and experimented on after you pulled her from the incubator, branded her w-with *demon* runes when she was just a baby."

Thunder cracked in the distance, my frayed restraint touching the *real* night sky too.

"Did I scream when you branded me?" His silence was answer enough. I stabbed my hands into my curls, and the billowing night charged forward, devouring the first and the second row of security, lapping up their calves, wild and unchecked. "You raised me just to torture me—a-and for what? For *data*? You used me, abused me, *hurt* me."

Crack-boom. Thunder detonated directly above us, and while Albert Abbott took it without flinching, his colleagues clapped their hands over their ears, a few scurrying back inside the lobby.

"All I wanted was *love*," I spat, eyes watery, throat clogged with a knot the size of a grapefruit, all my baggage spilling out. "I just wanted to feel safe and protected and *loved*."

Half the floodlights burst, sparks and glass flying, and I closed my eyes again when Arawn's hand cradled the nape of my neck. He stroked me with his thumb, Balor pacing with a *click, click, click* to the right, and I grabbed at Arawn's wrist, holding tight as I stared that *man* down for the last time. "I have all that now. This is your only warning for Cronus at large... Leave us alone."

I scanned the crowd, the building, the courtyard I used to love taking a quiet, thoughtful lunch in on fall days.

"If you come for us again..." The memories of this place would fade in time; I had so many new ones to make with my beautiful tatters of an old god's cloak. "I promise, I'll—"

"You'll what?" *Doctor* Albert Abbott hurled the question my way with some bite this time. "You'll burn it all to the ground?" He gestured to the building, to the pale-faced woman in her white coat behind him. "All these innocent people, Selene. These men and women *you* have known your whole life. You're not like them. You're not a monster—"

"I know I'm not a *monster*!" The rest of the floodlights exploded, the entire courtyard lost to darkness. Security scrambled for headlights and flashlights, one by one snapping to life in the black. My influence soared, stormy night licking up the splintered windows and the walls of a building full of prisoners, data, experiment subjects—but not *this* experiment. Not now, not ever again.

But he had a point.

So many innocents lived in there, around this building and on the base, human and otherwise. Albert Abbott had hundreds of shields. They didn't deserve to die for *his* sins. If I lived forever, just like Nyx, then I refused to wear their blood on my hands for the rest of time.

"You thought I was a monster from my first *breath*, and you did what you could to control me. I am not a monster, but if you hurt these three..." I spread my arms, sweeping all my loves into the fold. "If you come after us again, I'll show you exactly what I can do, and maybe *someone* will survive long enough to record it in my file."

While the threat had good ol' *Dad* rolling up his sleeves and flaring that clenched jaw at me, a few in the security lines suddenly lowered their weapons. Officers with rank insignia assumed an at-ease position, firearms no doubt still live—but no longer aimed at my head. A few more followed in their team leaders' footsteps, and, stunned, I retracted the night, drawing the stormy black close until it only touched me and my loves.

Tit for tat, I guess. If they could deescalate, so could I.

"It's done." I finally gave that *man* one of his famous dismissive up-and-down sweeps, the same he gave me every morning from the time I learned to dress myself. If only I could go back and hug little Selene, hold her tight as she hiccupped and sniffled and panicked in front of her pocket-sized dresser, trying to find the *perfect* outfit so she wouldn't get one of those fucking *looks*. If only I could tell her she was good enough, strong enough—*enough*. He was the problem. *He* was the sickness, the disease, the grain of sand in an otherwise finely tuned microchip. Not her.

With a deep breath, I drew on Draco's frustrating neutrality so that *thing* would walk away with absolutely nothing to cling onto; the days of him using the hurt in my eyes, the pain in my expression, were *over*. "We're done, Albert Abbott. Don't test me again. You'll lose."

Head held high, I turned my back on him—and a gun *clicked*. Balor snarled, charging forward, and Arawn went straight for me.

But I raised my hand, and he stopped. Draco culled the black mists before they swarmed me. A soft throat-clear stilled Balor's clacking claws, and I slowly turned around.

What did I just *say?*

There he was, the big man who devoted his life to torturing the little girl who called him *Dad*.

A gun in his hand. Just a basic pistol, standard issue to infantry troops on base.

Aimed at me.

And it was shaking.

"Enough of this, *Selene*," he spat, sweat beaded on his brow, his cruel eyes narrowed. "G-get inside—*now*."

The predator in me drooled; I'd never heard him stumble like that before. Never a stutter. Always so confident.

"If you leave, I will find a way to bind them." He flicked the gun toward each of my loves, Arawn, then Balor, then Draco. "You know our r-resources. You know what we can do with enough time. I'll bind them *here*, in Sub-level Z, and you—"

Night slithered up his calves, and he flailed backward with a yelp. A lone shot *cracked*, his finger resting on the trigger even as he tumbled off-balance. My slinking shadows had crept in a thin line across the courtyard, driven by rage and fear and pride, long before I noticed their reach. The white coats around him sprang out of the way, a few nearby officers pointing their guns at the darkness as it snaked around Albert Abbott's body.

Instinctively protective, my precious night.

Beautiful.

With a serene smile, I watched it engulf that monster's body. It surged up his nose and into his screaming mouth, then plumed out his ears—exploded from his eye sockets.

Albert Abbott ceased to exist about thirty seconds later, smothered, strangled by night and a lifetime of his own actions.

And the good folks at Cronus just watched.

No one raced to his side.

No one shot at the swirling darkness.

No one fired at *me*.

They let it happen, and for that, I withdrew my exquisite night completely, the storm tucked safe inside, the only shadows dancing across the cobblestone now courtesy of my three loves.

I zeroed in on another high-ranking grey-haired lab coat, waiting, unblinking, until he hesitantly met my eyes. Once I had him, I wouldn't let him go—not until I was sure he had heard every last word.

"I want nothing to do with Cronus unless *I* decide." Ah, good. He started nodding before I finished the sentence. "And if you find another feather..." I pursed my lips, cutting him loose to scan the familiar architecture all around us, the courtyard, the security details who had watched my back inside cells and labs alike. "If you find another of Nyx's feathers, don't put it in a fucking incubator." The stars flared to drive my point home, thunder rumbling and wind rustling. "Or, I swear, there won't be a Cronus headquarters on this planet that survives the night..."

I then marched into the shadowy fold of my beloved Arawn, Draco, and Balor, the three closing in on all sides, engulfing me in darkness, and we left my prison for the last time.

Free to do what we wanted, love how we wanted, and be wherever we wanted, in this realm and the next, until the end of days.

Or, you know, until Cronus tested me again.

Let them see what happened.

Let them learn the hard way that there was no weapon, no monster, no power, no *love* greater than the union of night and dark.

But, come on, they couldn't be *that* stupid...

Right?

EPILOGUE

Six Months Later

"Well then..." Arawn flung open the oak library door, golden sunbeams streaming into the otherwise dim, slightly musty foyer. "He was a wonderful speaker, wasn't he? Very crisp and concise. Exceptional pronunciation of the old terms."

Holding back a giggle, I hurried to keep up with his exuberant strides, a herd of fellow lecture attendees at our heels, and snagged his arm, the insistent tug a reminder that I would never match those long legs. With his pace tempered, we then strolled hand in hand down the cracked stone steps together, noon in Bellevue, Massachusetts, delightfully temperate on the brink of June, wildflowers hanging from streetlamp baskets and happy tulips in raised beds on either side of the stair railings.

"How much of it was true?"

"Very grey, I'm afraid," he mused, black brows taking a turn for the conflicted. Far too posh for such a small town, he had eyes on him from the second we landed about four hours ago, men *and* women studying the fitted black suit, his silky waves especially soft and bouncy in the late-spring sunshine.

And he was all mine. Divine *and* stylish, his charm touched everyone in a ten-mile radius, the library's lecture hall all warm and hazy courtesy of his good-natured interest.

Curls bobbing with every step, I peeked back at the poster tacked on the bulletin board next to the main doors. *Greek Mythology in the Modern Era.* For the last three hours, the lecturer from Boston had beguiled his audience of about sixty with tales of gods and monsters, heroes and tragedies, and how they still played out today in film, literature, and music. Interesting stuff. Worth the transatlantic jump, but as good as the lecturer presented, none of it was really new—not really.

Not when you'd actually met some of the gods in question, but whatever. A solid effort.

Even if I walked away from the presentation with lukewarm feelings, Arawn's enthusiasm was infectious, his breathtaking smile touching everyone, myself included, his black eyes twinkly and very, very alive.

But he was a nerd for all my lectures. In the last six months, I bought a new laptop—one *not* monitored by Cronus at large as far as I could tell—and researched university courses around the world. If a topic or syllabus caught my eye, Arawn chauffeured me to class without hesitation. Denmark. England. Scotland. Canada. All around the US and even down to New Zealand. After twenty-five years in a bubble, I craved culture, knowledge, and experience. I studied what I wanted, when I wanted, and usually found a cozy, dark corner in the lecture hall to make mine. Arawn, meanwhile, always sat at the edge of his seat, intense and maybe a bit much whenever he cornered the professor after class for a light theoretical grilling.

Today, however, our lecturer had been swarmed by Bellevue's historical society, a gaggle of white-haired women trapping him at the podium and literally body-blocking the class of senior history and classics kids from the local high school while their teacher huffed and constantly checked his watch.

Bit of a strange crowd, young and old—and then us, the gothic weirdos in all black at the back. Arawn rocked his suit, while I went for a toned-down sundress with capped sleeves and a scooped neckline, the fabric stretchy and clingy and comfy as hell. Throw in a pair of star-dusted sneakers and a big droopy purse Arawn charmed from a merchant in Florence and I was golden.

"Always so cruel to Aphrodite, this world," Arawn muttered when we hit the sidewalk and meandered toward a huge flowerpot of daisies.

"Oh yeah?" Fingers loosely entwined with his, I popped my sunglasses on, then did a quick sweep of the library's steepled rooftop for—oh, yup. There they were. Six ravens, perched in pairs. Always lurking. Always watching. I gave them a little finger wave, smitten with the way the sun highlighted all the details in their plumage. "Is she much different from the myths?"

Arawn shrugged in the corner of my eye, studying my ravens with a charmed expression. "Sometimes yes, sometimes no. She's great fun at a party."

I snorted and rolled my eyes, cuddling back into his side. "Cryptic as ever."

"We like to make you *work* for it, little one," Arawn purred as he kissed the top of my head. Library patrons swarming the sidewalk, the crowd eventually pushed us to the curb, and while my beloved scanned our surroundings—most likely on the hunt for a diner, forever attuned to my body's cycles and *very* wary of the hangrier moods—I stiffened.

The darkness in my chest sniffed *deep*.

A buoyancy filled my limbs, electricity sparking in my veins and the urge to *move* taking over.

"Where to now, little one?"

Leaning into the daze, I pulled away from him and fidgeted with my dress. Six months after leaving Fort Beacham and I *still* got the feeling someone was watching. It hit less and less as time went on, that prickly feeling in your belly, the hairs on the back of your neck shooting up. We were quite the group when the four of us went out together; people were always looking, frowning, leering, ogling.

But the sensation of being *hunted* by a hunter who had no idea he'd stumbled across an apex predator was... different.

And rare.

Cronus had pulled way, way, *way* back. Occasionally, I noted buildings around the world that would make a good secret headquarters in some of the larger cities. Once, the guy in line behind us at a Starbucks still had his ID badge hanging off a lanyard around his neck; he went deathly pale when Balor suggested he put some serious space between us, *now*—and I tucked that ID badge in his breast pocket and patted his chest with just enough preternatural strength to leave a bruise.

Things might have gone differently had I leveled the base that night.

Cronus had global ties to governments, agencies, terrorist groups—the works. If I obliterated one of their headquarters, destroying all the prisoners and test subjects and decades of research inside, all the innocent humans who did dull shit like data entry and janitorial—I'd be a persona non grata.

Enemy number one.

The organization would have made it their mission to put me down. Maybe they'd find a way to succeed. Maybe they would actually figure out how to bind the elusive tatters of Erebus's cloak—broken my heart into a million pieces, made me burn the world.

But my restraint mattered.

At the end of the day, we had settled on a tense truce. While I had no doubt they kept a file on me and the boys, there were higher supernatural priorities out there, monsters who craved the utter destruction of every living thing on this planet. We just wanted to exist. If they left us alone, I'd leave them alone.

No world burning.

No night apocalypse.

No Balor unleashed.

Live and let live.

And they had. This sudden *feeling* wasn't them.

No, it ran far deeper—with a much greater purpose.

The monster in me purred at the memory of Nyx's hand on my chest, the *jolt* when she declared me a guardian. Then, as awareness trickled back in, the sights, sounds, and golden sunlight of noon on Bellevue's Main Street sharpening, I went left, following the pull down the sidewalk.

"I don't know yet," I told him absently, and all of them knew when I was in one of these moods, that was the honest truth. When it started, I legitimately had no idea where we were headed or for what reason, but I let instinct guide me.

Arawn followed behind for about two blocks, allowing me space to do my thing, then eventually captured my hand, holding it and chatting away over the next two hours. From town to farmland to town again, then way out to the winding roads of rural northeastern nothingness, I followed my feet. Greenery thrived on either side of the two-lane road with gravel shoulders and electric-fenced fields, sheep and cattle grazing in pastures, the odd truck rumbling by few and far between.

I didn't stop, didn't even consider it, until I spotted a box in a ditch. Then, sliding my hand from Arawn's, I tiptoed down the steep dip, squishing through puddled rainwater under the flattened grass. While the cardboard wasn't exactly taped shut, someone had folded the flaps in a way that made it as good as. Scowling, I crouched and pushed my curls back, then gently pried it open—

"Oh." I sat back on my haunches, maternal warmth heating me from the inside out. "Hello, Mama."

Some asshole had stuffed a much-too-skinny black cat in there with her six newborn kittens. She blinked tawny eyes up at me, purrs immediate, small paws kneading as her kittens nursed.

"Aren't you a good mama," I crooned, scratching her ears and the velvety top of her head, "feeding your babies so *good* when I bet you're starving."

Of all the charges bestowed by Nyx, I took guardianship of black cats the most serious.

Humans seemed to hate them more than I remembered, the world overrun with strays and superstition. It would have been easy to lose my cool, to set my sights on finding whoever had trapped this precious girl and her babies in a cardboard coffin and tossed it in the ditch. Rainwater seeped in through the bottom, the cardboard soft—like it had been out in the storm.

I *could* have gone full wrath.

But I preferred the cozy warmth, the kinship between two mothers who just wanted what was best for their babies. So, I swaddled them all in night, starry darkness settling like a silk blanket around her, beneath her, blotting out the elements for good.

"Is this an animal dumping ground?" Arawn asked from above. I sniffed, carefully checking each kitten to ensure they were all breathing—and they were.

"I don't know." Six full bellies and closed eyes. Perfect. My smile softened, and I went back to Mama, rubbing her cheeks as her purr revved from a whisper to a roar. "Maybe... Why?"

A symphony of little *yips* answered, and I twisted around to Arawn with two squirmy blackish-brown pups under his arms. Mutts, probably. Big paws and floppy ears. Short coats, wagging tails—no doubt full of bugs.

Nothing we couldn't handle.

"I think we've got space in the nursery," I said as I scooped the kitty box up and stood. Arawn materialized behind me in a flash, puppies in tow with their big blue eyes and pale pink tongues, their whines and whimpers tugging at my heartstrings.

"Come on, then," Arawn urged, right at my heels in case I slipped, tailing me the whole way up the ditch side and back to the gravel shoulder. "Home for the day, everyone."

Shadows and black mist swirled around us, and our latest additions to *home* went still and quiet as Arawn ushered the whole group away. Cradled in darkness, in calm nothingness, I hugged the box tight, hoping Mama wasn't too stressed and that the pups didn't mind floating in a black void for a bit. While my night vision was solid, the darkness of my three loves was the one thing I couldn't see through.

However, as soon as my feet touched down on a crumbling stone wall, ancient but still standing, dating back centuries and in need of some patchwork, everyone appeared in one piece. Mama and all her kittens nuzzled under my night-conjured blanket in their box, and as Arawn solidified, he hugged the wiggly puppies to his chest with one arm, then offered the other to me, crooked and steady, as I climbed off the wall. Hands full of sodden cardboard, I just leaned into him where I could, hopping into the long yellowing grasses with a grin.

While *home* was Arawn, Balor, and Draco, the more literal version was this: an abandoned olive grove in Tuscany. Rolling hills and endless skies, overgrown pastures and neglected trees, it suited us just fine, and once Arawn charmed city officials into drafting actual deeds of purchase, we four fixed up the dilapidated villa and barn and slowly got to work on healing the forgotten trees. We still had a long way to go before they were happy enough to produce again, but the difference five and a half months could make was *wild*. Maybe next year we might have a proper harvest. In the meantime, a few potted baby olive trees by the main house supplied us with spotty growth and a pet project that everyone had a hand in.

"What's this? *More?*" came a deliciously deep rumble from the shadows of a nearby tree. Balor emerged a few moments later, finally at home as the sinful Italian heir who wasted his time on a yacht, forever sporting a sun-kissed glow and a haunting smile. That olive complexion suited the Tuscan countryside, the rest of us pale and sickly by comparison. He strode through the long, yellowy-green grasses with his huge hands in his pockets, rocking a white Armani polo and breezy black slacks. Aviators. Hair slicked. *Effortlessly* cool and suave—except for the legion of cats at his heels.

Fifteen of our current rescues who had full run of the property trailed after him, tails up and curled at the ends, following Balor like little black feline ducklings.

"Blame Nyx if you're going to blame anyone," I said with a huff and a barely contained smirk, twisting my box away from him—then offering him a peek when his eyes narrowed. Ever the giant, Balor peered over, then crouched to tickle the new mama's ears, her purrs ramping up again under his attention. "I'm just doing my job... I know it's *such* a burden."

"She's got pretty eyes... Yes, *yes*, you *do*," he whispered, his grin tinged with a sharklike affection that, a year ago, would have sent me running. Now, it tugged at my heartstrings as the rest of my rescues rubbed around our legs, purring and meowing—and then scattering the second Arawn set the pups down. Up trees, onto the pasture walls, they bolted with staticky tails and arched backs, hisses aplenty as the mutts barreled after them.

They changed course in a flash, however, two clumsy disasters on their too-big paws, as soon as Draco materialized nearby, darkness clinging to him like morning mist. He stopped, stiff as a board, and stared down at our newest troublemakers.

"Dogs are not our calling," he remarked hesitantly before offering each puppy's head a rigid *pat, pat, pat*, one in each hand. "Ravens, bats, and lost black cats, remember?"

"They are now," Arawn countered, which earned him an indignant side-eye. It softened when it settled on me, and I just popped my sunglasses up on my head and grinned wider, wholly aware that those two rascals were outside of the guardianship duties charged by Nyx—but they were just so freakin' *cute*. Like I'd ever leave them behind on that empty road to starve or get hit by a car. Here, they had acres and acres of olive groves to explore, but I already knew they'd like the house best, especially the wood-burning stove on cool nights and the cushy shadowy pet beds in the nursery.

Throaty croaks and squawks greeted me from the surrounding trees, our local raven conspiracy tucked in for the evening. With the sun just shy of setting, they had all found their favorite trees. We, on the other hand, made our way across the rolling hills for the main house, passing bat boxes Draco crafted from shadow and darkness, there for any wayward travelers who needed to rest for the day. *Pipistrelli* to locals, they were the smallest, sweetest, *babyiest* little bats I had ever seen, and those who roamed the property too close to dawn made good use of our safe havens. Come nightfall, they were out hunting mosquitos again, then back to the larger colony elsewhere.

Box of kittens and their mama safe in my arms, I trod familiar paths through the olive trees in a blissful quiet, Arawn to my right, Balor to my left—all the cats with him— and Draco a little way behind with two puppies who had fallen hard and fast for his aloof affection. A setting sun. A cool spring evening. Darkness painting the sky purple. Nature and quiet and space to just *be*.

Six months with these three had flown by, full of life and laughter, adventures and day trips, lovemaking and darkness birthed again and again in this very grove. There was still so much I planned to do, but I had come to really crave evenings like this, sun low and air thick, the four of us in for another night of taste-testing regional wines around a bonfire, fresh local sausages, cheeses, and breads waiting for me in the pantry. Just a simple night beneath a starry sky with my loves, talking and laughing and teasing, our animals dozing in the shadows.

After living all my life in a drugged stupor, I wanted the world.

But we had all eternity for that.

Just a feather and some torn cloak tatters.

For now, we took it day by day, really *living* for each other, for all the new experiences—for love.

Forever and always.

THE END

ACKNOWLEDGMENTS

First and forever, thank you to my amazing beta reader Amanda for always trudging through my first drafts and being my hype queen from day one. Big props to Sandra at One Love Editing for making my books sparkle. Linda, my typo checker — you are a GODDESS and I always so appreciate your time.

Shoutout to my reader group for making me laugh literally every single day.

Thank you to my sun and stars for listening to all my fears, and then making them disappear. You are the inspiration for all my heroes.

And finally, thank you to my readers. Without you, none of this would be possible.

xoxo,
Rhea

ABOUT THE AUTHOR

Rhea Watson is a Canadian reverse harem author who loves a good paranormal romance. She writes layered alpha heroes with rough exteriors who melt for their strong, independent soulmates.

In her spare time, Rhea babies her herb garden, bows to her cat's every whim, and flies through Netflix shows like it's her day job.

Want to keep in touch with Rhea about her life, writing cave shenanigans, and upcoming releases? Opt into her monthly newsletter here.

FACEBOOK READER GROUP

Reverse harem and menage romances from Rhea:

CRONUS SOCIETY
Secret Society Paranormal Romance RH Standalones, Same World
Bride of Shadows
Kiss of Death (June 2022)
Cambion (Early 2023)

ALL THE QUEEN'S MEN SERIES
(Paranormal Romance RH Standalones, Same Universe)

Reaper's Pack
Caged Kitten
Root Rot Academy: The Complete Trilogy
Bloodline: The Complete Trilogy

RHEA WATSON TRILOGIES & DUETS:

ROOT ROT
(*Professors-Only Academy Reverse Harem*)
Term 1
Term 2
Term 3

BLOODLINE TRILOGY
(*Wolf Shifters & Fated Mates*)
Raised by Wolves (#1)
Hunted by Wolves (#2)
Loved by Wolves (#3)

RHEA WATSON WRITING AS EVIE KENT

Evie Kent is a dark paranormal romance author who loves a possessive anti-hero and a strong-willed heroine. She has been #teamvillain for as long as she can remember, and thinks the dark side definitely has more fun.

Her work errs toward soft dark, and features soulmate-level romances with dubious beginnings, along with a dash of angst and a dollop of kink.

Dark M/F paranormal romances from Evie:

LILY OF THE VALLEY SERIES
(Dark-ish M/F Paranormal Romance Standalones)
To Love a God
Surrender: A Lily of the Valley Novella

Smoke and Mirrors: A Dark Space Standalone

BOOKS BY RHEA & EVIE:
Dark-ish Menage/Reverse Harem Paranormal Romances

BIRDS OF A FEATHER SERIES
Magpie's Song
Mourning Dove (2022)